The Cat, the Devil, the Last Escape

ALSO BY SHIRLEY ROUSSEAU MURPHY

The Cat, the Devil, the Last Escape

**Shirley Rousseau Murphy
and Pat J. J. Murphy**

HARPER LUXE

An Imprint of HarperCollins*Publishers*

To Janet and Bob

To Dr. Roy Dillon

and

Captain Weston H. Ament Sr.

THE CAT, THE DEVIL, THE LAST ESCAPE. Copyright © 2015 by Shirley Rousseau Murphy. All rights reserved. Printed in the United States of America. No part of this book may be used or reproduced in any manner whatsoever without written permission except in the case of brief quotations embodied in critical articles and reviews. For information address HarperCollins Publishers, 195 Broadway, New York, NY 10007.

HarperCollins books may be purchased for educational, business, or sales promotional use. For information please e-mail the Special Markets Department at SPsales@harpercollins.com.

FIRST HARPERLUXE EDITION

HarperLuxe™ is a trademark of HarperCollins Publishers

Library of Congress Cataloging-in-Publication Data is available upon request.

ISBN: 978-0-06-237016-7

15 ID/RRD 10 9 8 7 6 5 4 3 2 1

1

The cat prowled the prison rooftops invisible to human eyes, a ghost cat, a spirit cat unseen by anyone living. He could make himself visible when he chose but that wasn't often. A big, rangy tomcat, long and lank, his golden ears ragged from past battles during his earthly lives. Now, floating free between those lives, his mission was keen as he searched for his quarry, for his dark and indestructible adversary.

Padding across the shingles he paused at a noise from the walk below, dropped to a predator's stalk and slipped to the edge, to peer over.

But it was only a guard passing between the buildings with a pair of inmates, the men's shadows cast tall by the lowering sun. The shadow that Misto sought was not among them. When, in the softening light, some unease made the men glance up to the roofline they saw only wind-scattered leaves dancing across the shingles.

The men moved on and so did the ghost cat, scanning the walks below him, alert for that errant shade, for the demon that, unlike the cat himself, harbored no trace of goodness. For the wraith that haunted his human companion, that tormented Lee Fontana. In the windows of the prison offices warped reflections moved about as prison staff finished up for the day. He heard the casual click of a door closing but not a stealthy sound. Across the roofs the prairie wind scudded, tickling through his fur, turning him suddenly so giddy that he ran in circles, tail lashing, his yellow eyes gleaming. He played and raced unseen until the light shifted, far clouds dimmed the dropping sun and, sobering, the cat turned steady again and watchful.

Away at the far reaches of the prison grounds the vegetable gardens shone bright green in the sun's last rays. Ears sharp forward, he surveyed the dim corridors between the young fruit trees that the prisoners tended, but nothing stirred there, he saw no foreign presence. Tail twitching, he looked up past the gardens, out past the prison wall to the blowing wheat that rolled to the horizon. The ghost cat had, earlier in the day, sailed weightless on the wheat's flowing crest, diving and somersaulting, giddy with play, forgetting his quarry as he reveled in his ghostly powers, in his weightless and windblown freedom. Now he could see nothing spectral waiting there within that golden pelt. Nor did anything unwelcome move among the farm buildings or within the fenced paddocks where the cows and sheep browsed, casting their own docile shadows. The animals remained content, nothing evil lingered among them. They would know, the animals always knew.

The scent of the farm beasts, carried on the wind, comforted the ghost cat. Their warmth and familiarity, their steady and incorruptible innocence were as balm to Misto's restless nature. He turned away only when the stink of the prison pig farm reached him; he wheeled away then, his lips drawn back in a flehmen grin of disgust.

Galloping across the roofs, he paused to study the lighted factory windows where the inmates produced clothing and shoes and furniture. Nothing seemed amiss within those busy rooms, only the usual whine of machines, the pounding of hammers, and warped movement beyond the glass as the men went about their work. He watched for a few moments more, his ears down to keep out the wind, then headed for the roof of the hospital. There he settled on the shingles, his paws tucked under, to wait for his human cell-mate, for crusty old Lee Fontana to finish his daily session with the prison doctor and return to his solitary cell.

But even here, peering down through the hospital windows, still Misto watched for the dark presence that had followed Lee these many years, intent on his destruction. Had followed Lee long before he was transferred here to Springfield Federal Prison. The dark spirit that had followed him across the country from California and, months earlier, had shadowed him as he departed McNeil Island Federal Prison on parole, had followed Lee down the coast of Washington State and Oregon, down into California's southern desert. Tenacious and devious, hell's spirit sought to possess and destroy the vulnerable old man, in a vendetta that ranged back three generations of Lee's family. Back to the time of Lee's grandpappy, when train robber Russell Dobbs, late in the last century, made a wager with the devil and won it.

Satan didn't take kindly to defeat, he hadn't liked losing that bargain. Russell Dobbs, having miraculously bested the devil at his own game, had brashly stirred Lucifer's rage. The curse Satan laid on Dobbs's heirs led the dark spirit, long after Dobbs's own death, to return again and again into Lee's life attempting, with each visit, to suck away Lee's soul, to establish final victory.

So far Lucifer had not won the battle. Often enough he had masterfully tempted Lee, but still he could not possess him. Always, one way or another, Lee resisted. When recently in the California desert Lee had out-maneuvered Satan so stubbornly in a clashing of wills that the devil had drawn back, the cat thought Lee had won at last, he thought that was the end of the devil's harassment, that Lee would face the haunt no more.

This was not the case. Fairness means nothing to Satan, the devil keeps his own rules. Though there in the desert Lee had clearly bested Lucifer, the wraith wasn't done with him. The ghost cat had fought beside Lee, as much as one small cat *can* defy hell's forces; sometimes they had watched Satan falter, but the battle was far from ended.

The yellow tom had been with Lee for all this present ghostly interval between his earthbound lives, but he had known Lee far longer. Misto had known Lee Fontana before the cat's previous life ended. The two of them, both loners, had been close at McNeil Island. Misto, the boldest of the motley collection of cats that roamed the prison grounds, had moved as he pleased within the compound, strolling the dining room, demanding food from the friendlier inmates, slipping in and out of the cells as he chose. Though most of the time he remained in Lee's company, spending his days on the prison farm where Lee had worked as a trustee caring for the milk cows and chickens and sheep, a job Lee much preferred to working indoors in prison industries, where dust and sawdust from the machinery irritated his sick lungs.

When, at McNeil, Misto died from the quick but painful complications of old age, Lee, one of the guards, and a cortege of prisoners had buried him outside the prison wall. But even during the ceremony, before the first shovelful of earth tumbled down on his carefully wrapped body, Misto's spirit had risen up from that somber grave light and free. Riding the breeze above two dozen mourners he had watched his own funeral and listened to his friends' rough eulogies, and the ghost cat had smiled, touched by the men's awkward sentiment.

As ghost he had remained on McNeil with Lee until Lee was paroled. The old man might be a thief and a train robber, but Misto saw something more. He saw a vulnerability in Lee Fontana, a tenderness that Lee, all his life, had tried to conceal. The ghost cat saw qualities within the old convict that made him purr, that kept him close, determined to shield Lee from the fate the dark prince held in store for the crusty old train robber. When Lee was paroled, Misto followed him off the island. Balanced invisibly on the rail of the prison launch that carried them across Puget Sound, amused by the icy spray in his face, the ghost cat raced along the rail as the boat plied the rough, deep waters drawing near to the small town of Steilacoom, to the railway stop where Lee would board his train for California.

Once Lee was settled on the southbound train, claiming a long bench seat for himself, the ghost cat had moved invisibly through the rocking cars staring up at the passengers and nosing into their lunch bags. But soon enough he had returned to Lee to curl up beside him on the cracked leather seat. It was a long journey. Misto had napped close to Lee but then, when he grew bored, he would drift up through the iron roof to ride atop the train; galloping the length of the racing cars in the gusting wind, Misto was part of the wind. As ghost, the small spirit was far more frivolous than ever he had been as a living, earthbound tomcat.

That had been only a few months back, in early March, when Lee headed down the West Coast to take a job in the Coachella Valley at the parole board's direction, working one of the vast vegetable farms that fed half of California. Leaving Steilacoom, their train had swayed along beside the sea through green pastures and through small cozy towns dwarfed by Washington's snowcapped peaks. When, along the ever-changing coastline, flocks of birds exploded away, the cat leaped after them into the wind, diving and banking, gulping the small, winged morsels as a hawk or eagle might feast.

Only near the end of their three-day journey did the land abruptly change. As they moved south through green miles of orange and avocado groves, suddenly the groves ended. They were racing across pale, dry desert. As they descended a rocky, parched mountain the ghost cat crowded between Lee and the window, watching the flat desert, dry as bone, stretching to the horizon.

But soon, startling them both, the sandy expanse was broken by green farms laid out in emerald squares on the pale bare desert. A patchwork of vegetable fields, each as lush as a jungle, where river water fed the land, water piped in from the great Colorado. They could see men with trucks and tractors working the fields, harvesting rich crops of beans, melons, strawberries, and produce Lee couldn't name—but the ghost cat, ascending again to the top of the train for a wider look, was suddenly engulfed in blackness. Darkness hid the sun and from it a man-shape emerged towering over him, its eyes gleaming.

Hissing, the cat stood his ground, ears back, teeth bared. "What do you want?" He had no physical power over the wraith, he had only the power of the spirit—his will against Satan's eternal and devious lust. "You've done your work," Misto growled, "or tried to. You've made your pitch too many times over the years. Every time, you've failed. At none of the crimes you've laid out have you succeeded in corrupting Lee. Whatever robbery he undertook, he did it his way, not yours."

His yellow eyes raked the devil. "You think the curse you laid on Lee's family is still to be won? No," the tomcat rumbled. "You've failed in your vow to take down the heir of Russell Dobbs, you're the loser. Go torture someone else, you have no business here."

Satan's smile made the cat's fur stand rigid, but the next moment the wraith was gone, vanished, his lingering look of promise stirring a shiver along the tomcat's spine.

It was only a few weeks later that Lucifer appeared on the farm where Lee was working. Again, after weeks of sparring, Lee refused to commit the crime Satan pressed on him. It was that refusal that had led Lee here to Springfield. Lee had chosen, against the devil's seduction, a robbery that, instead of maiming and destroying lives, would harm no one. Scoffing at the devil, he had devised a foolproof alibi that would remove him from the crime scene but leave him with a wealth of stolen cash. And that would burden him with only a few months' prison time on a less serious misdemeanor.

But even then, the wraith continued to torment Lee. And, as well, to ply his evil on the little child back in Georgia who was the other half of the puzzle that so fascinated the ghost cat, the child about whom Lee knew nothing.

Though in a previous life Misto had lived with Sammie, had been her own cat, she was still a mystery to him. He knew only that there was, somehow, an inexplicable connection between nine-year-old Sammie Blake and Lee Fontana.

Lee, nearly all his life, had carried with him the small framed photograph of his little sister Mae, taken some sixty years ago on the Dakota ranch. Mae was eight then, and Lee was twelve. He carried the picture when he left the ranch, a boy of sixteen setting out to conquer the world. Setting out to learn, on his own, to rob the steam trains as skillfully as Russell Dobbs could ever do. Lee didn't seek to join Dobbs or to find him, Dobbs would have had none of that. To him Lee was only a boy.

Lee hadn't seen Mae since he'd left the ranch; he'd seen none of his family again and didn't know if they were still alive, except for his granddaddy. The legends and stories he heard of Dobbs's feats, and the newspaper headlines, were fodder to his young mind. But, like Dobbs, Lee was a loner. He had gone his way, and the rest of his family had gone theirs. Still, he thought about Mae often and always carried the small tintype wrapped in cloth, bent from being stuffed into a saddlebag or in his pocket.

It was only the ghost cat who knew and worried over the likeness between Lee's little sister of some sixty years gone, and the child now in Georgia, the child Misto loved and had so recently lived with. The mirror images shared by the two children teased at the tomcat. But even now, as a ghost with his wider vision, he was not all-seeing: The puzzle was as stubborn as a knot of tangled yarn.

Was there a connection between the two children? How could there not be when they were so alike, and when fate had put them both so close to Misto as he moved through time and space? It seemed to him that Lee, and present-day Sammie Blake, were being inexorably drawn together; he felt himself part of a drama that was only beginning to play out. A pattern was forming within the vastness of eternity, but he didn't know why. Were these events driven by the will of the dark one? Or were they happening in defiance of Satan's efforts? That was the heart of the question.

Misto's short life in Georgia occurred between the moment he died at McNeil Island and the instant that he, moving back in time, rose from his own grave as a ghost cat. A whole life lived outside the linear view of time. He was given to Sammie when she was five, when her daddy first went in the navy. Now, as a spirit, he saw his various lives floating on the realm of eternity as fishing skiffs might float rocking and shifting on an endless sea.

Now, stepping off the hospital roof, Misto rode the wind, floating along peering in through the rows of windows, one window to the next until he found Lee in a small examining room. There he rested on the fitful breeze, watching.

The old convict looked so vulnerable sitting on the metal table with his shirt off, his thin, ropy shoulders, his chest ivory white and frail. But his lower arms, his neck and wrinkled face were hard-looking, tanned to leather. Dr. Donovan, stethoscope in hand, was listening to Lee's lungs. Ed Donovan was young and lean, short blond hair, deep blue eyes. He was a runner, Misto would see him of an early morning circling the paths inside the prison complex, his pale hair mussed, his pace easy. He was patient with Lee, and at each visit he seemed to read precisely Lee's state of health, even before he examined the old man. He could tell by Lee's expression, and the way he moved, how Lee felt, though he always did examine him, designing Lee's treatments according to what he observed. Under Donovan's guidance, Misto thought Lee would grow as healthy as he could ever expect to be, considering the debilitation caused by the emphysema.

The cat thought about Lee's hope that within a few months, under the good care at Springfield, he would be pronounced healthy, would be discharged from the federal medical facility, would be back on parole heading for Blythe to retrieve the stolen money and then down to Mexico beyond easy reach of the feds.

Misto didn't think so. Trying to see the future, he felt his fur crawl. He sensed a far longer journey ahead, a more complicated and dangerous tangle than Lee dreamed before he reached California again to claim the treasure. Misto's fragmented glimpses into the future were often like the abandoned skiffs in high water, visible for only an instant: the shadow of a prow or of a coiled line obscured by engulfing waves. Now the yellow tom prayed for the old train robber in the journey that lay ahead; he prayed that Lee might find a new kind of treasure, more tender than Lee would ever imagine.

2

Drifting on the wind peering in through the hospital window at Lee and the doctor, the yellow tom soon grew bored with waiting. Lee had pulled on his shirt but the two men were deep in conversation. Lee laughed, the old man's eyes sparkling at some joke the doc had told him. Misto rose to the roof again thinking about the long, circuitous journey that had brought them there to Springfield, wondering which way fate would push Lee now. The cat hissed softly, knowing that Lee's crime in California might yet be discovered.

When, in Blythe, Lee committed the payroll robbery, he had, within an hour, surfaced two hundred miles away, drunk and disorderly in a Las Vegas casino. What better witnesses to his presence there than the cops who arrested him, booked and jailed him? No way he could have been in two places at once. By car, it was a four-hour drive, and little chance he could have flown. This was 1947; the few commercial airlines that had started up after the war flew only between the larger cities.

And a small plane? Few records were kept of the private planes in the area. That night, there was no record of a two-seat duster plane leaving the desert town of Blythe, winging above the Colorado River between the low mountains. The ghost cat had ridden with Lee, warmed by the old man's success, by the stolen money that was Lee's nest egg for the rest of his life, for whatever time he had left as he was dragged down by the emphysema.

In Vegas, Lee expected to do a few months' jail time, to be released with more federal time tacked on his parole and to be returned to his farm job in Blythe. He didn't mean to stay on the job. He meant to dig up the money at once and head for Mexico, lose himself across the border. Why would the feds look for him when they already had the man who appeared to have committed the robbery, the escapee Lee had set up for the job? When they'd already found the dead convict in the wrecked truck with some of the stolen money?

Lee never thought that in the Vegas jail his lungs would turn so bad he'd be sent back to California, housed in the San Bernardino County jail and, a few days later, shipped off to the new federal medical facility in Missouri, a plan set up by his parole officer and the San Bernardino County medical officer, Dr. Lou Thomas. Misto had stretched out unseen on the bookcase in Thomas's office, amused at the interview but concerned for Lee.

Dr. Thomas was a soft man with thinning hair, a high forehead above rimless glasses. Removing his glasses, he rubbed his eyes, looking quietly at Lee. "The emphysema is pretty severe, Fontana." Thomas looked from Lee to the young parole officer, waiting for him to take the lead.

George Raygor was maybe thirty, healthier looking than the portly physician. Crisp brown hair cut short, a rangy body and a deep tan, dressed in his usual suit, white shirt, and tie. "That field work," Raygor said, "driving for the pickers, the dust didn't help your condition. I feel partly responsible for that. I wish you'd said something, Lee, we could have found some other work. Didn't you think to tie on a bandana to breathe through?" He looked at Lou Thomas. "Can they do anything for him at Springfield?"

"They can't cure you," Thomas told Lee, "but they can treat the symptoms, the shortness of breath, the coughing. Teach you how to breathe differently, how to take in more oxygen. Springfield takes good care of the men, we're sending federal patients there from all over the country."

He glanced at Raygor. "I'll make the recommendation, I'll call the parole board this morning." But then the two looked at Lee, their expressions changing in a way Lee didn't much like.

"I stopped by the FBI office earlier," Raygor said. "You want to talk about the Blythe post office robbery?"

Lee had looked at Raygor, puzzled. "I heard about that in Vegas. I heard they found the guy, that he'd wrecked his car in a ditch or something."

Raygor said, "The bureau found a body in a wrecked truck, at the bottom of a canyon. Guy's name was Luke Zigler. Did you know him?"

Lee shook his head. "His picture was in the paper. No, I didn't know him. The paper said he'd been in prison."

"While you were being transported back to California," Raygor said, "I made a run down to Blythe and talked with your boss. Jake Ellson said you'd taken some time off, starting the day of the robbery. Said you hadn't quit your job, said you just wanted a break, a few days' rest. He said he didn't know where you went, said he didn't babysit his employees."

Among the bookshelves Misto had risen nervously and begun to pace. Lee didn't need this, he didn't need questioning. As he moved behind Dr. Thomas, he let the faintest breeze touch the man. Thomas flinched, distracted, and glanced around. When he saw nothing, he settled down again.

Across from him, Raygor leaned back in the metal chair, looking hard at Lee. "Jake covered for you, Fontana. He knew you weren't allowed to leave the state. And *you* knew it." He studied Lee, frowning. "If you did pull that post office job, you're better off telling us now. It will go easier for you."

Lee looked at him blankly. "How could I rob the Blythe post office? I was in Vegas when that happened. I read the papers, the robbery was the same night I was arrested. And why, even if I'd *been* in Blythe, would I pull a federal job and blow my parole?"

"Before I left Delgado Ranch," Raygor said, "I had a look in your cabin. No clothes in the drawers or in the closet. I talked with some of the pickers but I didn't learn much." Raygor's gaze was stubborn; Lee didn't think he'd turn loose of this.

"I stopped by the army airfield," Raygor said, and that gave Lee a jolt. "There aren't many private planes in Blythe, to get you to Vegas. Not much action since the war ended and the army shut the field down. The postal authorities checked for small planes leaving that night but didn't find anything. Maybe some duster pilot headed for an early job," Raygor said, watching Lee. "No one keeps records of those flights." Raygor said no more, he didn't push it any further.

Lee had thought maybe Raygor felt sorry for him, an insulting idea, but useful. There was something in Raygor that Lee liked; that made him hope the PO would back off, would let matters lie the way they looked. Hoped the feds would do the same. They had their case, and Zigler was a no-good, he had deserved to die. Lee had killed Zigler in self-defense to save his own life, and he didn't feel bad about that. He'd known enough of Zigler's kind, twisted killers more dangerous than a nest of rattlesnakes. If, in death, Zigler had helped Lee out, it might be the only favor he'd done in his coldhearted life.

But still, the bureau didn't have the rest of the stolen money and Lee knew those guys would keep looking. Searching the desert for shovel marks, tire marks, for the place where he had buried the cash, and that made him some nervous.

Misto, seeing Lee's restricted breathing, knew how shaky the old man felt. It was then the ghost cat became visible, prancing along the shelf behind the men's backs, lashing his tail and clowning. He vanished again at once, but Lee knew he was there and found it hard to keep a straight face; the ghost cat made him feel stronger, filled him with an amused courage.

But the next day when Lee found himself in a big black car headed for the L.A. airport accompanied by two deputy U.S. marshals, he had no sense of the ghost cat. At the airport, getting out of the car handcuffed and leg chained to board their flight for Missouri, Lee still didn't sense the cat's presence and felt painfully alone.

Lee drew stares as they boarded, chained to the heavyset deputy. When they were settled, the other deputy, who'd been driving, left them. Lee's companion took up most of their two seats, crushing Lee against the window. Weak and uncertain again after yesterday's interview, Lee wished mightily for some awareness of the ghost cat. He wanted to hear the invisible cat's purr; he wondered for a moment if Misto had left him for good, wondered if, with this trip, the yellow tom had ended their journey together.

But why would Misto do that, at this juncture in Lee's life? Sick as he was, he didn't relish all the prison hassle soon to come, the prodding and power plays of the established inmates; he longed for the cat's steady support. He wanted to feel the ghost cat draped warm and unseen across his shoulder, lending him courage;

he wanted that small and steady spirit near, to share this new turn in his journey. The one soul in all the world that he could trust, could talk with in the privacy of his cot at night, the cat's whisper hardly a sound at all beneath the prison blanket. Misto must know Lee needed him. Where was he, that was more urgent than easing the distress of his cellmate?

Seated beside the hard-faced deputy, wrenched with fits of coughing, avoiding the deputy's scowl, Lee felt so miserable he wondered if he'd make it to the prison hospital before he gave out. The day seemed endless until they deplaned at Kansas City, Lee stumbling down the metal stairs in his leg chains, crossing the wide strip of tarmac to the small terminal. He was allowed to use the men's room, still chained to the deputy, then was ushered into the backseat of another black touring car driven by another deputy marshal who had joined them there. Heading south for Missouri beneath heavy gray clouds, the car had sped through miles of wheat fields stretching away flat as the sea. Trying to ignore the belly chain that dug into his backbone, he'd still had no sense of the ghost cat. He'd felt used up, empty, cold, and aching tired.

His companions hadn't talked much. Both were silent, sour-faced men filled with the power of their own authority, and that had been fine with Lee. He didn't like small talk and he didn't have a damned thing to say to a deputy marshal. As night gathered, the clouds thickened; soon they raced through blackness. The deputies kept the interior of the car dimly lit by the overhead so they could watch him. But soon, far away across the wheat fields, a brighter light had appeared. Tiny at first, but slowly drawing nearer until it turned into an island of lights thrusting bright above the black wheat fields. As Lee took in his first sight of Springfield, suddenly the ghost cat returned. Lee sensed the yellow tom and felt his warmth stretched out across his shoulder, felt the tremble of Misto's silent purr, and Lee's interest in life revived.

"Times will be better at Springfield," the tomcat whispered so softly the two men couldn't hear. The cat didn't say there would be bad times, too, but Lee knew that. That's what life was about. As long as Misto was near, he knew they would prevail. In the dim car, Lee's desolation dwindled away and he had to smile. The ghost cat had never meant to leave him.

"What are *you* grinning about?" the deputy snapped, scowling at Lee.

"Hoping they'll give me some supper," Lee said. "I could sure use it, that sandwich at lunch didn't go far."

The deputy just looked at him. What did he care that Lee had barely gotten down a ham sandwich while the deputies wolfed two hamburgers each. No one had asked if he wanted anything more.

The sky was full dark when they drew up to the massive federal prison, its security lights pushing back the night to reveal well-lit buildings and a manicured lawn. Lee could see a guard tower rising up, probably with rifles trained on the approaching car. All he could think about was a hot meal and a warm bed. Even with Misto near, it had been a long day, a long trip crowded by the damned deputy.

Within minutes of pulling up before the brightly lit prison Lee, still cuffed to his surly companion, was ushered up the steps into the vast, five-story main building. He was searched, all his personal possessions taken from him except the small framed photograph of his little sister. Pictures were the only item the men were allowed to keep. Stripped of his clothes, he luxuriated in the hot shower, getting warm for the first time all day, feeling his muscles ease.

He dressed in the clean prison clothes he was issued, shorts and socks, a blue shirt and a blue jumper with white pinstripes. He was allowed to wear his own boots. A trustee had led him to the dining room, where he'd joined the last dinner shift. The big bowl of hot beef stew tasted mighty good, and there was fresh, homemade bread, and coffee and apple pie. He'd left the table feeling good, was escorted to his quarters, which were not a cell, as he'd expected, but a small hospital room. It was larger than any single cell he'd ever occupied, and far cleaner, freshly painted pale green, and the battleship-gray linoleum looked newly scrubbed. A decent-looking single bed stood in one corner, made up with real sheets and three rough, heavy blankets. There was even a small dresser for his clothes, and a real window, with glass outside the bars. This wasn't a prison, it was a hotel. He'd looked at the young, wide-shouldered guard. "How long will I stay here before I'm moved to a cell?"

"No cells for hospital inmates, Fontana. The prison-camp men, they're in a dorm, and some in a cellblock, in another building. They're on loan, mostly. Trusties from other facilities. They do the heavy work of the plant, maintenance, heavy kitchen work."

The young, freckle-faced guard had grinned at Lee's look. "Your job, at Springfield, is to get well. You'll like the stay," the guard said, smiling. "Your door isn't locked at night, but there's a guard outside, always on duty. And where would you go if you walked out? In your condition, you want to wade through a hundred miles of wheat fields?"

Lee laughed. This was a whole new game, a new kind of incarceration, and it was pretty nice. When at last he was alone he stripped, folded his clothes and laid them on the dresser. He crawled under the heavy blankets and lay floating in the warm comfort of the simple prison bed. He felt a little edgy at sleeping with an unlocked door, wondering what kind of guys might be roaming the halls, but he was too tired to think much about it. He might as well enjoy the freedom, he'd be out of here in a month or so, as soon as he was well enough. Would be back in California digging up the money and heading for Mexico, where the hot sun could bake away the last of the sickness, could ease comfort into his tired bones.

He'd find a small adobe cottage in one of the fishing villages along the Baja coast, he'd learn to speak enough Spanish to get by, he'd get to know the folks around him. If a Mexican liked you, he'd hide you. If he didn't, you were done for. In just a few months from now he'd have his own home, have all the good food, all the chilies and tortillas he'd ever wanted, all the clams he could dig from the shore. It wouldn't be hard to find a woman to cook for him, Lee thought, to keep his house and maybe warm his bed.

Smiling, Lee was nearly asleep when a fit of coughing jarred him awake again. He sat up, painfully sucking air, angered at the betrayal of his weakening body. He was so deep down tired that for one panicked moment he wondered if he would live long enough to retrieve the stolen money and luxuriate, for even a short time, in the hot, bright embrace of that Mexican village.

But then as he'd eased down into sleep once more he'd felt the ghost cat leap on the bed, heavy and purring. With the small spirit curled warm beside him, Lee had known he'd make it to Mexico. Had known for sure that no matter what lay ahead until he got back to the desert, the ghost cat would be with him. That his partner would stay close, traveling beside him.

3

Misto, waiting on the roof for his prisonmate to leave the doctor's office, was half asleep when he sensed Lee's departure. He didn't see Lee emerge from the building but he could hear his footsteps. The old convict had moved down the inner stairs into one of the subterranean passages that connected most of the buildings. His steady pace echoed along the tunnel from the hospital to the building that held the dining room, the kitchen, the big auditorium, and the prison library.

Lee had found, early on, that not only was the library a comfortable retreat but that librarian Nancy Trousdale, with her bobbed gray hair and laughing brown eyes, was nice to be around. She knew her collection, and the shelves held a surprising number of nonfiction books for inmates with a variety of interests, whether from their own professional backgrounds or prisoners planning to branch out into new endeavors. On Lee's first visit Nancy had guided him to exactly the history section he wanted. She made Lee feel at home as he pursued information about the old train robbers of the last century, looking for mention of his grand-pappy. She had helped him find a surprising number of volumes about Russell Dobbs's time, many with a wealth of information on Russell himself. There were clear descriptions of Russell's train robberies plus a number of tall tales about the old robber and the devil, stories that Lee knew were more than fiction.

As the ghost cat prowled the library, invisible to Nancy and to the inmates reading at the various tables, Lee moved to the desk to return four books. Nancy looked up at him, smiling as she retrieved three new books that she'd saved for him. "You're looking fine, Fontana. Our weather agrees with you?"

"The weather," Lee said, "the good food—and the good company," he said, giving her a wink.

"And you're finding what you want about Russell Dobbs?"

"Thanks to you," Lee said.

"He was a colorful man. You have me reading about him, too. Colorful and bold, a good man to have on *your* side," she said shyly. "According to the folktales about him, as well as his history, he was bold enough to face up to true evil."

They exchanged the friendly look of a shared interest; Lee checked out his books, gave her a parting smile, and headed back to his room. Misto followed and passed Lee, a breath of warm wind brushing Lee's face. The tomcat was crouched on the windowsill when Lee came in, but not until Lee shut the door did the cat materialize, first his furry yellow tail lashing against the barred pane, his whiskers curved in a sly smile, then the rest of him.

Lee laid his books on the small night table and stretched out on the bed. As he doubled the pillow behind him and selected a heavy volume, the cat leaped to the blanket and settled against his knee. Lee checked the index, found the sections on Dobbs, and marked them with some torn slips of paper that he kept on the nightstand. He knew well enough the more spectacular events of his grandpappy's history, the tales that had been told over campfires or were in the local papers. What he was looking for were the periods in Russell's life that, whenever he'd asked questions of his mother or Pa, they would ignore and abruptly change the subject to something more "respectable." Lee had wanted, even as a child, to understand better the long-standing curse on Russell. He hadn't known, then, that this curse would spill over to harass him as well.

He'd been twelve years old that morning on their South Dakota ranch when he stood beside his grandpappy watching Satan's shadow move across the open prairie.

No figure walked there, only the tall, drifting shadow where there should be no blemish against the pale ground and cloudless sky. The haunt had frightened Russell's horse so he reared back where he was tied and broke his reins, and had made the steers in the pasture wheel away running. The shadow had frightened Lee's grandpappy in a way Lee would never have guessed. It was the only time ever that he'd seen Russell Dobbs show fear

But Russell was his idol. Lee had put aside his grandpappy's unease, had put aside the strangeness of that day. As Lee grew older he'd patterned his life on that of Russell Dobbs. Before he was twenty-one, most often working alone, he had taken down some nice hauls of cash—and spent most of the money as fast as he stole it, on women, cards, and whiskey.

Only when the old steam trains began to vanish, replaced by diesels too fast for any horseman, did Russell change his methods. He took on a few partners and moved into the new era. But Lee didn't like the diesels; he stuck to the few steam trains remaining, on the smaller lines. He had stayed away from the large and vicious train gangs that Russell sometimes confronted. Detective Pinkerton had long ago become a whole army of Pinkertons, and for a long while Russell avoided them, too, as he avoided the shadow that hounded him.

The cat looked down from the dresser at Lee so deeply lost in tales of the past century, then nosed with curiosity at the picture of Lee's little sister that Lee had placed beside the lamp, the tintype of Mae taken some sixty years ago, the picture that could easily be of Misto's own Sammie.

Sometimes in Misto's spirit life distant events came to him clearly; other times they remained uncertain, endlessly frustrating. Lee knew nothing of Sammie Blake, but Misto felt clearly that the child and the old man would meet.

The ghost cat lost in speculation, and Lee lost in the past, were jerked back to the present when the noon whistle blasted.

Carefully closing the book, Lee rose, washed his hands and face, and headed out to the mess hall. Misto, leaping on the bed, knowing Lee would return to his room directly after lunch for the noon count, pawed out a warm nest among the covers and snuggled down, purring. A count was taken every morning, another after lunch, a third count before supper. Lee had no work detail at Springfield. It still amused Lee and amused Misto that the prison work, the gardening and kitchen, the farm work, the cleaning and maintenance was handled by trusties from other prisons. Men assigned from Leavenworth, from El Reno, or from the Atlanta Pen, first offenders chosen as the most responsible among their prison populations.

Once Lee had left for lunch, closing the door behind him, the cat's thoughts turned back to Georgia where the murder trial of Sammie's daddy was about to begin. The tomcat was well aware of Morgan Blake's arrest. He knew Morgan hadn't committed the murder he was charged with, he had suffered with Sammie when her daddy was jailed. He didn't doubt this trial would herald a painful time in the lives of the Blake family; he didn't like to think what life would be like if Morgan was found guilty and sent to federal prison on a life sentence. Bank robbery and murder weren't looked upon kindly in rural Georgia. Morgan was just a young man, a clean-living, hardworking man who did not deserve the bad luck, the cold and deliberate evil that now surrounded him and his family.

The ghost cat, vanishing and reappearing as he pleased, visited Sammie often. He would snuggle into her dreams at night and into her arms to comfort her. Though he remained unseen, Sammie stroked and cuddled him, put out a finger to feel his soft paw or gently scratched his ragged ears the way she'd done when he was alive. She didn't question that he was a ghost, she loved and needed him. But when, deep in the night, Sammie slept soundly, at peace again, Misto would return to Lee.

Often at night Misto was filled with Lee's sickness; he could feel within his own body Lee's struggle for breath, his fear of what lay ahead, his desperate bouts of depression. And often at night Misto puzzled mightily over the connection between Mae and Sammie. Always the future blurred, as undefined as if the dark spirit himself had stepped between the ghost cat and whatever beckoned, whatever waited for Lee.

4

Late afternoon sunlight shone in through the Blakes' living room windows, brightening the white wicker furniture and flowered cushions, the potted red geraniums on the sill, the hooked rug Becky's mother had made. Slanting sunlight heightened the carved details of the antique pie safe that had belonged to a great-aunt Becky had never known. All her treasures gathering the afternoon glow would normally comfort her, warm and welcoming; but now, at this moment, Becky's beloved retreat seemed close and constricting, the colors too bright, the sunlight brassy. She sat stiffly on the edge of a chair like a stranger in her own house, holding her white purse awkwardly on her knees, her dark hair damp with perspiration. She had no idea how long she had sat there. Thinking too much and then not thinking at all, just sitting, numb and unfeeling, incapable of thought.

The trial was over. After a long and shattering three days in the hot, crowded courtroom, Morgan had been found guilty on one count of murder, three counts of assault and attempted murder, and one count of armed robbery, sentence to be pronounced after an extended noon break.

During the trial she hadn't slept much at night, had lain awake staring into the dark, unable to deal with the concept of a death sentence. Praying, *praying* it would at least be a life sentence, but then wondering what that would do to Morgan. Wondering if all the rest of his life spent in prison was better than death, when he had done nothing? When he had not killed that man?

In court this afternoon waiting for the judge to pronounce sentence she had been so shaky and so terribly cold. She had attended all of the trial alone, unwilling to bring Sammie into the courtroom, make the child listen to the ugly accusations. Alone, she had listened as Morgan received sentence. Life plus twenty-five years.

She didn't remember leaving the building. The last formalities of the trial had swirled around her without meaning. She had been allowed to embrace Morgan and kiss him awkwardly as he stood handcuffed and desolate between the two guards. He had been taken away to a cell, shackled and helpless. He would be driven to Atlanta tomorrow morning, in a U.S. marshal's car. She and Sammie must be there by eight if they were to say good-bye. A few minutes with him at the jail before he was taken away. After that she and Sammie would see him only when they drove down to Atlanta to visit with him like a stranger inside the prison walls.

She felt uncertain about taking Sammie to the jail in the morning to say good-bye. Sammie having to part with him there behind bars, part with him maybe forever. But how could she not take her? The child had a right to be there no matter how painful the parting. To be excluded would be far more heartbreaking.

She didn't remember coming home after the sentencing. She remembered coming in the house, sitting down in the chair. She didn't know how long she had sat there, but evening was falling, the sun slanting low. She had not gone to her mother's, where she and Sammie were staying. She'd needed to pull herself together before she faced Sammie, before she went to tell Sammie.

Tell her they must begin now to live the rest of their lives without him.

Unless they could get an appeal, could win an appeal. That was the only chance they had. The only chance for Morgan to come home, to ever set foot inside his own house again, for him to live his life in freedom, the only chance for them to hold each other close, to be a family again.

Was he never again to play ball with Sammie, take her to the automotive shop to hand him his tools, as she so loved to do? Tomorrow he would leave Rome for the last time, to be locked in that vast concrete prison that rose on the south side of Atlanta, its high gray walls austere and forbidding, its guard towers catching light where loaded rifles shone in the hands of grim-faced guards. The world they had built together had ended. Their family's carefully nurtured life, their gentle protection of one another against whatever chaos existed in the world, had all been for nothing. Morgan's war years fighting against the tyranny of Japan and Germany, his safe return, had been for nothing.

But, she thought, Morgan's contribution to his country, to America's successful campaigns, had not been for nothing. And yet now, after all he had given, Morgan himself had been betrayed.

The jury of their own neighbors had believed—all of them believed—that Morgan had murdered the bank guard, had beaten those women and taken the bank money. The jury's unanimous vote was beyond her comprehension. Such unfairness didn't happen, not under the free government which, in the war, Morgan and so many men had fought to preserve. Morgan faced the rest of his life behind prison walls for crimes he'd had nothing to do with, to be harried by armed guards, harassed and maybe beaten by other prisoners, at the mercy of men as vicious as caged beasts. He didn't belong in there, she didn't want him in there; she wanted to scream and never stop screaming, wanted to put her fist through the window and smash it, hurt and bloody herself. She wanted to arm herself and find Brad Falon and kill him, wanted to destroy Falon just as he had destroyed Morgan and shattered the life of their little girl. She *would* kill him, except for Sammie, for what that would do to Sammie.

Falon had always been hateful. When they were kids in high school Morgan hadn't seen how twisted Falon was, he'd seen Falon's adventurous side, his boldness, had admired Brad Falon for the brash things he did that Morgan was reluctant to do. Though Morgan hadn't wanted Falon hanging around her. She'd never told Morgan the extent of Falon's unwanted attention when he found her alone; she'd tried never to be alone with him. Falon was possessed of a cruelty that she guessed some young men, with all that animal energy, found exciting. They were halfway through high school before Morgan realized how twisted Falon was and backed off, leaving Falon to pull his petty thefts alone. But after Morgan left for the navy, Falon started coming around, increasingly pushy, refusing to leave her alone. He had frightened her then. Now he terrified her.

There was no doubt Falon had set Morgan up, had drugged him, left him unconscious in Morgan's own car that afternoon. Had left him parked there in the woods overnight while Falon himself, disguised as Morgan, had walked into the bank, killed the guard, beaten the bank clerks, locked them in the vault and walked out with the money. Falon's planted evidence, the scattered hundred-dollar bills and canvas bank bag in Morgan's car, had incriminated Morgan well enough, coupled with Morgan's inability to remember where he'd been all afternoon and night. Though it was Natalie Hooper's testimony that, in the end, had sealed the conviction.

Anyone with common sense could see that the woman was lying, but the jury hadn't seen it. Gullible and unthinking, they had bought Natalie's story that Falon had spent the afternoon and all night with her, in her apartment. It was Natalie's lies that the jury believed. That fact alone left Becky hating her neighbors.

Rome was a small town, everyone knew Morgan, knew he was a good man, knew how hard he worked at the automotive shop he had built. And everyone knew

Brad Falon, knew he'd been in trouble all through school, had been in Juvenile Hall and later in prison. Everyone knew that Falon meant trouble, and that Natalie wasn't much better. What dark and twisted leverage, what illusion, had been at work in the courtroom while that slovenly woman occupied the witness stand? That slattern with her wild black hair and tight skirts and jangling jewelry who had already gone through three husbands and a dozen lovers? What magnetism had been in play among the unseeing jury of townspeople, of six men and six women, to make them believe Natalie, to allow her to successfully hoodwink them?

Becky didn't know how she was going to tell Sammie that her daddy wasn't coming home. She felt drained, wanted to be with her own mother, wanted Caroline to hold and comfort her as if she herself were a child again. Wanted Caroline to reassure and strengthen her as they must now support Sammie. She wanted to be the little girl again, to be held and soothed, to be told what to do, told how to live her life, now that they were alone.

After the verdict Becky had phoned Caroline from the glassed-in phone booth at the courthouse, trying not to cry. Later, after the sentencing, she had phoned her mother again, had stood with her back to the glass door that faced the courthouse hallway, avoiding the eyes of her neighbors as they crowded out of the court-room glancing at her with righteous or with embar-rassed stares. She had wanted only to be away from them, to remove herself even from the few awkward attempts at sympathy. She hated her neighbors, she hated the jury that was made up of her neighbors, she hated the courts, hated the judge, the police, hated the damned attorney who had lost for them.

Sitting rigid on the edge of the chair, she thought of making herself a cup of tea. She hadn't eaten since last night, but she didn't care enough to get up and put the kettle on or to rummage in the refrigerator for some-thing she thought she could keep down. She needed to pull herself together, needed to go on over to her mother's and tell Sammie. She didn't know how to face Sammie, didn't known how to present the truth to her. Even if she talked about an appeal, tried to say he might be coming home, that wouldn't be straightforward, the hope was too slim. If one attorney couldn't win for them, how could another? She and Morgan had always been honest with Sammie. With the perceptive dreams Sammie had, one couldn't be otherwise, couldn't side-step the true facts even though they were painful.

Sammie knew as well as she did that Brad Falon had set Morgan up, that the child feared and hated Falon and with good cause. While Morgan was overseas Falon broke into their house, terrified them both, and killed Sammie's cat: Sammie knew too well what he was. The fact that *this* man had destroyed her daddy made the blow all the more frightening. That night when he broke in, Sammie's yellow tomcat had leaped on Falon and done considerable damage before Falon killed him with a shard of broken glass. Sammie had never gotten over Misto's death, she still dreamed of him. Sometimes she imagined he was there in bed snuggled close to her, she imagined that Misto's ghost had come back to her. But lots of children had imaginary companions. The dreams comforted Sammie, and they hurt no one.

It was Sammie's dreams of future events that were upsetting. Powerful predictions that, days or weeks later, would turn out to come true: the courthouse fire that Sammie dreamed in surprising detail exactly as it would later happen, its fallen brick walls, every detail occurring just as she'd seen.

There were happy dreams, too, the birth of the neighbor's kittens, each with the same exact coloring that Sammie saw in her dream. But then had come the terrifying nightmare that brought Sammie up screaming that her daddy had been arrested and shoved behind bars, that he had been locked in a cell by the very officers who had been Morgan's friends. That was the beginning. It had all happened, the robbery, Morgan's arrest, Morgan locked in jail just as she'd dreamed.

On the witness stand, Falon told the jury that, originally, Morgan had driven over to look at Falon's stalled Ford coupe, which was parked in front of Natalie's apartment building. He said Morgan had noted the parts he must order and then had left, saying he was going back to the shop. Morgan's mechanic testified that Morgan had never returned there, that at closing time he'd locked the shop up himself and gone home.

Falon said when Morgan came to look at his car he had acted nervous and seemed anxious to get away. He said he'd gone back upstairs to Natalie's after Morgan left. Said he'd come down again shortly before three, walked across the street to the corner store and bought some candy and gum. The shopkeeper had testified to that, he said he'd seen Falon go back to the apartment building and in the front door. Falon testified that he had been with Natalie the rest of the afternoon and all night. When Natalie took the stand to corroborate his testimony she had blushed and tried to act shy that they had spent the night together. Right, Becky had thought angrily, and how many dozen other men over the years.

The court had allowed Becky to sit at the table with Morgan and Sed Williams, their attorney. She'd had a hard time avoiding the stares of the packed gallery. She had listened to the bank tellers identify Morgan's voice, identify his hands with the thin lines of grease that clung in deep creases and around his nails, from his work in the auto shop when he forgot to wear gloves. The empty bootleg whiskey bottle the police found in Morgan's car had Morgan's fingerprints on it. Everyone in town knew that Morgan and she didn't drink. A shopkeeper across the street from the bank had heard the shots, had seen Morgan's car pull away, and had written down the license number.

Why couldn't the jury see that Falon had planted it all? Why couldn't they see that? Her helplessness there in the courtroom, her inability to speak up and correct this evil, had made her physically ill.

Now, when she rose from the wicker chair to go into the kitchen to make a cup of tea, her stomach twisted so hard that she ran for the bathroom. She threw up in the sink, angrily cleaned the sink and scrubbed it with cleanser, then began to pace the house, living room to the two small bedrooms to kitchen, then back again, aimless and lost, desperate with rage.

An appeal was the only chance they had, was all they had to cling to. She had to think about that. How to get the money together? The best way to find a more competent attorney. She shouldn't have hired Williams; he was too quiet, too low-key. She had thought he was a family friend, that he really cared about Morgan and would work hard for him. She'd thought that his quiet, professional manner in the courtroom would help them get to the truth. But when he had a witness on the stand she'd seen how weak he was, with no ability to defend his client.

She didn't know how to start an appeal. She didn't know if there was a waiting period, didn't know how appeals worked. She'd been so sure Morgan would be acquitted that she hadn't bothered to find out. She had to find a new attorney and figure out how to pay him. They'd bought the house after Morgan went in the navy, with the smallest payments they could obtain. Maybe she could get a second mortgage or borrow money on the shop. She wanted an attorney who would dig harder, a man strong enough to make a new jury see the truth. She tried to cheer herself that an appeal would end the nightmare, that Morgan would be out soon, that it wouldn't be long and he'd be home again. Meantime she could run the shop just fine. Albert, the new mechanic, was a skilled worker even if he was dull about everything else. She knew she could take on more bookkeeping jobs, she always had a waiting list. Sammie would be in school, and she'd have plenty of time to work. Long empty nights in which to work. Long, empty weekends.

She supposed, if they were to get a new trial, there would have to be new evidence. Where and how would she, or even a new attorney, find evidence after the police had been over everything, had collected and presented in court all the evidence to be found? She stood in the middle of the living room frantic with fear, her mind circling like a caged animal searching for a way to escape.

At last she picked up her purse and headed for Mama's, to tell Sammie what must be told. Try to explain to her nine-year-old child that the law, which was meant to protect them, had turned against them. That the grown-ups on the jury whom Sammie knew and trusted, did not believe her daddy, that the whole town had betrayed him.

5

In the visiting room of the Rome jail, Morgan stiffened as two deputy U.S. marshals pulled him away from Becky and Sammie. It took all the resolve he had not to fight them as they jerked his arms behind him, snapped on handcuffs and forced him toward the door. The time was eight-fifteen, the morning after he was sentenced in Rome's U.S. courthouse by the town's one federal judge. He and Becky and Sammie had been allowed only a few moments to say good-bye, the three of them clinging together. As if they might form an unbreakable chain that could never be wrenched apart. Sammie, when she looked up at him, was so vulnerable and perplexed. He knew Becky had debated a long time whether to bring her this morning. But the pain Sammie was experiencing now was preferable to his being taken away without seeing her, to Sammie learning later that Morgan was gone for good, that he might never come home again.

From the hall, he looked back for as long as he could see them, Sammie biting her lip, the tears streaming down. Becky stone-faced, holding the child close, trying not to cry. Then he couldn't see them anymore, he was forced down the hall, through the jail's back door and into the backseat of a U.S. marshal's car. A heavy metal grid separated him from the front seat as if, despite handcuffs and a belly chain, they thought he would attack the driver from the rear.

In the backseat of the official vehicle, handcuffed to a second deputy, he watched the driver get settled, listened to the engine of the heavy Packard start up smooth and powerful. As the black car headed through Rome in the direction of Atlanta, he imagined Becky and Sammie getting in their car, holding each other, comforting each other. Imagined them driving the few blocks to Caroline's, and he was mighty glad for Becky's strong and caring mother.

Becky had been so still during the trial, sitting near him at the attorney's table, never moving, and so very pale. After the verdict, when he was back in his cell he kept reliving that moment: "Life and twenty-five years, life and twenty-five years." He kept seeing her face, closed and still, trying to hide the pain. Kept seeing the faces of his neighbors, members of his church, his automotive customers—the hard faces of strangers. In less than four weeks from the day Falon walked into the shop asking Morgan to come look at his car, nearly the whole town had turned against them. Their lives had been blown away as thoroughly as a landing craft sunk by a destroyer.

During the two-hour ride to Atlanta, handcuffed to the deputy marshal, he experienced every bitter emotion, desolation, helplessness, a violent rage that he had no way to act upon. He had always viewed the U.S. legal system as carefully designed to protect honest men, to confine those who threatened ordered society. How dumb was that?

If a federal jury could do this to an innocent man, what other destruction might the courts be capable of?

He and Becky had made their marriage vows for life; they had joined as a team not to be parted. Now Morgan himself, in one moment of bad judgment, had wrenched their family apart. In going with Falon to look at his car, he had broken all his promises to Becky and had shattered their little girl's life. Now, if he hadn't been chained he would have tried to grab the deputy's weapon, would have done his best to break away and get the hell out of there. Watching

the thin, scowling deputy, he grew increasingly res-
tive. Only when the deputy's hand edged toward his
gun did Morgan try to sit easier. These men didn't
know him, they didn't know what he might try. He
was dealing with a different world now. He had no
rights anymore. He would soon be surrounded by
guards like these who lived by power, and by inmates
just as power hungry, and he'd sure have to watch
himself.

After the trial he had suggested to Becky that she
file for divorce, that she try to make a new life for herself and Sammie. Her face had gone red with anger, her
eyes blazing, then she had clung to him, weeping. Not
since a mortar shell had ripped through the hull of his
ship in the Pacific, the water gushing in through splintered metal, had he realized how frail and precious life
was. Falon's deliberate destruction of their lives had
been as brutal as any enemy attack.

They entered the outskirts of Atlanta, passed the Fox
Theater and then the hotel where he and Becky had
had dinner before he left with the navy. She'd ended up
crying halfway through the meal. The future then, as
he went off to war, had seemed irrevocably black and
empty.

He'd come home from that one—but maybe he'd
had better odds, even in war, than he had now.

South of Atlanta the modest little houses gave way to mottled fields and then the Federal Pen loomed, tall and gray and cold, its fortress face and guard towers challenging all comers. Parking their black limo before the front door, the deputies pulled him out, forced him up the steps and inside.

He was booked and told to strip. His clothes were taken away, and a guard searched the cavities of his body, stirring his rage. He showered as he was told. He dressed in the prison blues he was issued, then moved into the cellblock followed by a guard. The cells stood five tiers high. He climbed the narrow metal stairs to the third level, walked ahead of the guard along the steel catwalk. He was locked into a single cell, and was grateful for that. He hoped he wouldn't be moved later into one of the bigger cells with multiple cots and with unrestrained roommates. Sitting down on his narrow bunk, he didn't look at the men in the cells across the way, didn't make eye contact. Some of them watched him idly; others stared directly at him, caged predators assessing new prey.

6

The night before Sammie said good-bye to Daddy she dreamed she was there in the police station. Sleeping next to Mama, Misto close in her arms, she saw their good-bye there in the jail and she hugged Misto tight, trying not to cry and wake Mama.

"It will be all right," Misto murmured, his whiskers tickling her ear. "It isn't over, Sammie. Your daddy will be all right."

"The cowboy will come?" Sammie whispered. "He will help Daddy?"

"You dreamed he would," Misto said.

She hadn't answered, she'd hugged the big cat tight and he pressed his cool nose against her cheek. "You are my Sammie, you will endure." He purred against her so hard she thought his rumble would wake Mama, but it didn't, she was too tired from the courtroom trial.

"It must have been ugly and mean," she whispered, "if Mama wouldn't take me."

"It was ugly. But your daddy will prevail, and so will you." And Misto had leaped from her arms, raced around the night-dim room, raced up the curtains never moving them and making no sound, only delighting Sammie. He sailed from the curtain rod to the dresser with not a stir of air, then to the top of the open closet door and back to the bed, then up, up to the ceiling. His joy and wildness, his cat-madness made her want to race and fly with him, and maybe that would make the pain go away. He sailed around the room twice, then pounced down again and snuggled close, still and warm against her, purring and purring. Misto was with her all the rest of the night, snuggled in her arms. In the morning when she and Mama drove to the jail she knew he was near; sometimes she could feel his whiskers on her cheek or feel a brush of fur, and that helped her to be strong for Daddy.

At the jail when they said good-bye she clung to Daddy and so did Mama but that cop pulled him away and forced him from the room. She could see Daddy's anger, she knew he wanted to fight them but what good would it do? They'd hardly had time to hug each other and then he was gone, was marched away down the hall. He glanced back once, then she and Mama were alone. Everything was empty, the whole world empty. She felt Misto's warmth against her cheek, but now even her loving cat couldn't help.

"You know we'll visit him at the prison," Mama said. "They have visiting hours, we'll be with him then."

"In a cage," Sammie said. "We can't *be* with him at home. We have to *visit* Daddy, like a stranger in a *cage*."

Another cop walked them out to the front door. They crossed the parking lot, got in their car and sat holding each other. Mama tried to stop crying but she couldn't. Sammie pressed so close that when Mama started the car she could hardly drive; she drove one-handed, her arm tight around Sammie. Sammie was nine but she felt like a tiny child, pressing her face against Mama. Now, without Daddy, they weren't a family, they needed to be together to be a real family. When Daddy went overseas, when she was little, he told her he was going to fight for freedom. Freedom for their world, he said. Freedom for their country and for every person in it. But instead of freedom for all, like the history books said, those people in the federal court and even their own neighbors had stolen her daddy's freedom from him, and Daddy had done nothing wrong.

Ever since the trial began, she and Mama had stayed with Grandma, and Sammie had been with Grandma every day. Mama didn't want her in school, when Brad Falon with the narrow eyes might still be in town, might follow her. And where the kids would bully her and say her daddy was guilty.

During the trial Grandma had gone right on running her baking business; she said the money she made was even more important now, and you couldn't just tell longtime customers there would be no more pies and cakes until the trial was over. Grandma said that would lose all her good customers and she had already lost some of them because of what people thought Daddy had done. Grandma was up every morning at three; the smell of baking always woke Sammie. A lady came in to help her, and once the cakes and pies and bread were out and cooling they would stop long enough to make breakfast, but Sammie could never eat very much. Later when the cakes were iced and everything was boxed and ready, Sammie would ride with Grandma in the van to deliver them to the local restaurants. And every night, during the trial, Misto was with her.

Now, after saying good-bye to Daddy they came in the house, through the closed-in porch, and straight into Grandma Caroline's arms. They stood in the middle of the living room clinging together hugging each other, needing each other, hurting and lost.

The whole house smelled of sausage biscuits. In the kitchen, Grandma had already poured a cup of hot tea for Mama and milk for Sammie. Grandma always wore jeans, and this morning a faded plaid shirt covered by a bright apron of patchwork, one of the aprons she liked to sew late at night when she couldn't sleep. She must be awake a lot because she sure had a lot of aprons, all as bright as picture books.

Caroline Tanner wore no makeup, her high coloring and short, dark hair needing no enhancement. She set a tray of sausage biscuits on the table beside a strawberry shortcake. Comfort food, Becky thought, watching her mother, never ceasing to wonder at her calm strength. Becky had been seven when her father was killed in a tractor accident. Two weeks after the funeral Caroline began baking and selling her goods. She was a Rome girl, and the town had given her its support. They had lived on what she made, Becky and her two brothers helping all they could.

Becky was ten, her brother Ron twelve and James fifteen when Caroline got a loan from the bank and extended the kitchen of their little house into a bigger and more efficient bakery and storeroom. Becky and her brothers had helped the carpenter after school and on weekends, as he built and dried in the new walls, then tore out the original walls. The children had learned how to paint properly, how to clean their tools, and her brothers had learned how to plaster. After the stainless steel counters were installed, and the two big commercial refrigerators and two sinks, they had taken the bakery van into Atlanta and brought home the new ovens, the big stovetop, and the smaller commercial appliances. The big window over the sink looked out on the side yard beneath a pair of live oak trees.

Before the remodel, Caroline had done all her baking in their small, inadequate kitchen, her equipment and trays of baked goods spilling over into the dining room, where cookies and breads and cakes cooled on racks, along with those already boxed and ready for delivery. The two iceboxes never had enough space for the salads and casseroles for the parties that Caroline catered. Their own simple meals had been eaten in the living room, worked around the urgent business of making a living. When the new bakery was finished, they'd had a little party, just the four of them, to celebrate the new and more accommodating kitchen, to reclaim their own house.

Within three years Caroline had paid off the van and equipment and could hire more help for the catered weddings and parties, though still, the whole family pitched in for those. All the years Becky was growing up, her mother would be out of bed and dressed by three in the morning, rolling out pie crusts, baking cakes. Becky's brothers made breakfast until Becky was old enough to cook. Her brothers, as soon as they could drive legally, had done the bakery deliveries before school.

Becky missed her brothers. Even after Ron was killed in the Pacific, she still felt often that he was near her. And though their older brother, James, was still in Japan he was close to them, he liked to write home of that very different part of the world. She looked forward to his return next year when his tour of duty ended.

By the time Becky turned sixteen and got her driver's license, her brothers had moved on with their lives. She had felt very grown-up, handling the deliveries herself, before and after school. She had helped with them after she and Morgan were married, until Sammie was born. Even during the war years Caroline made an adequate living, using special recipes that took little of the precious rationed sugar but were still delicious.

Now, at forty-eight, Caroline was as energetic and slim as ever, a tall, strong woman whom Becky, at this time in her life, deeply envied. She wished she had half her mother's resilience, wished she could follow better Caroline's hardheaded approach to life. Caroline Tanner had always tackled problems head-on, stubbornly weighing each possible solution, choosing the most viable one, then plunging ahead with no holds barred. If Caroline had tears during those hard years, she cried them in private.

They were halfway through supper when Caroline said, "The next thing is to go for an appeal. You need a better lawyer." She looked steadily at Becky. "I plan to help with his fees. I want Falon taken down, I want to see *him* in prison. I want Morgan out of that place."

"Mama, I don't—"

"It's family money. Half of it will be yours one day and you need it now. If it bothers you to take it, you can pay me back after Morgan gets out."

"If he gets out."

Caroline stared at her. "*When* he gets out. Morgan is in prison unjustly. We keep at it until we find a better lawyer, get an appeal and a new trial. A fair trial. But not in Rome," she said bitterly.

Becky laid her hand over Caroline's. "You make it sound so simple."

"There's no other way. First thing is to find an attorney."

"I've already made some inquiries," Becky said. "There are several lawyers in Atlanta I want to see. But, Mama, we need new evidence, stronger evidence, for an appeal. I want to talk with the tellers, with Mrs. Herron and Betty Holmes, and the younger teller. I want to talk with the bank manager, and the witness who saw Morgan's car leave the bank." She sighed. "I mean to talk with Natalie Hooper, though I don't look forward to facing that piece of trash."

Caroline gave Becky a long look. "That's not the way to go." She rose to cut the shortcake and lathered on whipped cream. "Let the lawyer do that. You could compromise the case."

Watching her mother, Becky thought about that. She watched Sammie, too. Though the child made quick work of her dessert she was too quiet, hurting so bad inside, missing her daddy.

Still, though, after the good meal Sammie seemed steadier. Her color brightened; she seemed more alive, less subdued than when they'd left the jail. "Can I go outside and play?"

Becky and Caroline looked at each other. "In the front yard," Becky said. "Stay in front of the big window where we can see you."

Sammie nodded. She walked quietly through the house and out the front door, not running as she normally would. Becky and Caroline moved into the living room to sit on the couch looking out the bay window, watching her.

"The new attorney should talk to the witnesses," Caroline repeated. "Particularly Falon's girlfriend, his key witness. What if Falon found out you'd questioned her? Don't you think he'd make trouble?"

"Mama, I . . . tried to speak to her yesterday, in the parking lot after the sentencing. He probably knows that. She was still nervous, even more upset than she showed on the witness stand. I thought if I could get her to say something incriminating . . ."

Watching her mother, Becky wilted. "I guess that was foolish. I approached her as she was getting in her car. She scowled and turned away, said she couldn't talk to me. But," she said, her hand on Caroline's, "it gave me satisfaction that she was so shaky. I . . . hoped to scare her, make her think about what she'd done."

"Leave her alone, Becky. That's your attorney's job." Caroline was quiet for a moment, then her look softened. "When you're the most determined, the most set on something, I see your father in you."

Becky grinned. "You don't see yourself?"

Caroline laughed.

"I didn't understand until I got older," Becky said, "how hard it was for you, raising us alone."

"We did it together," Caroline said, "the four of us. It was our life and it's been a good one. It's still a good life," she said. "We'll get through this hard part, this isn't forever."

Becky hoped it wasn't forever, hoped her mother was right. "No one could have had a better childhood," she said, "or a closer, stronger family."

Watching Sammie out the window, where she was petting the neighbors' collie, Becky smiled as Sammie tried to push the dog into the bushes as if in some new game. When he wouldn't go, and Sammie herself crept in beneath the shrubs, a chill touched Becky.

Rising, she moved quickly to the window. Sammie was out of sight. A sleek black convertible came slowly down the street, the top up. As Falon's Ford coupe eased to a crawl they raced for the front door. As they crossed the glassed porch, Falon was in the yard. Behind him the driver's door stood open, they could hear the engine running. They lost sight of him beyond the porch blinds. When they burst out to the walk the car door slammed and the car sped away.

The yard was empty. They couldn't see Sammie, and couldn't see if she was in the car. Becky parted the bushes, peering in, but saw only shadows. The dog had disappeared, too. She screamed for Sammie, then ran, chasing the car, ran until she heard Caroline shout.

"She's here—she's all right."

Becky turned, saw Caroline kneeling, hugging Sammie. The dog was there, too, pressing against them. Becky knelt beside them, holding Sammie close, the dog licking their faces. Picking Sammie up, Becky carried her in the house like a very small child. They locked the door, and as Caroline checked the back door, Becky sat at the table holding Sammie. "What did he say? What did he do, what did he say to you?"

"He came to the bushes and looked in. We were down at the end. When Brownie growled, Falon backed away. But he kept looking." She shivered against Becky. "He told me to come out. Brownie growled again and he turned away. I heard his door slam, heard him drive away."

Caroline had picked up the phone to call the police. At Becky's look she put the receiver down.

"What good," Becky said, "after the way we were treated in court? The Rome cops don't like us. They'll write it up as grandstanding, trying to get attention. Who knows what the report would say?" She stared over Sammie's head at Caroline. Could Falon have come in retaliation because she'd talked to Natalie? She should have left the woman alone. She cuddled Sammie, kissing her, terrified for her.

Caroline sat down at the table. "I think you can't stay in Rome. You'll have to get out, move where he won't find you."

"Where, Mama? I can't afford to rent somewhere. And my work, my bookkeeping accounts are all here."

Caroline's look was conflicted. "There's my sister, Anne. I doubt many people know where she is or even know I have a sister. I never talk about her, she never comes to see us."

"I couldn't go there. I haven't seen her since I was in high school. She wouldn't want me and Sammie, she doesn't even like children." The only time they heard from Anne was an occasional phone call, a familiar duty in which she'd ask after everyone's health but didn't seem to really care. She would send a stiff little card at Christmas, cool and impersonal.

Caroline and Anne, even when they were young children, had been at odds, Anne an austere and withdrawn little girl, disdaining the small pleasures that brought joy to Caroline and her friends. She didn't care to climb trees, play ball, compose and act out complicated stage plays with wildly fancy costumes. Aloof and judgmental, Anne had seemed caught in her own solemn world. As if, Caroline said, Anne had never *been* a child, not in the normal sense. Over the years, after Becky's father died, their family had visited Anne twice in Atlanta. They weren't comfortable in her big, elegant home, with her formal ways. She had never come up to Rome, though Caroline had invited her many times.

Anne had left Rome very young to work as a secretary in Atlanta. She had married young, and some years later was divorced. She had remained in Atlanta in her Morningside home, comfortable with the money her philandering husband had settled on her. Becky thought that asking to move in with Anne, begging to be taken in like a charity case, was not something she could handle.

But she had to get away from Falon, she had to get Sammie away.

"I'll call her," Caroline said. "Let me see what I can do."

"Mama, she won't want us. She certainly won't want a little girl in the house. And to know she'd be harboring a convict's family . . . No, I don't want to go there."

"We have to try. Sammie can't stay here, it's too dangerous." She put her hand over Becky's. "Only a few people in town would remember Anne. I doubt they'd know where she went or that she married and later divorced. I doubt anyone would know what her name is now."

Becky wasn't so sure. In a small town, everyone knew your business. And this small town had turned vicious; people might dredge up anything they could find.

"You have to get Sammie out of Rome, she's the one vulnerable weapon Falon has. He'll use her if he can, to make you stop going for an appeal. He has to be terrified of an appeal, of a new trial."

Becky watched her mother. "I'll look for a room in Atlanta, I can find a job there. You can keep Sammie close for a few days, keep her inside with you. Once we're settled she'll be in school. Maybe I can get a job with short hours, or take work home as I do here."

"If Anne will invite you, she won't want rent. Let me try. You'd be better off there, among other people, if you mean to keep Sammie safe."

It was late that night, Becky and Sammie asleep tucked up in Caroline's guest bed, when Sammie woke shivering, clinging to Becky, her body sticky with sweat. When Becky gathered her up, holding her tight, the child said nothing, but lay against Becky in silence. Becky would never force Sammie to tell a dream, that could make her reluctant to reveal any others in the future. Silently she held Sammie until at last the child dozed again, but restlessly, as if still trying to drive away whatever vision haunted her. Only in the small hours did Sammie sleep soundly. Becky slept then, exhausted, holding Sammie close.

In Sammie's dream Daddy was inside the bars and the man with the cold eyes and the narrow head was looking in at him but then he turned and looked hard at her, too. When he reached out for her she woke up. In the dark room she could hear her own heart pounding. Mama held her and kissed her, she clung to Mama for a long time but she was still afraid.

But then when she slept again her dream was nice. She was with the old man, the cowboy, his thin, tanned face, his gray eyes that seemed to see everything. He was in a big airplane looking out the window down at the world laid out below him, the green hills, the tall mountains. Then he was in a big black car with two men in uniform. He was coming now. Soon he would be with Daddy. And in sleep Sammie smiled, snuggling easier against Mama.

Becky woke at dawn, her eyes dry and grainy, her body aching. Whatever Sammie had experienced last night had left Becky herself uncertain and distraught. She rose, pulled on her robe, stood looking down at the sleeping child, wanting to touch her soft, innocent cheek but not wanting to wake her.

But when Becky left the room, Misto did wake Sammie. His purr rumbled, his fur was thick and warm, his whiskers tickled her face. In the dim, early light, as she recalled her dream of the cowboy she hugged Misto so tight he wriggled. The cowboy was coming now, and she didn't feel afraid anymore. When she slept again, cocooned with the invisible tomcat, it was a sleep filled with hope that her daddy would come home. That he would come home again, safe.

7

With the summer heat soaking into Lee's bones, with plenty of good food and rest and with the help of the prison doc, Lee's condition slowly improved. As he grew stronger and wanted something to do, he was assigned light work on the prison farm. Feeding and caring for the four plow horses suited him just fine; they were placid, loving animals and he liked to baby them, to groom them, bring them carrots from the kitchen, trim their hooves when they grew too long. As fall approached, Lee settled comfortably into the pleasant routine of morning work in the stable, then breathing and gym exercises, and late afternoons on his cot with a stack of library books. He was in Dr. Donovan's examining room when the blow struck, when his cozy life changed abruptly and not for the better.

Donovan, finished examining him, paused beside the table, his look solemn, his eyes way too serious. Lee waited uneasily. Were his lungs worse, even though he felt better? But then Donovan smiled, running a hand through his short, pale hair.

"I know you like it here, Lee. I hate to tell you this, but it looks like you're being transferred."

"What the hell? I'm just starting to get better. Transferred where? Why would—"

"Down to Atlanta," Donovan said. "We're receiving two dozen incoming patients, men from a number of states. They're all pretty sick, we need every space we can muster."

No one had asked what Lee wanted. His choices weren't a concern of the U.S. prison system. Scowling at Donovan, he finished buttoning his shirt.

"You're fit enough to move on, Lee. It'll be cold here pretty soon, but should still be warm down south. Atlanta will be good for you."

"Sure it will," Lee said. "Thrown in a cage of felons again where every minute I have to watch my back."

Donovan looked apologetic. Lee knew there was nothing the man could do. They said their good-byes, and early the next morning Lee was out of there, handcuffed, belly-chained, and shoved in the back of another big limo by two surly deputy marshals.

The deputy in the backseat took up most of the space and stunk of cigar smoke. The early morning road was empty, the yellow wheat towering tall on both sides of the two-lane. In the distance Lee could see a row of combines working, cutting wheat just as they would soon be doing outside the prison walls. Crowded into the small space, he couldn't get comfortable, couldn't move his arms much, and the belly chain was already digging in. Did they have to leave him chained like a mass killer?

His temper eased only when he felt a breeze behind him where there was no wind, then felt a soft paw press slyly against his cheek. He imagined the ghost cat stretched out on the wide shelf, enjoying the view through the back window—enjoying a little game, Lee realized when the deputy began to scratch a tickle along his neck. Lee hid a smile as the deputy scratched his ear, then his jaw. When the portly man slapped at his balding head, Lee had trouble not laughing out loud. When he scowled at Lee as if his prisoner was causing the trouble, Lee glanced sternly toward the shelf behind him—kitty-play was all right, but the cranky deputy looked like he wanted to pound someone, and Lee was the only one visible.

Misto stopped the teasing when Lee frowned. He rolled over away from the deputy, hissing softly at the way the heavy lawman hogged the seat, squeezing Lee against the door, deliberately crowding him in the hot car. When Lee's companion lit up a cigar Misto wanted to snake out his paw again and slap the stogie from the fat man's face.

And wouldn't *that* make trouble, when the unpredictable lawman felt his burning cigar jerked from his mouth and saw it flying across the car—an armed and unpredictable lawman. Smiling, Misto guessed he wouldn't try the man's temper that far.

Lee said nothing about the cigar smoke, but sat trying not to cough. Neither deputy had said much to him and he didn't want to get them started; he'd take the smoke and the silence. He looked out the window at the yellow wheat fields stretching away; he stared at the back of the driver's head until the thin deputy met Lee's eyes in the rearview mirror, his glance cold and ungiving. Soon the car was so thick with smoke that Lee couldn't help coughing.

"Can I crack open the window? The emphysema's getting to me."

The fat deputy scowled, but grunted.

Taking that as a yes, Lee managed, despite the handcuffs, to roll down his window, and sat sucking in the fresh breeze. The warm wind made him think of the desert, of Blythe, of the buried post office money and the simple pleasures it would buy.

"What're you smiling about, Fontana?" the fat deputy said. "You know something we don't?"

Lee shrugged. "Hungering for a good Mexican meal. They ever serve Mexican in the Atlanta pen?"

In the front seat, the thin deputy drawled, "Atlanta, you'll get Brunswick stew. That can be as hot as you'll want to try." When Lee began to cough hard despite the open window, the driver glanced back at his partner. "The doc at Springfield told you, Ray, no smoking in the car. That cough gets bad, he keeps it up, we'll have to turn around and take him back."

Scowling, Ray opened his window and threw the burning cigar out on the shoulder of the highway. Lee hoped to hell he didn't set the wheat afire. This wasn't going to improve the man's temper, if he couldn't smoke. And it was a two-day drive to Atlanta.

Soon, with the cigar smoke sucked away by the wind, Lee was able to breathe again. As he settled back, easing pressure off the belly chain, trying to get comfortable, he felt the weight of the ghost cat stretch out along his shoulder. Felt the insolent tickle of bold whiskers, and again he tried not to smile. Lee wished they were flying instead of driving, he liked looking down at the world below, the patterns of farms and cities, the snaking rivers. He'd been startled when, during the flight out from L.A. to Springfield, they'd passed right over the country he had known as a boy. He'd pressed his forehead to the plane's tiny window seeing, in a new way, the wrinkled face of Arizona, the great plains broken by dry, ragged mountains. He saw Flagstaff, the San Francisco peaks rising behind. Where the highway moved north of Winslow, and the Little Colorado River made a sharp turn, a lonely feeling had clutched at him. Off to his left, three fields formed a triangle with trees marking their borders. Those had to be the north fields of the ranch where they'd moved when they left South Dakota, when his dad sold out, sold all the stock, hoping for a better living.

The ranch his father had bought was no better for grass except in early spring, and that new green grass had been without much substance to put any fat on a steer. Sparse grazing land again, hot as hell in the summers, and the well water tasted bitterly of iron. He'd worked long hours, as a boy, doctoring and branding their scruffy cattle. He could still smell the dust, could still feel his favorite bay gelding under him, could still bring back the sweet smell of new grass bruised by a horse's hooves. He could taste the vinegar-soaked beefsteak his mother would cook for breakfast, for the few neighbors who helped each other during roundup, moving from one ranch to the next. Fresh-killed range beef was tough as hell if you didn't soak it overnight in vinegar.

He'd been fourteen when they moved west to Winslow. His brother Howard was fifteen but as useless in Arizona as he'd been in South Dakota, making more work for others than if you did the job yourself. Ma had kept the girls busy tending the garden and chickens, and canning what she could from their pitiful garden. His two older sisters didn't want to work with the cattle, but Mae had yearned after horses. She rode whenever she could sneak away, she would have grown into a good ranch hand if Ma had let her.

The year they moved to the Flagstaff land, Russell Dobbs had followed them all the way out from the Dakotas. Lee had been thrilled when his grandpappy showed up, but his mother was cold with rage. She'd been so relieved to come west to get away from her renegade, train-robbing father.

Grandpappy would be with them for a few days, then gone for a few. Shortly after he arrived, the Flagstaff paper reported a train robbery just north of Prescott. Two weeks later a second train was held up, east of Flagstaff. That was the start of a dozen successful jobs, all at night when Russell might have been there at the ranch, asleep in his bed. Russell knew, if the feds came looking, his daughter would lie for him despite her disapproval. It was at that time that Lee's mother turned inward. She didn't speak to her father much when he was at the ranch and she didn't smile often. After Russell left them for good and moved on again, she lived the rest of her life blaming him for everything that went wrong in the family. It was his influence, she said, that had soured their lives.

As a boy, Lee had known exactly how his grandpappy felt, had known the wild need that kept Dobbs robbing the trains and moving on to rob again. On the ranch, even when Lee stood on a knoll looking across emptiness as far as he could see in every direction, he felt the same trapped need to move on. He could still see that look in Dobbs's eyes, the intensity in Dobbs's movements and in his impatient ways.

Lee, with his own hunger for the fast trains, would do anything as a kid to get into town to see the train pull in, to watch that thin line of smoke curling up from the bell-mouthed stack, the black engine belching steam, steam sighing from the big pistons and drive wheels. His father always wanted Lee to go with him to the stockyard, to take an interest in the cattle trading. But the minute their buggy hit town Lee would sneak off to the station and beg the engineer to let him aboard. He could still feel the warm iron floor under his bare feet as he stood inside the engineer's cab looking at the bright brass gauges and levers, drinking in the power of the engine, a power that filled him right up like a dipper of water on a hot day.

But then his eyes would turn to the engineer's heavy thirty-thirty hanging beside the seat in its scarred leather scabbard, and he would imagine that weapon turned on his grandpappy during a robbery, imagine his grandpappy shot, twisting and falling, and Lee's excitement would turn to fear.

When the engineer shooed him off the train again he would wait beside the track feeling the ground rumble as the engine got moving, would stand there caught in the scream of the whistle and the jolt of the drive wheels as she gathered speed. Would stare up, entranced, at the big pistons pushing to a gallop and the rocking cars heaving past him.

Now, remembering that day flying from the West Coast to Kansas City looking down from the airliner at his old home, he had that same sense of living in two times. As if part of him was still a young man back on the prairie sixty years in the past, while part of him stumbled along toward the end of his life's journey.

In the end, what was it all about? What did it all add up to?

But when he paid attention to the ghost cat draped over his shoulder, one paw resting playfully against

Lee's neck, to the frisky, small ghost, he knew what it all added up to: If Misto had transcended from earthly life into a vast and more complicated dimension, why would humans be different?

Lee felt uncomfortable thinking about such matters, but Misto *was* the living—more than living—example that something more lay ahead, after this life. Not just the dark weight of evil, that was only part of it. Something more, so bright it shamed the golden wheat fields through which the car sped. Crushed in the limo beside the cigar-stinking deputy, Lee was embarrassed by such thoughts, but the proof of a better life was right there, draped over his shoulder, warm, heavy, invisible.

It was a long pull, a two-day trip moving south, crowded against the sweaty deputy. And the layover in Tennessee was no picnic. Lee was lodged in Jackson's dirty county jail while the two deputies went off to a hotel and a steak dinner. Lee's meal, shoved through the cell bars, was some kind of watery stew that had been around too long. The coffee was the color of dishwater and tasted like it. He ached from sitting in the car and his back was sore where the belly chain gouged him. He lay on the jail's dirty cot thinking there wasn't one damned person in the world who cared whether he made it to Atlanta or dropped dead before he got there. But then the ghost cat nudged him, and Lee smiled; and soon, eased by the insistent presence of the ghost cat, Lee slept.

The next day's travel was worse than the first. The weather grew hot and humid, and Lee's seat partner, without his smokes, grew increasingly cranky. They made half a dozen extra stops, pulling over at some turnout or campground so Ray could light up a stogy. Afterward he would heave himself back in the car stinking all the worse. At seven that evening when they pulled into Atlanta, Lee was done in. He wanted only to fall into a prison cot, to stretch out with no chains binding him, and ease into sleep. Moving through the city he could see, off to the right, a fancy section of big, beautiful homes with their spreading shade streets. "Buckhead," the driver said when he saw Lee looking. "Too fancy for you, or me neither."

They moved down Peachtree past closed, softly lit shops until they hit narrower streets, shabby little houses packed close together. In the fading evening, kids played ball in the street, running and shouting. The deputy honked impatiently at a bunch of Negro boys in a game of kick-the-can. Ahead loomed the penitentiary: thick concrete walls, one guard tower that Lee could see, the glint of rifles reflected from big spotlights glaring across the entry doors.

Belly-chained, Lee slid awkwardly out of the car and climbed the marble steps, aching tired. Once inside and through the sally port the deputy marshals freed him of the cuffs and chain. He stood rubbing his sore wrists where the cuffs had eaten in, rubbing his back, listening to the hum of the heavy barred gate sliding closed behind him.

Down both sides of the long passage were vaulted openings that led to the cellblocks. He followed along beside the uniformed admissions officer, a trim, dark-haired young man with a full mustache. Down at the end of the corridor he could see open double doors and could smell greasy dishwater and boiled cabbage, could hear pans clanging and male voices. The corridor was hung with inmates' paintings, some crazy paranoid, some nostalgic. An oil painting of a cowhand riding across open prairie struck him hard.

When he had showered and been issued prison clothes he was led into a cellblock five tiers high. He had stuffed his savings book and Mae's picture, which he was allowed to keep, into the pocket of his loose cotton shirt. He followed the officer up the metal stairs that zigzagged back and forth between metal catwalks. Some fifty feet above the main floor were barred clerestory windows, their glass arching up another thirty feet. He craned his neck to look up, the height dizzying him. "Some hotel, Lieutenant."

"Sorry, no elevator," the officer said in his soft Southern speech. "You'll be on the third tier." They climbed in silence as the rumble of a train broke the night from behind the prison, its scream shrill and demanding. By the time Lee reached his tier he was breathing so hard he had to stop twice to get enough air. "Long drop," he said when the train had passed and he could talk again. "Anyone ever cash it in and jump?"

"It's happened," the guard said. "Not often."

At midpoint of the catwalk he was ushered into a single cell.

"You'll see Mr. Hamilton, the section custodian, in the morning. Then the classification officer. After that you'll be able to move around the prison."

His cell was no different than the others he'd lived in: stainless steel washbowl, stained metal toilet. A cot bolted to the wall, with a cotton pad, a worn-out pillow, and a gray prison blanket. He didn't bother to undress. He pulled off his shoes, lay down and drew the blanket up around him, listening to the familiar prison noises, men snoring, metal clanging, the crinkle of paper as a candy bar was unwrapped. Maybe life was just one long cellblock after another until they planted you outside the wall.

But this thought brought a flurry of hissing. The cat leaped heavily onto the cot, right in Lee's face, as solid as any living beast. Solid and very visible, shocking Lee. Quickly he looked up and down the corridor at the cells on the other side.

He saw no one looking back, and saw no guard near. Misto grinned, flicked his tail, and vanished again—but when Lee lifted the blanket the invisible cat crawled underneath, warm against Lee's shoulder, the comfort of his purr easing Lee into sleep.

8

The clang of metal and the echo of men's voices woke Lee. Morning light flooded the cellblock, striking down from the high clerestory windows. He staggered out of his bunk in automatic response to the wake-up call, stood at his barred door in his wrinkled prison clothes and stocking feet while the count was taken, then turned to the metal basin. He splashed water on his face, used the toothbrush and toothpaste he'd been issued. He was sitting on his bunk putting on his prison-issued shoes when a big-bellied custodian in blue pants and white shirt slid the barred door open. His nametag read *HAMILTON*. He stood looking Lee over.

"You sleep in those clothes?'

Lee pulled the shirt straight, tried to brush out the wrinkles.

"Once you've made up your bunk, Fontana, you can go from here to the mess hall. Then to classifications, then return to your cell. You'll stay here until you're notified, until you're allowed to move around the prison and exercise yard."

Lee listened to Hamilton's directions to the various buildings, then followed him out, moving away along the metal catwalk among straggling inmates and down the iron stairs.

The prison cafeteria smelled of powdered eggs, bacon fat, and overcooked coffee. Inmates pushed in around him half awake, grumbling and arguing or shuffling along silent and morose. Again a train rumbled and screamed passing outside the wall. None of the men paid any attention. Lee guessed they were used to it. Maybe the siren's call didn't stir their blood the way it excited him, the way it made him want out of there, made him feel all the more shackled. He kept to himself in the crowded line until he was jolted hard from behind by two men horsing around, pummeling each other. Lee didn't look at them, he left it alone, he didn't want to start anything.

Not until one of them bumped him hard, did he turn. The man was right in his face. Lee stood his ground. The guy would be a fool to start something here, with half a dozen guards watching. He stared challengingly at Lee, his face hatched by deep lines pinched into a scowl. Dark hair in a short prison cut, a high, balding forehead. It was the look in his black eyes that brought Lee up short, a stare so brutal Lee paused, startled by the sense of another presence within that dark gaze.

But just as quickly the man's look changed to the insolence of any prison no-good. Lee could see the guards watching them, ready to move in. He took a good look at the man's companion: blond pompadour combed high above his weathered face, pale, ice-blue eyes. A pair of twisted inmates that a fellow wanted to avoid. Lee moved on with the line, picked up a tray and collected his breakfast. Turning away, he crossed the room to a small, empty table.

The two men joined a crowded table in the center of the big cafeteria and in a moment all seven inmates turned to watch Lee. He ate quickly, ignoring them, trying not to think about the spark he'd seen in those dark eyes, that quick glimpse of something foreign peering out.

He didn't look at the crowded table as he left the mess hall. Pushing out into the prison yard, he headed for the counselor's office. To his right rose the stone buildings that would be prison industries. Beyond, at a lower level, sprawled the exercise yard, surrounded by the massive stone wall that enclosed the prison grounds.

The wall must be thirty feet high. From this position he could see only one guard tower, two guards looking down, rifle barrels glinting in the morning sun. He had started toward the classifications building when a short man crossing the yard stopped, stared at him, then approached Lee with a dragging limp, a stocky man with husky arms and shoulders. His voice was grainy. "Hey, Boxcar, is that you?"

Lee hadn't heard that name in fifty years. "Gimpy, you old safecracking buzzard."

Hobbling along fast, Gimpy joined him, his eyes laughing beneath bushy gray brows. His hair was gray now, and he was maybe some heavier. "When the hell did you get in, Boxcar?"

"Just transferred in from Springfield. How long have you been here?"

"Two years, doing five. I might make parole one of these days." The little man scowled. "My last safe job went sour."

They'd been just kids when they'd pulled a few jobs together, Gimpy opening the train safes slick and fast. He was the best man with a punch and hand sledge Lee had ever seen. "Do you remember . . ." Lee began. He was silenced by the loud blast of a Klaxon, the sudden blare brought ice gripping his stomach. Gimpy nudged him out of the way as four guards ran by, followed by two medics carrying black bags and a stretcher, their white coats flapping.

"It's in the furniture plant," Gimpy said. They moved toward the industries building, where a short spur track ran from the loading platform out through a sally port in the prison wall. A freight car sat on the track, guards and inmates milling around its open door, pulling out heavy crates.

"Furniture crates," Gimpy said, "desks for the military." There was a lot of shouting, the sound of wood being pried and splintered. A guard and two prisoners eased a body out from the collapsed wooden crate, lifted the bloody figure onto a stretcher.

Once the injured man had been carried off, four inmates pulled the crate out. Lee could see the false bottom the man had built, splintered now and crushed. Gimpy said, "He must have squeezed into it after the crate was loaded. Maybe the crates on top shifted. Doesn't say much for his carpentry."

Lee shook his head. "An ugly way to go."

"Hell, Boxcar, no one's ever broke out of this joint, something always goes bad. One guy had a gun smuggled in by a guard, got himself rifle shot before he got through the main corridor."

Lee looked up with speculation at the thirty-foot wall, but Gimpy snorted. "Not over that wall, nor under it neither. Wall's a dozen feet thick at the bottom, and sitting on solid rock. I'll do my time right here," he said, shifting his weight. "No one could get over that baby."

When they parted company Lee headed for the classifications office, moving up the steps and inside past rows of desks where prison personnel sorted though files or sat talking with inmates, men fidgeting nervously in straight-backed chairs or slouching with bored disdain. The room stunk of sweaty bodies and stale cigarette smoke. Lee's classification officer was a soft little fellow in his forties: slick bald head, white rumpled shirt, his tie pulled loose and his collar unbuttoned. He laid his unlit pipe on the desk among stacks of jumbled papers. "I'm Paul Camp. You're Lee Fontana? You just came in from Springfield."

Lee nodded. Camp gestured for Lee to sit down and handed across a printed set of rules, a meal schedule, and a laundry and mail schedule. "I do three jobs here. Classification, parole, and counseling."

"You think I can get a job in industries? I like to be doing something."

"You'll have to see the doctor first. When I get a slip from him, you'll have more freedom, we'll see what we can do. You can go on over to the hospital from here." Camp gave him directions. "He'll want to see you every week for a while, to check on the emphysema." Then the jolt came. "Twice a week," Camp said, "you'll be attending group counseling sessions." He handed Lee another short schedule.

"I don't need group counseling. What do I want with that?"

Camp studied him, then thumbed through Lee's file. "You may not think you need the sessions, but I do. If you had used a little restraint, Fontana, if you hadn't gotten into trouble in Vegas, you'd still be out on parole." He fixed Lee with a hard look. "Unless, of course, you wanted to be back behind bars."

Lee's belly twisted. "Sure I did. I have what the shrinks call a subliminal need to be confined, to be shut in by high walls, safe from the outside world and with all the prison amenities."

Camp just looked at him. Lee couldn't decide whether the counselor's eyes reflected anger, suspicion, or a suppressed desire to laugh. "The Federal Bureau of Prisons, Fontana, has moved into the age of treatment. Just go to counseling, it's the policy. Just go and endure it."

He left Camp's office swallowing back a cough, hating modern prison ways. He'd rather take a beating than be forced into their fancy headshrinking show. Why couldn't they leave him alone? They'd locked him up, they had him where they wanted, so why couldn't they leave him be?

As he headed for the dispensary beyond the officers' mess, the thirty-foot concrete wall loomed over him and over the big exercise yard. He could see two tennis courts laid out, where six inmates in cut-offs were batting the little white balls. Two more guys were playing handball, and beyond the empty baseball diamond, on the oval track, several men were jogging laps—the place was a regular country club. His own first time behind bars, when he was eighteen, he'd had a rock pile to exercise on. Did the guards here in the South spoon-feed these punks and wipe their runny noses before they sent them out to play?

The dispensary waiting room was painted pale green like most government offices he'd seen, a color that was supposed to be restful. He wondered how many billions of gallons of that stuff the government had bought, allowing some big company to make a killing. Half a dozen inmates sat on folding metal chairs waiting to be seen by the duty doctor. Lee took a chair. He'd waited maybe twenty minutes when he got a shock that spun him around, looking.

"Lee Fontana?" a woman's voice called out. A woman? In a men's prison?

A young woman stood in the doorway holding a clipboard, and she was some classy lady. Dark, wavy hair cut short and neat, curled softly around her smooth face, dark eyes smiling at him through large oval glasses. The skirt of her short white uniform hit her just at the knee, the uniform accenting the curve of her hips, and was zipped down the front low enough to show the soft curve of her tanned breasts. He stared at the nametag on her lapel, but taking in a lot more. Karen Turner. Every male in the room was staring, their expressions just short of a drool. She smiled and motioned to Lee. Rising, he followed her as eagerly as a hungry pup. When he glanced back, the men were still looking. She led him into an office, handed his file to the thin-faced doctor, smiled at Lee again and left, brushing past him. She smelled good, a clean soap-and-water scent. He stood looking after her, then turned to the drawn, tired-looking doctor. His nametag read JAMES FLOYD, M.D.

Lee took off his shirt as Dr. Floyd directed, trying not to flinch as the icy stethoscope pressed against his bare chest. The doctor listened to his heart and chest as Lee breathed deeply, in and out, taking in as much air as he could manage. He took Lee's blood pressure, looked down his throat, thumped his back. While Lee pulled on his shirt again, Floyd made a number of notations in Lee's file.

"Everything's as fine as it can be, Fontana. You had excellent treatment at Springfield." Floyd handed him a slip of paper. "Give this to your counselor. I want you back here in three days. After that, once a week."

"Will I be allowed to work?"

"I think you could take a job, something that won't stress the breathing." He filled out a release-to-work form and handed it to Lee.

Lee said, "I've never seen a woman working in a men's prison."

"Karen Turner?" Floyd smiled. "It's good for the men's morale to see a woman once in a while. She's a premed student at the university, works for me part-time. She cheers the place up considerably; I think it's a good change in the system."

Sure it is, Lee thought. Until you get her hurt.

He doubled back to Paul Camp's office, where he dropped off the medical form and the work form. Camp handed him a slip for his custodian that would let him move around the area more freely. When Lee asked about the jobs available, Camp said, "I'll let you know later, Fontana. I'll see what's open in industries."

Outside again, as Lee cut across the yard from classifications, Gimpy turned away from a group of men and limped to join him. "They getting you squared away, Boxcar?"

"Camp put me in one of those group counseling sessions," Lee said sourly. "I start this afternoon,"

Gimpy chuckled, and scratched his bald spot. "They had me in there for a while. Guess they gave up on me. But hell, Boxcar, it passes the time."

"I'd rather pass it somewhere else."

"Maybe you could work in the cotton mill with me. Noisier than hell, but I like it. I like the clatter and activity."

Lee nodded, interested. He'd feel better when he was doing something. "Let me know if they could use another hand." He wondered if the doctor would allow it. Maybe, if he promised to wear a mask or kerchief, something to catch the lint, he could get permission.

"I'll talk to the foreman," Gimpy said, and swung away with his uneven, rolling gait. Lee stood looking after him; a lot of years had gone by, but Gimpy was still the same. Lee turned away, smiling, heading back to his cell, thinking about the old days.

He was moving along the narrow third-tier catwalk when a man came out of a cell walking slowly, his eyes fixed on the pages of an open book. He was heavy boned, prison pale but built like a barrel, was dressed not in prison blue but in the white pants and white shirt worn in the kitchen, the whiteness stark against the thick black hair on his arms. Lee stepped to one side to let him pass. "I guess we're neighbors."

The dark-eyed man smiled. "Al Bronski. I saw you come in last night."

"Lee Fontana."

"You looked bushed yesterday. Still feel a little pale?"

"It's a long pull from Springfield. What are we having for the noon meal?"

"Beef stew and French bread."

"Sounds good. If I get bored with the routine, are there any jobs in the kitchen?"

"Always use help in the kitchen," Bronski said. "See me when you're ready."

Lee thought he might like the relative quiet of the kitchen better than the noise of the cotton mill, but he'd like to work with Gimpy. Behind Bronski, coming along the catwalk headed for the stairs, were the two men from breakfast this morning, the dark-haired one in the lead, his face frozen in the same pinched scowl, his black eyes fixed on Lee. Behind him, the blond man's masklike face and pale eyes telegraphed a malice that Lee knew too well. They didn't move over for Lee and Bronski. When Lee stepped aside on the narrow catwalk to let them pass, the dark man elbowed him against the rail. "Ain't no place for a gab fest."

Bronski stiffened and reached for him. The man sidestepped, rounding on Bronski. Bronski crouched, waiting—but a guard shouted from the main floor, and he drew back. The two men pushed on past, pressing them both to the rail and giving them the finger.

"Their cells are down beyond yours," Bronski said, watching the two swagger away along the catwalk. "The dark one's Fred Coker. The blond is Sam Delone. There's been more than one knifing involving those two."

Lee kept the two in sight until they disappeared down the stairs and outside. He watched Bronski amble along behind them, reading again, then Lee moved on to his cell. Swept by a wave of exhaustion, he lay down on his bunk. Nobody had to spell it out for him. He was back in a big joint, crazy hotheads around him. And more than hotheads, too, with the shadow that fit so easily among Coker and his kind. As much as he'd admired his grandpappy, he wished Russell had never bargained with the devil, wished that in that one instance Russell had backed off and turned away.

The position he was in now, Lee thought, it was time to get himself a weapon. It was one thing to be threatened by prison scum when you were young and strong, when you could handle a battle bare-handed. It was different this late in life, when every move was an effort, when in every threat you saw the face of defeat. Suddenly cold, pulling the blanket over him, bleak and alone, he felt the weight of the ghost cat hit the bed, crowding against him purring like a small engine. He almost laughed when the ghost cat clawed the mattress, licked Lee's hand with his rough tongue, and said softly, "Screw Coker. Screw Delone. There's more to this prison, Lee, than you yet know."

"What? What are you getting at?" But Lee felt the cat curl up as if he'd tucked his head under, and in a moment the ghost was softly snoring. Lee smiled, turned over easy so as not to disturb him, and soon they both slept, Lee drifting off to Misto's rumbling purr, soothed in his apprehension of the days to come.

9

Driving south to the Atlanta Penitentiary to visit Morgan for the first time, Becky made herself sick thinking every ugly thought about his life inside, so upsetting herself that her driving was off. Twice, passing another car on the two-lane highway, she had to swerve fast into a tight space to avoid hitting an oncoming vehicle. She felt as if she was turning into one of those women so ruled by sick nerves they couldn't do anything right.

Coming into Atlanta, where they would be moving in a few days, driving down Peachtree and on south through mixed commercial and small cottages, she was shaky, her hands unsteady on the wheel. When she drew into the parking area outside the prison wall she sat in the car for a long time trying to pull herself together. She felt so nauseous she was afraid if she went in she'd be sick in the visiting room.

Thinking about leaving Rome didn't help, about leaving Caroline, thinking how much she depended on her mother—to take care of Sammie, but most of all to *be* there for them. Caroline was her friend, her best friend except for Morgan. Life was shattered without Morgan and now would be more empty still without Caroline nearby.

But at least living in Atlanta she'd be closer to Morgan, not an all-day trip to visit him. She and Sammie could run over to the prison in just a few minutes, she thought bitterly, just swing by the prison after school like any mother and child.

She got out of the car at last, feeling the stare of the guards from their towers. They would be wondering why she'd sat there for so long. Would they call down for extra security measures because she seemed suspicious? Her neck prickling from their stares, she hurried up the walk, up the steps. She pressed a buzzer, waited for the lock to click, and pushed through the iron door into a six-foot-square sally port, bars and heavy glass trapping her in the small space.

Through the slot in a thick glass barrier she told the guard her name and Morgan's name. A second guard stepped out of the glassed area, a tall, pale-haired man who asked for her purse. She watched, embarrassed, as he searched around a pack of tampons. Satisfied she wasn't carrying a weapon he handed it back and motioned her through a door into the prison's visiting room.

The room didn't look anything like part of a prison, was far more welcoming than she had expected: tan tweed carpeting, white walls, beige couches, and soft chairs set about in little groups. Half of the seating was already occupied, wives and children, elderly couples, each group gathered around an inmate dressed in prison blue. Most of the men were somber and withdrawn even among their friends and family. One man was so emotional, hugging his wife and children, he was almost in tears. Only two of the prisoners seemed relaxed and at home, chatting away, one man holding two little boys on his lap. She chose an empty couch, stood beside it watching an inner door where Morgan would most likely enter.

What would they talk about? For the first time in their lives she couldn't be open with him. She didn't want to tell him about her aborted effort to question Natalie Hooper. She was so sorry she'd done that. And she didn't dare tell him how Falon had come to Caroline's and gone after Sammie.

She didn't understand Falon. If he wanted *her*, Becky, as he'd always said, why did he go after Sammie?

Caroline said he showed psychopathic tendencies; Becky had to agree but the thought terrified her. She could cope with a normal person, but how did you deal with a psychopath?

She couldn't tell Morgan about this morning at work, before she left for Atlanta. Couldn't tell him that Falon had cornered her in the storeroom of Rome Hardware as she was getting together the bills to do their books. He must have waited hidden behind the shelves of stock as she came in. She was standing at an open file drawer when he grabbed her from behind and backed her against the shelves, his voice a low whisper.

"Keep your mouth shut, I can hurt you bad." His slimy tone sickened her. "You haven't any man in your bed now, Becky."

She came alive, kicking him and shouting. He slapped his hand over her mouth. She bit him so hard he grunted and slapped her again, harder. She yelled louder, so the clerks up front had to hear her. "Get out of here! Help! Help me!" When footsteps came pounding he slammed her against the wall, spun away, and was gone, vanishing between the shelves. She heard the back door open and scrape closed, heard the latch click.

The storeroom was empty, only her fear remained.

She had gotten through the confusion with the two clerks and the assistant manager who came running in, had fielded their questions, begged them not to call the police. She'd said she didn't know who the man was. The Rome police would do nothing to help her, she couldn't handle their patronization, and she didn't want Falon's added rage if she filed a report on him. When she'd mollified the staff, calmed them down, she'd hurried home to Caroline's to change clothes, to head for Atlanta.

When she told Caroline what had happened, her mother said, "That settles it. You'll have to move down to Anne's."

"But—"

"I talked with her this morning. She was—"

"She doesn't want us, Mama."

"Let's say she was reluctant. She'll get over it. You have to go, as soon as you can, at least until you find an apartment. As long as you're here Falon won't leave you alone, won't leave Sammie alone."

Caroline put her arm around Becky. "Anne will soften up once you're settled in. Once she gets to know you better, and gets to know Sammie."

Becky said nothing more. This plan would have to do for the moment.

"We can trade cars," Caroline said, "I keep mine in the garage, he can't see in there. I always drive the van. I'll leave your car out, park it in different parts of the drive so he knows it's being used."

"It will take me a while to wrap up my accounts," Becky said, "to give notice and pack a few things." The thought of moving in with Anne unwanted wasn't pleasant, she felt like a charity case.

"When you're ready, we'll pack the car at night and you can leave before dawn. You said Natalie and Falon sleep late?"

Becky nodded. "I think so, as much as I can tell from the street." She'd driven by Natalie's apartment several mornings, looking up at the windows. The curtains were never open until mid-morning, and twice when she drove by at midnight she'd seen the living room and kitchen lights burning. Maybe she could slip away before daylight without Falon knowing.

Now she watched the door into the visiting room open, repeatedly letting other prisoners through, but all were strangers. She watched openly as inmates, each with a black identification number stenciled on his shirt, were hugged and kissed and made over. She needed Morgan to comfort and hold her; and she couldn't imagine how lost he felt, lost and alone. She didn't want to think what his life was like within these high, cold walls.

She'd promised herself she'd tell him only hopeful things, that she'd make the move to Atlanta sound like exciting news: She'd be near the prison, she could come every visiting day. If she found a lawyer in Atlanta it would be easier to see him often. But she'd have to lie to him, tell him Anne had invited her. Of course he'd ask questions; he knew the cool relationship between Anne and Caroline. Maybe she could distract him with the four Atlanta attorneys she'd seen this week. She'd leave the best one for last, she thought, smiling.

When a guard ushered Morgan in, for an instant she didn't recognize him: another reserved figure in prison blues, his eyes cast down, his face expressionless, his hands limp at his sides, his walk stilted as if every ounce of fight had been taken from him.

Or was this rage she was seeing? Confined, bottled-up rage? As if even the smallest movement might stir a violence of rebellion that he dare not unleash? She stood looking, then ran across the big room, flinging herself at him. They held each other close, Morgan's face against hers, then kissing her neck, her hair, coming alive again. It was all right now, they were together.

Morgan held her away, searching her face. "I was afraid you'd bring Sammie. Does she know you're here?"

"I didn't tell her. She's with Mama. I don't think she's ready to come but she would have insisted. She's still so upset, I wanted to give her more time."

Ever since Sammie had run from Falon into the bushes she had slept badly, had had nightmares that she wouldn't talk about, and during most of the day was quiet and withdrawn. Only in the mornings did she seem easier. She would appear from the bedroom after Becky was up, relaxed and sunny and willing to smile. As if something about that last sleep strengthened her, as if her predawn dreams were happy ones. This morning Becky had heard her in her room talking to herself or maybe to her imaginary playmate. Whatever Sammie had found to comfort her was surely needed now.

Sitting on the couch, Morgan's arm around Becky, comforted by their closeness, they didn't talk for a long while. Becky wanted to know what it was like inside but she couldn't ask. She prayed he wouldn't ask how her work was going. She'd lost so many of her accounts that if she didn't find a job in Atlanta she'd have to sell the house to hire a new attorney and to rid herself of the mortgage payments. Even some of her oldest bookkeeping jobs had gone sour, so many people believing Morgan guilty had turned against them. She'd lost more than half her customers, though the folks at the hardware had remained loyal. And business at the automotive shop was no better.

She told Morgan that her work and work at the shop were just fine. She hated lying to him. As natural and upbeat as she tried to be, no color returned to his face, no laughter to his eyes. He didn't brighten when she told him about the four Atlanta lawyers, though he listened carefully, trying to assess each. She had so wanted to find a man she could have confidence in, someone sympathetic but capable and strong, who would give them hope.

"I think," she said, "Quaker Lowe might be the man. He didn't sit tapping his fingers on the desk or making lengthy notes on a legal pad as the others did. He focused on me, he really listened to me."

Lowe was a florid, square-faced man, big and rangy. Wide hands, like a farmer, his suit and white shirt limp from the heat, an active-looking man who seemed out of place in his cramped office. But his blue eyes showed a keen intelligence and, deep down, an easy wit. From the moment she sat down facing him across his desk she had liked him. "He took in what I had to say, all the details of Falon's setup. I told him about the witnesses, recalled as much of the testimony as I could.

"He said he was booked solid with court cases but he'd do his best to rearrange his schedule, said his assistant would handle some of the court work. He seemed . . . as if he *wanted* to help. I didn't get that from the other three.

"He said that if he could take the case he'd come up to Rome within the week and go through the court records." She laid her hand over Morgan's. "He really listened, Morgan. He . . . I think he might really care about how you've been treated."

She knew there was only a slim chance that Lowe would have time for them, but it was all they had. She prayed with every breath that he would make the time; she didn't let herself think that Quaker Lowe would let them down.

Snuggling close to Morgan she knew that the longer they were apart the more difficult it would be to talk, the more different their lives would become, the less they would have to share. Morgan absorbed into the regimen of prison life, she struggling to keep them financially afloat, trying to keep Sammie safe, trying to appease an aunt who didn't want them in her house. The one thing they had to share, besides Sammie herself, *was* the appeal.

When she told Morgan they'd be moving to Atlanta, that Aunt Anne had invited them, he knew she was leaving out half the story but he didn't push her. He said he was glad she'd be near and wouldn't have to make the long drive, and he left it at that. This wasn't pleasant for either of them, this tiptoeing around a subject; it made her feel as stiff as a stranger. Nor did she mention Sammie's continuing dreams of the cowboy—those parts of the dreams Sammie was willing to share with her.

She longed to tell him the dream from the previous night, which Sammie had shared; she wanted Morgan's response. But somehow, she was wary of that response. It was two in the morning when Sammie sat straight up in bed, wide awake, not screaming with fear but instead solemn and demanding. "Mama! Mama!"

Becky had turned on a light and drawn Sammie close. The child wasn't afraid, she was quiet and composed, her dark eyes serious. "He's here, Mama. The cowboy is here. He's in the prison, he's behind the wall with Daddy."

Becky had visualized the thin, leathery old man Sammie had once described. She hadn't known what to make of the dream, this one couldn't be real. Yet she never took Sammie's dreams lightly; they were not to be brushed aside.

"He came to help Daddy, help him get out of that place, help him come home again." Becky told herself this *was* a fantasy, how could it be anything else? It was nothing like Sammie's dreams of the believable though painful events one might expect from life, the death of Sammie's puppy, the courthouse fire.

But what about that last terrible nightmare where Morgan was locked in the Rome jail? They had known that was a fantasy, dark and impossible. And that nightmare had come true in all its terror and ugliness. Now, sitting close to Morgan, she knew she had to tell him, to share one more disturbing vision.

She described Sammie's waking, so different from other nightmares. "She woke so alert, more certain than with anything she's ever experienced. She kept repeating, 'He's here. He's here to help Daddy. The cowboy's here to help Daddy get away, help Daddy prove who robbed that bank and then Daddy will go free.'"

Morgan said nothing, he sat looking at Becky trying to take a matter-of-fact approach. Over the years Sammie's predictions had made a believer of him, but how could this dream ever be based in fact? This fanciful idea was impossible. He said, "I haven't noticed anyone like Sammie described. No thin wrinkled old con who walks bowlegged. Maybe this time, maybe it *is* just a dream." But somewhere in Morgan's heart a web of hope had begun to gather, a shadow of promise to weave itself into his thoughts, ready to spring to life.

10

Morgan went about his prison routine in the days that followed, putting aside the small hope he'd found in Sammie's dream. This time there was no substance, her idea of escape was wishful thinking. He settled into life behind bars as best he could except for the group counseling session. He didn't need counseling, he needed justice.

The courts had locked him up for the rest of his life, but why force him to listen to a bunch of bickering inmates air their petty complaints? Or to the sanctimonious platitudes of the fresh-faced counselor who led the others in their pointless rankling? He didn't want to share his pain.

The problem was, the day the counselor started working on him he ended up bellyaching just like the rest of the group. Afterward he felt cheap and ashamed. He'd let it all out, the unfairness of the jury, the uncaring judge and U.S. attorney, the incompetence of his own lawyer. He'd gone on about being used, manipulated like a rat in a lab experiment. The counseling he got, in front of the whole group, only made it worse. At least the counselor had gotten him a job in the automotive shop, but only because they needed skilled men. Now, thankful for that good luck, he crossed the prison yard on his way to another "shrink" session, for another hour of misery.

It was just one o'clock when Lee found the group counseling room and stepped inside. A gray metal desk stood across the room, arranged so the group leader sat with his back to the wall facing three rows of folding chairs, all empty. The young counselor looked up from his paperwork, then glanced at a list. "Lee Fontana?"

Lee nodded. The first one there, he took a seat in the middle so he wouldn't have men pushing by stepping on his feet. The young man was all of twenty-some, a college type with an almost pretty face, a deep tan, a blond crew cut. He wore a V-necked red sweater with turned-up sleeves over a starched white shirt. He gave Lee a charming smile, introduced himself as Tom

Randall, and returned to his loose-leaf notebook. He didn't look up again until a broad-shouldered black man entered. He looked Lee over and slid into the chair next to him. Lee hoped he wasn't going to be talkative, he wasn't here to be social.

But the man's smile drew Lee, his eyes alive with intelligence and humor. He was middle-aged, square faced and clean-cut, with flecks of gray through his short hair. He extended his broad, lined hand. "Andy Trotter," he said in a polished British accent.

"Lee Fontana." Lee shook the man's hand. "You're a Brit? What are you doing in here?"

Trotter grinned and pulled a bag of Bull Durham from his shirt pocket. "Born right here in Georgia. But I spent most of my childhood in Jamaica with my granny, she made sure I could speak the King's English. Smoke?" He extended the makings.

Lee shook his head. As Andy rolled a cigarette quickly and neatly, three more men wandered in. Two of them were the dregs of prison population, scruffy, edgy types. Lee could smell the body odor of the frazzled, dirty one before he sat down at the end of the row. The man's hair was greasy, his eyes darted restlessly, and he couldn't keep his hands still, his twitching fingers rubbing and fidgeting. This fellow didn't need counseling, he needed to dry out.

The man who took the chair next to Lee held himself rigidly, staring straight ahead to avoid eye contact. His thin red hair was combed straight back over a premature baldness, his mouth and chin dwarfed by a large beaked nose.

The third man, who came in behind them, was younger, clean-cut, probably in his late twenties, an honest-John citizen type. Lee watched him with interest, wondering what he was in for. Open, friendly face like that, he'd make a great con artist. Only when their eyes met did Lee see his deep, embedded anger.

The young man grinned at Andy, received a smile in return, and took the seat on the other side of him. When Andy made introductions, when Morgan Blake reached across to shake Lee's hand, Lee saw something else in his look. Not the buried anger now, but a spark of surprise, a puzzled frown as he studied Lee. A surprise and confusion he found hard to conceal. What was that about? Around them more men drifted in jostling, scraping chairs along the floor as they settled down.

Morgan Blake's look lasted only a minute, then was gone. Turning away he gave his attention to Tom Randall. With only two chairs vacant, Randall closed his notebook, glanced at his watch, and looked up at the group. In the open doorway, Sam Delone sauntered in, his blond pompadour catching light from the overhead bulb, his cold eyes scanning the group. His gaze settled on Lee.

The counselor looked Delone over. "Glad you could join us, Delone," he said coolly.

"Sorry," Delone said. "Those dummies in the laundry took forever, farting around slow as hell."

Randall introduced Lee to the group. Ralph Smee was the one with greasy hair and nervous eyes; he barely flicked a glance in Lee's direction. Red Foster stared straight ahead over his big nose and didn't acknowledge Lee. Sam Delone lit a cigarette and took a deep drag. "I'm afraid Gramps and I have already met."

"Who wants to start?" the counselor said, pushing up the sleeves of his sweater. "Anything where you think the group, in an exchange of ideas, can be of help."

Delone flicked his burnt match onto the linoleum. "Why the hell can't they hire someone in the kitchen who knows how to cook? Those dumb bastards can't even cook an egg without pounding it into leather."

Lee tried not to smile, but Delone caught his look. "You think that's funny, old man?" Turning, he fixed his gaze on Trotter. "And what are you grinning about, darky?"

"Perhaps," said Andy slowly, "Mr. Randall has something more important in mind than your gourmet sensitivities."

"And maybe," Lee said evenly, "you ought to be more careful what you call people."

The counselor adjusted his sleeves again. "These sessions are not for petty gripes, you men know that. How about you, Blake? You settle into the automotive shop okay?"

Morgan Blake nodded. "Yes, sir. I appreciate getting the job."

"Have you heard anything on your appeal?"

Lee saw Blake's jaw tighten. "Not yet," Blake said, "but my wife's found a new attorney. One who might really try."

Sam Delone snorted.

"I didn't rob that bank," Blake snapped at him, "and I didn't kill anyone." He looked hard at the counselor. "The courts don't want justice, all they want are bodies to fill up their prisons, any scapegoat they can lay the blame on."

Lee watched Blake with interest. If he was lying, he was pretty good.

But Lee had seen plenty of scams in his time, a man could fake anything if he practiced long enough.

Delone ground out his cigarette with his heel, glaring at the counselor. "Ralph, here, he has the same problem, don't you, Ralphy? Tell us, Ralph, how you didn't rape that little girl, up at Stone Mountain. Tell us how the park ranger and that girl made it all up just to get at you."

Smee darted a hasty look at Delone and laughed raggedly.

Delone said, "You see, Blake, everyone in here is innocent."

Lee leaned back, watching the group and watching the ineffective young counselor. Morgan Blake said no more, but sat quietly, his hands tense, his face flushed.

"Anyway, Blake," Delone said with mock sympathy, "there's always parole. Don't forget parole. You might be old by then, as old as this old fart here," he said, glancing at Lee. "But maybe you'll have some time left, a year or two to spend with your little wife and family."

The counselor tried to take things in hand, shooting Delone a look to shut him up, then looking at Morgan. "You haven't told us your whole story, Blake. Would it help to talk about it?"

Blake was silent. Randall nodded encouragement. "How long is your sentence?"

"I'll be eligible for parole in twenty-three years," Blake said reluctantly, and Lee could see that he needed to talk. "Fifteen on the life term, eight on the twenty-five-year jolt." He had turned, was talking to Lee and Andy, glancing up at the counselor only to be polite.

"For the next twenty-three years I'll get to see my little girl grow up, from right here behind the bars. I'll be here on visiting days to talk with her, to help with her problems, to help shape what kind of a young woman she'll be. When I get out, she'll be grown and married. My wife will be over fifty years old."

Blake seemed, once he got started, to need badly to spill it all out. He looked deeply at Lee, again that puzzled look that made Lee uneasy. "My life, their lives, are down the drain because of a crime I didn't commit. But what do the courts care? No one in law enforcement, no one in the courts will listen."

"Even if you lose your appeal," the counselor said, "you know you can try again."

"What good is a second try?" Morgan said. "The first jury didn't believe me. If we lose an appeal, why bother with another? The witnesses who lied in court, they'll keep on lying." Morgan flushed deeply. "If I were guilty I'd figure I had it coming, I'd figure I had to get used to prison. But I'm not guilty and every day I'm in here is hard time, unfair time. I don't know how to get used to it."

Andy stubbed out his cigarette, his broad, dark hands catching the light. His look at Morgan was gentle and patient. "The reality is, you are here. You cannot change that, not until the appeal. You can only take each day as it comes. You are fortunate, you know, to have such a loyal and loving wife working to help you, and to have your little girl to visit you, to hold her and love her, even here in the prison setting."

Morgan nodded. He looked companionably at Andy and was quiet.

Randall listened to several more petty complaints from other inmates, then he tried to draw Lee out. "You were transferred down from Springfield, Fontana. That means your health has improved."

Lee didn't care to discuss his weakness in front of these men. Didn't Randall have any sense? "Springfield had a new bunch of men coming in, they needed the space," he said. He clammed up and would answer no more questions, scowling at Randall until the counselor turned to another inmate.

At the end of the session, as they headed for the door Andy Trotter laid a hand on Morgan Blake's arm. "Stay steady, man. I'd like to talk, have a cup of coffee, but I have to get to work."

Lee moved out behind them. The ground shook as, beyond the wall, a train thundered and screamed, passing the prison. Lee was getting used to their freedom call, to their beckoning. He'd started to turn away from the other men when Blake fell into step with him, and again that searching look. "Sorry I came on so strong back there. I know that doesn't do any good." Blake's frown as he watched Lee seemed to hold some question about Lee himself.

Warily Lee said, "Why do you care what I think?"

Blake colored, lowered his gaze, and moved away. Lee felt relief but then, on impulse, he stepped up beside Blake again. "Come on, kid. Let's go down to the mess hall, see if we can wrangle that coffee."

Even as he said it, he wondered what he was doing. A few minutes over a cup of coffee could get him uncomfortably involved, could gain him a persistent sidekick that he didn't want hanging around. This guy needed a friend. And Lee wasn't interested. He knew nothing about Blake or about Blake's crime. He didn't know whether Blake's trial had been fair or rigged. He didn't want to know. He knew only that any friendship, in prison, could end up the kiss of death.

11

Brad Falon wasn't finished with the Blake family. Having skillfully finessed Morgan into the federal pen, his full attention turned to Becky and the child. They had been staying with Caroline Tanner but it looked now as if they'd moved back home again just as he'd hoped they'd do. Last night he had cruised by meaning, if he saw no one about, to jimmy the back door and slip inside.

But the Tanner woman's white van was parked in the drive beside Becky's car, there was another car behind it that he didn't recognize, and the living room and kitchen lights burned bright behind the drawn drapes. Easing his car along past the house beneath the overhanging oaks he had parked for a few minutes, looking back, watching the house, wondering what was going on, wondering what Becky might be up to.

But now, this late morning, there was no car at all in the drive. There was no room for a car in the small garage, he knew it was stacked with boxes of automotive parts and new tires for Morgan's shop. He remained parked for a few moments, scanning the neighborhood. He saw no one in any of the yards, no one looking out a window. Parking half a block down, he walked back beneath the tree shadows to Becky's front porch.

Having studied the lock on earlier visits, he quickly inserted a thin screwdriver, tripped the simple device, and let himself in. Locking the door behind him he made a leisurely tour of the rooms to be certain the place was empty. In the kitchen he opened the refrigerator, drank some milk from the bottle, took out a bowl of cold spaghetti, found a spoon in one of the drawers. He ate half of it, then put the bowl back. The kitchen was too neat, the counters scrubbed, everything put away behind cupboard doors. None of the easy clutter his mother kept on the counter, the cookie jars filled with flour and packages of staples where she could reach them, the pots of miniature cacti, the pictures and lists she kept stuck to the refrigerator and to the walls between hooks bearing limp dish towels and greasy potholders. His mother still lived alone, the house too big for her.

The rest of his clothes were there, but he didn't stop by often, they had their differences. She seemed sometimes almost afraid of him, he thought, smiling.

Moving down the hall to the front bedroom he opened the closet, stroked Becky's neatly arranged dresses and fondled them. Morgan's clothes still hung beside hers—as if they thought he was coming home again. He chose a pale blue cotton dress Becky had worn during the trial. Stretching it tight on the hanger he slashed it with his pocketknife, ripped it nearly in half and dropped the pieces on the floor. He'd reached for a second dress when a chill ran through him, a sense that he was watched.

He stared into the shadowed end of the closet where Morgan's clothes hung but saw nothing to threaten him. He looked foolishly up at the shadowed shelf as if someone could hide among the half-dozen shoe boxes and the battered suitcase. Nothing there of course, and no one behind him in the small bedroom. He checked the hall, went through the rest of the house, then returned. On the dresser stood a cluster of framed photographs, one of Becky and Morgan standing before the house, their hands clasped, and several pictures of the child, from baby to little girl. One by one he smashed the glass, pulled the pictures out and broke the frames. But even as he tore the pictures into small pieces and dropped them on the floor he felt watched again, felt that he was not alone. Nervously he began to open dresser drawers. He removed Becky's panties and bras one at a time, dropped his pants, and rubbed them over himself. She wore only cotton, not silk, but the garments felt smooth and cool. From the next drawer he lifted out nighties and some stockings and did the same with these, leaving the drawers in a tangle ripe with his male scent.

He left Morgan's side of the dresser alone except for the top drawer, which was locked. That interested him, and he was examining the lock when he heard a car door slam. As he stepped to the closed window a faint breeze touched the back of his neck, making him shiver. But when he turned, nothing was there. Outside, a car had parked at the curb. A strange man was heading for the house as Becky's car pulled into the drive, a big man, broad of shoulder, his tie loosened over a white shirt, his gray suit wrinkled. Quickly Falon headed for the kitchen, eased open the bolt on the back door and left, shutting the door softly behind him.

Becky came into the house ahead of Quaker Lowe. She made him comfortable in the living room, then went to make some coffee. They had met outside the courthouse where Lowe had spent the morning going over the transcripts of the trial. They hadn't talked there, Lowe had followed her directly home. She was comfortable with Lowe, he seemed to understand clearly her lone battle and her helpless frustration.

He had driven up from Atlanta two days before to talk with the bank employees who had witnessed the guard's murder and then been beaten and locked in the vault. He was staying at the nicest of Rome's three motels. So far he had seemed content with the five-hundred-dollar retainer she'd given him, which was all the money she had in their savings account. She had seen him for only a few minutes the day he arrived and then again last night when they'd had a simple dinner here at the house, when Caroline had joined them bringing a hot casserole. Now, as she carried the tray of cookies and coffee into the living room, Lowe was reading his copies of the police reports.

"I read the transcripts," he said, smiling up at her, "and talked the court steno out of a set of her carbons." He spooned sugar into his coffee. "Last night after I left you I tried again to see Natalie Hooper. There was a light in the living room, but she didn't answer the door. I tried again this morning. She didn't respond and she isn't answering her phone."

He added cream to the brew and slid three cookies onto his saucer. "It wasn't much good sitting in the car watching the front entrance to the lobby when she could slip out the back. I parked around the corner, borrowed a chair from the building manager, and sat in the hall. When she did come down, she wasn't happy to see me," Lowe said, smiling.

"I told her we could either go upstairs to her place or talk there in the hall. Reluctantly she took me upstairs. I spent over an hour with her but I didn't get much, just the same lies she told in court. Except for one small discrepancy.

"On the stand, she said Falon left her apartment at two-thirty, the day of the robbery, to go across the street to the corner store. This morning she told me two-fifteen, I got her to say it twice." He looked evenly at Becky. "I don't see how she could forget what she said on the witness stand, though the woman doesn't seem too swift.

"It may be nothing," he said, "but it flustered her. I'll talk with the store manager when I leave here. But the biggest hole in Falon's story," Lowe said, "is that double entry to the apartment building, the fact that when he left the grocery he could have gone in the front door and out the back. But with no witness, there's nothing to support that. Can you think of anything that might have been overlooked?"

She couldn't. Yet despite that discouragement she had faith in Lowe, he was far more positive than their trial attorney, he left her feeling so much more hopeful. She was thankful he'd taken the case, though she didn't know where she was going to find the money to pay him, and she hated taking it from her mother. Lowe had told her to take her time to make payments, that what he was interested in right now was getting the appeal and winning it.

This morning when she'd met Lowe at the courthouse she had just come from taking the ledgers over to Farley's Dime Store and collecting her last paycheck. Farley would no longer need her services, and he had been pretty cool. He hadn't apologized for letting her go, he had just abruptly fired her. Last Thursday she had lost three accounts including Brennan's Dress Shop, and she'd known Beverly Brennan all her life. She couldn't believe Morgan's trial and conviction had caused such a change among people she'd thought would stand by them. And business at the automotive shop was so bad she wasn't sure she could pay Morgan's mechanic.

Selling the automotive shop would help pay the bills. But would destroy what Morgan had worked so hard to build, destroy another big piece of his life.

Lowe finished his coffee. "You can think of nothing else?" When she shook her head, he stood up to leave. "I want to check the records on Falon, see if the police missed any old outstanding warrants here or out on the coast, maybe in Washington State or while he was in California." He put out his hand. "Please take care. Doors locked, that kind of thing." He took both her hands in his, looking at her kindly. "Will you and Sammie be all right? You'll be moving to Atlanta in a few days, to your aunt's? You'll be near the office then, when we need to talk."

She handed him the paper where she'd written Anne's address and phone number. "Maybe we'll be lucky, maybe he won't know about Anne. His mother might remember, but they don't get along, I'd guess he seldom sees her. We're taking Mama's car to Anne's. Mine will be here, in Mama's garage."

On impulse Lowe gave her a big bear hug that made tears start. "I'll call you before I leave Rome, let you know what else I find, and of course I'll call you at Anne's." He turned and left her, swinging out the front door heading for his car. Getting in and pulling away, he waved. She stood at the front door, tears gushing in spite of herself, watching him drive away.

It was twenty minutes after Quaker Lowe left that she discovered someone had been in the house. She hadn't gone into the bedroom when she got home. Now when she went in to change to a pair of slacks she stopped, looking down at scattered shards of smashed glass, at broken frames and the torn pieces of their family pictures. She spun around, her back to the dresser facing the closet door.

Reaching up, she snatched the dresser key from where it clung to a magnet behind the mirror. She unlocked the dresser drawer and took out Morgan's loaded and holstered .38. Only when she was armed did she open the closet door.

No one there. Her blue dress, Morgan's favorite, lay on the floor torn into rags.

No other clothes had been disturbed but when she turned to the dresser and pulled out the drawers she found her bras and panties tangled in a mess and they smelled; every piece of her more intimate clothing reeked with an ammonialike male smell. Her sweaters, blouses, everything had been pulled out, wadded up, and stuffed back again. Morgan's clothes had not been touched.

Carrying the gun pointed down, her thumb on the hammer, she walked slowly through the rest of the small house, stepping back as she flung open each door: Sammie's room, Sammie's closet, the coat closet, the bathroom, the kitchen. When she checked the service porch, the back door was unlocked. She locked it and called the police.

From now on she'd keep the loaded gun with her. She would train Sammie, she'd gun-proof Sammie just as she knew the children of police officers were trained. She should have done that before. Now she would drill Sammie over and over in the rules for caution and safety, she had no other choice.

Standing at the front window she waited nervously for the police, but then when Sergeant Leonard did arrive, the stern older man made her feel that she had called him out for nothing. Leonard was a beefy man, forty pounds overweight with soft, thick jowls and an attitude of boredom. He made little effort to conceal his amusement even when, entering the bedroom among the broken and torn pictures, she showed him her ruined dress and the wadded clothes in her dresser. When he looked at them, stone-faced, embarrassedly she asked him to smell them. He sniffed her clothes with distaste and gave her another amused look. "Is anything missing?" he said as if she had made up the intrusion, had made this mess herself.

"Nothing's missing that I've found." She told him she had locked both doors when she left the house that morning, and that just now, when she went through the house, the back door was unlocked, the bolt slid back.

When she moved to the front door and asked him to look at the lock, the pry marks were easy to see, bright scratches in the weathered brass. When, in the kitchen, she showed him that the milk bottle had been left out and the leftover spaghetti had been dug into, she felt awkward and stupid. She said Sammie was at Caroline's, that she hadn't been home at all to enjoy a little snack. Everything she showed him or told him seemed to amuse him. He moved back to the living room, stood by the front door asking questions about what time she had left the house this morning, how long she had been gone, and where she had been. He didn't make any notes, though he carried his field book in his hand.

She said, "Can you take fingerprints, can you find out who was in here?"

"If there's nothing missing, no break-in, no door or window broken, we don't take fingerprints."

"But the pry marks on the front door. That *is* the sign of a break-in."

Carelessly he scribbled a few lines in his field book as if to humor her. His disdain, his refusal to take prints made her feel totally helpless. This was not how the police handled a problem, this was not what she'd been raised to expect of them, in Rome or anywhere else. Enraged by his lack of concern, by his sarcasm, all she could think was that the entire Rome PD was against Morgan, was sure Morgan was guilty, and had lost respect for their family. Leonard said nothing more. He turned, let himself out the front door. She watched from the window as his patrol car pulled away.

When he had gone she locked the door and checked the bolt again on the back door. Tonight she would either booby-trap both doors or go back to Caroline's. She had moved home yesterday, leaving Sammie cosseted at Caroline's, so she could get her bills and papers in order and pack what they'd need in Atlanta.

In the bedroom she removed her clothes from the drawers, her panties and nighties, bras and slips, and put them in the washer. She washed everything twice, with a little bleach. But for months afterward the touch of her undergarments against her skin made her feel violated and unclean.

While she was running the wash she called Quaker at the motel. He was out but she left a message. When he called back and learned what had happened he made her promise to go back to Caroline's, where at least the neighbors were younger and more able to come if they were needed. "How soon can you leave for Atlanta? How soon can you be out of Rome?"

"A day, maybe two. As soon as I can wrap up the figures for my last job."

He said to call him when she left, and again when she got to Atlanta, he wanted to know she was safe. "As soon as I get back to Atlanta myself, I'll set up a meeting with Morgan, go over the transcript with him, see if he can come up with anything else, even the smallest lead I might follow."

"Don't tell him Falon broke in. I've told him nothing about Falon's attacks, it would only worry him when there's nothing he can do." She was still shaky when they hung up. She put her clothes in the dryer, dragged out their old battered suitcase and some grocery bags, and got to work packing.

Sammie snuggled deeper under the quilt, pulling Misto warm against her. "You'll come with me tomorrow, you'll come to Aunt Anne's house. No one will know." It was late after supper, Mama hadn't come to bed yet, she could hear Mama and Grandma in the kitchen, the bright rattle of silverware as they washed dishes, the soft murmur of their "good-bye" voices, their sad voices. "You can ride on top of my new suitcase or anywhere in the car you want and Mama can't see you."

Sammie's small brown suitcase, the one Grandma had given her, stood packed and ready, across the room on the cedar chest beside Mama's battered one. She didn't want to leave Grandma, she didn't want to move to Atlanta, she wanted Daddy home again, not gone away like when he was in the war. Why did things have to change? Mama said *life* was change, she said the important things stayed the same because the important things were inside you. Like loving each other and being strong.

Ducking her head under the covers she pressed her face against Misto. When she stroked his ragged ears and tickled him under the chin the way he liked, he purred and patted a soft paw against her cheek and she knew he loved her just the way she loved him. That would never change.

Misto thought about Falon in Becky's house rummaging through Becky's clothes, peering up at the closet shelf knowing something was there, never guessing that a ghost crouched inches from his face, an angry invisible tomcat who could have clawed and bloodied him if he'd wanted. Misto had simply crouched there entertained by Falon's fear, he could still see Falon shiver and back away. Falon had been even more afraid when Misto streaked through the air letting his tail trail across Falon's neck. Falon's reaction would make any cat laugh.

Now as Sammie drifted into sleep Misto slept, too, as deep and restorative a sleep as if he was a mortal cat; a sleep that helped embolden him against the dark that not only tormented Lee but so often traveled with Falon. As the little cat slept he knew in his enduring feline soul that he was not alone, that neither he nor Sammie was alone, that they could never be abandoned; eternity didn't work in that way.

12

Anne Chesserson had grave reservations about allowing Becky and the child to move in with her. She had never been close to Caroline, even when they were children, for reasons her younger sister wouldn't have understood. Now she was already sorry she'd let Caroline manipulate her into letting Becky and the little girl live there. What had possessed her? She wasn't comfortable with children, she had never wanted a family, she liked her life as it was. She didn't like changes in her routine. She didn't care much for houseguests, though she had room for them, and of course she had Mariol to wait on the few visitors she did invite.

Anne was a handsome woman, meticulously turned out, her black hair coiffed in a sleek French twist, her dresses custom made of pale silks which, on anyone else, might become quickly spotted or watermarked. Her winter coats were confections of beautifully draped cashmere. Her couturière, in Morningside, was so well situated that she had an unlisted phone. Anne had invested wisely the money John had settled on her when he left. While Caroline, with much lower goals, ran a bakery business that couldn't be very profitable. Anne couldn't find much sympathy for Caroline or her niece in this present situation. Becky knew, when she married Morgan Blake, that he ran with a troublemaker in high school. Caroline should never have allowed her to marry the boy—Morgan *had* been only a boy when they married. Then when Morgan came out of the navy all he wanted to do with his life was become an auto mechanic. No one could support a wife as a simple mechanic; no wonder he'd resorted to theft. The Atlanta papers had been full of the robbery and murder, it was an ugly business that she would prefer to keep at a distance. She could hardly do that if Becky was staying with her. But the decision had been made, so she wouldn't back out.

At least Becky and the child would have the basement suite, downstairs where Becky's early rising to go to work, and the child's noisy play, might not disturb her. Mariol lived on the main floor in the back bedroom; Anne's own bedroom suite took up the smaller, second floor where she could look out over the rooftops of Atlanta. Anne believed in stairs; the exercise kept her waist and legs trim. She liked to cook, and on the nights she was home she prepared their meals, though Mariol did the shopping. Anne had been a temperamental, nervous child, and had been treated with extra care. Their mother had kept her perfectly groomed, immaculately dressed, not a wrinkle allowed nor a hair out of place, while she let Caroline run as she pleased in ragged dresses or boy's jeans. Caroline had been a sturdy child, Anne had not. Anne's interest in perfecting her outer self had helped to build a wall of protection, hiding her inner fears; that was the best shelter their mother could provide for her.

Becky and Sammie moved into the basement suite on a Friday afternoon, slipping almost subserviently down the carpeted stairs from the foyer carrying their tattered suitcases. The Tudor house was built all of pale stone, with sharply peaked slate roofs and diamond leaded windows. From the basement sitting area one could step out onto a stone patio surrounded by an expanse of velvet lawn and carefully shaped azalea and rhododendron bushes. The downstairs suite seemed as big as Becky's whole house, occupying three fourths of the large basement, with a laundry off to one side. The bedroom wing had twin beds done up with elegant satin spreads. This room could be hidden by cream velvet draperies drawn across. The other wing of the guest suite, the sitting area, featured a Louis XV–style desk and a rose marble fireplace. The rooms were carpeted in off-white wool carved in a Chinese pattern, the cost per square yard a sum that would have kept Becky and Sammie in luxury for months. The storage chests and dressing table were finished in hand-laid gold leaf. The room terrified Becky. She couldn't feel comfortable here; she was afraid that either she or Sammie would mar the furniture or leave a stain on the carpet, on the velvet settee or on the two brocade chairs, would mar this perfect grouping arranged before the marble mantel and gas log. Even now with the chill nights of early fall she wouldn't dare light a fire.

There was no kitchenette and no possible place to comfortably open a can of tuna and a package of crackers except the bathroom. That room was done in mauve marble and mauve tile with both a shower and a tub, the shower protected by three layers of shower curtains, the outer, mauve one deeply ruffled. Stepping in the shower made Becky feel as if she was slipping into a closet filled with lacy ball gowns. The one new addition to the bedroom was the phone with a private line that Anne had had installed for her. Whether this was added out of thoughtfulness or to keep Becky from interrupting Anne's own calls, the phone was welcome and made her feel more accepted.

She had brought half a dozen of her own bedsheets to spread over the carpet where they would walk the most and to cover a six-foot square between Sammie's bed and the wall so Sammie would have a play area. She had not allowed Sammie to bring paints or crayons, only a drawing pad and pencils. Sammie had specific instructions about keeping the carpet clean—Becky gave her more instructions than either of them wanted to deal with. Sammie was a good child, she was never intentionally destructive, but children were children and Becky worried obsessively about damaging Anne's perfect house.

For the first few days she made their breakfasts and dinners from cans, she and Sammie sitting on the bathroom floor on a folded sheet pretending they were having a picnic. Maybe she was making too much of trying to keep the rooms clean, but she hadn't been invited here, she couldn't help feeling like an intruder.

She had turned the bedspreads wrong side up to keep them clean and now, after her third day of job hunting, she lay across her bed, exhausted. Her feet ached from walking the streets, her head ached from filling out countless job applications, answering the same probing questions over and over, and dealing with countless interviews. The questions always included the same inquiry about her marital status and her husband's occupation. In the last week and a half she had applied for eighteen jobs and had been told eighteen times, after filling out all the applications, that there were no openings or that she didn't fit the qualifications or that they would call her if something came up. What did she expect when she told the truth, that Morgan was in the Atlanta pen for a robbery and murder that he hadn't committed, that she was working with an attorney on an appeal?

On the nineteenth application, where she must check either married, single, divorced, or widowed, she marked widowed, and she used her maiden name, Tanner. She had to find a job, and soon, and then a small apartment near a school for Sammie. The problem of after-school weighed heavily, she hadn't solved that one yet. Now, when she was out job hunting, Sammie stayed quietly in their room but she couldn't leave Sammie alone in an apartment.

On their visits to Morgan she found it increasingly hard to hide her despair at the lack of a job. When she was with him she talked hopefully about their request for an appeal, but too often he would simply hug her and change the subject, knowing she was holding back her stress and doubts. She worried, too, because Sammie wasn't sleeping well. And now Sammie wouldn't talk about her dreams, though she had never before been secretive. Sammie had started to make a picture book of small pencil drawings in a plain, unlined tablet, but she didn't want to show Becky, she made her promise not to look.

But soon, when Anne was out at one or another of her club meetings, Becky would come home to find Sammie upstairs in the kitchen with Mariol; at first that disturbed her, but Mariol herself put Becky at ease. The housekeeper was a handsome Negro woman to whom Becky had warmed at once. She had been with Anne since before John left, before the divorce. Soon Mariol was giving Sammie a hot lunch, and then she had them both coming upstairs to a hot breakfast. Anne was quiet during those meals but she seemed to tolerate the arrangement. Mariol would hug and cuddle Sammie, but of course Anne didn't put aside her own reserve, Becky knew she never would.

One thing was certain—Anne didn't want to talk about Morgan or the trial. If Becky mentioned Morgan, Anne grew ill at ease. Becky wanted her to understand that Morgan was innocent, but after three awkward attempts she gave up. Anne would think what she pleased. Becky was surprised when after only a few days, Mariol's kindness to Sammie seemed to stir a subtle change in Anne. Several times Becky found her watching Sammie with a puzzled frown and once, when Becky was tucking Sammie in bed and hearing her prayers, Sammie said, "Bless Aunt Anne and please make her less lonely."

But then came the night when Sammie woke screaming, "Look out! Look out! Get away from him! Get away!" Becky lunged for the lamp switch, turned it on to find Sammie sitting up in bed still half asleep but trembling and terrified. Becky crawled into bed with her, holding her close. "What was it?" she said softly. "What did you dream?"

"I don't remember," Sammie said, clearly lying. "It's gone now. I want to go to sleep now." What *were* these new dreams, that she wouldn't talk about them? Prison dreams? Ugly prison incidents that no child should see and that Becky couldn't stop her from seeing?

"Whatever you dreamed," Becky said, "there's more good in life than ugliness. We have to hold on to the bright part, so we'll be stronger." They lay holding each other until at last Sammie slept—leaving Becky wakeful, certain that Sammie had seen Morgan hurt. No matter what she told Sammie, she couldn't shake her own fear. She had no notion that across the room brightness did touch them; that the yellow tomcat sat on the mantel watching them, reaching out an invisible paw to ease them as he, too, considered Sammie's dream.

Misto had seen the child's drawings, had looked carefully at the little sketches. In one a man was falling a great distance tied to a rope, and that puzzled him. The tomcat had been in and out of the Chesserson house ever since Becky and Sammie had arrived; he had prowled the opulent rooms getting to know Anne and Mariol, seeing how each interacted with Sammie. He had rolled luxuriously on the fine upholstered furniture and the dense imported carpets, leaving no mark; he had sampled Mariol's good cooking, licking his whiskers; he had stalked the neighborhood rooftops. Galloping along the steep angles of the Tudor's slate roof, leaping into the high foliage of the great oaks and across the roofs of the big Morningside homes, he had spied down through mullioned windows, and peered down into lush, shaded gardens; but always he returned to Sammie. He was shocked to a rigid stillness when Anne Chesserson realized that something unseen wandered the house.

If Misto drifted into the room with her, she would turn in his direction with a puzzled frown. If he stood on the kitchen table licking a plate or peering down at Sammie's drawings, Anne would look around the room, frowning. She never seemed afraid. When she became too intently aware of him Misto would vacate the house, would return to prowl the prison beside Lee, abandoning the luxury of Morningside, watching for the shadow that, too often, followed his cellmate.

13

Lee's morning was brightened considerably on his next visit to the dispensary by the sight of Karen Turner coming down the corridor carrying a sheaf of files, the zipper of her short uniform pulled low, her dark hair clean and bouncy. "Hi, Fontana. You look chipper today."

Lee grinned at her, the very sight of her made him feel lighter. "Guess I do feel pretty good, I just got myself a job." Thanks to Gimpy, when a job had opened up in the cotton mill, Lee was in—with some reservation from his counselor, on a try-and-see basis. He was to start the next afternoon on a short, three o'clock shift.

"I'm glad for you, Fontana." Karen's smile warmed him clear to his toes. She went on past him, but before she entered the next office she turned and gave him a wink and a thumbs-up.

His counselor had been hesitant about the job, but Lee persisted until Camp said he could give it a try. "Wear a handkerchief over your face, Fontana. Or get a mask from the dispensary, the air isn't the best in there."

Lee said he would, but he wasn't going to go in there acting like a sissy, with some kerchief tied around his face.

He moved on down the hall to the doctor's office, still thinking about Karen's smile and wink. Swinging up onto the examining table, he took off his shirt, wincing as Dr. Floyd slapped the cold stethoscope on him. With the doctor preoccupied, thumping his chest and back, telling him to take deep breaths and listening to his heart, Lee scanned the small, square room. A tray of several sizes of adhesive tape and bandages sat beside the sink, along with a bottle of antiseptic. There were no small, sharp tools to be easily slipped into a guy's pocket. But across the room on the wall hung dispensers for rubber gloves and paper towels, a disposal bin for waste products and another one for used razor blades: a simple metal box with a handle that operated a dump bin at the bottom. Lee studied this as Dr. Floyd took his blood pressure. He was looking innocently at the doctor when an orderly stuck his head in the door, a thin guy in a pale blue lab coat. "Can you take a phone call from the warden?"

Floyd glanced uneasily at Lee, then looked around the room, making sure that no sharp instruments had been left out. "Stay put, Fontana." He moved away, leaving the door wide open, stopping to speak to the orderly. The orderly disappeared from Lee's sight and Lee moved fast. When the orderly reappeared, stepping into the room, Lee sat on the table as before, his legs dangling.

Dr. Floyd wasn't gone much longer. Returning, he nodded to Lee. "You can put on your shirt, Fontana. So far you look good. Keep doing your breathing exercises. I want to see you in a week." As Floyd moved to the sink to wash his hands, Lee left the room walking carefully, conscious of the tangle of double-edged razor blades wrapped in a paper towel; he had slipped them into his pants pocket in the second before the orderly stepped in, blades that must have been used to shave around wounds before they were stitched and bandaged.

As he left the clinic, pushing out through the iron door, an icy wind hit him, cutting down the open walk. As he passed the cotton mill he casually checked its trash bins, glanced around, and removed a length of cotton cord from among the detritus.

From there he headed for the automotive shop, where the sound of hammering on metal rang sharply. Even from a distance the wind carried the smell of oil and solvent and wet paint. He found Morgan at work on a sleek red roadster. They could hardly talk for the noise echoing through the busy shop, and then the rumble and cry of a freight train. At least a dozen men worked in the shop, sanding car parts, carefully tapping out dents with rubber mallets, filling tiny flaws in fenders and door panels, spraying on primer. Three men at the far end stood under a lift working on the axle of an old Model T. Lee smiled, watching Morgan. It was clear that Blake liked his work. When Blake turned to look at Lee his usual anger was gone, his expression almost happy. Lee made small talk, admiring the red roadster and the work Morgan was doing, the newly painted fender replacement, the new tan upholstery. They visited for only a few minutes. As Lee turned to leave, blowing his nose, he managed to drop his handkerchief over a lost machine nut that had rolled beneath a tire. Picking up both, he left the auto shop with everything he needed for a good, no-nonsense weapon.

So far he had been passive with Coker and Delone, had played it low-key. But those two were half crazy, the kind who got a jolt from bullying and hurting and worse. That night after supper, alone in his cell, Lee checked the cells across the way to be sure no one was idly watching. The custodian had already done the count, the cells were locked for the night and that was the most privacy he'd get. He glanced the length of the cellblock, then, sitting on his bunk with his back to the bars, a pillow behind him as if he was reading, he got to work.

In the half-light from the corridor, keeping the materials close in his lap so he could pull the blanket up, he cut the cotton cord in two and unraveled the shorter piece to produce lengths of heavy-duty thread. He stretched out the other cord, and at one end he tied the heavy, half-inch-thick machine nut. Moving down the length of the cord he commenced to tie on the double-edged blades with the heavy thread, taking care not to slice his fingers. He was lucky to have gotten them. In the cellblocks the guards kept tight count of every razor blade a fellow was issued and collected them again pretty quick.

Down at the end of Lee's cot the tomcat appeared as the faintest shadow watching with kneading claws the enticing lengths of thread twist and writhe as they unraveled, watching the heavier, snakelike behavior of the long cord. He wanted to leap into the tangle playing and rolling, biting at the threads. The sharp blades stopped him—though they couldn't hurt a ghost, memories of past lives and sharp tools were too indelibly a part of his nature. Restraining himself, he only let his shadowy tail lash as Lee fished each thread through the narrow slot of a blade and around the cord and back.

In order for the weapon to be effective each blade had to be strongly secured at both ends. Working on the garrote Lee found himself thinking about Morgan Blake, puzzling over the young man's story. Why did it keep nudging at him, why did he keep thinking about Blake's version of the crime and the trial? He'd heard a million sob stories, all of them as fake as counterfeit twenties, so why did he believe this one?

But somehow he did believe, and that bothered him. They'd had breakfast together several times when Blake sought him out; each time Blake got onto the bank robbery and the events leading up to that day. Lee didn't want to listen, but his instinct said Blake was telling the truth, said Blake *had* been set up, that a carefully planned robbery and killing had been smoothly pulled off at the young man's expense.

Lee was irritated that he believed Blake; it bothered him that he'd begun to care about the guy's predicament. Getting involved in someone else's life, in prison, was the best way Lee knew to jeopardize his own life. There was no way he could help Blake even if he was stupid enough to try. Yet he couldn't shake his growing interest.

It was late when Lee finished tying on the razor blades, working in the dim light of his own shadow. Every time he heard the guard's soft footsteps walking the rounds he pulled up the blanket, picked up his pulp novel and bent over it. Sometimes he rattled and wadded up a candy wrapper, tossing it on the floor. When the guard had moved on, Lee would continue with the garrote. The weapon was about twenty inches long. At the opposite end to the nut he tied a loop large enough to slip his finger through. The blades, crowded close together, started ten inches from the loop and ended four inches from the steel nut. Turning to check the cellblock, Lee let the weapon hang from his right forefinger.

Along the rows of cells, the men he could see were either asleep or busy with their own concerns, lying in bed reading, writing letters. Satisfied no one was watching, he moved back into the shadows. "Get out of here," he hissed at the ghost cat. Misto disappeared but reappeared at the head of Lee's cot, the faintest shadow. Lee could just see his whiskers and ears flat to his head, but Misto's toothy hiss was all bravado. Free of the cat, he swung the garrote in a circle, letting the weight of the nut pull the cord taut, whirling it until a faint light flashed off the sharp blades, then the garrote began a faint whistle. At the sound he stopped its motion, glancing across the way. Carefully he rolled the nut and blades up inside the cord until the finished product looked like no more than a ball of string. He dropped this in a Bull Durham bag he'd fished out of the trash behind the mess hall, slipped it under his mattress, and crawled into bed. If Coker and Delone wanted to play rough, he was ready.

14

The cotton looms thrashed and banged as if they'd tear themselves from the floor; the big room rocked with rows of clattering looms, the thread feeding into them faster than Lee could follow. His job was to keep the spindles supplied to machines fourteen and fifteen so they'd never stop running, and he had to stay on his toes. Red lines painted on the floor cautioned him where to keep clear. As the canvas fabric edged its way out of each loom, Lee's freckle-faced partner guided its dropping in folds onto a rubber-wheeled cart.

Gimpy had warned him that no matter what job a man did in here, he had to be careful, everything in the place was dangerous. When Gimpy had introduced him to the foreman, the middle-aged, military-looking man walked Lee through the routine just once and then put him to work. The cotton came into the mill already ginned, the seeds removed. It was air-blown in a big metal hopper up on the second-level loft, was sent from there through a large tube to machines that spun it into thread, wound the thread on spindles, and the spindles sent down to the busy looms. The room's thunder seemed to rip right through Lee. He had put cotton wads in his ears, as his partner wore, but it didn't help much. The air was murky with cotton dust, but he wasn't wearing a sissy mask. He thought he could breathe shallowly until he was out in the fresh air again. Only when he left his machine to get more spindles did he find something to laugh about.

Glancing into the adjoining room he saw the woven canvas being sewn into large bags, and each stamped in black letters, *U.S. MAIL.* He was helping make the exact same bags he'd buried in the desert full of hundred-dollar bills. The bags he'd taken at gunpoint from the Blythe post office. And didn't that make him smile.

By the end of his shift his cough was bad and his body ached from the noise, the clatter penetrated clear to his bones. The most positive thing about the job, he thought, was that it allowed him to drop out of group counseling—but even that didn't work. As he left the noisy cotton mill, the guard stopped him.

"You're to go from here to your counselor, Fontana." The man had a face like a bloodhound, drooping jowls, no smile. "He'll set up a new time for your group sessions."

Lee swallowed back his reply, which would only have gotten him in trouble. Heading for Paul Camp's building, walking back between rows of desks, he found Camp leaning over his own desk tamping tobacco into a dark, carved pipe. Leaning back in his chair, Camp took his time lighting up. Drawing the smoke in deeply, he handed Lee his new counseling schedule. Lee wanted to argue, but what good?

Camp sat looking him over in a way Lee didn't like. "I have a request from Morgan Blake."

Lee waited. Why tell him about Blake's problems?

"Blake wants you to accompany him on his wife's visiting days, says she'd like to meet you."

"Why would she do that? What the hell is that about? Visiting is for families." Why would Blake want him there during that private time? Why would the woman want to meet *him*?

"It's an unusual request," Camp said. "Did you know Blake before you were transferred to Atlanta?"

"Never heard of him. Why would I want to get involved in someone else's family?"

Camp leaned back until his wooden chair creaked. "You've gotten friendly with Blake pretty fast."

"He's a nice enough kid. But visiting day? I don't think so."

Camp just looked at him.

"I listen to him," Lee said, "the kid needs someone to vent to, but I sure didn't put it in his head to meet his family."

"Morgan says that talking to you has helped him accept his situation. You think you're some kind of counselor?"

"I listen good," Lee said, hiding his amusement.

"Whatever you're doing," Camp said, "seems to be working. I've noticed a change in Blake."

"So what do I get, a medal? Maybe I can counsel the whole family."

Camp gave him another long, hard gaze. Lee was about to rise and leave, but his curiosity got the best of him. What harm would it do, a few minutes in the visiting room? It might answer some questions about the way Blake watched him, frowning and puzzled. "What the hell," he said. "I can give it a try."

Camp studied him, made a notation on a pad, and handed Lee a list of visiting hours. Lee moved on out of the office wondering why he'd agreed. Wondering why Blake had made the request. If there was something

Morgan knew that Lee didn't, maybe now he'd find out.

Bushed from the cotton mill, he skipped supper and headed for his cell. One day on the job and his cough was bad. His body ached, his head pounded, he knew he should have taken the kitchen job.

But he wasn't going to call it quits, he'd *wear* a damned handkerchief around his face, he'd get *used* to the noise.

In the cellblock, as he climbed the metal stairs and moved in through his barred door, his bunk looked mighty good. He collapsed onto it, his strength gone. He was getting old. The thought sent a chill through him. He was deep asleep when Misto dropped onto the cot and stretched out beside him, lying close, listening to Lee's ragged breathing.

"She will come now," the cat whispered, placing a soft paw on Lee's cheek, sending his words deep into Lee's dreams. "The child will come now. You'll know soon enough why Morgan watches you. You'll know soon enough why, all these years, you've carried Mae's picture with you. You'll begin to see now that you can defeat the dark spirit. You will take strength not only from me, but from the child."

Lee didn't wake until morning, to the sounds of men starting the day, coughing and grumbling, the water running, an angry shout, springs creaking and metal clanging. He washed, dressed, stood for the count and then headed for breakfast. Collecting his tray, he found Morgan already at a small table.

"What's that about?" he said, setting down his tray. "Why would your wife want me to visit? What kind of scam is this?"

Morgan looked down at his plate, his face coloring. "Actually, it's my child who wants you there, it's Sammie who asked for you."

Lee scowled at him. "How does your kid even know about me? What have you told her? Why would . . . ?"

Morgan drizzled syrup over his pancakes. "I didn't tell her anything about you. She . . . she dreamed about you. She . . . said you came here from California."

Lee looked hard at him.

"She's only a little girl," Morgan said, forking pancakes. The clatter of breakfast dishes and the staccato of men's voices echoed around them, bouncing off the concrete walls. "She . . . Sammie has these dreams. About people, about things that will happen. Sometimes," he said, looking almost shyly at Lee, "sometimes her dreams turn out to be real."

"What do you mean, real?" Lee said uneasily.

"She knows what you look like. She knows you worked in the desert, driving a truck, and she dreamed of you flying in a small, open plane. She knows you, Lee, though you've never met."

Morgan's words chilled Lee, pulled a memory from deep within and nearly forgotten, incidents from childhood that he'd put away from him, that he hadn't wanted to think about. Secrets came alive again, his sister Mae's secrets when she would whisper her dreams to him, dreams that later turned out to be real.

Once Mae told him that their milk cow, Lucy, would birth triplet calves, and triplet calves were rare. Lucy bore three live calves, all healthy little bull calves. The predictions frightened Mae; she would tell them shyly, painfully but earnestly, only hoping the adults would listen. Once she told Pa that he'd better fix the roof of the hay barn before the next snow or it would cave it in. Pa didn't fix the roof. In the heavy winter it did collapse, ruined half a barn full of good hay, but luckily none of the animals was hurt. Pa was angry at Mae that the roof fell in, like it was her fault, and that was the last dream she ever told Pa.

By the time Lee left home, either the dreams had stopped or Mae stopped talking about them. Pa grew angry if she mentioned a dream, and their mother didn't want to hear it, either. Lee was the only one who listened, uncomfortably, then he'd put the dreams away from him. Mae never knew how much they frightened him, this seeing into the future, predicting a future that hadn't yet happened, that no one should be able to see. Now again the shadowed memories from that long-ago time filled him. "Your little girl dreams of something that hasn't happened?" he asked softly.

Morgan nodded. "She described you exactly. She dreams of you and feels close to you. She wants you there on visiting day," he said awkwardly.

Lee shivered.

"She's only nine, Lee. She's my child and I love her and she has these dreams, that's all I can say. What will it hurt to humor her?"

"She dreamed about me because you talked about me." Lee said nothing about Mae, he wasn't telling Morgan about Mae.

Morgan laid down his fork, fixing his attention on Lee. "I never talked about you. I never mentioned you. I can't explain why she dreams of you. She dreamed of you and me talking together in the automotive shop."

"That's because you told her you were working there. That's where she pictures you, in a place like your shop in Rome."

"In her dream there was a red Buick roadster up on the rack."

"How would a little girl know a Buick roadster from a hay wagon?"

Morgan smiled. "She helps . . . used to help me in the shop, handing me tools. From the time I came home from the navy she's hung around the shop, she knows all my automotive tools. She knows the makes of most cars, she can stand on the street and rattle off the make, model, and year of nearly every car that passes.

"It was hard on her," Morgan said, "being without a father. Hard on all the service kids, those years without a dad to lean on and to learn from. Becky took the best care of her, but when I got home Sammie clung to me, wanted to be with me in the shop." Morgan shook his head. "We were so happy, the three of us together again, our life starting again as it should be. And then, long before the robbery and murder, Sammie dreamed about me being locked behind prison bars.

"Becky and I thought this dream was just a simple nightmare, we knew such a thing couldn't happen. But then it did happen," Morgan said. "The afternoon and night I was drugged? Sammie, at the exact same time, reacted in the same way; she was groggy, she kept falling asleep, she couldn't stay awake."

Lee said nothing. To believe in the ghost cat was one thing, and to know the dark spirit was real, he had learned to adjust to that unseen world. But to bring alive the future as Mae had done, to reach forward into unformed time—that bruised something young and painful in Lee, brought back an unsteady fear he didn't want to deal with.

"Yesterday," Morgan said, "Sammie told me that when she dreamed of you in the shop, you dropped your handkerchief on the floor. She said when you picked it up, you picked up a metal nut off the shop floor, that you made sure it was hidden in the handkerchief that you put in your pocket."

Lee choked, couldn't swallow. When at last he got the coughing under control, Morgan said, "Come on, Lee, humor a little girl. What can it hurt to meet her, to spend a little while with us next visiting day?"

Lee knew now that he'd better do that. This kind of thing would turn a man crazy unless he knew what it was about.

15

Becky left the drugstore at five feeling good after her first day at work. She'd found a bookkeeping job at last, after multiple tries. She liked the people she was working with; she liked the fact that the Latham family had slowly, over the years, established a small chain that gave five areas of Atlanta excellent pharmacy service. She would be paid at the end of each week and she badly needed the money to pay their attorney. The shop windows along Peachtree were bright with Thanksgiving color, a hint of Christmas scattered among them, and the air had turned crisp and chill. She had started to cross the street to the department store meaning to buy some stockings before her last pair gave way when she thought she saw Brad Falon.

Catching her breath, she drew back into the shadow of a doorway. The man moved swiftly away from her; she could see only his back, a slim man, Falon's height. Same narrow head, light brown hair combed into a thick ducktail. He turned the corner and was gone and she hadn't seen his face. Had he seen *her,* was that why he hurried away? She wanted to follow him, but that wasn't wise. Instead she returned to the pharmacy, stood in the shadow of the doorway for a long time watching the street.

He didn't return. Maybe it wasn't Falon, maybe only someone who resembled him. The man had been visible for only a minute, and was half hidden by shoppers. How could Falon have found out so soon where she'd gone? Moving on into the drugstore as if she had forgotten something she smiled at Amy, the small, blond clerk, and went on into the back office. She sat down at her desk, feeling shaky. She stared at the neatly stacked ledgers, at the chrysanthemums that Mr. Latham had brought from his garden to brighten her first day on the job, a homey, kindly gesture.

The Latham's pharmacies were small shops selling prescriptions only and over-the-counter medications, no ice cream counter, no magazines or toys. The plate-glass windows were kept sparkling, the marble floors immaculate. Near the front door were two benches where customers could wait for their orders. Behind the pharmacist's counter was a large safe where cash and a few narcotic drugs were kept, a refrigerator, and shelves of prescription medicines. The inner office was lined with file cabinets facing the two desks. Becky's job was to keep daily accounts for the five stores. Invoices and sales records were put on her desk each night, after John Latham had made his rounds. Latham was a slim, quiet man, with a habit of smoothing the top of his head, where his hair was thinning.

Becky had found the job through an agency after two weeks of looking on her own. She had chosen the agency with the most comfortable atmosphere, and had indicated on her registration forms that she was a widow. Two days later she had the job. The previous bookkeeper, who was leaving to have a baby, had interviewed her, and then Mr. Latham had talked with her. Her salary was more than she had hoped, and this downtown branch was a five-minute drive from Anne's, an equal distance from the grammar school. Sammie should already be in school, but Becky was still reluctant to send her off by herself. Now, if she *had* seen Falon, she would have to keep Sammie home.

If he had tracked her this far, he would find the house—or had already found it, was already watching the Morningside neighborhood. Fear and anger made her heart pound. She breathed deeply, trying to relax. She couldn't let panic paralyze her, she had to think what to do, had to watch more carefully around her, further caution to her aunt and Anne's housekeeper to be aware, to keep the doors locked. And she'd have to carry the .38. An empty gun was no good, lying in the bottom of a suitcase.

She waited at her desk for twenty minutes, then left by the back door, crossing the small parking area to her car. She drove home to Anne's by a circuitous route, watching for Falon's black coupe. The next morning when she dressed for work she unlocked the .38 from her battered overnight bag, loaded it and put it in her purse.

Leaving Sammie at home with Mariol, Becky drove to work, warily watching the streets. Pulling into the narrow parking area behind the redbrick building, she left the gun under the seat of the locked car. Maybe she was being paranoid, carrying a gun, and maybe not. Falon had been in their house more than once. He had killed one man that she knew of, and he had nearly killed bank teller Betty Holmes. He might well have killed her and Sammie that night when Sammie was small, when he broke into their house and Sammie's good cat attacked him. Sammie was so little then. Neither of them had forgotten Misto's bravery and the terrible shock of his death.

Could she shoot Falon if she must? Oh, yes. If he came at Sammie, she'd kill him. She had warned Anne and Mariol about Falon, though she wasn't sure that either one took the threat seriously enough. She had made them promise not to open the door to any stranger and not to let Sammie play outside alone.

On her second day, arriving at work, she didn't glimpse Falon or his car, and when she didn't see him the next day or the next, her tension began to ease. Very likely that wasn't Falon she'd seen, but a stranger, a coincidence not a threat. She had been at work a week when she came out of the drugstore at four feeling good, her first week's pay in her purse, feeling strong and secure to be making a regular salary again. Things were better at Anne's, too; something was changing that puzzled her, Anne seemed almost pleased that they were staying there, she wasn't nearly so grim and cold as when they arrived.

To further lighten her mood, Quaker Lowe had called not fifteen minutes ago, just before she left work. He said he should know about the appeal within the week, and he had sounded hopeful. That cheered her considerably. She didn't let herself think they might be denied. Leaving the pharmacy by the rear door, she checked the alley, glanced between the parked cars, then moved toward her own car. She unlocked the driver's door, tossed her purse on the seat—and was jerked backward. Hard fingers dug into her shoulder, jerked her off balance, she hit her head on the door frame. Falon spun her around, threw her to the ground, the rough surface ripping her outthrust hands.

He crouched over her, pawing at her dress. She tried to shout but was mute with fear. When he shoved his hand under her skirt she clawed him and tried again to scream. It was broad daylight, four o'clock, there were people on the street, people in the drugstore, someone had to hear her if only she could make some sound. He grabbed her hair, jerked her up so hard blackness swam, pulled her close, pawing and stroking her. When he leaned down as if to kiss her she bit him in the throat. He struck her hard across the cheek. She grabbed his face, dug her fingers in his eyes. He let go, knocked her hands away, and bent over, pawing at his eyes. Free of him, she pulled herself up into the car, but again he lunged at her. She kicked him in the crotch and reached frantically under the seat, feeling for the gun.

She couldn't find it. Searching, she hit her head on the steering wheel. Behind her Falon was bent over groaning, holding himself. She spun around and shoved him off balance. He stumbled back. She jerked the door closed and locked it, snatched the key from her pocket, jammed it in the ignition and started the car. As the engine roared she pressed her face to the window, he was getting up. She backed out fast. She'd like to put the car in low and ram him. Careening out of the parking lot she swung into traffic nearly hitting an oncoming car. Falon would be parked nearby, would be behind her in seconds, and she didn't dare lead him to Anne's. Turning off Peachtree she sped two blocks to a gas station and swung in. Staying in the locked car with the window half down, she asked the attendant to call the police. The grizzled old man stared at the black car swerving in behind her and raced for the office phone. Falon paused, watching the attendant, then swung a U-turn, narrowly missing the gas pumps, and took off again.

When the police arrived she told them only that a man had attacked her behind the drugstore, that he had chased her, that she didn't know who he was. The attendant gave them the make and model of the Ford but he hadn't been able, at the angle and speed it moved, to see the license plate. She gave the police her Rome address, she said she was in town only for the day. If Falon didn't know where she was staying, she didn't want him finding out by some fluke at the police station, by some clerical indiscretion. If her lies caught up with her, she'd deal with them later.

Falon would be back, she was only grateful that he had come after her and not Sammie. Driving around the business district watching behind her and watching the side streets, she kept seeing the look in his eyes.

She drove around for half an hour and didn't see the sporty black Ford. She hurried on to Anne's, got out quickly, opened the garage door, pulled her car in beside Anne's Cadillac, jerked the door closed from within. Locking it, she could hear the fiery music of Stravinsky coming from the living room. Mariol had told her Anne didn't use the record player often, usually when she was upset, perhaps after some conflict in one of her women's club meetings. Fishing her compact from her purse, looking in the little mirror, she frowned at the bruises already darkening her forehead and cheek, wondering how she was going to explain that. Carefully she combed her hair, straightened her blouse and jacket, tried to put herself in some kind of order.

Letting herself into the foyer, she looked into the empty living room, its ivory-toned velvet furniture and pale Oriental carpet pristine and untouched. The cream-colored afghan lay tangled on the couch among the throw pillows as if Sammie might have been napping. Following the scent of hot chocolate she headed past the dining room to the kitchen, pausing just outside the half-closed door.

Sammie was crying, a shaky sniffle; then she blew her nose. Anne's voice was soft. "I cried, too, I cried after such a dream. Oh, so many times. But she's all right, Sammie. Your mother's all right now."

"But she *isn't* all right. That man hurt her, that Brad Falon—the man who watches us, who broke into our house. The man who killed my Misto."

Becky stood dismayed. Had Sammie had a daytime nightmare, had awakened from seeing Falon's attack? Awakened frightened and crying—and Anne had been there for her, had reached out to her? Something tender in Anne had reached out?

She moved into the kitchen. Anne sat at the big kitchen table, her back to Becky, holding Sammie in her lap, cuddling her close and tenderly in a way Becky would never have guessed. "I cried, too," Anne repeated softly, "but your mother's all right. And you and I are all right."

Sammie looked up at Anne and reached to touch her face. Around them the airy white kitchen was fresh and welcoming with its mullioned-glass cabinet doors, white tile counters, and the three deep-set windows crowded with pots of green herbs. Mariol stood at the double sink washing vegetables, her back to Anne and the child.

"We're together now," Anne said. "Now, when the nightmares come, you have not only your mother to tell, you have me and Mariol to tell, if you want to."

When the child glanced across at Mariol, the slim, mulatto woman turned to look kindly at her. Anne said, "Until now I have trusted only Mariol to keep my secret. But you have all three of us, Mariol and me and your mama, to hold you when the ugly dreams come, to hold you and keep you safe."

"But you can't change what I see," Sammie said. "No one can. He hurt Mama and he'll try again."

Shaken, Becky moved on into the kitchen. Sammie leaped from Anne's lap and flew at her, hugging her. "Are you all right, Mama? He hurt you." When Becky knelt, holding her, Sammie gently touched Becky's bruised forehead and cheek. Pulling out a chair, Becky sat cuddling Sammie as Anne had done, smiling across at her aunt.

"He got away?" Anne said. "How badly are you hurt?"

"Just bruises," Becky lied, not mentioning the pain where she'd fallen and where he'd hit her. She watched Mariol empty an ice tray, wrap ice in a dish towel, and hand it across to her. As she pressed the coldness to her face, the pain and bruises didn't matter, only Anne's words mattered. *I cried, too, after such a dream. Oh, so many times.* What was this, where had this come from? To hear Anne confess to the same prescience as Sammie's left her indeed shaken. Did Sammie's strange talent, then, belong within their family?

Two half-empty mugs of cocoa stood on the table beside Sammie's open picture book, and a third mug where Mariol had been sitting. That was another strange thing about Anne, Becky thought, that while most Southern households would not permit colored help to sit at the table with their employers, this was not the case here. In this house, even as proper as Anne was in other matters, she and Mariol were equals, were dear friends. Mariol might, Becky thought, be the closest friend Anne had, maybe her only true friend.

Mariol poured fresh cocoa from a pan on the stove, set the mug on the table before Becky, then took her own place again, her dark eyes, when she looked up at Becky, filled with concern. "You *are* all right?"

Becky nodded, drawn to her kindness.

"She's a special child," Mariol said. "She's fortunate to have parents who understand." She looked at Anne companionably. "And lucky, too, to have an aunt who understands." And Becky wondered if Anne, in her own childhood, had not been so lucky.

16

Lee paused in the doorway, watching across the visiting room where Morgan stood hugging his family. The minute Morgan entered, the little girl had flung herself at him, he'd hugged her tight and drawn his wife close. Lee couldn't see much of the child from the back, her long blond hair, one strand caught on the collar of her blue gingham dress. Her gangly legs with several scratches, tomboy legs. And the eager way she clung to Morgan, the three of them wrapped around one another, their voices soft and caressing. Lee wanted to turn away, this emotional family reunion had nothing to do with him. Painfully out of place, he'd rather head back to his cell and crawl in his bunk.

The room itself seemed out of place, had no relationship to the rest of the prison; even the bars on the wide windows were half disguised by the potted white flowers on the sills. He stood not on hard concrete but on a tan tweed carpet, the walls painted white instead of government green. Soft-looking couches and chairs were set about in little family groupings, the effect cozy and unreal. Taking in the unnatural scene, he turned to leave—but he didn't leave. He had promised Morgan.

And something else held him, the child held him, her likeness to Mae made him turn to watch her. From the back she looked so like Mae that he felt jerked into the past, returned to their childhood. Her thin body as light-boned as a fledgling bird, just like Mae, her long legs and the way she stood as if she might leap away any instant. He wished she'd turn around, but he was afraid of what he'd see.

Last night he hadn't slept well, he'd coughed all night, after the cotton mill. Awake and choking, he had tossed restlessly thinking about today, thinking about the child who was so like Mae, who dreamed as Mae dreamed. Periodically he had sat up on his bunk and done his breathing exercises, but it had been impossible to get enough air. He'd skipped breakfast this morning, had drunk some coffee and then sat in the thin winter sun hoping it would warm him. It would be Christmas soon; some wag had tied a red bow on the railing of the stairs that led down from the industries buildings. He had stood looking at it and thinking about this visit, about Sammie and about Mae, feeling curious and uneasy.

Now he sat down in the nearest chair watching the cozy family. Watched Morgan draw his wife and child to a couch where they sat close together. Becky was tall and slim, built like her daughter but with dark hair falling to her shoulders. She wore a plain tan coat over her skirt and white blouse, sheer stockings and flat shoes. He was watching the way Morgan held her so tenderly when the little girl turned, looking across the room at him. The shock sent him weak.

He was looking at Mae. This was Mae, this was his sister. The long-ago memories flooded back. Holding her hand as they waded in the drying stream on a scorching summer day—bundling Mae up in scarves and gloves in the freezing winter, lifting her onto his homemade sled. Mae slipping away from their mother to the saddled horses, scrambling up into the saddle by herself.

Mae crossed the room to him . . . *But not Mae.* This was Sammie. She ran to him reaching for him, same dark brown eyes as Mae, same long blond hair tangled around her ears, Mae's own elfin smile. She stopped a few feet from him, shy suddenly. But then she flew at him, she was in his lap, her arms around him as if she'd known him forever. How warm she was, like a hound pup, shockingly warm and sweet smelling. This *was* Mae, this was his little sister, her hug infinitely comforting.

But of course she wasn't Mae, this was Morgan Blake's child, this was Sammie Blake who had dreamed of him in the same inexplicable way that Mae dreamed, seeing what she couldn't know.

Seeing his unease, Sammie lowered her eyes and drew back, her look as coolly shuttered as any grown-up's, shy and removed suddenly, plucking at the doll she carried. From the couch, Morgan and Becky watched them in silence, Becky's hands twisting in her lap, the moment as brittle as glass—until Sammie reached to touch his face.

"Where is your horse?"

Lee stared at her.

"Where is your gray horse?"

No one knew about the gray, Lee had never talked to Morgan about horses, the young mechanic had no interest in horses. Certainly he would never mention the gelding on which he had escaped after the post office robbery; he had never told Morgan about the robbery. "I don't have a horse. You can't have a horse in prison."

"But you do. You have a horse. The gray horse. Where is he?"

If she had dreamed of the gray, had she dreamed of the robbery, too? "Sorry," he said. "No horse. The prison guards won't let me keep one."

This child knew secrets she shouldn't know, she had seen into his life as no normal person could do. He didn't know what else she might have dreamed, he was sorry he'd come, today. When he looked up, Becky's face was closed and unreadable, her hands joined with Morgan's, their fingers gripped together telegraphing their unease. When again Sammie started to speak, Lee rose, lifting her. He needed to get out of there. But when he tried to put her in her father's lap she clutched him around the neck and wouldn't let go.

He pried her arms loose. "You have to stay with your daddy, I have to leave now." He handed her forcibly to Morgan, muttered a weak good-bye, and quickly turned away. Hurrying across the big room he could feel Sammie's hurt and disappointment. Unfinished business weighed on the child—and weighed on Becky and Morgan. Too much had been left unsaid, urging him to turn back. But he didn't turn; he pushed on out through the heavy door, nodded to the guard and hurried through the corridors to the safety of his cell. Crawling under the blanket shivering, he didn't want to deal with this. But at the same time, he was drawn to Sammie and to the mystery of the Blake family that seemed, that had to be a part of his own life.

Lee woke when the Klaxon rang for first shift supper. He had slept for over an hour. He thought of skipping the meal, he didn't want to sit with Morgan, didn't want to try to explain how uncomfortable the child made him, he didn't want to talk. But in the end he decided he'd better eat something. Maybe Morgan would eat later, slip in at second shift. He washed his face, combed his hair, pulled on the wool jacket the prison had issued when the weather turned cool, and headed out along the catwalk. They'd have to talk sometime, he just hoped it wasn't tonight.

In the mess hall, getting his tray, he chose a table in the farthest corner, hoping Morgan wouldn't show. But of course when he looked back at the line, there he was. In a few minutes he set his tray down across from Lee.

Lee had invented a number of fake explanations for departing the visiting room so abruptly; but this morning, leaving his cell, something had made him slip Mae's picture in his pocket. Now, when Morgan began quizzing him, he handed it across the table.

Morgan looked at the picture, frowning. Sammie was dressed as he had never seen her in a white pinafore, shiny black shoes, and white socks. She was standing before a three-rail pasture fence, a couple of steers off in the distance, a place Morgan had never been.

"My sister," Lee said. "Taken when we were kids. Mae was about eight."

Morgan frowned at Sammie's dark eyes and perky smile, Sammie's pale hair hanging down her thin shoulders. Except for her old-fashioned clothes, this child *was* Sammie. Morgan looked for a very long time, then looked up at Lee.

"Mae had dreams," Lee said, "the same as Sammie. Not often, but she would dream of the future. She didn't talk much about them except to me, they upset our mother. And Pa would pitch a fit. Mae wasn't very old when she quit telling Pa what she saw, telling him what would happen."

Morgan handed the picture back, treating it with care. "Where is Mae now?"

Lee shook his head. "I didn't keep in touch, I lost track. I tried to find them in North Carolina, in a town where I thought they might be, but my letters were sent back. Someone wrote on one, 'Try Canada,' but they didn't say where, in Canada. I had an older brother, and two sisters older than Mae, I knew they'd take care of her.

"I heard from our neighbor when Pa died, there was a saloon where he knew to get in touch. It took a couple months before I rode that way. He said Ma and the kids had moved to North Carolina, that's when I tried to write to them. He wasn't certain about the address. I never heard from them, but I wouldn't have, I was always on the move." He knew he could have tried harder. He was ashamed about that. Well, hell, he was so caught up in his own life. All that young wildness, always another train to test him, another woman's smile to entice him.

"I was fourteen when we moved to Arizona. Two years later I went off on my own. I took the best two cow horses we had and I know Pa wasn't happy about that." He didn't know what made him talk so much. Maybe the fact of Mae's and Sammie's strange likeness made him ramble on, drew him to confide in Morgan.

It was long after supper and lights out, as Lee lay coughing and sleepless, when the tomcat joined him as he liked to do—as if he was tucking his wards in for the night. Landing hard on Lee's bed, this time the cat was fully visible in the overhead lights. Quickly Lee rose up from the covers, effectively hiding Misto, and turned to scan the cells across the way.

No one seemed to be looking back. He guessed the cat would know. Misto pricked his ears as a train thundered, its small earthquake deafening the cellblock. The ghost cat seemed quite to like the noise and hustle, the excitement. When the train had faded, he sat watching Lee again, alert and waiting.

Lee said, "That child is the spittin' image of Mae. You're the spirit, you know these things. You tell me what that's about."

Misto lashed his tail but said nothing.

"Talk to me." Lee scratched the cat's ragged ears.

"I can't know everything. But I can tell you this. You are meant to be together, you and Morgan and Sammie. A path is taking shape, just as certain as the route of that train. A path that you and I have followed, just as the devil follows."

Lee looked up again along the tiers of cells. Still no one was looking or seemed to be listening.

"He not only wants your soul," Misto said, "he would take Sammie if he could. There is something in the child that he can't touch, but still she is part of his plan."

Misto licked his paw. "The child is strong. Her deepest nature is to resist him, so deep an instinct that often she is hardly aware of him. She will help you, just as I will—as best a child and a small ghost *can* help, *can* try to save your scrawny neck."

17

The full moon was hidden by clouds, the Morningside neighborhood cast in shadow except where an occasional porch light had been left to burn past midnight. No light illuminated Anne Chesserson's large Tudor house as Brad Falon approached, his footsteps silent passing broad gardens and luxurious homes. He had sat in his car for some time parked on the hill several doors away, had seen the lights come on in the Chesserson woman's second-floor bedroom, had seen her come to the window, close it, and pull the shutters across as if the night air had turned too cold. No light reflected from the basement suite where Becky and Sammie were staying. He had watched the house at different hours of the day and night until he felt sure of the layout and the sleeping arrangements. This morning he had surveyed from the backyard, dressed in gray pants and shirt like those worn by the local meter readers.

Now, with the house dark, he headed down the sloping lawn between the Chesserson house and its plantation-style neighbor, descending a cover of pine straw between manicured rhododendron and azalea bushes. In his pocket he carried a roll of masking tape, a glass cutter, a rubber mallet, and a crowbar. His left eye was swollen and black where Becky had hit him, in the parking lot. Even after three days his throat was still torn and bruised where she'd bitten him, the vicious bitch. He'd known, when he attacked her at her car, that she'd fight. He hadn't thought she'd bite like a wild animal.

Heading for the wide French doors that opened to the spacious downstairs, he stood in the dark garden listening, looking around him. Had something moved in the shadows, had he heard some small, stealthy sound? He waited, puzzled. Something had alerted him, made him uneasy. He waited for some time; when nothing more bothered him he moved on up the three steps to look in through the wide glass panels. The rooms within were dark, the drapes partly open as if Becky might have pulled them back after she turned out the lights. Silently he tried the handle. Of course the door was locked. Fishing the tape from his pocket he tore off four short lengths, stuck them to the glass to form a small square that, when cut and removed, would leave an opening big enough to put his hand through.

When again he felt uneasy he turned to survey the garden. The clouds were shifting, the exposed moon sending more light. He wasn't armed, wasn't carrying the new S&W automatic, he didn't need it to take care of Becky Blake. If something happened to screw him up, he didn't want to be caught armed. Though of course he wasn't in possession of the .38 that had killed the bank guard, that gun was where no one would find it.

When the wary feeling subsided he applied the glass cutter in four quick, precise strokes, then used the rubber mallet. One small, sure tap neatly loosened the glass square. He removed it. Nothing stirred now behind him. Within the rooms, all was still. He had seen, this morning, that this door led into a sitting area. Beyond was the sleeping wing, one corner of a bed visible. Beside the bed, the carpeted floor was covered with a sheet spread out to full size and scattered with the child's drawing books. Reaching through, quietly he turned the knob of the lock. He was easing the door open when the kid screamed. The piercing ululation sent his heart racing, it went on and on, driving him off the terrace into the bushes.

As he crouched among the foliage, his dark clothes blended with the shadows. Had the girl heard that smallest tap when his hammer hit the glass? Or heard the lock turning? Inside, a faint light came on. From this angle he could see most of the bedroom. Sammie sat up rigid in bed, still screaming, her shrill voice jangling his nerves. He watched Becky slip out of her own bed into the child's and take the girl in her arms. For one moment, as they clung together, Becky's back was to him, her shoulder blocking Sammie's view. Quickly he slipped from the bushes, slid the door open enough to enter, silently closed it and eased behind the couch out of sight.

"Someone's there," Sammie said softly. "In the other room."

"It was the dream, it was in the dream," Becky said, hugging her.

"No. Not this time."

With the small lamp switched on, Becky looked through to the sitting room, as much as she could see from the bed. No one was there. Thin moonlight slanted in, but picked out only the couch and two chairs. She could see no darker shadow at the French doors as if someone stood looking in. "It was a dream," she said again, holding Sammie close.

But something had awakened Becky, too. Before Sammie started to scream. She was trying to remember what had jerked her to consciousness when she saw that the drapery hung awry. The bottom corner was folded back as if it had been disturbed. Had she left it that way? She didn't think so.

Slipping out of bed she grabbed her purse and unholstered the loaded Colt revolver, the .38 that Morgan had so carefully taught her to handle. As she moved toward the sitting room, the scents of the garden and of freshly crushed grass were sharp. As if the night breeze had blown in, though she knew she'd left the door locked. The sitting room was empty—unless someone crouched behind a chair or behind the couch. Cocking the .38, she approached the shadowed furniture, shaky with the pounding of her own heart. She stopped suddenly when, behind her, Sammie screamed. Holding the gun down and away, she whirled toward the bedroom.

Sammie's cry stopped abruptly, turned into a muffled sound of rage. Falon clutched the child against him, Sammie twisting and kicking. Grunting, he jerked her arm behind her so hard she caught her breath—but suddenly Falon stumbled. He struck out at the air as if someone had hit him. There was no one, he swung at empty air. Becky, holding the weapon low, moved to the bedroom. "Drop the child. Do it now."

He swung Sammie down into her line of fire, nearly dropped the fighting child. Clutching her with one hand, again he swatted at empty air then ducked away. Grabbing Sammie to him, he ran straight past Becky, ignoring the gun, racing for the door. Did he think Becky wouldn't shoot? She lunged, grabbed him by the shirt to pull him off balance, aimed at his legs away from Sammie, and fired.

He jerked and dropped Sammie. She fled. Falon stumbled out the door ducking, swinging his arms, nearly fell down the shallow steps. He beat at his shoulder and chest as if something clung to him. Becky heard Sammie in the bedroom calling the police. Falon struggled up, pushed his unseen attacker away, and ran through the azaleas and up the hill. Becky fired once at his retreating back, but then he was too near the neighbor's house. She ran chasing him up to the street but didn't dare fire again among the many houses. His limping footsteps pounded into the shadows beneath the trees; she heard him stumble again then heard a car door slam, heard the engine start. Tires squealed, and the car careened away. Becky turned and ran, burst into the sitting room.

Sammie stood between the two beds pale and silent, the phone still in her hand. Becky, with four rounds still in the chamber, checked the suite for a second assailant, though she doubted Falon had a partner. She pulled on a robe over her gown and dropped the gun in her pocket, then sat on the bed holding Sammie, waiting for the police. If they didn't find Falon and lock him up, if they didn't *keep* him in jail, he'd be back.

Not tonight, but soon.

Maybe her one sure shot had damaged his leg enough so he'd look for a doctor, someone who would treat him without reporting the shooting. She knew he'd keep coming back, harassing them until he had hurt them both or killed them.

Or until she killed Falon.

Could she have wounded him bad enough to make him stay away? When she looked at the threshold, there was blood on the carpet and on the steps. She was sorry she hadn't killed him and put an end to it. If she had trained more, she might have been more effective in stopping him without harming Sammie. What training she'd had, Morgan had given her long ago. When the war was over and Morgan was home again, neither of them dreamed that her life and Sammie's might depend on added training. The world seemed at peace then. They were caught up with being a family again, with being together and being happy. She started when a shadow moved through the bushes toward the French door. She rose, her hand in her pocket on the gun, and stood waiting.

"Police," a man shouted. His back was to the light, he was only a silhouette, she couldn't see a uniform. At the same moment she heard Anne call from the top of the stairs, then the figure on the terrace moved into clearer view where the sitting room light struck across his badge and sergeant's stripes. A tall, thin man with sandy hair.

She told him she was armed, slowly drew the gun, opened the action, and laid it on the dresser. "Come in," she said dryly.

"Sergeant Krangdon," he said, entering, glancing at the gun. Anne was coming down the carpeted stairs beside a second officer. The two men searched the suite while two more officers searched for Falon outside, their lights moving among the bushes, circling the garden and the neighbors' gardens and then up the hill. The sergeant took samples of blood and photographed bloodstains, out to where Falon's trail disappeared among the mulch and bushes. Anne didn't stay downstairs long. Seeing that Becky and Sammie were safe, she went up again, as Sergeant Krangdon asked her to do, to avoid disturbing any evidence. Sammie stood huddled against Becky, cold with the aftermath of fear. But something else shone in Sammie's eyes.

She looked up at Becky with a deep and secret amazement. Becky looked back at her, shaken with what she'd seen.

Earlier, after Falon attacked Becky in the parking lot, Sammie had said, *Misto couldn't help you, Mama, the dark was too strong.*

If the cat couldn't help her then—if there *was* a real ghost cat, Becky thought—why had he been powerful enough tonight to attack Falon? To make Falon pause so she *could* get in that one telling shot?

Had the difference to do with Sammie? With the fact that *Sammie* was in danger?

When Sergeant Krangdon returned she watched him unload her gun and bag it for evidence. He didn't seem concerned that he was leaving her with no protection from Falon. Quietly she answered his questions. Told him how Sammie had awakened screaming, and that she had grabbed the gun from her purse. She showed him where she had stood when she fired. She didn't tell him who the man was, she didn't say she knew him, and Sammie remained silent.

"If you could ID him," Krangdon said, "if you would file a complaint, you can take him to court, put a restraining order on him."

"How can I? I don't know him. I can't identify a man I've never seen before."

If Falon were caught, if he learned that she had identified him, and if he were then released, as he likely would be, he would come after them with even more vengeance. And what did the police have, to hold him? They had only her word against Falon's. They couldn't hold him long on that. She had heard of women attacked, brutally beaten, where the story proliferated, in gossip, even in the papers, that they had led the man on, had enticed him. Maybe the day would come when women were treated more fairly, but it hadn't arrived yet and she wasn't taking chances.

Most damning of all, Falon's testimony had helped convict Morgan. If she identified Falon for the break-in, what would the police or the court say? That she'd filed the complaint to get back at Falon? That she had enticed Falon, had set him up?

She thought of calling Quaker Lowe, but maybe she didn't want to know what he would advise. If she called Lowe now, in front of the police, they'd know there was more to the story, that this hadn't been a random break-in. She was courteous to Krangdon, cooperative in every other way. When he'd finished the interview he assigned young Officer Bishop to stay on the premises so that Becky and Sammie might get some sleep. He suggested they get a carpenter to install a metal barrier over the French doors. "An open grid," he said, "that can be locked but will let in air in hot weather. Make sure he installs it so the drapes can be pulled. And," he said, "you could put better locks on some of the solid doors, replace the thumb locks with dead bolts."

When the thin-faced officer had left them, moving out into the yard, Anne came down again and sat on the bed, holding Sammie. "It's all right. The police are here, it's all right now." But Sammie, like Becky, didn't have much faith in the police, after Rome PD had abandoned Morgan, had done nothing to uncover the real facts of the Rome murder. When Anne had said good night, Becky turned out the lamp and crawled into bed with Sammie. Not until the next morning did she call Quaker Lowe.

When she told him about the break-in and that she had shot Falon, Lowe was quiet, noncommittal. Did he really understand why she had withheld Falon's name? He said, "A complaint against Falon might have been useful in getting the appeal. Did you think of that?"

"I did. And it might also have gotten me or Sammie killed." Had she been wrong in not identifying Falon? She didn't want to cross Lowe, she couldn't afford to turn him away. She didn't want to lose the appeal. She ended the phone call feeling alone and uncertain, more frightened and upset than she would have thought, at losing Lowe's sympathy.

18

Lee sat on the metal examining table, his shirt off, waiting for Dr. Floyd to come in and poke the cold stethoscope at him. He'd felt rotten this morning, he'd coughed so bad in the cotton mill that the foreman had fired him and sent him straight here to the infirmary. He wasn't sorry, he should have known when he started that it was a dumb thing to do. But even now, sitting on the table staring at the orderly who stood in the doorway, what Lee was seeing in his mind wasn't the cotton mill but Sammie Blake and Mae, their mirror images that had stayed with him ever since visiting day. He was fretting, wondering if Mae was still alive somewhere, when Dr. Floyd came in.

The doctor took one look at Lee and shook his head. "You're pale as a dead flounder." He pressed the stethoscope against Lee's chest, listened, moved it again and again, listening. "You should have known better. The slip from your counselor said you'd wear a mask. Why didn't you? Even so, it was iffy. What did you think that lint would do to your lungs? You don't have much room in those air sacs, at best."

"I didn't have any choice if I wanted to work." Lee didn't mention that he could have asked for kitchen duty. "I don't like just sitting around," he said crossly.

"You'll be sitting around now. You're done with the cotton mill, you're going to sit in the sun and do nothing until you feel better."

"You ruling out all jobs? What about the kitchen?"

Floyd hesitated. "The kitchen would be all right, if you can work around the steam equipment. Steam would be good for you." The doctor shook his head. "You're a stubborn SOB, Fontana. I'll talk to Bronski about a job."

Lee pulled on his shirt and slid down from the table. "I didn't see Karen Turner when I came in."

That made Floyd laugh. "You're as bad as the young bucks. I think she's down in the lab."

"Guess you were right," Lee said, "it's nice to see a pretty face, gives a guy a lift."

Heading out, he was halfway along the corridor when he paused beside a closed door, listening. A series of soft thuds, then a muffled cry. He grabbed the knob and flung the door open.

Karen writhed on the floor beside a desk, fighting Coker. He crouched over her, pinning her down with his knee, blood streaking his dark hair. She hit and struck at him, her white uniform open to her waist and bloodstained, her brassiere torn away. Coker had wrapped a telephone cord around her neck and was pressing a prison-made knife to her throat. Lee lunged, brought the toe of his shoe crashing up under Cocker's arm, lifting the knife away. Coker came up swinging at him. Lee got in a kick to Coker's groin and dodged, shouting for help. Coker grabbed him, threw him against the desk, and bolted out the door, his eyes cold with hate and with promise.

Lee knelt over Karen, unwinding the cord from her neck. Long red lines circled her throat. Her forehead was already swelling and turning dark; she was bleeding pretty bad, red stains soaking her uniform. Lee propped her up against the side of the desk and ran for the hall, shouting again, but already Dr. Floyd was there, an orderly behind him. They dropped to their knees beside Karen.

"Who was it?" Floyd said, glancing up at Lee. "Did you see him?"

"Coker," Lee croaked, coughing hard, then he ran, chasing Coker.

By the time he reached the double doors of the dispensary he was gasping for air. He saw Coker between the buildings, making for the mess hall. Lee slowed, moved across the yard taking deep, slow breaths. Why chase him? There was no place Coker could hide for long. When Coker turned and saw him he quickened his pace and headed for the cellblock. Moving fast across the compound, his crew cut dark against the pale buildings, he swung in through the heavy door. Lee ran, pushing into the cellblock behind him.

From the entry he had a full view of the zigzag metal stair leading up. Hamilton, at his desk, saw Lee looking and followed his gaze. Coker was already scrambling onto the third tier. Ahead of Coker on the catwalk, Bronski was coming along, his eyes down on the book open in his hands, reading as he walked slowly toward the stairs. Lee thought Coker meant to play it innocent, to go on casually by Bronski and into his cell, but when Bronski glanced up at him, then looked over the rail toward Lee, Coker froze.

He stared down at Lee and Hamilton watching him, knew he couldn't go down again, that he was cornered. Swinging around he charged Bronski, his knife flashing. Bronski crouched, dropped his book, grabbed

Coker's arm, diverting the knife inches from his own face. Bronski clutched Coker's belt and in one move lifted and rolled Coker up over the rail. Coker hung for an instant over open space, then fell, arms flailing, his body twisting down the three tiers. He hit the concrete headfirst with a sound that sickened Lee.

Behind Lee the big doors burst open and armed guards came running. Shaken, Lee headed for the stairs and his cell. They'd be locked down now, until the guards got it sorted out.

He sat on his bunk hoping Karen Turner would be all right, seeing her blood-smeared uniform, the red marks circling her throat. He'd been right in the first place, the authorities were damn fools bringing a woman in here. He heard the guards' shouted orders, heard the prisoners moving in for the lockdown. He didn't see Karen Turner again.

The prison staff got the action sifted out in a hurry when Karen told them what had happened. Lee heard that she'd left the prison, that she was working in a civilian hospital. A week later, Dr. Floyd was gone, too. Whether he was fired or took an "early retirement," as they called it, Lee never knew. And even though he was glad Karen was out of there, he missed that pretty smile. Two days later he was working again, this time in the warm, steamy kitchen.

19

Anne sat at the kitchen table sipping coffee. "Did you and Sammie sleep at all?" Becky and Sammie had just come upstairs, Sammie moving to the stove to watch Mariol flip pancakes. Becky poured a cup of coffee and sat down.

"Surprisingly, we did sleep." She didn't say they'd slept with a warm cat between them, Sammie's arms circling that unseen presence who had comforted Becky, too.

"Last night . . ." Anne said, "I wish you'd killed him." That shocked Becky, coming from her proper aunt.

"I've prayed every night," Anne told her, "that Brad Falon was dead." She seemed amused at Becky's expression. "He tried to kill you, he's made nothing but trouble, he's doing his best to ruin your lives. What good is he, in the world?" This Aunt Anne whom she was seeing now was far different, indeed, from the way Becky had always thought of her.

Beside the stove, Sammie turned. "I dreamed he broke in, I dreamed of a hand reaching through."

Anne nodded. "That dream may have saved your lives." And, as if half to herself, "The same . . . *affliction* . . . our mother called it, that our aunt Mae endured. She had the dreams, too," Anne said softly. "Mother did tell me that, because of my own dreams, but she told me as if they were shameful. Otherwise she seldom talked about family, I know only a smattering of our history. I know that Mae was the youngest of our great-aunt Nell's five children.

"Nell and her three girls moved to North Carolina after the children's father died. He left them with very little, they sold their Arizona land for practically nothing, they had nowhere else to go but to her sister there. Mae's two older brothers had already left home. Later Mae's sister Nora married and settled in Georgia, our mother Nora."

Becky laid her hand over Anne's. "Do you know where Mae is now?"

Anne shook her head. "I don't. It's strange, embarrassing sometimes, shameful knowing so little about our family. Most Southern families are steeped in their history, from before the Civil War. But that's the way we grew up. No discussion, so Caroline or I weren't really interested. I didn't realize then the emptiness that left in me, having no real ties to our past."

Anne sipped her coffee, looked up at Becky. "I had a sense, too, that there might be more in our past even than the dreams, other 'shameful' things that Mama didn't want to talk about."

Becky, too, sometimes felt adrift not knowing their family history. Caroline had kept no letters, no pictures, nothing to define the past. She watched Mariol pour a glass of milk for Sammie and set her breakfast on the table. When Sammie slid into her chair, reaching for the syrup, Mariol kissed the top of her head, then turned away to test the skillet and pour more batter. Interesting, Becky thought, how comfortable Mariol seemed with the mention of prophetic dreams. As if she and Anne might have talked openly about Anne's dreams. Maybe, in Mariol's family, such talents were not considered strange. Whatever the case, Mariol's acceptance comforted Becky, made her feel easier.

Three days after Fred Coker died on the cellblock floor, Coker's friend Delone cornered Lee between the buildings, flashing a thin, a prison-made knife. Lee had just left the kitchen after his shift and was heading for the automotive shop, when he heard the crunch of gravel behind him. He spun around, saw Delone coming on him fast, a blade shining in his palm.

"You cruddy old bastard, it's your fault he's dead."

Lee wanted to reach for the garrote but something told him no, told him to get away. Puzzled, not used to backing off, he swung in through a side door of the masonry shop, a big, cavernous room. He saw no one, heard no sound. Dodging away among the freestanding practice walls and tall piles of stones and bricks, he lost himself in their shadows. He heard Delone behind him, heard him trip, maybe over a wooden support that steadied the masonry barriers. Dodging toward the back of the building where, Lee knew, another door led out again, he didn't see above him the yellow shadow slipping across the tops of the stone and block walls, a shadow thin as smoke.

The tomcat could not have materialized if he'd wanted to. He was spent, his attack last night on Falon, as he diverted the intruder to protect Sammie, had left him weak as a new kitten. If this was Satan's influence, he didn't like it much. This happened sometimes when he sought to function in both worlds; and he had heard, last night as he dropped into sleep, the cold laughter of the dark prince; he didn't like that much, either. Now he followed Lee along the tops of the freestanding walls until, at the far corner of the dim room, Lee slipped into darkness between the back door and tall piles of blocks.

Lee tried the door and found it locked. There was no knob to turn, no key in the keyhole. He shouldered uselessly against it, was unable to force it open, and, at the scuff of shoes behind him, swung around, waiting. Stood palming the ball of string, his finger in the loop.

It all happened too fast. A chunk of concrete fell and Delone rushed him, the knife-edged ice pick low and lethal. Lee saw too late there was no room to swing his weapon. He dodged but Delone was on him, the knife flashing as Delone rammed him into the wall. Lee felt the knife go in, low in his side.

Delone jerked the blade free, blood spurted. The weapon flashed again. Lee kicked Delone in the knee and kicked the blade from his hand. The effort doubled Lee over, the cat could feel the pain of his wound as if it were his own. He crouched to leap as Delone closed in, but instinctively backed off when Lee swung the garrote. He watched it circle Delone's leg. Lee jerked the cord hard, the blades cut through cloth and flesh, Delone stumbled, clutching his torn leg. But when Lee jerked the weapon free again, Delone lunged. Lee dodged and swung higher, the cord whistled, light shattered off its arsenal of blades as it snaked around Delone's throat. Lee grabbed the heavy nut, yanked the cord hard. Delone fell, clutching his torn throat. The ghost cat crouched lower, his yellow eyes burning, his own fear eased, his sense of Satan's presence fading.

Lee, watching Delone die, knew *he* could have been dead in Delone's place. He worked the garrote loose and backed away from the body. He found the lavatory, untied the nut from the cord, washed it off, and tossed it in the corner. He flushed the bladed cord down the toilet, stringing it out long, hoping it wouldn't get stuck. He washed the blood off his hands and pressed a wad of paper towels under his shirt against the knife wound. The blade had gone through at an angle, piercing the flesh along his side and maybe cracking a rib; it hurt like hell. He prayed it hadn't reached anything vital.

He stripped off his shirt and pants, soaked and scrubbed the blood out as best he could and dried them with paper towels. Tearing the towels in pieces, he flushed them down a little at a time. He cleaned his shoes and disposed of those towels the same way. He dressed in his wet clothes, securing the wadded towels under his belt. He scrubbed the floor, using the last of the towels; the pain turned him dizzy when he knelt.

He walked out slowly, stopping only once on his way to the cellblock, at the back door of the cotton mill.

He got up to his cell all right, keeping his arm over his side against the bleeding. He pushed inside, chilled not only with the pain but with fear. This could blow his release, could put him in prison for the rest of his life. He'd snuffed a few men in his time, every one of them trying to kill him. He'd been lucky so far. This time maybe his luck had run out?

Lying on his bunk keeping pressure against the wound, he must have dozed some. He heard the Klaxon for supper, he'd have to skip that meal. He rose from his cot meaning to clean the wound better. He was standing at the small steel basin, his back to the bars, his shirt open, washing the jagged knife hole with soap and water, when he heard a thump behind him. Turning, he saw no one. On the floor inside the bars lay a little rag bundle.

He retrieved it fast, going sick with pain when he bent over. Inside were adhesive bandages, gauze pads, iodine, and ten aspirin tablets wrapped in a tissue. Thanks, Gimpy. Gimpy hadn't batted an eye when Lee told him his needs. Lee swallowed three aspirin and, his back to the bars again, smeared on the iodine, working it in deep, clenching his jaw against the pain. He bandaged the wound, listening for the guard's footsteps on the catwalk. He tore the bloody paper towels into small pieces and flushed them. He changed to his other shirt, pulling on the thick, prison-issue T-shirt under it. He hung the wet shirt on the hook to dry, and why would the guard ask questions? He often came in from the kitchen splashed with dishwater. When he stretched out again on his bunk he felt the cat land on the bed.

"Does it bother you," Misto said softly, "that you killed him?"

"He tried to kill me," Lee said gruffly.

"Does it bother you?"

"Maybe," Lee growled. "What difference? If I hadn't done him, I'd be dead."

Misto lashed his tail against the blanket. Lee felt him curl up as if prepared for sleep. Maybe Lee slept, too, he wasn't sure. The wail of a Klaxon brought them both up rigid, the cat standing hard and alert beside Lee. The body had been found. The cellblocks would be locked down, double security set in place. Fear chilled him at thoughts of the search. Before the guards reached his cell he rose, took three more aspirin, and lay down again, listening to the clang of barred doors as the search began.

When the prison team reached Lee's cell, he stood in the middle of the small space, sucking in his gut when the guard patted him down. He willed the man not to feel the bandage under the heavy T-shirt. The guard jerked off his bedcovers, flipped and examined his mattress, inspected his damp shoes and wet shirt. "You fall in the dishwater, Fontana?"

"The guy works beside me," Lee said, "sloppy as hell." He waited, hiding his nervousness until the man finished his nosy prying and left, giving Lee a last appraising look. Alone again, Lee crawled back under the covers. That was when the devil returned, descending as if Delone's death had kept him near. Again the cat stiffened, the air grew icy, and Lucifer's grainy voice struck through Lee.

"That guard," Satan said, "he *could* have made you strip down, Fontana. He would have if I'd nudged him a little. Or," the devil said, "think of this. When you killed Delone, I *could* have led a guard in there at that moment, led him into the masonry room to find you standing over the body.

"I took pity on you, Fontana. Now, you can return the courtesy."

"Go to hell."

"I have a mission for you."

"I don't want to hear it. Get someone else for your lackey." Lee rolled over, turning his back, gritting his teeth against the pain.

The wraith shifted again so it faced Lee. "I want you to gain Morgan Blake's full confidence, I want him to completely depend on you."

Lee stared at the heavy shadow. "What do you want with Blake?"

"I want him to trust you in all matters, to follow you unquestioningly. In return, I will let up on you, Fontana. I will make your life easier. Blake is already your friend, you are special to him because of his child. Now he must seek your wisdom in whatever he undertakes. It should be easy enough to manipulate him in this way."

"Why? What do you mean to do?"

"Blake thinks you can help him, Fontana. And you can help. When you do so, my pressure on you will ease. The wound will heal, the pain will be gone. So easy to do, to gain Blake's absolute confidence no matter what you might ask him to do . . . A fine bargain," the devil said. "Think about it, Fontana . . ." And the voice faded, the shadow faded, the dark wraith was gone. Lee was left only with questions.

In the next days, as prison authorities investigated Delone's murder, Lee's wound continued to throb; everything he did, even eating a meal, left him chilled and weak. He didn't change his work routine, he took painkillers, went to the kitchen as usual and pulled his shift. The pain came bad when he carried the heavy trays. The third afternoon near the end of shift, as he hoisted a stack of trays, cold sweat beaded his face, and he saw Bronski watching him. Bronski stepped over and took the trays from him. "Go sit on the steps, Fontana. I'll take care of these." It was the only indication he ever had that Bronski knew how Delone died.

By the time security dropped back to normal, Lee's wound had begun to heal. Gimpy passed by the back door of the kitchen twice, slipping Lee more aspirin, iodine, some sulfa powder, and fresh bandages, turning away quickly as Lee slipped the package under his shirt. Lee and Gimpy went back a long way, and Lee was mighty thankful for his friendship. He had no idea that, within only a few days, he would abandon Gimpy, that the Atlanta pen would be the last time he would ever see the old safecracker.

20

Lee had started down toward the big yard, meaning to sit quietly in the thin morning sun and try to ease his hurting side, when he saw something that stirred a shock of challenge—but sent a jolt of fear through him, too. He was heading down the hillside steps when he noticed something different about the thirty-foot wall towering over him. The way the sunlight fell, he glimpsed a hint of shadow running up the concrete, the faintest blemish. Not a cloud shadow, it was too thin and straight. Some imperfection in the wall? He paused to look, leaning casually on the metal rail.

In the yard below, half a dozen younger inmates were jogging the track. Two men were playing handball against the wall itself, and beyond them three convicts were throwing a baseball, the figures dwarfed by the giant wall. He looked carefully at the thin line but when he started down the stairs for a closer view it disappeared, was lost in the way the light fell.

He moved on down, trying to recapture the shadow, but not until he reached the lowest step did he see it again. A thin vertical line running from the ground straight up thirty feet to the top. When Lee moved, the line disappeared. He moved back a step, and there it was. He propped his foot on the lower rail, looking. It must be an interlocking joint, though he couldn't find another like it. This was the only flaw he could see along the bare expanse between the near tower and the distant one, away at the far corner. Could this be a defect when the forms were up? So faint a blemish that when the forms were removed it was missed, had been left uncorrected with no last-minute touch of the trowel to smooth it away? His gaze was over halfway up, following the line, when he saw something else.

Some six inches on either side of the line he could see a small round indentation, the faintest dimple picked out by the slanting sun. Following the line itself, he found two more dots, and two above those, blemishes so indistinct that his slightest move made them vanish.

He noted where the line struck at the base of the wall in relation to the curve of the jogging track. Taking his time, he moved on down the stairs, across the yard and the jogging track. He sat down against the wall just at the joint, casually watching the joggers and ballplayers. No one paid him any attention. When he ran his hand behind him he could feel the joint. When he felt up and down, he found the lowest small dimple. He scraped it with his thumb, then pressed it hard and felt the heavy paint break away. He pushed his finger into the hole. A snug fit, but so deep he couldn't touch the end.

If all the dimples were this deep, a man had only to figure out how to use them. He found the chip that had fallen behind him, and took a good look. Layer after layer of dried paint hinted at the venerable age of the wall. He visualized it being built. First, a metal inter-structure, then the plywood or metal forms both inside and out to receive the wet cement. The line had to be a joint between two sheets of the form. The forms them-selves, angled in from the thicker base, would have had supports to keep the cement from collapsing as it dried.

There had to be other lines and other groups of holes. Or did there? Maybe the other holes *had* all been carefully filled, the lines smoothed away and plastered over. How could this one joint have been overlooked? Maybe this was where two workers met at quitting time? Maybe they had applied one coat of spackle, and the next day they moved on, forgetting to finish this joint? Soon it was painted over by other, uncaring workmen? Leaning back against the wall, he looked up its great height to where it rounded at the top.

If a fellow were to push an iron bar into each hole, he could climb this baby, easy as going up spikes in a telephone pole.

Except, the guards in the tower would pick you off like a cockroach on a barn door.

But when he looked up toward the tower, he couldn't see the windows that circled it, not from where he was sitting. He could see just a little of the room's base flaring out atop the wall. Frowning, he glanced toward the farther tower down at the end but couldn't see any more of that one. If he couldn't see the windows, the guards inside couldn't see him, unless they leaned dangerously far out.

Maybe they wouldn't see a climber scaling the wall until he got near the top, and that thought ripped a thrill of challenge through Lee.

When he looked down the full stretch of the wall, sighting in both directions, he could see that it bowed in. The forms had been bowed here, something had gone badly awry. Either no one noticed or no one wanted to take responsibility. No one had wanted to tear out the forms or maybe tear out part of the wall itself and rebuild it. Maybe some foreman thought no one would ever notice, and that it wouldn't matter anyway. Once the cement was dry and painted over, why would such a tiny flaw matter? Excitement made his hands tremble. Had he stumbled on something that maybe no one else in this entire prison knew or didn't think important? Sitting there against the wall, Lee had to smile.

You wouldn't need a bar at each hole. All you needed was three short iron rods to push in and out. One to hold on to, one to stand on, the third to set for the next step. Lean down, pull the lower pin, insert it over the handhold pin. Step higher, pull out the bottom pin, and replace it in the hole above you. At the top where the guards could see you, you'd have to be quick. You'd leave the last pin in, hook the looped end of a rope over it, and slide down the outside. Slide to freedom.

Lee's own time was so short that he had no need to escape. But Blake, if his appeal was denied, could be looking at the rest of his life in this trap.

If Blake was to get out of here, if he and Blake together left this joint and could find Brad Falon and get new evidence, maybe make Falon tell where he'd hidden the bank money, Blake would have a chance. The chance he'd never had when, before he knew there'd *been* a bank robbery, before he knew anything about the crime, he was handcuffed and hauled off to jail.

If they could get out of there, get their hands on Falon, make him tell where he hid the money . . . Maybe it was still in the canvas bank bags where the tellers had stuffed it, bags like the one Falon had planted in Morgan's car. That was the evidence Morgan needed. Those bank bags, most of them, were edged with leather around the top and had leather handles, and leather should retain fingerprints. If the cops got lucky and found Falon's prints, that was all Becky's lawyer would need. He could get a warrant based on new evidence, and the DA would have to indict Falon. There would be a new trial and, if it was a fair trial this time, Blake would be on his way to freedom.

Leaning back against the cool concrete, Lee wondered. Had he stumbled on this by accident? Or had he been led, could this discovery be Satan's trap? Had he been enticed into this view of the wall? Was he being teased to make an aborted try that could leave them both locked up for the rest of their lives or get them shot and killed?

Picking up a handful of dirt, he crammed it in the hole in the wall and smeared it across the concrete, then he rose and left the big yard. Crossing toward the cellblock he told himself he wasn't going to think about this, that the idea would never work. That he wasn't going to screw up his release and mess up what chance

Morgan might have for an appeal, he wasn't going to blow Morgan's possible new trial all to hell.

But in the next few days it wasn't easy to leave the idea alone. He thought about the wall at night when he woke with his side hurting. Thought about it when he woke in the morning and all during his shift in the kitchen, thought hard about it when a train rumbled screaming by headed across the country. Thought about it until he wished he'd never seen the damned flaw.

21

Two days after Becky shot Brad Falon, she and Sammie headed for Rome just for supper and to stay overnight. Despite Anne's and Mariol's support she needed to be with her mother, and Sammie needed her grandmother, they needed Caroline to talk with and to soothe them both. She watched the streets as they left Morningside but was sure that no black car followed them. She wondered if Falon might have made it back to Rome, to Natalie or to his long-suffering and usually ignored mother. She hoped he was holed up somewhere in Atlanta hurting bad from the wound she'd inflicted. They left directly after work, Becky swinging by Anne's to pick up Sammie and tuck their overnight bag in the car. The traffic wasn't heavy once they were out of the business and residential areas and on the two-lane highway heading north. Before they pulled away from the house she had slipped her new revolver from under the seat and belted it to her waist.

The day after the police took her gun for evidence she'd driven out to a gun shop on Decatur Road and bought a .32-caliber snub-nosed revolver and a holster, a gun small enough to wear under her suit jacket or under a two-piece dress. Such a move might seem silly, and even the .32 felt unnatural against her side, but it might save their lives. She'd given Sammie strict instructions about not handling the gun, and they had gone over the rules carefully. Becky had also shown her how the revolver worked, in order to fully understand the principles of safety. Maybe she was foolish to be driving to Rome when she didn't know where Falon was. Maybe he'd found a doctor who wouldn't report the wound, maybe he'd been properly treated and was up and moving again. She'd read that some psychopathic personalities could ignore a lot of pain. As they moved north between vegetable plots and chicken farms she was sharply aware of any car parked on a side road, as well as those few approaching from behind. Sammie wanted to know when she could start school, she talked about the hamsters they'd had in her classroom in Rome, the playhouse they'd built from cardboard cartons, about the colored Georgia map on the wall and the stories their teacher had read to them. Sammie didn't mention Falon's attack; she sat close to Becky, a favorite book in her lap, was soon buried in the story. Only when she'd turned the last page did she look up, her words startling Becky.

"Are you going to tell Daddy you shot Falon?"

"No, I'm not. Daddy has enough on his mind." Becky pulled Sammie closer, hugging her. "We don't need to worry him. I hope, after I shot Falon, he'll stay away from us." She looked down at Sammie. "We'll be watchful, though?" Sammie nodded. Becky knew the ugliness mustn't be buried, that they must talk about it. If they shared their fear, discussed what to do about it, tried to understand it, she thought Sammie could deal with it better. They were perhaps an hour north of Atlanta on the narrow, deserted two-lane when she saw a car pulling up fast behind them.

She thought it would pass them quickly, a black car, sleek and low, but there were plenty of black cars in the world. Probably some local farmer who had turned out of his gate behind them. Though few locals drove so fast, knowing there might be loose livestock or a dog on the road. This was all open country, pastures and woods separating the scattered farms. They were east of Kingston, had already left the larger town of Cartersville behind. They would not pass through

Kingston, only near it, and then there were no more towns until Rome. Feeling suddenly vulnerable, she eased her jacket open to better reach the revolver.

But when the car drew close she saw that it wasn't black at all, it was dark blue, and was pulling a small trailer. It passed them, a low, dark blue sedan driven by a white-haired woman, pulling a slat-sided trailer with a big yearling calf inside. Becky felt silly, as if she were too wildly dramatic. Falon was probably miles away, laid up from her gunshot. The next car that approached gained on her quickly, speeding up behind her. She slowed to let it pass, watching in her rearview mirror the lone driver—then staring at him, at the silhouette of his thin head and puffed hair, backlit behind the car's windshield. As he drew up on her tail, her rearview mirror reflected back to her Falon's thin, pinched face.

They were nearly ten miles from Rome, there would be no more gas stations, no towns before Rome, only small homeplaces that didn't have police but depended on the county sheriff, who might be miles away. She scanned the passing farms, praying to see a sheriff's car parked in one of the yards and wishing she had a more formidable weapon than the small revolver. When Sammie started to turn in the seat, to look back, Becky stopped her. "Don't, honey, don't turn. Don't let him know you see him."

Sammie sat very still, looking straight ahead. They were coming to a narrow bridge across a creek that fed the Etowah River. When, starting across, Becky gunned the car, Falon sped up beside her, crowding her against the rail. She floored it, burning rubber. He slammed against her so hard she skidded and careened, thought she'd go through the flimsy rail. She slammed on her brakes, grabbed Sammie to keep her from going into the dashboard. They were in the middle of the bridge, her fender crumpled against the rail. She spun the wheel, jammed the gas pedal to the floor, and swerved out. Their fenders caught, metal screaming against metal. She leaned on the gas; it took everything her car had to jerk free, bent metal squealing as she surged ahead. She was past him for only an instant, enough to careen off the bridge onto the rough road, and now his car was even with her again. She unholstered and cocked the .32, laid it on the edge of the open window. She fired, hardly taking her eyes from the road.

"Get that box in my purse. The bullets." She fired again, and a third time as Sammie scrambled to find the box. She wondered if she could reload while driving. But suddenly Falon's car slowed and fell behind. Had she hit him? Or he was only afraid she would? Wishing she'd killed him this time, she jammed her foot to the floor, took a curve on squealing tires, and headed fast for Rome.

22

They pulled into Rome still shaken, Becky still watching behind her though she'd seen no more of Falon's car. Easing along the familiar streets beneath the bright maples, their red leaves half fallen, past the familiar houses where she had played when she was small, she began to relax. The cold sky was silvering toward darkness, the shadows beneath the wide oaks pooling into night, the lighted windows beckoning. She didn't head for their own empty house but made straight for Caroline's. Pulling into the drive behind the bakery van, she gathered Sammie up as if she was still a small child, not a gangling nine-year-old, and hurried inside.

A fire burned on the hearth, in the big living room. Only when they were safe in Caroline's arms did Becky feel her pounding heart slow. Caroline held them quietly, seeing how upset they were. Her dark hair was tied back in a ponytail, her jeans old and faded, her apron a colorful patchwork. They stood for a long time holding each other, then moved into the big kitchen, the bright room warm from the ovens and filled with the scents of cinnamon and chocolate. The timers ticked away in a rhythm that was part of Becky's childhood. The bakery racks were filled with trays of brownies and cinnamon rolls, with lemon cakes and sweet potato pies. The aura of home, the rich patterns and scents of Caroline's kitchen seemed, for a moment, to wipe Brad Falon from their lives.

Becky hadn't stopped at the police station to file a report that Falon had tried to run her off the road and that she had shot at him. What good? Why face more of their disdain, their chill disbelief?

Not since Morgan was first arrested had she come to terms with the change in the officers of Rome PD, these men who had been his lifelong friends, with their cold disregard for Morgan's own version of what had happened to him the day of the robbery. All the time Morgan was in the Rome jail, and all through the trial, she couldn't believe the hard, judgmental testimony from those officers, from the men Morgan had trusted.

Granted, evidence of the robbery had been found in Morgan's car, the empty canvas bank bag with blood on it, the scattered hundred-dollar bills. But never once did a police witness suggest that those items could have been planted. These were men they had played with as children, men whose weddings they had attended, who went to the same church, the same picnics and celebrations. Even Morgan's own attorney, the lawyer Becky had picked herself only to regret it later, had done little to help him; everyone in town, it seemed, had thought him guilty.

Now, sitting at the bakery table as Caroline warmed up homemade soup and made sandwiches, Becky described Falon's midnight break-in, the shooting and his escape. She described how, this evening on the deserted road, he had forced them against the bridge rail. "Trying to drive and fire, I most likely missed him," she said regretfully. "But your poor car, Mama . . . You don't want to look at your car."

"It's only a car, Becky. You can leave it for Albert to work on," Caroline said, setting supper on the table. "You can take your own car now, he already knows how to find you. Did you stop by the station to report Falon?"

Becky shook her head. Caroline rose, turned to her planning desk, and picked up the phone.

"Don't, Mama. Don't call the police. What good will it do?"

Caroline turned to look at her. "You can't *not* call them. This is evidence against Falon. As is the break-in at Anne's," she said, starting to dial.

"Please, Mama. I didn't identify him for the break-in, either." She let her glance linger on Sammie. Caroline nodded but went right on, identifying herself, making the verbal report and discussing a written report. When she hung up, she was smiling. Becky was rigid with anger.

"The desk sergeant said they'd send someone out." She rose and moved to the table. "Becky, they've already talked with the Atlanta police. Sergeant Trevis is coming, let's have supper before he gets here."

Becky looked at her, puzzled. "They know about the break-in at Anne's? But why . . . ?" She picked up half a sandwich. She didn't feel like eating, but then found herself wolfing the lean roast beef and good homemade bread. "Atlanta PD knows I live in Rome, it's on my driver's license. But why would they *call* Rome?" She looked at Caroline. "To see if Rome knows me? To get a character witness?" she asked angrily.

"Falon lives in Rome," Caroline said. "Did Atlanta take fingerprints? Maybe they've identified him from those. Maybe they're interested, for some reason, even if you didn't file a report."

It was full dark when they'd finished supper and moved in by the fire to wait for Sergeant Trevis. As Caroline pulled the draperies to shut out prying eyes, Sammie leaned, yawning, against her grandmother. Caroline led her to the window seat, settled her among the cushions, and pulled a warm throw over her. Becky, watching them, was filled with nostalgia for when she was small and was sick. Caroline had tucked the same plaid blanket around her, warm and safe. Within minutes, Sammie was asleep. Becky and Caroline stood looking down at her until they heard a car pull up the drive, heard the static of the police radio.

Answering the door, Caroline led Sergeant Trevis through to the kitchen, where they wouldn't wake Sammie. She set a cup of coffee and a plate of brownies on the table before him, and coffee for her and Becky. Trevis took off his cap, laid it on the table beside his field book. The tall, lean officer had just had a haircut, leaving a pale line against his fading tan.

Becky described Falon's attack on the bridge and, at Caroline's insistent look, she told Trevis about the break-in, and that Falon had attacked her earlier behind the drugstore.

"You filed reports in both cases? And identified Falon?" Trevis looked doubtful. He knew she hadn't given Falon's name, the department had already talked with Atlanta.

"I filed a report only for the break-in. I said I didn't know who the man was," Becky told him.

"Why?" Trevis asked.

"I was afraid. That when they released him, if he knew I'd given his name, he'd be all the more dangerous."

"Is that the only reason?"

"I was afraid for Sammie." Trevis's look puzzled her. "What else would there be?"

"There's nothing between you and Falon?"

She stared at Trevis.

"I didn't tell her," Caroline said. "She hasn't heard the gossip."

Becky looked from her mother to Trevis. "What gossip?"

"There's a story around town," Trevis said, "that you're seeing Falon. That you and Falon planned the bank robbery, that the two of you set Morgan up, wanted him sent to prison, to get rid of him. Some folks say you're living with Falon, in Atlanta."

She looked at him in silence. Her closest friends couldn't think this. She found it hard to believe that Morgan's automotive customers, or even the book-keeping clients who had let her go, would believe it, and certainly not the members of their church.

Yet nearly the whole town seemed to have bought into what the jury believed, to the lies, under oath, on the witness stand. So why wouldn't they believe this? "Does everyone think that?" she said softly

"Where are you living?" Trevis said.

"With my aunt, Mama's sister. But if you talked with the Atlanta police, you already know that. How long . . ." she said, "how long have people been saying this?"

"Not everyone—" Trevis began.

"How long?"

"The stories began shortly after the trial."

She looked at her mother. "Why didn't you tell me? Is this part of why I lost my accounts, not just Morgan going to prison, but these lies?" She didn't know much about the rest of the world, but gossip, in a small Southern town, was a cherished commodity, a traditional and beloved pastime.

"For a long time," Caroline said, "I didn't hear the stories, no one said anything to me. I suppose they knew I'd be furious. No one treated me any differently, except maybe for a look or two, as if some people felt sorry for me. I didn't hear this story until you'd moved to Atlanta." She put her hand over Becky's. "When you had so many other troubles, I couldn't add one more ugliness, there seemed no point in it."

Across the table, Sergeant Trevis busied himself with his coffee and brownie. Becky said, "The police, all of you, believed Morgan was guilty. So when you heard this, you believed that, too."

"We didn't believe Morgan was guilty," Trevis said.

"You acted like you did. You were terrible to him."

"We are not supposed to voice judgment."

"You *showed* judgment," she snapped. "You're supposed to be fair. The way you treated Morgan, the way you acted, you believed he was guilty from the minute you hauled him out of the car that morning, after he'd been drugged. You thought he was drunk when you know he doesn't drink. You thought he killed the guard and robbed the bank. Afterward, when Morgan was in jail and Falon broke into my house, the officer who came was unforgivably rude."

"Sometimes," Trevis said, "when we have to keep a professional distance, we seem—gruff, I guess."

She just looked at him.

"Some of us were wrong," Trevis said. "Becky, we want Morgan to get an appeal." He looked at her evenly. "To be truthful, I don't know what made us so surly. We were all caught up in something, some violent feeling that I can't explain, that was not professional." Trevis's face colored. "Like a bunch of little boys torturing a hurt animal. You're right, we weren't fair to Morgan.

"Not until after the trial was over," he said, "after Morgan was down in Atlanta, did we seem to come to our senses, realize how ugly we'd been, how grossly we let him down. Becky, I don't believe the story about you and Falon. I went to school with Falon, I know what he's like." He was quiet, then, "I do have some good news." Trevis grinned, his tall frame easing back in his chair. "There's a warrant out for Falon."

"What, for the break-in? Not for the bank robbery?"

"No. He's wanted in California. The warrant came in this morning. That's why I got over here so fast. Seems he was involved in a series of real estate scams out there, and fraud by wire. The bureau traced him from California to Chattanooga, to some large bank accounts there under fictitious names, and then traced him here."

"Then when you find him, he'll be in jail? He'll be locked up where he can't reach us?"

"If you didn't kill him, on the bridge," Trevis said with the hint of a smile. "If we can find him, he'll be transported by the U.S. marshal's office to California, he'll be held in jail there to await arraignment and trial."

She wanted to hug Trevis. She couldn't stop smiling.

"The U.S. attorney in L.A. seems hot to move on him," Trevis said. "There were five men involved. The other four have been indicted. With any luck, Falon should be in federal court in L.A. fairly soon."

"And if he's convicted?" Becky said. "Oh, he won't be sent back here, to prison in Atlanta?" *He won't be imprisoned with Morgan,* she thought, *where Falon would hurt or kill him.*

"If he's convicted in California, there's no reason to return him to Georgia. Terminal Island, maybe, that's the closest to L.A. where he'd be tried."

"How long would he be there? How long would he get?"

"On those charges, the maximum might be thirty years, the minimum maybe twenty. With parole and good time, maybe half that."

"Ten years at least," she said softly. "Ten years, free of Falon."

"If he comes out on parole," Trevis said, "and is caught doing anything out of line, he'll be revoked and sent back." He swallowed the last of his coffee. "If you file a complaint now and amend the complaint you filed with Atlanta, give them his name, then the probation department will have that information. That means, if he comes out on parole they'll do their best to keep him away from you. Have you heard anything on the appeal? Quaker Lowe has been up from Atlanta several times, reading the reports, talking with the witnesses."

"He's working hard on it, Trevis."

Trevis rose. "He's a good man, good reputation." He came around the table and hugged Becky. That startled her. His closeness was caring and honest, this was the Trevis she knew. In that moment, she felt as soothed as Sammie must have felt when Grandma wrapped the plaid blanket around her.

23

In the night-dim cellblock, rain beat down on the high clerestory windows, sloughing across their steel mesh. Lightning flashed, bleaching the cells below as pale as bone. Lee paced his own small cubicle fighting the ache in his side. It had eased off some, until a bout of coughing brought the pain stabbing sharp again. Pain and the cold had kept him up most of the night. He thought Georgia was supposed to be hot and humid. He'd asked the guard twice for another blanket. At last, on his third round, the man had brought it, grumbling as he shoved it through the bars.

Back in his bunk, rolled up in the extra warmth, Lee tried to sleep, the thick scratchy wool pulled tight around him. He badly wanted a hot cup of coffee. He tossed restlessly until daylight crept gray and tentative

across the high glass, until he heard the guard's footsteps again, then the harsh clang of the lever as the
overhead bars were withdrawn and the cells unlocked.
Lee stood for the count, washed and dressed, pulled on
his coat, and moved out to the catwalk. Men crowded
him, hurrying him along, surging down the metal
stairs and outside into the rain, double-timing to the
mess hall hungering for coffee.

In the mess hall he poured two cups from the coffeepot and headed for a small, empty table. He sat with
his back to the wall shivering. Rain poured against the
glass, its cold breath biting to the bone. Not until the
hot brew had warmed him did he get in line, pick up
a tray of scrambled eggs, potatoes, toast, and two more
coffees, and return to the table. By the time he finished
eating, the worst of the storm had passed. He was on
second shift for the kitchen, hours away yet; leaving
the mess hall, he headed back for his cell. There were
advantages to his illness, that he could rest when he
pleased. The rain had stopped but wind whipped water
from the eaves down across the walk, wetting Lee's
pant legs. A lone slit of sun slanted down between the
heavy clouds, reflecting up from the puddles. Ahead on
the walk a flock of cowbirds was splashing, drinking,
screeching to wake the dead. They went quiet at his
approach, then exploded into the sky and were gone;

and a figure was walking beside him. Appearing out of nowhere, a tall man in prison blues, an inmate he had never seen. When Lee looked square at him his bony face seemed to shift and change, Lee couldn't look for long into those hollow eyes.

Where the man stepped through deep puddles the water didn't move, no ripple stirred. A flock of sparrows soared in on a gust of wind, paused in the sky hovering, then fell dead on the rain-slick walk. When Lee didn't alter his stride or look at the wraith again the dark presence grabbed his hand, its fingers cold as death, making Lee jerk away. "Leave me alone. Back off and leave me alone."

"I can offer you one more opportunity, Fontana. One you'd be a fool to refuse."

"I haven't done what you wanted yet. And I'm not doing it now." He headed for the cellblock, shivering. The dark one kept pace with him.

"If the authorities find the post office money, Lee, find any track leading to where it's buried—perhaps with a little help—they'll have all the evidence they need. They'll lift fingerprints you only thought you destroyed. You'll be in prison until you die. Unless," he said, "you are willing to strike this one bargain." The wraith looked at him so intently that Lee had to look back. One instant and he turned away again, colder than before.

"One small favor, Fontana, and it is not a difficult task. You will gain much, when your dream of Mexico is fulfilled."

Lee kept walking.

"You are seventy-two years old. You are sick. If I choose, I can cure the emphysema. I can make your lungs whole again, make you strong again. You will breathe as easily as a young man. I can give you new life, Lee, many more years of healthy, vigorous life, a whole new beginning."

"I'd pay hard for anything *you* offered."

"You would pay nothing, you would acquire the ultimate prize. Not only renewed health in this life, but a new life when this one ends, a new and unblemished future designed to your own choosing. A new life where you'll be anything you want to be. Meantime, you finish out this life in perfect health and comfort. All you need to do is help Morgan Blake."

The tall figure warped and shifted so darkness drifted through him, then he was whole again. "If you agree to help Blake, I will see that you escape from here undetected, free and unharmed."

Lee was silent as they passed other prisoners, though none took any notice, he didn't think they saw or heard his companion.

"Without my help, your lungs will quickly grow worse. The short time you have left will be even more miserable. When you can hardly breathe at all, panic will entrap you. You will slowly strangle to death, choked by the emphysema. Wouldn't you prefer perfect health and a long life? Wouldn't you prefer to escape this concrete trap and enjoy the benefits I promise?"

Coughing hard, Lee clutched at the wound in his side. "There's no way out of this cage. Even if there were, why would you want to help Blake?"

"I will help get Blake out of here, help him find Brad Falon, help him force Falon to confess. That is exactly what you are planning, so, you see, I simply want to assist in your venture."

Morgan's escape was what he'd planned, ever since Becky came to visiting day so excited she could hardly get it out fast enough, that there was a warrant for Falon. That as soon as Falon was found he'd be shipped off to L.A. for arraignment and trial, with a good chance he'd go to prison out there.

In the visiting room, Becky had spoken in heated whispers, sitting in the far corner on an isolated couch close between Morgan and Lee. She hadn't brought Sammie; she said Anne had taken the child to a movie. This was a different kind of visit, she was all business, was strung tight with her news and seemed to want no distraction.

But still she'd left a lot unsaid, questions to which Lee still wanted answers. Who had shot Falon? She said she didn't know but Lee thought she did know. Maybe, if Becky had shot him herself, she didn't want to upset Morgan? Maybe that was why she hadn't brought Sammie, because Sammie would say too much?

But Lee sensed, as well, something more left unrevealed. The way Becky looked at him puzzled and embarrassed him; she was holding something back. Yet how could it affect him, when he hardly knew her? Whatever it was, it left him with questions that, he thought, he might not want to ask.

Morgan had sat stone-faced, saying nothing. Lee hadn't been able to tell what either one was thinking. But questions or not, with a warrant out for Falon, Lee's plan had begun to take shape. If Falon was arrested, was out on the West Coast—if Lee and Morgan *could* get to him, could break out of prison, hightail it out there, get themselves arrested and locked in the same institution, they'd have Falon where he couldn't escape. Could force a confession from him, make him reveal where the bank money was hidden. Once the money was found, and maybe the murder weapon, Morgan should have more than enough to clear him.

A lot of ifs and maybes, Lee thought. But that was what life was made of.

But it was not the devil's plan that they force information from Falon. Now, standing there on the wet walkway, the wraith kept pressing at Lee. "Once you've broken out of here, Fontana, and Blake thinks you're helping him, you will be in a position to crush him. You will raise his hopes high. Then you will destroy him."

Lee glanced along the walks again, and now they were alone.

"With my help," Lucifer said, "you will arrange that Blake kills Falon. That a number of reliable witnesses are present, and that Blake is arrested. The prosecuting attorney will easily prove that Blake broke out of prison with the intention of killing Falon. This," Satan said, smiling, "will put an end to Morgan's bid for an appeal. When he attacks Falon, he destroys whatever chance he might have had."

"Why would you want him to kill Falon? Falon's one of yours."

"Falon has been useful. Now, when all is finished, he will join my ranks. He will work the game from the other side, and that should please him."

"And when Blake goes down, I would be arrested as his accomplice."

"Oh, no," the devil said. "I will see that you conveniently vanish, into any kind of life you choose. Healthy again, with wealth, with bawdy women, the finest horses, gold, whatever is your pleasure."

"If Morgan and I got out of here, if that was even possible—and if I didn't double-cross him, if I continued to help him and kept him out of trouble, what would you do then?"

"I would destroy you both."

"You haven't destroyed me so far. What makes you think you can take down Blake, either? The truth is," Lee said, "you're more bluff than substance."

Though, in fact, he knew better. He knew too well how Lucifer could twist human thought. If he and Morgan did escape, it might be more than they could do to fight off whatever influence Satan brought to bear. It might be more than they could handle, not to follow the dark's lead.

"Once I've helped you escape, *if* you are capable of that feat, and if then you tried to double-cross me and save Blake, tried to make Falon reveal the evidence, it will be easy enough to twist your plan to my own design."

"If you're that powerful, you don't need my help to destroy Blake."

"I need you to encourage Blake. He is—not an easy subject," said the dark spirit. "Too religious, for one thing, and what a waste that is. It is you who must show him the broader way, who must lay out the plan. But first, you must inflame his desire to break out. Blake would never have the courage on his own."

Lee looked hard at him. "Why Blake? What the hell do you *have* against Blake?"

The devil didn't answer. The tall inmate grew indistinct, blending into the building behind him, and he vanished on the rain-sodden wind. It was in that moment that Lee thought about Becky, about her secrecy in the visiting room and her shuttered looks, and he wondered what had made him think of that.

24

Becky woke to rain pounding at the windows, and to a residue of fear. In the night she had experienced again Falon's car careening at hers, had fought the wheel again to avoid going off the bridge. Now, waking fully, she lay listening to the comforting clatter from the kitchen, smelling the aromas of baking bread and pies and, this morning, the scent of bacon as Caroline made their breakfast. Rising, she showered and dressed quickly, then woke Sammie, watched as Sammie sleepily pulled her on clothes and ran a brush through her hair.

In the big kitchen Caroline and her assistant, red-headed Nettie Parks, were lifting pecan pies and fresh bread from the two big ovens. Nettie was a neighbor, a widow whose five children had left the nest. She liked getting up early, she liked the extra money, and most of all, she and Caroline enjoyed working together. Nettie was among the few who had stood by them during the trial. Nettie set their breakfast on a corner of the long, crowded table and hugged Becky. "I hope Brad Falon burns in hell."

That made Becky smile. Sitting down, she cupped her hands around the warm coffee cup while listening to the rain, watched her mother turn out muffins from their tins and ease them into the familiar bakery boxes stamped CAROLINE'S. They ate quickly this morning and didn't linger; it would take a while at the police station to file the complaints and go over the details of Falon's attacks. Their overnight stay with Caroline was too short, but they'd had a cozy visit after Sergeant Trevis left.

She had called Quaker Lowe last night, too, on the after-hours number he'd given her. He said, "I tried to call you, at your aunt's, Becky. Good news! There's a warrant out for Falon, he's wanted in California."

She laughed. "I know. I'm in Rome, Sergeant Trevis told me." She told Lowe about Falon's attack on the bridge, and that she was on her way to the station.

"But you're both all right?"

"We're fine. Sammie's a soldier."

"I'm glad you changed your mind about naming Falon, glad the police have a record of his attacks. This will be a big help if . . . if there are complaints on file against Falon," Lowe said quietly. His unspoken words *If we lose the appeal* resonated in silence between them. *If we lose the appeal and have to start over . . .*

Now, rising from the table, promising Caroline she'd call when they were safely home, she hugged her mother, hugged Nettie, and went to get her car from the garage—leaving Caroline to deal with her own poor, damaged vehicle.

Getting Sammie settled in the front seat with her books, they headed along the rain-sloughed streets for the station. Becky missed Caroline already. Sometimes she felt as needful of mothering as was Sammie. That amused and annoyed her.

At the station she filed a complaint for each offense: the highway assault, the break-in at Anne's, Falon's attack on her behind the drugstore, and the break-in at her house in Rome when Sergeant Leonard had refused to make a written report.

Detective Palmer, a thin, dark-haired officer of Cherokee background, asked that Caroline bring in her car. "Will you call her? I want to take paint samples. With luck, I can lift chips from it, left by Falon's car. And if we pick up his car, we should find scrapes there from Caroline's vehicle. One more piece of evidence," Palmer said. "Every small thing counts."

He stood looking down at her. "The FBI will want to talk with you, as part of the federal investigation on Falon's land scam. The Atlanta bureau will call you at your aunt's if you'll give me the number."

Becky wrote down both numbers, Anne's and her private one. She saw no animosity in Palmer, she didn't think he'd been among the many officers who'd turned against Morgan. She found it comforting that the FBI wanted to question her about Falon; that made her feel more in control. As she and Sammie headed for Atlanta she drove the narrow, rainy highway filled only with positive thoughts, with new hope. She wasn't in the habit of saying prayers to ask for special favors; such begging was, in her mind, self-serving. Her prayers were more often of thanks, for the many blessings they did have. But last night and now, this morning, she prayed hard that Falon would be found and sent to L.A., that a California judge or jury would convict him for the land scam, that he would be locked up for the maximum time. And that maybe, in prison, someone would kill him. If her prayers were a sin, so be it, that was what he deserved.

It rained all the way to Atlanta, harsh rain slanting across the road in gusts so sharp they rocked the car.

They were home at Anne's just before noon. Mariol had made hot vegetable soup and a plate of cornbread.

"I'm just going to grab a bite," Becky said, "and go on to work, it's payroll time."

Mariol nodded. "Go in the dining room first, take a look at what was in the attic."

Becky found Anne at the dining table leafing carefully through the pages of a black leather album, a thin folder so ancient and ragged that the disintegrating covers had shed bits of rotting leather onto the white runner.

"Mariol found it," Anne said. "I'd forgotten about those few boxes we'd stored away. We cleaned out most of the relics a couple of years ago, left a few family papers, this album, and a small trunk of antique clothes. I forgot, but Mariol remembered."

The faded pictures were all in sepia tones, some of men in coveralls standing by their teams of horses, or women in long dresses over laced-up boots, women with serious, unsmiling faces beneath hand-tucked sunbonnets. Becky touched the old pictures gently, thinking how it would be to live in that time when life was so hard. Raising and canning or curing all your food or going without, doing the laundry over a corrugated washboard, traveling on foot or in a horse-dawn wagon or by horseback, maybe sometimes by train. No telephone to call for the sheriff, if there even was one, only your own firearms and your courage to protect your children.

When Sammie came to stand beside them, Anne said, "This is our family, *your* family."

Sammie stood looking as Anne turned the pages, then excitedly she pointed. "Wait. That's the cowboy. That's Lee."

The boy was maybe fourteen. He did look like Lee, the same long bony face, same challenging look in his eyes, even at that young age. Sammie looked up at Becky, her dark eyes deep with pleasure. "I dream of him, Mama, we're family. Lee's part of our family."

Gently Becky touched the picture. All along, was this what Sammie's dreams had been about?

"Here's another of the boy," Anne said, turning the page. "And that's your great-aunt Mae."

The woman in the picture was maybe thirty, but Becky could see the resemblance to Sammie. "Mae . . . Mae was Lee's sister," she said.

Anne turned back several pages. "Here . . . here's Mae as a child." She looked from the picture to Sammie, looked at Becky, but said nothing more. The child was about ten. Becky studied her for a long while, as did Sammie. They were looking at Sammie's twin, except for Mae's long, old-fashioned skirt and laced boots.

Sammie reached out a hesitant hand, gently touching the faded likeness just as Becky had touched the picture of Lee. Mae's mirror image of Sammie made Becky shiver. How could any child be so like her own little girl?

She left Anne and Sammie at last, numb with putting the pieces together, with accepting the reality of a family she had never known. Sammie was doing a better job of it, seemed to have accepted it all: her great-uncle Lee, stepping out of a formless past; her great-aunt Mae, who had dreamed just as Sammie dreamed.

Returning to the kitchen, Becky ate her lunch quickly, then hurried downstairs to call Caroline, to tell her they'd arrived home safely, that they had seen no more of Falon. Upstairs again she pulled on her coat and was out the door into the rain ducking into her car. But, heading for work, she felt tired and worn out. She told herself she'd be better once she got into the books, began writing checks and adding up bills and charges. The neatness and logic of bookkeeping always eased her. She wished life could be as ordered, its problems as readily untangled and made right.

By five that afternoon she'd finished the payroll and billing for the five stores. Only in the car heading home did the tiredness hit her again, leave her longing for sleep. She found Sammie and Mariol in the kitchen, Mariol ironing, Sammie standing at the table folding and stacking towels. Mariol took one look at Becky and set down her iron. "Go take a nap. Take a couple of aspirin and cover up, you're white as these sheets. You don't want to be sick."

"I can't afford to be sick." She did as Mariol told her, headed obediently downstairs, took the aspirins, and collapsed on the bed, pulling the heavy quilt over her.

She didn't mean to sleep long. She was deep under when the ringing phone woke her, cutting harshly through the pounding of the rain. Reaching for the phone, she hesitated, frightened suddenly. This was a private line, no one had this number but Caroline and Quaker Lowe. And the prison.

The bedside clock said six-thirty. She could smell supper cooking, the aroma of frying onions and browned beef. She picked up the phone. Lowe's voice brought her wide awake. "What's wrong?" she said, sitting up, her heart pounding.

"Nothing's wrong. I—"

"The appeal . . ." Becky said. She didn't want to hear this, she didn't want to hear what was coming.

There was a long pause. Lowe said, "I have never found it so hard to give anyone bad news, as I find it now."

"Denied," she said woodenly. "It was denied."

"Insufficient new evidence. Of course I'll keep trying. Now, with the federal warrant, and the complaints you filed, we'll have a better chance. Neither is direct evidence of the robbery and murder, but they are evidence of Falon's destructive intent toward your family. I'm going up to Rome in the morning to dig some more, do some more interviewing."

"You've talked to everyone. What good—"

"It's possible, now that Falon is wanted by the feds, that Natalie Hooper will be less inclined to lie for him."

Becky didn't think Natalie would ever testify against Falon. The appeal had been denied, they were beaten, everything was over.

"We're not giving up," Lowe said.

Mutely she shook her head. Quaker was grasping at straws, they would never get an appeal, his continued effort would only lead Morgan on uselessly. And the added cost would be more than she could ever pay.

"I mean to charge only half the hourly rates," Lowe said, "for whatever time it takes to file again. Now, if Falon is picked up, I think Natalie will talk rather than getting crosswise with the bureau. I wish we could find the money or the gun," he said dryly. "I'll pick up copies of the complaints when I get to Rome. I don't mean to quit on this, Becky."

Becky ended up crying into the phone. The disappointment of the denial and then Lowe's kindness undid her. She wept so hard she couldn't talk and had to hang up. Shutting herself in the bathroom she gave over to painful sobs, she cried until she was limp, all the weeks of worry and stress shaking her. Her whole body felt drained, her eyes red and swollen. Her helplessness enraged her. She wanted to call Lowe back and apologize but what could she say? She didn't let herself think about visiting day, about telling Morgan tomorrow that they'd have to start over, that the appeal had been shot down.

Driving down Peachtree headed for the prison, Sammie sitting quietly in the seat beside her, Becky dreaded this visit. She'd wanted to leave Sammie home again, had wanted to tell Morgan alone about the appeal, not force him to deal with his rage in front of Sammie. But Sammie had been so insistent, wanting to see Lee, to show him the album. Becky wished Lee wouldn't come to visiting day either; she wanted only to be alone with Morgan. But, in the end, it was the album that saved her.

In the sally port, she cautioned the guard that the thin black folder was very old and fragile. She watched him page through it, making only a small show of being careful. When she and Sammie entered the visiting room, Becky handed Lee the album and glanced across to an unoccupied corner.

Lee accepted the disintegrating book, watching her face. Cradling the album, he took Sammie's hand and moved to the far lounge chair. With Sammie on his lap he sat turning the pages, looking at the pictures as Sammie pointed to various relatives and recited the names and what she could remember of the family relationships as Anne had told her. Becky, sitting quietly with Morgan, watched Lee's expression change as he pored over the old photos: at first he was startled, then his look turned vulnerable and uncertain. From across the room, Becky gave him a smile and a thumbs-up. Lee looked back at her and grinned, shy and embarrassed. She smiled, then turned away, took Morgan's hand, snuggling against him.

She told him she loved him, she wrapped her arms around him and pressed her face into his shoulder. He sat quietly, waiting. When she didn't speak, he said, "The appeal was denied."

"Quaker called last night," she said softly. When she looked up at Morgan, his eyes were hard and rage sculpted his face. He turned away, didn't want her to comfort him. She felt that the denial was her fault, felt that again she had chosen the wrong lawyer.

"Lowe is still trying," she said. "He's not a quitter, he's up in Rome now, seeing what more he can find. He's dropped his fees to half, he's been very kind, Morgan. He *wants* this appeal, he believes in you. Please give him a chance, don't lose faith. Somewhere there has to be more evidence."

He said nothing.

"But here's the good news," she said. "Morgan, please look at me."

He turned toward her, his face hard and closed.

"There's a warrant out for Falon. A federal warrant."

"A warrant for what? Not the robbery?"

"The FBI wants him. For some land scams out on the West Coast, and for fraud by wire. The other four men in it have already been indicted. If they're convicted, if Falon's convicted, Sergeant Trevis said he could get ten to twenty years."

"If they find him," Morgan said. "If they can get him to trial. If they *can* convict him."

"The FBI will find him. If he's arrested in Georgia, he'll be shipped out to the coast. Trevis says he'd be tried out there, that if he's convicted he'll most likely be in prison out there—far away from us."

Morgan took her in his arms, holding her close—but not believing Falon would ever be imprisoned.

"We have to go with this, Morgan. We have to put our faith in this. If Falon's wanted for another federal crime, the U.S. attorney will look at him differently. He'll look differently at our new try for an appeal."

"Maybe," he said noncommittally.

"Believe it will happen. We have to believe, have to hang on to something." Holding his hand, she looked across the room again at Lee and Sammie, so engrossed in the frail album. "Our family pictures," she said gently. "Lee as a child. His sister Mae, aunts and uncles, they all belong to us and to Lee."

Watching Morgan as he considered her words, as he considered the tough old man and Sammie, so comfortable together, she saw his face soften, saw the hint of a smile.

25

Brad Falon, after attempting to run Becky's car off the bridge, had slipped on into town behind her. He didn't think she'd go to the police, and the cops wouldn't listen anyway. They'd been down on Morgan ever since the robbery and they had no more use for Becky. He'd seen to that, had done enough one-on-one talking with selected officers to sour the validity of what either Morgan or Becky said. The rumors he'd spread about Becky and him, through a couple of friends, had further tarnished her credibility. Damn woman. Her gunshot wound in his leg hurt bad, and now, so did the crease in his shoulder where she'd winged him back there on the bridge. The pain made it hard to drive. Leaving the bridge he'd popped a couple of the Dover's Powder pills, the same pain pills with which he'd drugged Morgan before the bank robbery—only then, he'd used enough to leave Blake sleeping like a dead flounder.

Washing the pills down with the last of an open Coke, he threw the bottle out the window and, staying well behind Becky out of sight, headed for Natalie's place. He needed his shoulder bandaged, needed the bandage on his leg changed, needed someone to take care of him, cook for him, needed a place to hole up until he healed. He wouldn't go to his mother's, she was too judgmental, he didn't see her often. The cops would already have been there looking for him; they didn't waste time when there'd been a shooting no matter who the victim was. They would have searched Natalie's apartment, too, late last night or maybe this morning. Natalie wouldn't rat on him, she wouldn't like the consequences.

He'd moved in, sent her out for a steak and a bottle of bootleg, was settled in just fine. He'd been there three days when the Rome cops found him. It was two A.M., he was asleep in Natalie's bed tossing with fever from the wound in his leg. Earlier that evening just after supper, the first time the cops showed up, they didn't have a warrant. Natalie had helped him hide in the attic crawl space. It hurt like hell getting up the folding stairs, his leg burning like fire. Natalie had refused to let the law in without the proper paperwork. When they'd gone, he'd been too sick to leave. He'd gone back to bed, had thought, if the cops came back with a warrant, he could make it out onto the balcony, could handle the five-foot drop to the concrete. The damn cops wouldn't be looking for him if Becky hadn't reported the bridge incident. She'd sure as hell sworn out a warrant, why else would they be there?

Natalie had been careful to keep his presence secret, had made no increased purchases of food, had pulled the drapes at dusk as was her habit. She had some anti-septic and an old sheet to tear up, so she needn't buy anything incriminating; she had nursed him as best she knew how. When, at night, he grew too fevered and restless to lie still she'd brought him cold compresses for his leg; and she'd moved out of the double bed into the living room, and slept on the couch. She was asleep there when, two hours past midnight, the cops pounded on her door again.

When they kept pounding, she shouted at them to shut up and go away. When Falon himself, groggy from the Dover's Powder, heard the sharp bite of a cop's voice, he rolled out of bed, shocked to wakefulness, pain jarring through him. He'd pulled on his pants and was sliding the balcony door open when he heard the front door crash open and two cops stormed in. One of them lunged and grabbed him, jerked his arms behind him, striking pain through him. The other cuffed him, and it was all over. They searched his pockets and found a set of car keys. They looked at his bandaged wounds. Once they were done questioning him and jerking him around, he pulled on his shirt, Natalie tied his shoes for him, crying, and handed him his jacket. She had a talent for crying on cue, she had done that to perfection in the courtroom when she took the stand at Blake's trial.

Two of the cops escorted him out of the apartment, forced him down the stairs and out the back door to a squad car, hustling him along, making no effort to allow for the pain he was experiencing. A third officer went to try Falon's keys in the cars that were parked behind the building. Falon's Ford coupe wasn't among them; he and Natalie had ditched it outside town behind an empty barn, returning in her car.

Falon was housed in the Rome city jail in a private cell to increase security while Rome police waited for the U.S. marshals to pick him up. His shoulder began bleeding again, soaking through the bandage and through his shirt. He was treated by the doctor who tended the prisoners, his wound was rebandaged, and he was given a shot for the infection. His rage at being arrested was directed equally at Becky Blake, at every bastard cop on the Rome force, and at Natalie for not alerting him soon enough to get him out of the apartment—but most of all at Becky. Somewhere down the line she'd pay for this and for all the snubs and injustices she'd forced on him over the years.

It was five A.M. the next morning that the ringing phone jerked Becky from a heavy sleep. She rolled over, fighting the covers, grabbing for the receiver—afraid it was the prison, that Morgan was hurt.

"It's Quaker. I'm sorry to wake you."

She sat up in bed, glancing over at Sammie, who had come wide awake and lay watching her. "Quaker? What is it? What's happened?" His last call hadn't been good news. What had happened now?

But there was a smile in Quaker's voice. "Becky? The Rome police have picked up Falon. He's locked down tight. They hauled him out of Natalie's at two-thirty this morning. He was hurting real bad from your gunshot wounds," he said cheerfully.

"Can they keep him locked up, now that they have the warrants?"

"They can. Do you want me to tell Morgan? I have an early appointment down that way."

"Oh yes, please. That's the best news he could have. It's a pain to try to call. I tried twice in the last weeks;

they said I could talk to him on visiting day. But, Quaker, you won't tell him that Falon attacked us? I've told him none of that, I couldn't bear to worry him, he has enough to deal with."

"Not a word," Lowe said. "Becky, the bureau will be all over Falon. With the crimes out on the coast, and after the bridge incident and the break-in there at your aunt's, I think we'll see some action."

When Lowe had hung up, Becky climbed into bed with Sammie, hugging her and laughing. "He's in jail, Falon's in jail, he can't touch us." And as Sammie chimed in, "He's in jail, he's in jail," Misto was suddenly there snuggling close and warm against them, big and golden and ragged-eared, his whole body rumbling with purrs.

26

Morgan parted from Quaker Lowe outside the prison office that was used by attorneys and their clients. Shaking hands with Lowe, he wanted to hug the man; they were both smiling as Lowe turned away toward the sally port. Morgan, double-timing to the mess hall, shouldered in among the stragglers looking for Lee. The kitchen staff was cleaning up the last of breakfast, the clanging of metal and crockery, the smell of overcooked food and soapy water. Lee sat at a table across the room where he'd pushed aside his empty plate. Morgan grabbed a plate, served himself from what was left in a few big pans, the eggs and pancakes limp and cold. Heading across among the empty tables, setting down his tray, he gave Lee a thumbs-up, "Falon's in jail. Locked up tight."

Lee let out a whoop that made the men in the kitchen turn and stare. "Hot damn! *That's* what Lowe came out here for. To give you the news in person. Becky knows?"

"He called her at five this morning, said she laughed like a kid. Rome cops picked him up on the federal warrant. Lowe agrees with them, if Falon's convicted in L.A., they'll keep him out there, maybe at Terminal Island."

Lee smiled. Morgan grinned back at Lee's pleasure, which seemed to wipe away the years. But Lee's eyes were bright with challenge, too. And that turned Morgan uneasy.

"He went over parts of the trial transcript again," Morgan said, watching Lee. "Wanted to know if there was anything I'd forgotten, that might have seemed unimportant at the time. I couldn't think of one detail." Morgan made a face at the cold eggs but shoveled them in. "This has set him up, Lee. The guy really wants to burn Falon. I like him, he doesn't act superior like the lawyers I've known. They come in the shop to get their car fixed, they want it yesterday and they know exactly what's wrong with it, they want it done exactly the way they tell me, even when they're dead wrong."

"You couldn't think of any new leads." Lee said. "Anything he can move on."

"Nothing." Morgan stirred sugar into his coffee; at least the coffee was hot. "It's the money that would fry him. If we knew where he hid the money."

Lee was quiet, watching Morgan.

"He was good at hiding things," Morgan said. "When we were kids, he knew places to stash car radios and batteries that I never thought of. He'd dig stuff out of the big flour bin in his mother's kitchen or an old water heater lying in the lot next door, dig out all the stash we'd lifted so we could take it to the fence."

Still, Lee said nothing. Morgan finished his breakfast; they returned their trays to the counter and moved out into the exercise yard. The morning's rain had stopped. As they moved down the concrete walk, puddles splashed their shoes. "The bank money," Morgan said, "he wouldn't trust that to some water heater—or to Natalie, either. She lied for him, but that doesn't mean he'd trust her with money. Falon's opinion of women is on a level with hogs in a mud hole."

"I wonder," Lee said, "if he's already retrieved the stash. He's had plenty of time to split it up, hide it in half a dozen places or maybe in banks. Maybe the bureau didn't find all the accounts. Maybe some small deposits, say, over in Kentucky and Alabama, accounts he might have already set up."

"Lowe's checking the banks in several states. That takes a while, when they'd be under false names. Harder still if he opened them some time ago, so they wouldn't show up under new accounts." Two joggers passed them moving swiftly, glancing at them without interest.

"If the feds haul him out to California," Morgan said, "he won't get his hands on the cash for some long time." He looked up at the sky, the clouds dark and low above them. "Or maybe he buried it, maybe thought that was safer than banks. He knows the land around Rome real well."

"And so do you," Lee said.

"So? You think I can look for it, locked in this damn prison?"

"There might be a way," Lee said. Over the last days, working in the steamy kitchen, he'd laid out a plan. Even now, with this new turn in Falon's fate, Lowe's try for an appeal could fail. If that happened, what Lee had in mind might be Morgan's only shot at a new trial, his only chance at freedom.

Lee didn't tell Morgan what he had in mind, he wanted Blake to think of it himself. He'd been working on Blake, planting the notion of escape, describing prison breaks he'd heard about, but then moving on to a colorful crime or a well-known inmate. Whether or not Blake knew what he was doing, the idea of escape was planted. Now, watching Morgan, Lee said, "What if we could find the money?"

"That's all the proof Lowe would need, he could get him back in court." Morgan looked hard at Lee. "If somehow I could get my hands on Falon before they ship him off . . . Get him alone and make him spill where he hid it . . ."

"How would you do that? Even if you broke out, he's locked up." Lee kicked at a pebble. "And by tomorrow or the next day, he'll be gone. On his way to the West Coast." He visualized Falon belly-chained in a DC-3 between a couple of deputy marshals. He hoped they were hard-nosed bastards; he wished Falon a miserable flight.

"If he's acquitted of the land scam," Morgan said, "he'll come back for the money. If I *could* get out of here, I could watch him and follow him."

"Slim chance he'll walk, if the feds are this hot to convict him."

"I want to get the bastard, Lee. *Make* him talk, *make him* tell where the money is. If I could get out, get my hands on him . . ."

Lee looked hard at Morgan. "You think *you* could take down Falon?"

Morgan looked uncertain. Lee said, "Together we could. We could hurt him bad enough so he'd tell whatever we want." And, watching Morgan, he knew Blake had grabbed the bait.

But what lay ahead would take all the planning, all the wiliness and strength the two of them had. Lee tried not to think how dangerous it was. His agenda wasn't only crazy, it was pushing suicide.

"You sure they'd put him in Terminal Island?" Morgan said.

"That's the closest to L.A. Why go to the expense of bringing him back here?"

"If there was a way to get transferred out there, if I could get into T.I. with him, I swear I'd beat the truth out of him."

"Well, sure, if you could get out there," Lee said. "The prison system does that all the time. You just tell your counselor you're unhappy here, that you'd like the California climate better, he'll put in for a transfer and you'll be on your way."

They moved over as four more joggers surged by, stinking of sweat. Morgan had taken the bait real well. "If he's sent to T.I.," he said stubbornly, "and I *could* get out there, I'd have a chance at him. I had no chance after the bank robbery. When I came to, groggy from the drugs, I was already on my way to jail. But now, if I could break out somehow, get out to California . . ."

"Then what? You camp on the doorstep of T.I. waiting for Falon to be released? Wait there how many years for him to walk out the prison door, then you nail him?"

"I have to do something. Becky and Sammie and I have our whole lives ahead of us. I don't want to watch from behind this damned wall as Sammie grows up. I want my life back."

Lee waited.

"If he *is* convicted, if he *does* do his time out there, there has to be some way I can get into the joint." Morgan looked helplessly at Lee. "I know it's impossible, but . . . Maybe I could get out through the train gate, where that guy got crushed. Maybe I could do a better job of it than he did."

"And what if you screw up? End up crushed, like him?"

Morgan slowed, looked at Lee a long time. "In here, I might as *well* be dead. In here, I'm nothing to Becky and Sammie. I can't work to support them, can't hold them and love them except in public at the exact place and time of day the prison says I can."

They had circled the exercise yard, had started around again when Morgan said, "If I did find a way to break out, if I got all the way out there, they wouldn't ship me back right away? I *am* a federal prisoner, wouldn't they hold me, maybe right there in T.I. for a few days, while they did the paperwork?"

Lee looked hard at Morgan. "They might not ship you back at all. It would be cheaper to keep you there." He shrugged. "Maybe T.I. Why not?"

"Then how do I do it? How do I get out, avoid the feds long enough to hop a freight or hitchhike, get on out to L.A.?"

Lee glanced up at the wall.

"I sure can't go over that baby," Morgan said, laughing sourly. "Thirty, forty feet. And the guards. Even if there was a way over, I wouldn't last two seconds, with those rifles trained on me."

"Maybe," Lee said. "Maybe there's a way. Come on," he said, heading across the big yard.

Sitting with their backs to the concrete barrier, Lee laid out the plan. He showed Morgan the dimples in the concrete. He watched Morgan glance up, as Lee himself had done, looking toward the towers that couldn't be seen from that position. He watched Morgan's expression change to disbelief and then to excitement, and Lee's own blood surged. They could do this. They could get out of there, in a way that no one had ever done, before.

Maybe something was pushing him, maybe not. This was what he meant to do and to hell with his short sentence. Beside him, Morgan began to smile. "Sammie was right," he said.

"Right about what?"

"That you'd come here to Atlanta and save me," Morgan said. "That you'd get me out of this cage."

27

Lee sat across the visiting room as far away from Morgan and Becky as he could get, holding Sammie on his lap hoping she couldn't hear Morgan's pitch as he laid out their escape plan to Becky. Though the child would know soon enough, he thought wryly. If she hadn't already dreamed of what they meant to do. Dreamed it, but had kept it from her mother?

Or had she dreamed of the outcome of their venture? But if she'd done that, now she'd be either tearful and grieving for Morgan or wildly excited that they would soon be free. She wouldn't be the quiet little girl sitting snuggled and uncertain in his lap, leaning against him, her small hand in his.

There were only a few other visitors in the room. Lee watched a lean young prisoner and his pillow-shaped wife, their smear-faced toddler fussing and crying as they passed him back and forth between them. Neither they nor the other three couples seemed to be listening to Morgan's soft, urgent voice.

Lee knew Becky would try to stop them, try to tear their plan apart. He watched her scowl grow deeper until suddenly she lit into Morgan, her whisper, even from across the room, as virulent as a snake's hiss.

He didn't like to see the two of them at odds but, more to the point, they needed Becky's help, needed help on the outside to make this work. As the two battled it out, their angry whispers drowned by the fussy baby, Lee hoped no one could hear. If any rumor of a planned escape was passed on to a guard, he and Morgan would be separated, confined to their cells, maybe one of them sent to another prison, and that would end their plan.

Now, though Sammie still sat quietly turning the pages of her book, her whole being was focused on her parents' whispered battle. Soon she laid down her book, pressed closer against Lee, her body rigid and still. Across the room, Becky grabbed Morgan by the shoulders, her fingers digging in. Lee rose, setting Sammie back in the chair. "Stay there, stay quiet." But before he could cross the room Becky was up, moving toward him, backing him away from the others into a corner. Her whisper was like a wasp sting.

"What have you been telling him? What crazy ideas have you been feeding Morgan? No one can do what you're planning." Her dark eyes flashed, her anger a force that made Lee step back. "This will get him killed. Morgan was a patsy once. I won't let him do this, this isn't going to happen."

Lee was shocked by the degree of her rage. "You won't *let* him do this?" he whispered. "What right have you to *let* him do anything! Morgan is the one who's in prison, not you. *He's* the one who was framed, not you. He wants a new trial. There's no chance without new, solid evidence." He wanted to shake her, he had drawn close, the others were looking now; without the bawling baby they'd hear every word. "This is the only way *I* know to get new evidence," he breathed.

He leaned over, racked by a fit of coughing, then faced her again. "Maybe Natalie Hooper will talk to your lawyer the way he thinks. And maybe she won't." He glanced across at Sammie, sitting rigid in the chair, her fists clenched.

"The best way to get real evidence," Lee said softly, "is from Falon himself. Find out where he hid the money. Tell the bureau so they can retrieve it." He swallowed back another cough. "The best way is to make him talk. And you won't *let* Morgan do this?"

"He'll get himself killed trying to escape. What good is that? You might not care if the guards shoot him, but I do. And even if you did get out," she breathed, "even if you made it all the way to California without being picked up, which isn't likely—even if you did turn yourselves in at Terminal Island and they kept you a few days, the minute you try to hustle Falon, he'll kill Morgan. Don't you understand how vicious Falon is?" Her jaw was clenched, her lips a thin line, her dark eyes huge with anger and pain. "What kind of scam is this, Fontana? What do you care if Morgan gets a new trial? Just because we're related doesn't mean I can trust you or that Morgan can. Leave him alone. Keep your nose out of our business."

"I can do that," Lee said quietly. "I can tell him the plan's no good, that we'll have to scratch it, and he'll back off. He knows he can't get out of here alone without help, without a partner. We trash the plan, and you'll go right on visiting him here until he's an old man. You two can sit on the couch holding hands, you can watch him grow bitter, watch him turn into an empty shell with nothing inside but rage. And watch yourself do the same. And Sammie will grow up seeing her father for an hour at a time, a few days a week at best, right here in this visiting room with iron bars at the windows. If you stop him from trying," Lee said, "you'll never sleep well again. You'll never sleep with Morgan again, never hold him close at night."

Beneath the anger, Becky's look had gone naked and still.

"This is a pretty visiting room, isn't it, Becky? The nice furniture and clean walls, the expensive carpeting, the plants along the window. And the rest of the prison is just as pretty and clean, it smells just as nice, and is just as comfortable and safe. We're all just loving brothers in here, behind these bars and walls."

She wiped at her eyes. "I know it's hard, that it's ugly, but—"

"You don't know anything, you don't have a clue. You wouldn't last five minutes behind those doors." Lee looked at her coldly. "That world in there peels away all the layers, lady. Right down to the worst ugliness you can think of, and worse than you can think of." He choked and swallowed. "You don't know anything about what it's like in there, about what Morgan's life is like. But that doesn't matter," he whispered. "You want Morgan to stay locked in here, maybe until he dies. He's only a young man, but you want him to stay here until he rots to nothing for a crime he didn't commit."

She turned away, her head bowed. He put a hand on her shoulder. She was still for a long time. When she turned back, she faced him squarely, pale and quiet, her look so vulnerable that he wanted to hold her just as he had held Sammie. She stood silent looking at him until he started to turn away. Quietly she pulled him down on the nearest couch, sat facing him.

"What about the second appeal?" she said softly. "Why would you do this before we know if it's granted?"

"There won't be a second appeal without new evidence, no matter how hard Lowe works at it. The complaints you filed are supporting evidence, but not enough, not the kind of evidence you need for a sure win. Lowe knows that, that's why he's still digging.

"So far he has nothing. Morgan doesn't think he'll get it from Natalie and neither do you. Not the solid, irrefutable evidence he needs. Maybe he'll find flaws in her story, inconsistencies, but that's far from solid."

She was silent again, looking down at her lap. As he rose to leave she looked up. "Tell me what to do," she said. "Tell me how I can help."

He hugged her and then settled back, his shoulder against hers, his voice so low she had to lean close. "We'll need clothes, old jeans. Old shirts, nothing fancy or new. Old, warm jackets. Good heavy boots, waterproof if you can find them." He found a scrap of paper in his pocket and wrote down his shoe size. "And money," he said, "all the money you can lay your hands on." He read her alarm at that. "At some point," Lee said, "once we're out on the coast, we'll need to hire a lawyer."

He watched Morgan rise to join them, sitting down close on Becky's other side. "Get the clothes at some charity shop," Morgan said. "Wash them in lye soap, we don't want lice."

"The other thing," Lee said, "we need to know what's on the other side of the wall. The train track has to be close, the whistles damn near take your head off, but we need to know the layout, what's on beyond."

"There's a General Motors plant," Morgan said, "a car distribution center. On behind that, unless things have changed, there's an open field. But check it all out, see if it's still the same, see how the field lies in relation to the wall and the track."

Lee told her where to leave the clothes and money. "We'll let you know later when to drop it. Once we're out of here, there'll be no contact. Morgan won't be making any calls from some pay phone, the bureau boys would pick it up in a minute.

"Once we're gone," Lee said, "you won't be finished with it, Becky. Make no mistake, the feds will be all over you, they'll question you and question Sammie. Doesn't matter that she's just a child, they'll try to drag information out of her, try for anything they think they can use."

"Why do you want to go with Morgan?" Becky said. "If you stay here, you'll be getting out soon."

"I don't know why," Lee snapped. "Because I'm crazy. Because he can't do it alone, he doesn't know anything about hopping the trains, about avoiding the law. He doesn't know anything much that will help him." He took her hand. "Don't tell Sammie any more than she's overheard or guessed. Whatever she knows will put her on the spot. If she dreams this you'll have to make her understand, make her swear to keep silent.

"You'd better start teaching her now," Lee said. "Not to talk to anyone about this, not to your aunt, not to the maid, not to your mother. Sure as hell not to a bureau agent. Anything she says, even if it's only a dream, an agent might run with it." Lee glanced up past Becky toward the half-open door, at the shadow of the guard standing in the hall. "Morgan will let you know the rest, let you know the timing. We've been talking too long, I need to get out of here." He rose and left them, and didn't look back.

Telling Becky about the plan scared him, that she wouldn't keep their secret, but they needed her. The idea of Sammie's dreams disturbed him all the more, the thought that she might innocently let a hint drop, meaning no harm. But Sammie was a wise child. He told himself that with Becky's help she'd learn to be still, would learn to lie for her daddy.

28

That's not a wall, it's a mountain," Morgan said. "There's no way we can get over that baby." They stood on the steps leaning against the rail where Lee had first seen the flaw in the concrete. It was two days after they'd told Becky their plan. Below them the big yard gleamed with puddles, bouts of rain had swept through all day.

"People climb mountains," Lee said dryly. "You've already made the rods. What's the matter with you, what did Becky say?" Morgan had just come from visiting hour. Lee had skipped this one; it was the last time the two would be together. "She's not angry again?" Lee said warily. "Did she get the clothes, the money? Or did she . . . ?"

"She got everything we asked for," Morgan said, pulling his coat tighter against the chill. "She's not mad. She's . . . quiet. Trying to hold it in. This is hard on her, Lee. What if . . . ?" Morgan shook his head. "I'm not sure I can do this to her."

"It'll be harder on her if you don't. If you never get out of here, never get an appeal."

Morgan stared up at the guard tower, his hands clutched white on the rail. "She drove the roads behind the wall, she's done everything you asked. She's just . . . She said there were still open fields back there, the weeds waist-high from the rain. She thought the distance from the wall to the train track was about five hundred yards. Said there's a signal pole beside the track, she'll leave the bundle of clothes in the weeds near its base. Said she'd stuff them in a greasy gunny-sack the way you said, smear it with mud and lay some dead weeds over it."

Lee had to smile at Becky crouched in the weeds, messing around in the mud like a kid herself.

"She went to the city library, found a map of the railway lines, drew a rough copy. She took half a day off from work to get everything together, buy the used clothes, draw out the money. That's all the money we have, Lee. She has nothing to pay Quaker Lowe, she . . ." Morgan shook his head. "She said that from Atlanta the freight will go either to Birmingham or Chattanooga depending on the timing, she couldn't find a schedule for that. Then on to Memphis, Little

Rock, across Oklahoma and the Texas Panhandle to Albuquerque."

"Then Arizona," Lee said, "and into California." He wanted to stop in Blythe, draw out the prison-earned money he'd deposited. Money he'd carried with him when he was paroled from McNeil, plus what he'd earned in Blythe; he thought they'd need every penny.

Right. Stop in Blythe, and what if he were spotted approaching the bank or inside, when he tried to close his account? Who could say how much more the feds knew by now about the post office robbery? What other details might they have picked up? If they had anything more pointing to him, they'd have put an alert on his account. If they had and he showed up to draw his cash, the clerk would call the local cops. He and Morgan would end their journey right there, in the Blythe slammer.

Don't borrow trouble, Lee told himself. *Quit worrying. Wait until we reach Blythe, then play it the way it falls.*

"Becky followed the track as best she could in the car," Morgan said. "There's a switching yard to the left about three miles. She couldn't tell how much security they have, she saw only one guard moving among the workmen. But the cars were crowded close, so maybe we can keep out of sight. We'll have to watch it, not ride out of town in the wrong direction."

"Doesn't matter," Lee said. "Either way, Chattanooga or Birmingham, we'll be all right, we'll take whichever we draw." They had already timed the sweep of the spotlight beams, where they crossed each other. There was some two hundred feet of open yard to cross to reach the flaw and the blind spot. They had ten seconds between sweeps, to cover the distance, and Lee was no track star. He didn't know if he was fast enough or if he'd blow it right there.

"I'll work my regular supper shift," he said. "Then we haul out. Hope to hell the storm passes." He didn't like to think about climbing those metal rods if they were slick with rain. But maybe it would clear by tomorrow. He was having trouble breathing. He told himself it was from the pain of the healing wound, but he knew it was from worry—worry over the moves to come, worry over Morgan's sudden reluctance. He'd like to know what more Becky had said to make him pull back. When the rain came hard again, driving down at them, they hurried under the nearest overhang.

Misto followed them floating close to Lee and reaching out a paw to softly touch Lee's ear. Lee glanced his way, scowling, but then with a crooked smile. The ghost cat—his coat perfectly dry in the downpour—having listened to their plans and to Morgan's hesitance, now shadowed them as they headed away to supper.

But at the door to the crowded mess hall with its smell of overcooked vegetables and limp sauerkraut, he left them again, returning to his dance in the rain. Leaping through the pelting onslaught dry and untouched, he rolled and tumbled thirty feet above the exercise yard, landed atop the prison wall and crouched a few feet from the guard tower, looking in.

The room atop the tower extended out over the wall on both sides, a round dome with windows circling it, the windows open, the glass angled up like awnings keeping out the rain and affording the guards a better view through the storm. Within, the two uniformed guards paced or paused to look out, their rifles slung over their shoulders. Both looked sour, as if they'd rather be anywhere else. Bored men, Misto thought, who might easily be distracted. Leaping in through the nearest window, he narrowly missed the taller man, brushing past his shoulder and rifle. The man shivered, looked around, and buttoned his jacket higher.

Dropping onto the small table that stood in the center of the crowded space, the ghost cat patted idly at a plate of ham sandwiches and enjoyed a few bites from one. Invisible, he prowled between a thermos bottle, two empty cups reeking of stale coffee, a tall black telephone, a newspaper folded to the crossword puzzle, six clips for the rifles, and five boxes of ammunition marked Winchester .30-06. He listened to the short, barrel-chested guard grouse that his wife wanted to have another child and that three kids were all he wanted. When the man's tall, half-bald partner started telling dirty jokes, Misto lost interest and left them.

Drifting out a window and back along the wall listening to the thunder roll, the tomcat looked down at the fault in the wall and, for only an instant, he hoped Lee and Morgan would make it over. For that one instant the tomcat knew uncertainty.

But his dismay, he thought, was most likely born of Morgan Blake's own doubt, just as was Lee's hesitation. The escape tomorrow night was destined for success, Misto told himself. It would come off just fine. Among Misto's earlier lives, and often between lives, he'd witnessed the escapes of other imprisoned men. Some escapees were good men, others were blood-hungry rebels bent on destruction. Once, in Africa, Misto was carried in the arms of a small slave boy, both of them hoping that somewhere there was a safe haven for them and knowing there was not. He had watched the terror of peasants fleeing from medieval slave makers, and once he had died in the confusion of battle as free men were snatched away on the bloody streets of Rome.

This world of humans was not a kind place. Joy was a rare treasure; compassion and joy and a clear assessment of life were gifts too often lost beneath the hand of the dark spirit.

Now, diving from the wall and spinning through the rain, Misto thought to join Lee and Morgan at supper despite the unappealing scents in the mess hall. Drifting into the crowded room, dropping down to the steam table, he padded along between the big pans sniffing, then delicately picking out morsels to his liking: a bit of hot dog, half a biscuit. He skipped whatever was disgusting, but lingered over the spaghetti.

Quickly the pan's contents disappeared, vanished behind men's backs or while heads were turned. When the tomcat was replete he drifted away to join his friends, dropping unseen onto the table between Lee's and Morgan's trays. His tail twitching, he watched them wolf down sauerkraut, hot dogs, and biscuits as, in low voices, they went over again their moves of the next night. Misto thought they had honed the plan as well as they could, except for Morgan's nerves; he only hoped the rain would move on away. But even a talented ghost can't do much about weather; that was an act of power beyond the most stubborn spirit.

Watching the two men, Misto knew Lee was worn out, was cold, that his healing wound hurt him, that he wanted his bunk and warm blankets. He watched Lee rise stiffly, leaving Morgan to finish his pie; he followed Lee, hovering close, moving through driving rain for the cellblock.

Tomorrow night, Lee thought as he crossed the wet grounds, rain soaking into his coat and pants. *Tomorrow night we'll be out of here, headed for California, we're as ready as we can be.* He slowly climbed the three flights of metal stairs and moved down the catwalk to his cell. He tried to sense the ghost cat near. He had no hint of Misto, though the company would be welcome. Pulling off his wet clothes, he crawled in his bunk and pulled the covers around him. He smiled when he felt the ghost cat land on the bed. The tomcat stretched out against Lee's side as warm as an oversized heating pad. With the added warmth and the hypnotic rumble of Misto's purrs, Lee soon drifted into sleep, deep and dreamless. No whispers tonight from the dark spirit, no nightmare that he was falling from the wall or from a moving freight car, just peaceful sleep.

He woke to continued rain, the cellblock dark and silent. The ghost cat was gone, the blankets awry, the space the cat had occupied was cold to the touch. Rain sluiced across the clerestory windows like buckets of water dumped from the sky. Lightning whitened the high glass, too, nearly blinding him. He hadn't *dreamed* of climbing the wall, but now his mind was filled with the effort. He lay wondering if they'd make it over or be shot down, crippled like a pair of clumsy pigeons.

Twenty years ago he would have found the challenge a lark. Two weeks ago when he'd first thought of the plan, he'd been hot to get on with it. Now he felt only tired, daunted by the moves ahead, discouraged by Morgan's loss of nerve and by the failure of his own strength, the debilitation of his aging body.

Well, they weren't backing off. He might feel like hell some days, but other times he was pretty good. No one said it would be easy. No one had ever gone over that wall. He and Morgan would be the first, and he meant to do it right.

Half asleep, he didn't let himself think that his powerful urge to conquer the wall was encouraged by the dark spirit. He wasn't being led. This wasn't Satan's pushing. He and Morgan were beholden to no one. He was nearly asleep again when he felt the ghost cat return. Misto was fully visible now, bold and ragged, clearly seen in the glow of the cellblock lights, sharply outlined when lightning flashed. The yellow tomcat didn't want petting now. He stood stiff-legged, staring at the back of the cell. His snarl keened so loud that

Lee stared across to the other cells. No one seemed to be looking, maybe no one else heard the cat's yowl, no one but the shadow that stood against the cell wall, the wraith's voice pounding heavy against the beating rain.

"You fret over Morgan's loss of courage, Lee. Don't let his fear dishearten you. *You* can bring this off, *you* have the courage to do this, even if Blake falters. *You* won't fail, I'll see to that. This will be an easy escape. Tomorrow night you'll be over the wall and on your way riding the freights, free and unimpeded—if you do as I require."

The cat snarled again. The shadow shifted and thinned, but then it darkened and drew close to Lee, its cold embracing him. "If you follow where I lead, you can thumb your nose at the feds. And," Satan said, "you will reap substantial profits from your venture."

"*What* do you want? What do you think I'd be willing to do for *you*?"

Beside Lee the ghost cat paced, his eyes blazing, his claws flexing above the blanket.

"This is what I want, only this one small favor. In return I will guarantee the success of your long journey. When you reach Terminal Island," Satan said, "or perhaps before you reach the coast, you will turn Morgan Blake in to the authorities."

Lee wanted to smash the shadow. He knew he couldn't touch it, that nothing alive could invade that dark and shifting power.

"You will both be arrested for the escape," Lucifer said. "You, Lee, will swear that Blake forced you to help him. I will see that the arresting officers believe you, I am adept at that. *You* will go free, Fontana, while Morgan Blake remains behind bars." The devil smiled, a shadow within shadows twisting up eerie and tall. "You will receive a reward for Blake's capture, for the apprehension of a cold-blooded murderer. The amount will be considerable. *You alone, Lee,* will leave California, loaded with cash and enjoying great notoriety for the capture."

"What do I want with notoriety *or* with the curse of your money? Get the hell out of here."

"Didn't you want to be the first one to scale the wall? Isn't that notoriety? And," Lucifer said, "you turn Blake in, you'll not only be rewarded and admired, you'll most likely be pardoned for your heroism. You can head for Blythe a free man. Richer than you dreamed, no law enforcement tailing you, and with a long and satisfying retirement before you, just as you planned."

"No one's going to pat me on the head and turn me loose. If I double-crossed Blake, the reward I'd get would be an extended sentence for escaping, more time in the pen. The feds would laugh at some effort to play hero; they'd lock me up until they buried me."

The cat stalked down the bed snarling, tail lashing. The tall shadow shifted and grew thinner. Thunder shook the cellblock, the clerestory windows flashed white; and the shade was gone, vanished.

29

Lee found the rope behind a row of trash cans outside the mess hall where Gimpy had left it, a coil of half-inch hemp secured with a cotton cord. Gimpy hadn't asked questions when Lee made his request. His eyes had widened, then he'd clapped Lee on the shoulder and nodded. Because they were alone, no one watching, he'd given Lee a hug that brought tears to Lee's eyes.

Before heading for the kitchen Lee slipped the rope inside his shirt. Moving through the kitchen into the pantry, he pulled on a white cotton jacket with a stain on one sleeve. Opening a seldom-used cupboard, he hid the rope inside an iron pot he'd never seen Bronski remove from its dusty shelf. He worked steadily all evening. Adding hot water to the dishwater, plunging his hands in, he thought this might be the last time he'd feel warm for a good while. He thought about the cold, windy boxcars, about walking cold along the tracks in the night; and he hungered to get on with the job.

At the end of shift, after two short-termers finished mopping the floor, he wiped down the steam table, then set the chairs in place for breakfast. Bronski, busy around the stoves, nodded good night to the other five workers. "About ready, Fontana?"

"I'll be along as soon as I get the last load of trays out on the line." Lee shuffled the trays, watching Bronski's broad back as the big man moved through the dining area and shoved out through the double doors, heading for the cellblocks. There'd be a guard along in a minute to lock up. Beyond the mess hall windows, the outdoor lights were bright, the sweeping prison spotlights swinging back and forth, back and forth. A guard was clearing the building, moving through the dining area toward the kitchen. He gave Lee a long look, studied the stack of trays in Lee's arms, and glanced up at the wall clock. "Ready to wrap it up?"

Lee nodded, stacked the trays at the end of the counter, then turned back to the kitchen. He knew the guard would linger, waiting for him. Moving into the pantry he took off the white jacket, retrieved the rope from the iron pot, and slipped it inside his shirt. He pushed out the back door past the waiting guard into the darkness between the shop buildings, heard the door lock behind him, and from the shadows Morgan fell into step. They didn't speak.

They emerged from between the buildings at the top of the stairs, a story above the yard. Stood looking across at the prison wall, stroked by the tower's sweeping lights. Blinding light, and then dark. Punishing light, then dark. Lee told himself the thirty-foot rampart wasn't a barrier, it was a vertical concrete road, a road to freedom. It was all timing now, timing and speed.

Descending the stairs, they waited in the shadows underneath, Lee's heart pounding, Morgan silent and tense. The sweeping lights crossed, then swung apart. Crossed and swung away. Crossed . . . "Go!" Lee croaked. They broke from the shadows running.

Morgan quickly outdistanced him. Lee gave it all he had, sucking in ragged breath. The space seemed miles, not yards. Gulping air, he kept his feet flying. Dizziness gripped him. *Run. Run.* But an uneven patch tripped him, he fell sprawling, sharp pain stabbed his hand as he tried to catch himself, and the sweeping light headed straight at him.

"Run!" Sammie shouted, wide awake. "Run, the light's coming!

Becky heard her screams and came to kneel by the bathtub, trying to hold her, the child thrashing, her slick, soapy body flailing. She thrust forward so violently the bathwater surged and she lunged past Becky as if to grab someone. "Get up! Run! The lights . . ."

Becky gripped Sammie hard to keep her from hurting herself. The child stared past her, fixed on something Becky couldn't see; she was unaware of Becky. She cradled her left hand, tears of pain glistening. Then suddenly she went limp, turned blindly to Becky, wanting only to be held.

Becky lifted her from the tub, wrapped her in a towel, and kissed the hurt hand, though there was no abrasion, no redness. The child clung to Becky, but she was still far away, watching the violence unfold, so far removed from the safe, warm room where her mother held her.

At the moment Lee fell, the cat appeared in the guard tower, solid and real. His sudden yowl startled the two guards; they swung around, rifles pointed. Misto, on the table, glared at them. Both men backed away, but then the short, stocky guard paused, grinning. "How did you get in here?"

The tall guard still fingered his rifle. "How could a cat get up here? Get it out of here, Willy. I don't like cats. Where the hell did it come from?"

"It sure didn't climb the wall," Willy said. "Maybe followed us up the stairs when we came on shift. But there ain't no cat in the prison," he said, frowning. "I've never seen a cat around here."

"Wild ones, outside the wall," his tall companion said. "Why would one come in here? They run from people. What's it want in here?"

Willy reached to stroke the golden cat. "It's tame enough, Sam. Maybe it's hungry. Hand me a sandwich."

"No. That's our supper, damn it."

Willy laughed and stroked the cat's ragged ears. "Tomcat. Been fighting." His partner looked at Misto with distaste, their combined attention distracting both from the windows.

Misto held their attention, rolling over, hamming for Willy. He knew that Lee still lay sprawled on the blacktop, he knew when Morgan turned back to Lee. The tomcat, buying the few seconds the escapees needed, flirted with Willy, purring for him with all the charm he could muster. Sam watched them, disgusted.

"Go on," Lee hissed at Morgan. "Get the hell on, do it alone." As the light swept back at him, probing like a giant beast, he buried his face in his jacket and tucked his hands under. In that short moment before the light hit him, he felt Morgan's hand grab his. He stumbled up, Morgan pulling him into the dark.

They crouched against the wall, Lee hacking up phlegm, trying to stifle the sound. Damned lungs, everything he did, they screwed him up. Pressed tight into the wall's curve, he could only pray the sweeping blaze would miss them. "You okay?" Morgan whispered.

"I need a minute. Find the holes." He crouched trying to get his breath. The light was coming back. Quickly he wrapped his handkerchief around his hand to stop the bleeding. He couldn't climb the rods with a blood-slick hand. By the time he got his hand bound, Morgan had set the first two pins. Lee patted the coil of rope tied to his belt, grabbed the top pin, and stepped up on the lower one. He took a third pin from Morgan and set it into the third hole. Clinging to the face of the wall, he climbed. He was soon eight feet up, then ten, Morgan, with his own three pins, pressing up behind him. The light swept by never touching them. They moved up and up, the lights racing behind not inches from their backs. They were more than halfway up when Lee reached down for a pin and felt it slip from his hand. He made a grab. It bounced in his hand and fell. He saw Morgan lean out and catch it. Morgan handed it up to him.

"Christ," Lee breathed. "Lucky."

"I didn't make any spares," Morgan whispered, and Lee hoped he was lying. Soon the top of the wall was some six feet above him. His leg muscles had begun to quiver, and as he positioned the next pin to push it in the hole, it resisted. He could feel the paint break away but the rod wouldn't go in. He tried again, thrusting so hard he nearly unbalanced himself. Tried again, but the damn thing wouldn't go. He slipped it back under his belt and felt the hole with his finger. It felt too small, as if maybe the cement had sagged when the original pin was pulled away with the form. His holding hand was numb, his hold precarious. Switching hands, the wrapped hand slick again with blood, he looked down at Morgan. "I can't get the damn thing in."

"Try again. Maybe there's something in the mouth of the hole. Break it away."

Again he switched hands, lined up the pin, drew it back and hit the opening. It bounced off. He lined up again, spit on the wall, hit the hole with all the force in him.

The pin drove in and wedged tight.

No way he could get it out, but they were nearly over, they wouldn't need it now. With the last step set in place, Lee eased up onto the two-foot-wide concrete. Lying on his belly staring down at the prison yard and the sweeping lights, he unfastened the rope from his belt, slipped the looped end over the top peg, and dropped the free end down the outside. His wrapped hand wet with blood, he grabbed the rope with both hands and slid off, his feet against the wall, dropped hand over hand down the outside. He thought he'd never reach the bottom but at last his feet touched the ground. Above him Morgan was halfway down.

Morgan landed beside him, they lay hidden in the weeds among rusted cans, catching their breath, listening.

The night was still, no alarm blared. The diffused spill of light above the wall continued back and forth but softer now, unthreatening. To their right the automobile plant was bright, big spotlights mounted on poles inside its tall wire fence, gleaming off rows of new cars that awaited shipment. As their eyes adjusted to the dark they could see woods beyond and, nearer, just across the weedy field, what looked like the signal pole beside the shine of railroad tracks. Beyond ran an empty street, no cars, no headlights moving in either direction. Crouching, slipping through the weeds, stumbling among unidentifiable trash, they headed for the lone pole.

Lee kept watch as Morgan searched, watched him pull a muddy gunnysack out of the weeds, haul out a canvas bag with a drawstring top. Morgan had started to open it when Lee heard the faint sound of the train, quickly growing louder, approaching fast.

"We won't have time to change clothes." Lee grabbed the bundle from Morgan, tied it to his waist as the rocking sound of iron wheels came at them. "Drop," Lee snapped, and the engine broke out of the woods.

They lay belly down, the single headlight sweeping the weeds above them. The whistle screamed, screamed again, and as the engine passed the signal pole, the train reduced speed, boxcars bucking against each other. "Come on," Lee said, "follow me. Do what I do. Be quick, don't hesitate. We're headed up on top." He broke into a fast trot as the train continued to slow. He picked a car, grabbed a rung on the steel ladder and jumped, landed safe on the bottom rung.

He climbed fast, glancing down to see that Morgan had made it, then sprawled on his belly atop the boxcar. Morgan slid up beside him. They lay flat, faces hidden as the train crept past the automobile plant, past the high prison wall and guard towers and then through a dark industrial area that smelled of gas fumes. Lee shoved the bundle at Morgan, then wriggled to the edge of the boxcar to look down.

Below him the door was ajar some two inches. "Hang tight until I get down, then hand me the bundle."

He reached down, grabbed the rail that ran along the top of the sliding door, and swung over the side. Raising his legs, he pushed the door open with his feet, swallowing back the cough in his lungs. Before he swung inside, Morgan handed the bundle down and then followed him.

They changed clothes inside the boxcar, checking first behind half a dozen big crates, but there was no one else aboard. They rolled their prison blues into a ball and threw them into the weeds along the track. The soft, worn jeans and dark wool shirts felt good. Becky had put in heavy, lined jackets, thick gloves, and wool socks. The worn boots she had found fit just fine. They kept their prison shoes for spares, shoving them in the bag. The money was in their left-hand jeans pockets, she had split it half and half, three hundred dollars each and change. A little over six hundred dollars to get them across the country and pay the lawyer—if some slime didn't catch them off guard and take them down. The train rolled around the edge of the city past office buildings with softly lit windows, past a church spire whose bell tolled nine o'clock, striking counterpoint to the slow clacking of the train. "Evening count's been taken," Lee said. "They know we're gone."

Morgan stepped to the door, stood in the shadows looking back. The train bucked and slowed again, its couplings groaning; they were moving into the switching yard. Lee pulled the door nearly shut, stood looking out the crack as the long line of cars ground to a halt and yardmen began walking its length, lanterns swinging. "They're going to drop some cars. If they slide the door open," Lee said, "dive for the crates, stay in the shadows."

But the workmen passed without incident. They waited in silence. Only when the train jerked hard did Lee lean out for a quick look toward the tail. "They've dropped a dozen cars." The train lurched again, traveled forward a distance, stopped, and backed onto another siding. There was a jolt as the end car was coupled with another car. Leaning out again Lee could see they'd taken on a stand of flatcars. "We're good," he said, "we're on our way." They picked up speed again, heading out from the switching yard moving south, passing another set of tracks that likely ran north. "We're headed for Birmingham," Lee said, grinning, and he settled down on the moldy straw that covered the bed of the boxcar.

"I can't believe we did it," Morgan said. "Can't believe we're out of there. It feels— Hey, Fontana, it feels pretty good."

Lee smiled. "I told you we'd make it," and he forgot his earlier uncertainty.

Now that they were clear of the yard he rolled the door open and sat with his back against its edge looking out at the city slipping by, at the little stores, their windows softly lit, many with Christmas decorations, at the little box houses with Christmas trees in their windows. But then soon they were in open country, gathering speed, the mournful cries of the whistle echoing across the night, a siren call that eased and comforted Lee. They were moving on, fast and free, heading toward a different kind of job than he'd ever pulled. Not a robbery but an adventure that would, if all went well, set straight the lives of those he cared about. He was sitting with his back against the wall of the boxcar, thinking about Sammie, when he felt the ghost cat walk across his legs. Unseen, the big tom settled down in the straw, his head on Lee's outstretched knee. Had the tomcat been with them all along? Was Lee more aware of him when he paused to rest, when he was not distracted, his senses more alert to the ghost cat?

And, he wondered, did Misto like the trains, too? Did the ghost cat like their galloping rattle and screaming whistle as they ate up the miles? Sure as hell the spirit cat seemed mighty pleased with himself.

Maybe he, too, was happy they were out of there, that they were on their way?

Their bold and chancy plan might be infinitesimal, Lee thought, in the vast scheme of the universe.

Or, in that eternally unwinding tangle, did even the smallest blow for good matter? Was the very effort to right a wrong, in fact, the *heart* of mortal life? Was this the secret that made life real?

30

The train's speed altered, jerking Lee awake as they passed through a switch. He'd slept cold, and the ghost cat had left him. When he eased the door open, the icy night chilled his bones. As the train slowed to a creep he cracked the door wider and looked ahead.

They were approaching a freight yard, he could see the edge of the dark platform, a lighted tower marked Birmingham. He shook Morgan awake. There'd been a couple of stops during the night when Morgan had risen to keep watch, but then they'd moved on again. Now as Lee reached for the canvas bag, out of the blackness half a dozen men swarmed off the platform running in both directions, fanning out along the train.

"They're searching," Lee hissed, grabbing the canvas bag. "Move it."

They dropped to the track bed running, ducked under a line of standing cars, ran dodging across the freight yard behind and under boxcars, Morgan still half asleep. Beyond a row of freight cars the beams of powerful flashlights swung toward them. Four lights, five, leaping up the sides of the boxcars, searching along their tops, then down among the train's wheels. They followed behind the lights' wake, but were stopped by a six-foot wall.

They scaled the brick barrier fast, helping each other over. Were the cops checking every train heading out of Atlanta? If they searched this yard, would they hit *every* yard, every station, one town to the next? That meant they'd have to drop off each train before they reached the station, keep away from the freight yards, stay to the outlying fields until they were past each town, catch another train on beyond, and that would sure slow them.

On the other side of the wall they lay flat, listening, until the reflection of lights stopped roaming above and the sound of running feet faded. Rising, double-timing away from the walled yard, they moved on past a metal plant, a junked-car lot, a pipe yard. In the dark, the rough, weed-tangled ground slowed them. They made their way through the industrial section of Birmingham, avoiding occasional security lights mounted on rooftops or cyclone fences, but trying to stay near the tracks.

But soon the sky lightened toward dawn and the rough industries gave way to run-down houses. In another half hour of shabby streets they were beyond the city in another industrial area. They could see a railroad signal ahead, then an overhead crane lifting sheets of metal, maybe a steel fabrication plant. They were both hungry, and Lee's back ached from the hard jolting floor of the boxcar. "Men working down there," he said, "there should be a food wagon."

Moving on fast, they soon stood on a low hill above the steel plant, the top of the crane just at eye level. The yard below was surrounded by a six-foot wire fence, its gate open. A snack truck stood just inside, surrounded by men swilling coffee, eating doughnuts.

Leaving Morgan, Lee angled down the embankment and in through the open gate to mingle with the crowd of workmen. At the truck's coffee urn he drew two paper cups of brew, then gathered up a dozen doughnuts and a couple of sandwiches, dropping them in a paper bag from a little rack. The vendor, watching him, took his five-dollar bill, punched out some coins from his belt and added three ones. "Haven't seen you before. Just start on the job?"

Lee nodded, and dropped the change in his pocket. "Just this morning."

The vendor raised an eyebrow. "Big appetite."

"My buddy missed breakfast." Turning away, he eased back through the crowd toward the nearest metal building, and glanced around. When he thought no one was watching he doubled back between two sheds, behind some parked cars, and up the hill again to where Morgan waited. They ate as they walked, devouring half the doughnuts, sucking in air to cool the coffee. They tucked the rest of the doughnuts and the sandwiches in their jacket pockets, ground the empty cups down into the weeds and kicked dirt over them.

"We need blanket rolls," Lee said, glancing at the meager canvas bundle Morgan carried. "Some food staples, couple of cook pans. Too risky to eat in restaurants. The less we're seen the better."

Morgan had stopped and was listening. Then Lee heard it too, the wailing whistle of an approaching train, and across a winter-brown field they could see the raised track bed. They left the road, crossed the field running, crouched low beside the track. They had no way to know if the train would slow, but here on the industrial outskirts it was likely. They could hear the rumble in the tracks now, they watched the black speck grow nearer. "It'll be different this time,"

Lee said. "If it only slows some, we'll have to run like hell."

Approaching the steel plant the train dropped its speed, its whistle screaming short, hard blasts. They could see it didn't mean to stop. As the engine sped by, Lee picked a car and ran, gave it all he had. He grabbed the iron rung and jumped. The forward momentum slammed his body against the ladder knocking the wind out. He held tight, gasping for breath. When he looked back, Morgan was still running, losing ground trying to make the next car, a flatcar with a row of heavy crates down the center covered by a canvas tarp. Lee was about to drop off again, keep from getting separated, when a man appeared from under the canvas, knelt, grabbed Morgan's hand, and lofted him up onto the flatcar.

The hobo and Morgan stood beside the canvas tarp looking up along the cars at Lee. Carefully he worked his way along the side of the car to the back, clinging to the metal handholds, sucking air, trying to get his breath. He was sweating hard when he'd crossed the swaying coupling to the flatcar. As he scrambled onto it, Morgan and the hobo grabbed his hands to steady him. The hobo was maybe twenty-some, his stubble of beard grizzled brown and gray over thin, caved-in cheeks. He wore loose jeans with threadbare knees, a rusty leather coat, and, on his head, a war surplus helmet liner. "Name's Beanie." He looked Lee over, took another good look at Morgan, seemed comfortable with what he saw. "Come on in, it's nice and warm inside."

They followed him in under the tarp to a small, cozy space between the crates, as snug as a little house. Blanket folded lengthwise to form a sitting pad, a Sterno burner snuffling away under a blackened coffeepot, a second Sterno rig burning under a stewpot that bubbled with meat and vegetables. Lee and Morgan held their hands near the little flames as Beanie dug tin cups, tin plates, and half a loaf of French bread from a canvas duffel.

"Mighty fine camp," Lee said, accepting a plate of hot stew, sitting cross-legged at one end of the pad.

Beanie grinned. "Latched onto this out of Waycross. A fellow learns to make do. Had to roll up camp twice before that, once going through Atlanta—railroad dicks all over the place. Don't know what they were after." He gave Lee a long look. "I dropped off, waited until they checked the cars, slipped back on as she was pulling out." His accent was as Southern as Morgan's, but his diction was not that of most hobos.

Lee was quiet, mopping up gravy with the good French bread. When they were finished he passed

Beanie the bag of doughnuts and settled back against the vibrating crate. "Feels mighty good to have something warm in the belly and a warm, fine shelter."

"It's all woods along here," Beanie said. "The trees in those woods? They're full of Civil War shot. I found an old musket along here once, buried in a trench, nearly all rusted away. I used to make camp along in these woods. There are several old Confederate trenches in there." He looked at Lee. "Guess they fought that war different out in the West where you come from."

Lee nodded. "Most Westerners were for the Union, but a lot of the Western Indian nations, they sent men to fight for the South."

"A terrible war, the Civil War—those old single-shot powder rifles and the cold," Beanie said. "Men froze to death, starved to death, died of infection and every kind of sickness."

"You were in the military," Lee said.

"Career army, starting in World War I. But that's all behind me." He dumped some water from his canteen onto his plate and put it to heat, to wash their dishes. "I'm heading for Memphis, the riverbank south of the bridge, real nice camp there. You're welcome to join me."

Lee smiled. "Not many good camps left anymore. But I guess we'll keep moving."

It was mid-afternoon when they hit the outskirts of Memphis. They said their good-byes to Beanie, knowing they'd likely never meet again. One of those chance encounters you'd carry with you for the rest of your life, a nostalgic and lasting memory that saddened Lee. Dropping off as the train slowed, they hit the ground running.

Cutting away from the track they were soon in a quiet neighborhood of neatly kept houses. Lighted Christmas trees shone in the windows, and beyond the cozy houses were several blocks of small businesses decorated up with candles, holly, red and green lights. Morgan said, "It's nearly Christmas, and they'll be alone . . . except for Becky's family. But not the three of us together." He turned to look at Lee, trying to shake off the loneliness. Up ahead stood a small brick church, its brass cross cutting the low skyline, and on the lawn, racks of used clothing and a small hand-painted sign: THRIFT SHOP.

"Tacky," Morgan said, "old used stuff cluttering up a church yard." But the door of the church basement was framed with Christmas lights, and when they'd moved down the steps and inside, Lee began to grin. The shop had everything they wanted. From the crowded tables they selected four thick blankets, a coffeepot, a saucepan, two tin plates, tin cups, and some soft cotton rope. Lee found a good canteen and a couple of switch-blade knives, which surprised him. He picked up a can of heavy grease to coat their aging waterproof boots, and a couple of burlap feed bags. The two old women who ran the shop sat side by side behind the counter, knitting colored squares for an afghan. Lee remem-bered his mother making afghan squares, as well as quilt squares to be stuffed with goose and duck down, to keep them warm in the harsh Dakota winters.

He paid for the gear, shoved the small stuff in the two gunnysacks except for the knives, which they pocketed. He laid the folded blankets on top, cut the rope in half, and tied the bags closed. Two blocks down the street at a dark little grocery they bought coffee, bacon, bread, a slab of cheese, and four cans of beans. It was dark by the time they'd crossed Memphis and set up camp in a little woods. They cleared a space of brush, made a small campfire, heated up the beans, and made coffee. Morgan said, "Think I'll get to a phone tomorrow, some little store maybe, and call Becky. Let her know we're all right."

"The hell you will."

"The hell I won't. She's got to be worried."

"I told you, no phone calls. The bureau boys have questioned her by now. They sure have her place staked out and her telephone tapped. You phone her, not only will the feds trace the call and find us, pick us up, Becky will be charged with aiding our escape."

"I didn't think," Morgan said, picking up a stick and poking at the coals. "I just—I know she's worried."

"Better worried than getting us caught." Lee doused the fire with the last of the coffee and rolled up in his blankets. "We've got a long pull ahead, important things to do. Let's concentrate on that." He shivered even in the thick blankets. And before they reached warm country again, the weather would get colder. The newspaper Morgan had picked from the trash, in the last town, said the Midwest was having the coldest winter in twenty years. Lee thought about Christmas when he was a kid, snow piled high against the house and barn, great chunks of snow sliding off the steep roofs. A spindly little Christmas tree with homemade paper ornaments. A wild turkey for their Christmas dinner, or one of the pheasants his mother canned, the prairie was overrun with pheasants. That always amused him. Back then, on the prairie, pheasants might be all a starving family had to live on. The exact same delicacy which, not many miles away in some fancy city restaurant, would cost them a small fortune.

From that night on, moving west, they were always cold, slogging through snow in boots that took up water in spite of the aging waterproofing and the grease they applied. They continued to avoid the cities, dropping off the train to circle through farms and open country or through slums. Most of the farms had Christmas lights, as did some of the slum houses. It was in such an area that they faced a surly, mean-tempered drunk and Lee saw in the man's eyes not drunken bleariness but the dark's cold presence, eyes hard with promise as the man crouched, his knife flashing. They dodged, circling him. Lee received a slice across his arm before Morgan had the guy down; and now the man's eyes went dull again, reflecting only the bleary look of a common drunk.

"Why would a bum be interested in us?" Morgan said when they'd turned away. "Do we look like we have money?"

Lee laughed, but he was sickened by what he'd seen in that brief moment. They moved on fast, leaving the drunk sitting against a building, his head in his hands, trying to recover from Morgan's blows. This time the devil's invasion had netted only a cut on Lee's arm. But what about the next time? Good luck they hadn't had to kill the man, Lee thought as he swabbed the wound with the iodine Becky had put in their pack. Sure, drunks got killed in brawls. But he'd rather not leave a dead body marking their trail. That kind of sloppiness annoyed him.

31

Circling the small towns with their Christmas lights, avoiding the switching yards and then racing to grab a train as it pulled out, they missed more than one ride. Often on the ramshackle edge of a town they dodged away from a patrolling cop car, or one slowed, pacing them, watching them. "Plenty of hobos around," Lee said, "they're just checking us out." But the law's scrutiny made him some nervous. In Oklahoma a hard blizzard caught them. The temperature dropped steadily, the chill cut through them like knives. Lee was sick of cold weather, and even Texas was icy. Why did they have to pick the coldest winter of the century? Out of Fort Worth when they missed a westbound, a semi driver picked them up, a slack-faced man with wide-set eyes. He didn't talk much, he just drove, and that was fine with Lee.

But then, after maybe thirty miles he began to ask questions. Lee answered him in one-syllable lies, then started with questions of his own. Were did he hail from? What was he hauling? That shut the man up. Lee pulled his hat over his face and went to sleep. It was some hours later that Morgan nudged him. The trucker had slowed, they were in a little cow town, two blocks of dusty wooden buildings and a small old café marked with a wooden sign: TRAIN STATION. The train track ran behind it, parallel to the highway. The trucker dropped them at the café, drove another eighth of a mile, and turned west on a dirt road that looked like it led to nowhere; maybe he was headed home.

Stepping into the wooden building, sitting on stools at the counter, they treated themselves to fried eggs, fried potatoes, and hot apple pie. The waitress, a pillow-fat blonde in her sixties with an understanding smile, looked them over as she poured their coffee. "The eastbound's due in half an hour," she said. "The westbound, an hour after that." And Lee guessed they weren't the only hobos traveling this route. Finishing their pie and coffee, Lee thanked her for the information, made sure he tipped her, and they hiked out along the train track to a stand of pale trees. Sitting down with their backs against the thick trunk of a giant cottonwood, they made themselves comfortable, listening for the far-off rumble, for a lone and distant whistle.

"It's nearly Christmas Eve," Morgan said. "A few more days. Will they go home to Caroline's or stay at Anne's? Maybe Caroline will drive down from Rome. I hope Sammie will be happy Christmas morning, excited to open a few presents?" he said doubtfully. "What's she seeing in her dreams? Maybe only the good times? Maybe she dreamed of Beanie's warm little house on the flatcar and the good hot stew?"

Lee only looked at him. They both knew Sammie would dream of the bad times, the brutal cold, the man with the knife and evil eyes.

"I can't hold her and comfort her," Morgan said. "I can't help her." He was in a dour mood when they left the cottonwoods running, swinging aboard a boxcar as the approaching train slowed for the small rural station.

Settling back to watch the land roll by, they managed to stay with this freight several days, slipping behind shipping crates when they made a stop. The nights grew warmer, the wind didn't cut like ice, Lee's cough subsided. New Mexico was cool but not freezing. Lee liked seeing sheep grazing, and the herds of antelope that hardly stirred as the train sped past them. Approaching Phoenix, they dropped off the car onto bare red land among the red bluffs and raw canyons. The Arizona sky was blue and clear, buzzards cruising the wind searching for the stink of anything dead. Walking through Phoenix, they replenished their supplies at a small, side-street grocery. Moving on past the freight yards, they saw no sign of cops. On the far side when they slipped aboard, the boxcar was crowded with men settled in small groups. They nodded at Lee and Morgan and didn't seem threatening. Most of them were *braceros*, keeping to themselves. West of Phoenix, Lee began to get nervous.

Maybe he was a fool, wanting to drop off in Blythe, take the chance of being seen. Would the feds figure, once they broke out, he'd head straight there, wanting the money from his savings account? Seemed likely, the way a federal agent's mind worked. He knew he shouldn't risk it, but once they found a lawyer they'd need every penny they could lay hands on, might need that eight hundred real bad to add to the six hundred Becky had scraped together.

He worried about the feds until they reached the desert north of Blythe. As they rolled up their blankets and tied up their packs, the smell of Blythe hit him, the salty tamarisk trees and the damp breath of the irrigation canals. When the train topped a rise, the Colorado River ran below them dark and turgid. They dropped off just outside town when the cars bucked and the train slowed, Lee hit the ground rolling. It was late afternoon. "Christmas Eve," Morgan said. "At least they're together, and with family."

They moved through a willow thicket to an irrigation ditch flowing with dark, fast water. Ragged cotton fields stretched away on both sides. They were past Delgado Ranch, three fourths of the way to town. It had been nearly a year since Lee pulled into Blythe straight out of the federal pen at McNeil, ready to go to work for Jake Ellson, thinking even that first day how he could cheat Ellson. In the end, he hadn't had the stomach for that.

On the bank of the irrigation ditch Lee dug the bar of soap from the burlap bag, the razor and the little mirror Becky had packed. Stripping off their clothes they bathed and shaved in the swift cold water. With the last of the soap they scrubbed their shirts, socks, and shorts, hung them on willow branches, and sat on a blanket letting the sun dry their wet bodies. Not a soul out there, only the lizards to see their white nakedness. Twice, jackrabbits leaped out in the fields and went racing away, stirring a cloud of dust. Both times, a second dust cloud followed, dodging and doubling close on the rabbit's tail—but they could see no second beast chasing. Nothing, just the detached swirl of dust pursuing the rabbit. Morgan turned to Lee, puzzled. Lee frowned and shrugged. "The wind, I guess." Did the ghost cat have to be such a show-off?

When their clothes were nearly dry they smoothed out the wrinkles and dressed again. The winter sun was setting as they made camp beneath the scruffy willows. The small clearing reminded Lee of the meadow where he'd kept the gray for a few days, the gelding that had helped him pull off the bank robbery. The good horse he'd used to get the stolen money away, to where he could bury it. He thought about riding the gray along the riverbank in the evenings, peaceful and serene, and that had been a good time.

They cooked a meal of Spam and potatoes, and made coffee, Morgan missing Becky and Sammie, Lee edgy with the prospect of entering the bank. "We'll have to lay over tomorrow," he said nervously. He'd prefer to get it over with. "Everything closed, Christmas Day."

"A day to give thanks," Morgan said. "To go to church with your family."

Lee looked at him and said nothing. When he was small they seldom went to church; it was half a day's ride away. His mother had read the Bible. His father didn't want to listen. Lee wasn't sure just what his pa thought about such matters. But Lee knew—he'd better know, after his own encounters—that there was more in the universe than a person saw. That amazements waited beyond this life, which a mortal might not want to consider.

"Early the morning after Christmas," Lee said, "we head into Blythe. We'll leave our gear here. If luck's with us, we won't need it anymore." Rolling into his blanket, he tried not to think about lying idle for a whole day. Tried not to think about entering Blythe, about what might happen, tried not to borrow trouble.

32

The Christmas tree shone bright in the Chesserson living room with its many-colored lights, its red and golden balls, silver ropes and bright tinsel. Sammie seemed hardly to notice the tree, nor did she gently rattle the colorful packages. This wasn't Christmas Eve. Christmas would be when Daddy came home. For days her stubborn spirit had remained with Morgan and Lee aboard a speeding train or walking cold beside the highway, two lone men crossing the vast, empty land.

When Anne put a Christmas record on to play softly, Sammie didn't want to hear the music. Rolling over on the couch she pulled the afghan over her face, pretending to sleep. In the dark beneath the cover she lay thinking of Christmas when she was little, when Daddy was there. When they were together in their own house decorating their own tree or having supper at Caroline's among the scents of Christmas baking. The music, then, had been wonderful, the boys' choir Sammie loved, the church music, but now music only brought tears. This Christmas week, her mother had gone to church several times, but Sammie didn't want to go, she didn't want to see the life-sized crèche or hear the story of the Christ child, they only made her sad.

Caroline drove down on Christmas Eve after making her last deliveries. They had arranged the dining table so they could see not only the living room fire but the Christmas tree. Though they sat down to a supper of Mariol's good shrimp gumbo, a fresh salad, and Caroline's pecan pie, Sammie was quiet and unresponsive. Only later, when she was given no choice but to share her bed with Grandma, had she snuggled down against Caroline.

Sammie was equally quiet Christmas morning, was slow getting up and dressing. Upstairs, even Mariol's baked eggs and cheese grits failed to cheer her. She was far away with her daddy and Lee, the night still dark on the desert, the low moon brightening the pale sand.

Mariol had laid a fire on the hearth, its flames reflecting rainbows among the bright decorations. Sammie tried to be cheerful. She looked up into the tree, touched a few boxes, and smiled at the adults, but she was only pretending. The joy they had hoped would blossom this morning was a thin parody. They could only be there for her, love her, could only try to ease her worry.

When she opened her presents, the Little House books Becky had bought for her, and the new winter coat in a soft, cozy red that was Sammie's favorite color, she pretended excitement. She tried the coat on and twirled around, smiling. She read the first pages of the first book, but her preoccupation and distress filled the room. Caroline had brought her a new bike, as Sammie had outgrown her small one. Anne and Mariol had chosen a small, carved chest from Anne's attic that had been in the family since Anne was a child, and had filled it with new drawing pads, crayons, colored pencils, and a watercolor set. Sammie tore off the wrappings, pretending excitement. She straddled the bike with its red ribbon tied to the handlebars. But her spirit walked the lonely roads, slept cold on the rumbling trains. It was not until later that morning when all the gifts had been unwrapped that suddenly Sammie brightened.

Mariol was putting another log on the fire. The living room was a comfortable shambles of torn Christmas paper, scattered boxes and ribbon. As Mariol rose from the hearth, turning toward the tree, she went hushed and still.

At the base of the tree among tangles of paper the lower branches were moving, branches shifted and sprang back, though there was nothing there to disturb them. A shiny red bell began to swing but nothing had touched it. A golden ball twirled, the tinsel shivered, another branch bowed down as if with a heavy weight.

Mariol didn't move, no one moved or spoke. Becky and Caroline remained intently watching as Sammie slipped toward the tree, reaching.

Anne, not moving from her chair, reached out involuntarily, just as Sammie was reaching; something within her was sharply stirred.

They watched Sammie kneel, holding out her arms, cuddling some invisible presence. The sleeve and collar of Sammie's robe were pulled and stretched as if something unseen scrambled up, to push against her face.

"Christmas ghost," Anne said softly.

They could see only joy in Sammie, bright pleasure as she stroked her invisible visitor. They watched for a long time, the four women silent and unmoving, Sammie hardly aware of them.

When she did look up, her face colored, she didn't know how to explain what was happening, she didn't want to explain.

Mariol said, "There were stories in my family, Cajun stories that ghosts will return on Christmas to be with their family, to share in the joy of the day. Ghosts of children usually, though often of family pets." Mariol looked over at Anne, and they shared a comfortable smile. When Mariol turned away, Anne rose too; soon they all four left the room, left Sammie and her friend to themselves. Only then did the ghost cat make himself seen.

Dropping heavily into Sammie's lap he reached a paw to her cheek. She held him tight and they sat for a long time beneath the bright tree, Sammie stroking, Misto snuggling and purring. And Sammie knew, wherever Daddy and Lee were, that this Christmas morning, for this moment, they were safe, they were all right.

Taking the three hundred dollars from his pocket, Lee handed it to Morgan. They were walking the dusty road, headed into Blythe. "If the feds spot me," Lee said, "you beat it out of there fast. Hop a ride to L.A. and go on with the plan. Find a lawyer you think you can trust, get settled with him, then turn yourself in to T.I. the way we laid it out." He knew it would be easier for Morgan if they stayed together. Lee knew L.A. a bit, he could find his way around the city. If they made it out of Blythe together, maybe their luck would hold.

It was a long walk into Blythe, they'd left well before the sun was up, eating cold Spam and stale crackers as they strode along. By the time they entered town the sun was up, there was traffic on the street, the stores were opening. Lee pulled his hat brim low and scanned the street for anyone he knew, for Jake Ellson's red truck or for Jake himself. When they neared the new bank, Morgan waited in a shop across the street, keeping watch for the law, for a cop or anyone in a suit who looked like a federal agent. The new bank, built after Lee had left Blythe, stood on the cleared site of the old, burned bank, next to the post office he had robbed. Entering the high-ceilinged lobby, Lee tailed onto the shortest line.

They had, before approaching the bank, turned down a side street where they could see several trucks parked behind the shops loaded with crated vegetables, and two refrigerator trucks. "Drivers are stoking up on breakfast," Lee had said, "before they head out." Within ten minutes they had lined up a ride to L.A. Now, in line, he stood tense, ready to move out fast if Morgan slipped in to alert him. Sure as hell, the feds had talked with Lee's PO and knew about his savings account.

Jake Ellson, his friend and boss, would have told them nothing. But his PO would be more than cooperative. Lee could see no back or side door leading out of the lobby, only the front, glass entry. As the man ahead of him finished and turned away counting a handful of bills, the heavy-jowled clerk watched Lee impatiently. "Next?"

Lee pushed his bankbook across the counter. "Like to draw out my savings, close my account."

The clerk looked Lee over, then thumbed open the savings book. "It's been almost a year since the last entry."

"Something wrong with that?"

"No. Just that most folks have more activity in their accounts."

"I've been traveling. Alaska. I'm in kind of a hurry, the wife's waiting."

The clerk started to say something more but changed his mind. "Excuse me for a moment." When he left his window, disappearing into the back, Lee was ready to bolt, to get the hell out of there.

But his quick departure could blow it, if there was nothing wrong. He didn't need a suspicious bank clerk nosing around. Waiting for the man to return, Lee began to fidget, glancing out the front window. When the clerk didn't return, the patrons behind Lee pressed closer, annoyed at the delay. Beyond the big windows, a slowing movement caught Lee's eye, and a police car slid into view, stopping at the curb. Lee forced himself to stay steady, but he was ready to move as one of the two officers got out.

When the officer headed away, down the street, Lee relaxed. The clerk was gone a long time. Some of the men behind Lee moved to another line. He watched the absent cop return carrying a paper bag and two paper cups sealed with paper lids. The cops were pulling away when the clerk did return.

"Sorry for the delay, Mr. Fontana. We've had a bookkeeping change, and what with the move and all . . . It took me a while to find your account and figure up the interest. The total is eight hundred and forty-two dollars. How would you like it?"

"Seven hundreds, the rest in small bills." Lee waited, still strung tight, while the clerk counted out the money. Stuffing it in his pocket he headed for the street. From the far curb, Morgan crossed over to join him.

They moved along the side street to the refrigerator truck parked behind the bank beside the half-dozen other rigs. There were storage sheds and a small warehouse back there, and the rear doors to the post office and small businesses. The driver stood wiping his mouth from breakfast: a young, ruddy-faced fellow with a short beard neatly trimmed, and clear blue eyes. He nodded to Lee, looked Morgan over, nodded again, and they stepped up into the cab.

The ride into L.A. was quiet, the driver uncommunicative. He drove the long rig like he was on a close schedule and didn't need any small talk. Morgan, sitting in the middle, looked white and tense, whether from their companion's aggressive driving or from thinking about turning themselves in, Lee didn't know. They hadn't talked much about that part of the plan, about being back inside prison walls. Morgan hadn't talked too much about facing Falon, but Lee knew he was scared.

Well, hell, they were both nervous. If you weren't nervous, you weren't on your toes. Traveling north, Morgan seemed diverted only by the desert. The flat, pale, treeless land fascinated the Georgia boy, who was used to miles of dense pine woods. The endless flat sand stretching away was foreign and strange. The sudden patches of crops laid on the sand as bright as green carpets were even more unnatural. The groves of tall palms flicking by, their precise rows fanning past at dizzying speed like cards shuffled too fast, all was new and exotic.

Lee dozed over Banning Pass and down into San Bernardino. The big diesel ate up the miles until, in east L.A., they parted from the driver at a wholesale warehouse. They found a bus stop and, jolted in their seats and breathing gas fumes, they arrived at last in downtown L.A. Fog softened the low commercial buildings, and it, too, smelled of gas or of some industrial residue. At the first phone booth they came to, Lee flipped through the yellow pages to the attorneys.

It was all instinct now. Jabbing his finger at a name he liked, he dropped a nickel in the slot. It might take a dozen calls or more before he found a lawyer who sounded right, but he had nothing else to go on.

The first five calls, he couldn't get past cold, officious secretaries. He gave the same story each time: they needed a lawyer to save a man's life, they could pay up front, and the details of the problem were confidential. On the sixth call the secretary, maybe taking pity on the older man's stumbling voice, put him through to Reginald Storm.

Storm sounded calm and direct. Lee remained devious, as circumspect as he could be. He laid out only enough of Morgan's story to stir Storm's interest. Storm asked a number of questions, as if he might be filling in more blanks than Lee liked. He had to convince Storm to see them, had to hint at their escape without telling him much; he couldn't let Storm blow the whistle on them. If the feds grabbed them before they turned themselves in at T.I., there was a chance they'd ship them straight back to Georgia. They talked for maybe twenty minutes, and Storm seemed to really listen. But when he said he'd make time right then, that they could come on up, his willingness put Lee off, left Lee nervous again.

Hanging up, he looked at Morgan. "I think he knows more than I told him, he makes me edgy." He shook his head. "But even so, I like the sound of him. He seems direct and no-nonsense. What do you think, you want to take a chance or forget him, try someone else?"

Morgan thought for only a minute. "We're taking a chance, no matter who we choose. Let's go for it."

Storm had given Lee directions. They walked the seven blocks at double time, Lee praying they weren't walking into trouble, that they'd made the right decision.

Reginald Storm's office was one flight up, in a plain redbrick building that looked clean and well kept. A narrow strip of lawn separated it from the street, bisected by a short walk of pale stone. The four name plaques mounted beside the glassed entry were those of Storm himself, a doctor, an accountant, and an estate attorney—all one might need when contemplating the end of life, except for spiritual attention.

"Come on," Morgan said, heading for the stairs, "before I lose my nerve."

33

Climbing the inner stairs, Lee and Morgan pushed through a second glass door into an office paneled in whitewashed oak. A blond secretary looked up from her desk, frowning at the hobo look of them. At the same moment, Storm appeared through an inner door waving them on past her to his office.

Storm was shorter than Lee, a solid man who looked to be more muscle than fat. Square face, creases at the corners of his gray eyes, the top of his head as bald as a mirror above a thick fringe of brown hair. His gray suit coat was off, hung neatly over the back of his desk chair, his shirtsleeves rolled up, his sinewy arms tanned, his pale blue tie loosened crookedly.

This room, too, was paneled in white-stained oak, with shelves of law books along one wall behind the plain oak desk. Two walls were hung with black-and-white photographs of rugged mountains, snow-covered peaks, and close-ups of rocky escarpments. A U.S. flag and a California State flag stood together in one corner. The windows of the fourth wall were open to the yellow-tinged fog. Storm nodded toward four easy chairs grouped around a conference table, and took a chair himself rather than retreat behind his desk. He sat quietly waiting, looking them over, taking stock of them.

Lee had not given his name on the phone; he'd said that Storm would understand why when they met. Now as he introduced themselves, the lawyer's eyes hardened with recognition.

"Our names were in the L.A. papers?" Lee asked.

"They were. You haven't seen the papers?"

"We've been traveling," Lee said.

Storm waited, quietly watching Lee.

"I don't know how we can convince you of this," Lee said. "In Atlanta, Morgan was doing life plus twenty-five for a robbery and murder he didn't commit. We went over the wall in order to correct that injustice. It would be pretty stupid for us to break out, come clear across the country, and then make ourselves known to a lawyer without a good reason—an honest reason. We'd be crazy to pull a stunt like that unless we're straight."

"And unless you have a plan laid out," Storm said. His hands were relaxed on the chair arms, but Lee could feel his tension. "As I recall," he said, looking at Morgan, "you were convicted for the bank robbery, killing a guard, and badly wounding one of the tellers."

"Wrongly convicted," Morgan said. "I know who robbed the bank and killed the guard. He's now in Terminal Island on an older, land-scam charge committed in San Diego. The other four men had already been indicted when they picked Falon up."

"I know the case," Storm said. He rose and stepped to his desk. When he touched the intercom, they both jerked to attention. They eased back when he said, "Nancy, try to reschedule my next appointment, and hold my calls." He picked up a yellow legal pad and a pen and returned to the table. He watched them carefully as Morgan told his story. Only when Morgan finished did Storm speak again.

"So Falon, who committed the murder, is now a short-termer at T.I. on another charge. You plan to turn yourselves in, where you can get at him before he goes into court on the land scam charge. You think you can make him talk, make him provide new evidence."

Lee nodded. "We mean to try."

"You understand how risky that is. And that, ethically, I should not be a party to your plan," Storm said.

"Also, Falon may not be kept at T.I. for long. He could be shipped off somewhere else. T.I. is still mainly a naval discipline barracks, has been for about three years. The Bureau of Prisons has a small section they use for civilian prisoners, men with federal convictions waiting to be transferred to a permanent facility. And they do keep a few short-termers. They might possibly keep Falon, depending on how crowded that part of the facility is. But you two . . . It isn't likely you'll be there long."

He looked at Lee. "They might keep you, Fontana, to finish out your sentence, or they might send you back to McNeil. But you, Blake . . . That's a medium-security institution, they won't want a man with a brutal murder conviction. I'd say they'll ship you right on out, maybe back to Atlanta or maybe Leavenworth."

"We've got to do this," Morgan said. "Even if we're in T.I. only a few days. It's my only chance, the only chance I've had to get close to Falon. I was locked up before I knew there was a robbery and murder, I've been behind bars ever since."

Storm shook his head. "You know that's coercion. You understand I shouldn't be a party to this. You think in that short time you can corner him, make him tell you where he hid the money? Those are pretty long odds. Slim chance you can even get near him."

"Slim, maybe," Lee said. "But it's what we mean to do. This is our only chance to get to him, where he can't get away."

"Why are you in this, Fontana?"

"It's something that needs doing," Lee said. "The only real evidence will be the money and maybe the gun. The money has to be stashed somewhere, and the most likely place is Georgia. We're guessing he hid it right after the robbery. If he knew, then, that the feds were getting close on the San Diego case, he'd want to ditch it fast before they came nosing around."

"And," Storm said, "there were no witnesses who could identify Falon at the bank? They saw only a man in a stocking mask?" The way Storm was looking at them, Lee thought the lawyer was going to refuse them. "You know the matter of coercion itself could tilt things the wrong way."

"If he bangs *us* up," Lee said, "how can he claim coercion? He could have attacked us, who's to say? If we can find where the money is—hopefully with his prints on it—that's hard evidence. That's what we're after."

Storm sat back, watching them. Lee, despite his own wariness, saw a keen challenge in Storm's gray eyes. "You know," Storm said, "you're putting me in a compromising position. What if you kill him? That makes me an accessory."

"We won't kill him," Lee said. "A dead man can't tell us anything, and he can't confess later. We just plan to scare him real bad."

"You're very confident," Storm said. "You turn yourselves in, Warden Iverson calls Atlanta, tells them he has their escapees, what do you think will happen? They'll make the connection to Falon, even if it takes a couple of days. As soon as Iverson puts it together he'll lock you down and ship you out of there, before he has a mess on his hands."

Storm moved to his desk again and dropped the pad on the blotter. "There's also the matter of your escape. You'll be charged and tried separately for that. I'm sure the brass in Atlanta didn't like you climbing their wall."

Lee grinned and shrugged. "If we can make Falon talk, maybe we won't be charged with escape. Anyway, with the time Morgan's looking at, what are a few years tacked on? He won't be any worse off than he is now. As for me, I'll take my chances."

Storm stood looking at them, his square face solemn. "You walk into T.I., what are you going to tell them? Iverson asks you why you turned yourselves in, what are you going to say?" Lee and Morgan just looked at him. Storm sighed. "You better have a story ready that doesn't involve Falon. And you're not to mention me.

Iverson and I are on good terms. Let's keep that relationship, we're going to need it."

"Then you'll take us on," Lee said.

Storm shifted his weight, put his hands in his pockets. "I've never committed to anything quite like this." He watched them rise. "How are you going to pay me?"

Morgan pulled the six hundred dollars from his pocket. Lee said, "Is that enough to get started, get the trial transcript, make some inquiries, talk to Morgan's Atlanta attorney?"

Storm nodded. He laid the money neatly on the yellow pad.

"Here's Quaker Lowe's phone number and address," Morgan said, handing Storm a battered slip of paper. "When you call him, he'll let Becky know we're safe. She's had a long wait, not hearing from us, a long time to worry. I'd like to know," he said softly, "if my wife and our little girl are all right. Can you get a message to me?"

Storm smiled. "I'll be in touch." They shook hands. "Once you're inside," he said, "you'll each be allowed two calls a week if you're in good standing. They'll keep a record of the numbers."

Lee smiled. "We'll let you know as soon as Falon talks."

Storm walked them out, through the outer office past the blond secretary. She watched them with curiosity, turning away only when Storm glanced at her.

Out on the hot L.A. street again, at the covered bus stop, they read the schedule tacked inside. They had half an hour before the bus arrived that would circle out past T.I. They settled down on the wooden bench to wait, not talking, not looking forward to the next step. They were both edgy, afraid they'd be shipped out again before they had a chance at Falon, a chance to get him alone.

The bus ride toward the ocean was hot, the humidity worse inside than on the street, the sky hazy and yellowish. Hot, sulfurous air blew in through the open bus windows. Smog, a passenger said. The result, the thin-looking woman told them, frowning, of too many cars and too many factories. They rolled through Florence sweating, passing row after row of little box houses, then some shops and billiard rooms along Gardena's main street, then more box houses crowded together. They listened to the other passengers complain about the heat, telling each other this wasn't a typical California winter and that they wished they'd get some rain. Not until they crossed a bridge leading to the main gate of Terminal Island did they feel the cool breath of the Pacific. They drank in the smell of the sea, but then came the ripe stink of the commercial fishing boats that nosed farther along the shore. The bus jolted to a stop in front of the federal penitentiary, jerking them hard.

Lee stumbled up and led the way down the steps. They alighted directly in front of the broad gray prison, on the walk that led to the main entrance. Here on the ocean the sky was clear and blue, the smog blown inland behind them. Overhead, wheeling gulls screamed, flaunting their winged freedom. Behind them the bus departed with a motorized fart. This was the first time Lee, in all his long life, had ever asked to be locked behind bars. First time he'd ever entered a federal prison out of choice. "Come on," he said. "We either hike on in or run like hell."

34

Misto drifted out of the bus beside Lee and Morgan just as he had floated into the vehicle and, during their ride through L.A., had snooped among the passengers' belongings and looked out the dirty windows at the city rolling by, at the green hills rising to the east with a glimpse of tile-roofed mansions. Lee's and Morgan's destination of another federal prison didn't thrill the ghost cat. Even though, of the three of them, only he could come and go as he pleased from the regimented environ. He alone could float out from the prison rooftops over the adjacent harbor where sailboats and fishing boats were moored, bristling with masts and sails, and great ships lay at anchor. As Lee and Morgan descended the bus, three young trusties looked up from where they mowed the green lawn;

the smell of freshly cut grass was sharp, mixed with the tang of the sea. Only one guard tower was visible, placed to view the front entry.

At the foot of the concrete steps Lee stood with Morgan before an open metal booth. Inside hung a microphone, with a speaker attached. As Lee reached for the mike, a voice from the speaker barked, "Identify yourselves. State your business."

"Lee Fontana," Lee said, looking up at the tower where the guard held a second mike. "And Morgan Blake. Escapees from the federal pen in Atlanta, come to turn ourselves in."

There was a long silence while the guard looked them over. Lee knew he had sounded an alarm inside the building. No surprise when suddenly the front doors were flung open and four guards burst out crouching, covering them with riot guns.

Their response was so dramatic they made the ghost cat laugh. Lee and Morgan had their hands up and, at the guards' orders, moved on into the prison. Misto floated beside them, protective and amused. He watched as they were searched. Still surrounded by armed guards, they were directed to sit in wooden chairs in front of the warden's office. Misto drifted on in through the warden's closed door, to have a look.

He floated beneath the ceiling of a typical prison office. Dark oak floors, government-green walls, prison-made oak desk and swivel chair, oak book-cases stacked with untidy pamphlets and file folders. Venetian blinds crossed at right angles to the vertical bars that secured the windows. Warden Iverson sat at his desk holding the earpiece of a black telephone as if waiting for his call to be answered. He was a tall, bony man, maybe sixty, pale skin wrinkled over prominent, bony cheeks, a military-short haircut emphasizing his large ears and prominent nose. He wore a brown, light-weight suit, crisp white shirt, and plain brown tie. As soon as he was connected he picked up the tall phone itself, leaned back in his chair, holding the mouthpiece close. Misto lay down atop a stack of reports, careful to disturb nothing, to make no sound. Iverson frowned a little, but had no idea anyone watched him and listened.

"Paulson? John Iverson. We've got your two escapees out here at T.I., they just turned themselves in."

Misto knew Paulson; the Atlanta warden was a slight, quick-tempered man about Iverson's age, a man he'd found was generally respected among Atlanta's prison population.

"What kind of a plant you running," Iverson said dryly, "to let those two go over your wall? I thought you were maximum security back there. You expect me to keep them corralled here? We don't even *have* a wall."

Misto padded up the desk beside Iverson where he could hear Paulson, as well. The Atlanta warden's voice at the other end sounded tinny. "What did they tell you?" he asked. "What crazy reason did they think up for turning themselves in? That old man, Fontana—"

Iverson said, "They told the guard they got tired of your place, said they wanted an ocean view."

Misto was suppressing a cat laugh when he carelessly brushed a pencil from the desk, sent it rolling to the floor. At Iverson's puzzled frown he retreated to the door, sat on the floor as decorous as a trained poodle. Iverson was saying, "You bet I will. When this business of escape has been handled, we'll give Blake an ocean view. Maybe from Alcatraz, they're not real crowded up there." He listened, then, "You'll send me copies of Fontana's record? And Blake's trial transcripts?" He nodded at the phone. "We'll keep Blake locked down until this is sorted out. They'll be confined to the civilian compound."

Again he listened, then, "No, we have plenty of room. The navy's winding down on its detention numbers, we're losing population every day."

He made no mention of Brad Falon. Neither had Paulson. Maybe, Misto thought, they wouldn't discover the relationship right away. Even if, in Atlanta, Paulson had read Morgan's transcript and come across Falon's name as a witness, why would that mean anything to him? He'd had no contact with Falon, Brad Falon had never been in the Atlanta pen.

But somehow, Misto knew, the two wardens would make the connection, it was only a matter of time.

Misto thought, when Iverson hung up, that he'd signal the guards to bring Lee and Morgan in so he could interrogate them, that maybe he'd pick up on the connection right then. He'd have Falon's file, and Falon was from Rome. When he questioned Morgan, he'd learn that Morgan was from Rome, and that was all he'd need. Two Georgia convicts showing up in California, in the same prison, one of them by choice?

Hanging up the receiver, Iverson set the phone down on the desk and looked at his watch. Switching on the intercom, he told the guard to go ahead and process the two escapees. "Let them eat lunch, whatever's left. Get their medical checks, then lock them in their cells." He rose, picked up his briefcase from the desk and added a few papers. Once Iverson had left the building, Misto returned to Lee and Morgan.

Within twenty minutes Lee and Morgan were body searched, had showered, and had dressed in prison blues. Their personal effects were locked in storage. They were marched away for the noon meal before the medical staff checked them over. The civilian unit of the naval disciplinary facility was small, isolated by a locked gate. It had its own small dining room, several rows of single cells and one dormitory. Misto followed them to the cafeteria, where only a few wrapped sandwiches and some desserts were visible, this long after the noon meal. Leaving his charges to partake of the lean pickings, Misto drifted away.

He hovered above groups of inmates, into rows of dull prison offices, through the larger, navy mess hall and the steamy kitchen. Out over the exercise yard, through the auto shop, machine shop, furniture and clothing workrooms, none much different from the other prisons Misto had prowled invisible and often amused. When he returned to the small civilian dining room he found Lee and Morgan alone at a table eating roast beef sandwiches. A guard stood against the wall watching them—and across the room sat Brad Falon at a table with two other inmates, his small eyes narrowed as he, too, watched Lee and Morgan. It had been easier to find Falon than they'd thought. Under the eyes of the guard, they couldn't approach Falon, but Misto had no such restraint.

Drifting close to Falon's face he let his fur brush the convict's cheek. The vibration sent Falon up from the table swatting at empty air. Misto, drifting away, smiled and lashed his tail.

From across the room, Lee watched Falon's gyrations with satisfaction. Morgan watched, perplexed. The guard rounded on Falon, his hand touching his weapon. Falon slapped at the air again, looked sheepishly at the guard, and sat down. But the guard jerked him up, spun him around, and quickly patted him down. Finding no weapon and no drugs, he looked at Falon a long time, then shoved him back in his chair.

Falon's face was flushed. Still the guard watched him. Falon hunched over his plate finishing his coffee and pie. He left the room quickly. Misto abandoned Falon, brushed Lee's arm, and received an amused smile.

It was after lunch when Morgan was locked in his cell, that Lee was ushered by two guards to Warden Iverson's office. He found the warden at his desk, his suit jacket dangling from a prison-made coat tree, his pale tie loosened, his thin, bony face flushed from the heat. "Sit down, Fontana."

Lee sat, in a hard wooden chair facing the desk.

"You want to tell me, Fontana, why you and Blake turned yourselves in? Why you took the trouble to climb the wall—no mean task—why you hitched all the way across the country only to give yourselves up? Headed right back to prison, as docile as starving dogs?"

"I guess that's the way we were feeling," Lee said. "Seemed like, every move we made, every train or truck we hitched, the cops were on our tail. Almost like they were pacing us. They never made a move, but they made us nervous, we couldn't seem to shake them." He looked levelly at the warden. "When we got to California we'd run out of steam. We were hungry and scared, and my emphysema was real bad from that blizzard weather. Right then, prison looked pretty good. Free bed, hot meals, a place to rest and quit running." His lie sounded plausible to him.

"This was the only place we knew," he said, "where the law would back off, stop tailing us, where we could rest easy for a while."

But, watching Iverson, he could see the warden wasn't buying it.

"Why did you scale the wall in the first place? What were you looking for, why make that hard trip all the way out here?" Iverson leaned back, watching him. "What's this really about, Fontana?"

"We thought by the time we got out to the coast we'd lose the tail on us, we'd be home free and could head either down into Mexico or up to Canada, somewhere we might shake the law. But then," Lee said, "by then, I was feeling too sick."

"You were practically *in* Mexico. We know you got off at Blythe, your PO called us. The bank called him. But it took them a while. Before they caught up with you, you could have made it across the border. You knew you had a good chance, right then. But you turned north instead. Why? And what about Blake's wife and child? Did he plan to send for them, down in Mexico? Or never to see them again?"

"He thought he could get them up to Canada," Lee said. "They have relatives up there that he thought would hide them."

Iverson wasn't warming to this.

"By the time we hit L.A.," Lee said, "I didn't think I could make it much farther. That's when Morgan said, 'Let's give it up.' Maybe he did it for me, maybe he thought I might die on him. He knew I'd get medical care in here. He swears not, swears he just didn't want to run anymore." Lee knew he was talking too much. He tried to look sicker than he felt, to look more despondent.

Iverson pressed a buzzer calling a guard, signaling the end of the interview. Did he believe any of what

Lee had told him? "You'll both be confined to the civilian unit. We used to enforce a month's complete isolation to prevent spread of disease, but with the war over and not many men coming in from overseas, we've lightened the rules. You'll see the doctor three times a week. When you're better, you can think about industries, something not too demanding. We like to keep the men busy." He nodded. Lee rose and turned away, meeting the guard at the door.

He was escorted to his cell and locked in, a cell like all the others except this one was cleaner and had the luxury of a small, barred window through which he could see a bit of the ocean. He looked out through the barred glass at a glimpse of the island, of boats and ships, and the mainland beyond. Long Beach, he thought, or maybe San Pedro, and beyond these, the far, green hills.

35

It was the next morning at breakfast that they saw Falon again, sitting alone at a small table as Morgan joined Lee in the chow line. Again Morgan was accompanied by a guard, but the uniformed man didn't linger. He watched them settle at a table, then turned away. Once he'd left the cafeteria, they picked up their trays again and joined Falon.

"Lots of empty tables. Go sit somewhere else."

"Does it bother you," Morgan asked, "to sit with the man you framed?"

"What're you doing here, Blake? What kind of stupid stunt was that, to break out, make it across the country, and then turn yourselves in? You get scared out in the big world, Morgy boy? Lose your nerve? What, were the feds on your tail? You crawl to them like a beaten dog that can't get away?"

Lee laid a hand on Morgan's arm until he eased back. Under the overhead lights the sleeves of Falon's prison shirt sparkled with tiny bits of steel, as if he'd been working the lathe or jigsaw in the metal shop. "Maybe," Lee said, "maybe after we've been here a while, Falon, our escape won't seem so stupid."

"What does that mean, you crazy old creep?" Falon rose, picking up his tray. "You'll stay out of my way, if you plan to leave here in one piece."

Lee smiled. "Doesn't take much to get you fluffed, does it, Falon?"

A wash of red moved up Fallon's face. "I don't know what you want, old man, but you'll be sorry you took up with this punk." They watched him cross the room, shove in where two men had just sat down. In a moment the other two turned, staring at Morgan and Lee.

"I thought it would be simple," Morgan said softly. "I thought when we showed up he'd get scared."

"You knew better than that. You never thought that, you know he's dangerous. Take your time," Lee said, "play it close." Lee was nervous, too, but they needed to move on with this, they didn't have much time. Once Iverson received the paperwork from Atlanta, he'd start putting it together, Morgan's connection to Rome and to Falon, Falon's testimony at Morgan's trial.

It was late that afternoon, after seeing both his doctor and his counselor again, that Lee got permission to work in the metal shop for a half shift. He was in luck, there was an opening, maybe things were turning their way. It was the ghost cat who didn't feel good about the plan.

"This isn't smart," Misto murmured softly, materializing on Lee's bunk. "That shop's dangerous. Falon knows the moves, and you don't."

Lee pulled off his shoes, eased back against the folded pillow. "I'm a quick learner." He stroked the cat's shaggy, invisible fur.

Misto sneezed with disgust. "You blow it in there, you get hurt and it's all over for Morgan, too."

"I don't have a choice. That's where Falon works." He watched the line of pawprints pace neatly down the bed, little indentations appearing one by one. "If I can get Falon alone in there," Lee said, "maybe in one of the storerooms, I can work on him."

"Is that *your* idea? Or is that another dark plan to trap you?" The cat, not waiting for an answer, vanished, hissing. Nothing remained but his anger. Lee stretched out on his bunk listening to the bellow of the foghorns, watching through his barred window the lights of the naval station blurred by mist. The foghorn's eerie cry rang through him like a train whistle, the lonely call he'd followed in his youth, the siren cry that had led him ever deeper into the life he had made for himself.

Every time he was locked up he grew nostalgic for the old times, for the open prairie. No locks, no bars, no one telling him what to do. Every time he was incarcerated he had to get used, all over again, to confinement and too many people and nowhere to get away.

Well, he could have stayed in Atlanta. Could have been out and free in a few months. Now, unless Storm came through not only for Morgan but for Lee himself, a whole new sentence could be tacked on. At his age, no matter how he dreamed of a new life in Mexico, he might never live to see the buried money.

Yet he wouldn't do it any differently, he'd climb that wall again in a damn minute. Coming after Falon was the right thing to do; he felt it in his gut that they were going to free Morgan. That this was what they were meant to do. He lay sleepless a long time listening to the foghorns, assessing just how much pressure it might take to unwind Brad Falon, to force from him the information they needed

36

Lee didn't expect, when he reported for work at the metal plant, to be paired with Falon. He'd only thought to position himself nearby, where he could get at Falon—not where Falon had the split-second upper hand.

The factory was a big, well-lit room with plenty of space between the equipment, but still, it was a dangerous workplace. There was a layout table, and near it a metal shear, a metal break, spot welders, pipe benders, and saws. Falon was working the metal break, pulling a lever that dropped the blade, lethal as a guillotine, onto a sheet of steel. At the far end of the room were paint vats and spraying equipment, and a bake room for drying painted items. The men were making machine parts for the military. As Lee cut across the room toward the glassed-in office at the back, the plant foreman, a broad-hipped man dressed in khaki, came out chewing on an unlit pipe. When he stopped to light up, Lee introduced himself and handed him the note from his counselor. Mr. Randolph glanced at the note, his square cheeks sucking in to get the pipe going. He stuck the paper in his pocket and motioned Lee to follow him, skirting past the layout table to the metal break, where Falon stood watching them.

"Falon will give you instructions," Randolph said, handing Lee a pair of leather gloves. "You'll operate this unit, Falon will work the machine next to you, see that you're doing the job right." He nodded to Lee, turned to leave, then glanced back. "Pay attention, Fontana. That machine's not a toy." He left them, moving on down the room.

As Lee stepped up to the machine Falon smiled, coiled tight as a rattlesnake. "Any retard could run it, old man. Stand in front of the machine. Take a square sheet of metal off that stack. Place the chalk line that runs down the metal directly under the blade, lined up with the line on the table." Falon stared at Lee. "You understand so far? You just step back, old man, reach over your head, and give the lever a hard pull. Don't ever forget to step back," Falon said. "You think you can reach up over your head and pull the lever?"

Lee pulled on the gloves, picked up a square of sheet metal and slid it onto the break table. He lined it up, stepped back, pulled the lever hard, watched the blade strike down powerfully, bending the metal to a neat, ninety-degree angle.

"Try it again."

Lee looked at Falon and reached for another sheet. But when he swung it onto the table it slipped, sliding beyond the raised break. Alarm touched him as he reached to retrieve it, darting his hand beyond the break line. He swung away fast when Falon grabbed the lever. The blade fell, catching the tip of Lee's glove as he jerked his hand out.

Swinging around, he grabbed Falon's collar, threw him against the break, and rammed Falon's arm under the blade, grabbing for the lever. Falon fought him, his face drained white, staring at Lee's hand on the lever. Beyond Falon at the other side of the room, Randolph had his back to them. Lee let Falon lie frozen against the blade until Randolph started to turn, only then did he release Falon. "I see how this thing works, Falon. And I see how you work. I don't think," he said softly, "that I'll have trouble with either one."

The next two days, working with Falon, Lee was mighty careful. He learned some of the other machines under Falon's supervision, learned them all with a wary respect for the man. He didn't like having Falon in a superior position, he hadn't planned on that. As short a time as Falon had been there, he must have sold the foreman a bill of goods—though he did know the equipment. It was the second evening after work that Lee got Falon alone between the buildings and goaded him, told him the feds were still working the case, that they'd picked up new information in Rome, had lined up new witnesses. Told Falon he could soon be arraigned for murder. Falon laughed at him, but Lee could see doubt in his eyes. The third evening, Lee went into the dormitory to locate Falon's cubicle.

The room was a typical military layout, freestanding partitions around the individual bunks, low enough so a guard could look over, high enough to give a man some sense of privacy. Falon was in his cubicle, Lee could see his narrow head and shoulders where he sat on his bunk, his back to Lee, talking with two other inmates. Two sleazy types slouched in the small space, half sitting against the low wall. Lee didn't pause long, but moved on past, smiling now that he knew where he might corner Falon.

But then before Lee could make a move, Morgan got Falon alone. He told Falon that Natalie Hooper was dating several men, said she'd talked pretty freely about the robbery. Told Falon that, with the feds still working the case, if he opened up to the law now, revealed where the money was hidden, they'd go easier on him, maybe he could go for a plea bargain and minimum time.

Of course Falon laughed at him; and with every passing hour the arrival of the court documents drew nearer, the time when Iverson would see their connection to Falon and move them where they couldn't get to him at all. Lee was growing edgy when, the fourth day on the job, Morgan joined him in the lunch line tense with excitement.

"He admitted it," Morgan said softly.

"Keep your voice down," Lee snapped. "Wait until we find a table." He thought Morgan would explode before they got settled. Morgan set down his tray next to Lee's and scooted his chair close, as bright faced as a kid. "I got him alone in the shower room, told him a lot of lies, got him so angry he lost it." Morgan smiled.

"I've seen him do that before, his temper flares, he didn't even hit at me, didn't try to fight, he just went kind of—glazed. Hissed right in my face, 'Damn right I robbed that bank, damn right I shot that guard. What was I supposed to do, old geezer couldn't even get his gun out of the holster.' He admitted it, Lee. Admitted the murder, stealing the money, admitted everything."

"But then," Morgan said, "then he laughed at me. He said, 'What are you going to do about it? You're the one got convicted.'"

"He didn't tell you where the money's hidden," Lee said quietly.

"No, he said he'd never admit anything in court. But it's . . ."

"It's what?" Lee said tiredly.

"It has to be proof. He *told* me. He—"

"But you *have* no proof. It doesn't matter what he tells either of us if we can't come up with the money or the gun. That's the proof. Nothing's any good until we have solid evidence."

"I did the best I could," Morgan said glumly. "I told him if the law could retrieve the money, if he told them where it is, he'd get a lighter sentence."

"You know that's a lot of bull and so does he. The charge for murder, they're not going to plea-bargain that. What did he say then?"

"He said, 'You're the one doing time. I'll be out in a few days.'" Morgan laid down his fork. "I won't let that happen, Lee. I have to make him talk. I tried naming places around Rome where he might have hidden the money, thought maybe he'd give himself away but he didn't. He's too good a liar," Morgan said glumly.

Lee's half-days in the metal shop grew agonizingly long; he was always tense and on guard. Trying to do his job while protecting himself from Falon, he was more bushed after each succeeding shift. He remembered wryly Dr. Floyd's advice to pace himself, to pick jobs that didn't stress him. And then suddenly Falon was taken off the job, he wasn't there when Lee checked in for work.

The foreman said he was being transferred, that Falon would be out of there in a couple of days, and Lee knew the court transcripts had come through. They were moving Falon out fast, before there was trouble. He wondered if they would move Morgan, too.

He finished his shift and then quit his job, forcing his cough, telling the foreman his emphysema was worse, that his chest hurt and he needed to see the doc. When he went on into the medical office he did have a ragged cough and did feel pale and cold, it wasn't hard to feign exhaustion. The examining doctor told him to quit his shift. Lee said he already had. The doc gave him a form with a note on it and sent him to his counselor.

He'd seen John Taylor only once since he and Morgan were checked in. Taylor was a short, tight-knit man, well tanned, who'd seemed fair enough with Lee. He nodded, signed and filed the form, and didn't suggest that Lee look for another job. It was that afternoon that Lee returned to the metal plant one last time.

The shift changed at four, men were leaving the industry shops. He hoped the metal shop wasn't locked. Earlier, while at work, he had hidden a piece of thin cable under a stack of metal. When he left, there had been too many men around, he couldn't retrieve it. Now he found a guard standing inside the door and gave him a sheepish smile. "I think I left the safety latch off on my machine—I'd like to go back and check it."

The guard looked wary. "Make it quick. The paint crew's cleaning up, I'm about to lock the door."

Lee hurried the length of the plant, past the break. Glancing in the guard's direction, he reached under the stack of metal sheets, scooped up the coiled cable, and slid it under his shirt. He pretended to check his machine, reaching as if to flip a safety latch, then moved on out of the building, nodding to the guard. He was strung tight, hot to get at Falon before he was gone. He told himself to slow down, to work out the moves, don't go off half-cocked. He'd already failed once, earlier in the day when he found Falon alone in the yard and came onto him. Falon had lunged viciously at Lee; he thought Falon had him until three inmates appeared from among the buildings, talking and laughing, and Falon had to back off.

They had little time to make Falon talk before the paperwork arrived from Atlanta. Lee didn't sleep well that night, and the next day he overheard from a guard that Falon's transfer to L.A. county jail was being processed in connection with the land-scam trial. Blake was so wild to get at Falon that Lee knew he should have kept his mouth shut, knew this could blow up in their faces—and the next afternoon, it did blow. Blew sky high, shutting down the entire prison, leaving Lee shocked, panicked, unable to do anything to help Morgan.

He was cutting across the yard when a small scuffing behind him made him pause, the sound of running feet made him spin around. Two guards came racing between the buildings, and behind them two white-coated medics moving fast carrying a stretcher with a body strapped to it. Lee saw blood, got a glimpse of Morgan's face, a gash across his forehead spurting blood. Lee ran, caught up with them just outside the medical ward. Morgan's head was drenched with blood, his face gray and still. Lee bent over him searching for a spark of life. The guards shoved him away hard, double-timed in through the ward door, and slammed it in his face. Lee heard the lock slide home.

37

Lee waited a long time by the infirmary door before the two guards came out again. When he tried to question them they would say nothing, they turned away, ignoring him. When a medic came out hurrying past, he wouldn't talk to Lee, either. No one would tell him anything, he didn't know whether Morgan was dead or alive. He was scared as hell and boiling with rage when he headed for Falon's dorm; he had a hunch the little scum would go to ground right there lounging on his bunk as if he'd been idling about for hours. Even as Lee entered the building he could hear Falon's laugh.

Telling himself to take it easy, cool down and not blow this, he moved silently along the hall past a short turn to the showers, past the doors to a janitor's room and a supply closet. He tried both doors, silently turning the knobs knowing they'd be locked. Janitor's room was locked, all right, but Lee paused, startled, when the door to the supply closet swung in. Shelves of sheets, blankets, towels pale in the dim light from the hall. He located the light switch but left it off, left the door barely cracked open. Moving on, he stood against the wall outside the open door to the dormitory, glancing in.

Above the low barriers he could just see just the top of Falon's head, and again his two friends stood leaning against the wall. Was that Falon's mode when he was in prison, to collect two or three sleazy sidekicks to play lackey for him? The pudgy kid was crossing his eyes and staggering around with his tongue out, grinning evilly.

"Knock it off," Falon snapped. He rose and pulled off his prison shirt, dark with bloodstains. "Now," he said softly, "I can't wait to bust the *old* son of a bitch. Hand me that towel and the soap—no, the big bar." Carrying the soiled shirt under his towel, he headed for the door. Lee drew back, stepped into the supply closet, and eased the door closed.

When Falon had passed, Lee followed, his bridled anger making his heart pound. Followed Falon down the short corridor to the showers. Just before Falon entered the tiled room, Lee grabbed his shoulder and swung him around. Falon lunged for Lee's throat. Stepping back fast, Lee judged his distance, brought his foot crashing into Falon's crotch. Falon doubled over holding himself, groaning, rocking back and forth.

It took all Lee's strength to drag him to the supply room and shove him inside; Falon sprawled on the floor, still holding himself. Lee pulled the door closed, switched on the light, and straddled Falon, whipping the cable around his neck. The man was hurting too bad to fight much, his blows were weak and off center. Lee locked his knees, pinning Falon's arms, tightening the cable around his throat. Writhing, Falon began to choke.

"I've killed men like this before, Falon. It isn't hard to do."

When he saw Falon was strangling he loosened the cable a little, let him gulp a breath, then tightened it again. "Tell me where you hid the money."

Falon slammed his body against Lee's imprisoning legs. Lee tightened the cable until Falon's face grew red, sucking for breath.

"What's the matter, Falon? You can't talk? Well, that's all right, just tap with your hand when you're ready to tell me and I'll loosen your tie."

Falon didn't respond. Lee increased the pressure, sinking the cable deeper. "Talk to me. Tell me where you hid the money." He pulled again, carefully. If he killed Falon, it would be all over. Nervous sweat ran down Lee's face. "Tell me or you're finished. Where's the bank money?" As he tightened the cable again a hot desire surged through Lee, to see Falon die, a viciousness that was not part of his plan. He fought to hold himself in check, tightening the cable only slowly. "Where?" he hissed. "Where did you hide it?" He felt himself losing control, filled with a hunger that was not his own, suddenly wild to kill, drawing the cable too tight. Falon's eyes began to bulge; fear made Lee loosen the cable, he watched Falon suck in air. Would Falon die before he talked? Tighter, gently tighter . . .

Falon gave a weak tap on his arm, staring up blearily at him. Lee released the pressure and leaned close, straining to hear.

"Georgia," Falon rasped. "North of Rome."

"Where north of Rome? Tell me where, or you're dead."

Falon's look became pleading. "You'll be getting out soon. I can't get at the money, but I know someone who can. I'll split it with you, I'll have them put it in a bank, send you the deposit book. Half of all the money, Fontana."

"That's hogwash." But even so, a hot greed hit Lee, his blood quickened at easy money. Shaking off the dark hunger, he pulled the cable and twisted and felt Falon's body jerk. "Tell me where. I don't want your deal."

Watching Lee, Falon grabbed at the cable. "North . . . North of Rome. Tur . . . Turkey Mountain Ridge," he whispered, gasping.

"Where is that? Where on the ridge?"

"Morgan will know," Falon said, choking. "East side—old homeplace."

"Where on the homeplace?"

Silence. Lee shoved his knee in Falon's belly, pulling . . .

"The bot . . . bottom of the well . . . abandoned well."

"Does anyone else know?

"No."

"Natalie Hooper?" Lee said, easing off a little.

"Not her, she'd have gone for it." Falon's eyes were begging. "Half the money if you let me live. We'll go together when I get out, I'll show you where."

"I don't need you to show me anything. If you're telling the truth," Lee said, shifting his weight but still holding Falon pinned. "You nearly killed Morgan. Now you're going to talk to the law, tell them where to find the money. You're going to do it now, tonight. You're going to swear to me, Falon, that you'll tell the law the whole story." He tightened the cable again. "If it's there, it should take only a few hours to find it. If you're lying, if they don't find anything, I'll kill you before you're out of here."

"I—I'll tell them," Falon wheezed.

There was little more Lee could do. He removed the cable, revealing angry red lines circling Falon's throat. "You go back on me, Falon, you refuse to talk, you're dead."

He knew Falon would sing a different tune as soon as he felt secure. "Once I talk to the warden, they won't release you until you tell what you know. And it better be straight talk." Lee stood up, coiled the cable, and dropped it in his pocket. Falon didn't rise, he rolled over, avoiding pressure on his tender crotch and one hand caressing his throat. Lee flipped off the light, casting the storeroom in blackness, peered out to check the hall, then left, shutting the door behind him. It must be nearly an hour since Morgan was taken to the infirmary. He wanted to go back there, wanted to see Morgan, but instead he headed for the administration building, before his counselor left for the day.

There had been no lockdown, no Klaxon, though he saw guards everywhere. He found John Taylor still at his desk, putting away files. Lee approached the desk, his adrenaline pumping hard. "I know it's late in the day, but it's important."

Taylor gestured for him to sit down.

Reaching in his pocket, Lee dropped Reginald Storm's business card on the desk. "Storm is my attorney and Morgan's. We need him bad, tonight. Could you call him, ask if he could come on out?"

Taylor studied Lee. "Why the hurry? I know Blake was taken to the infirmary. Tell me what's going on. Why suddenly an attorney?"

"*Because* Blake's hurt," Lee said. "I need to talk with Storm. In person, not on the phone. Afterward, Storm will fill you in."

Taylor sat watching him. Lee could read nothing in his expression. "How bad is he?" Lee said warily. "He's not . . . They wouldn't tell me a damn thing."

"He has a concussion. He's conscious only some of the time. They're doing their best to keep him awake, there's an orderly with him." He looked again at the attorney's card. "Tell me what's going on, and I'll see about calling Storm."

"I'll tell you after you call him. I promise you that. This could mean Morgan's life, if he makes it, there in the infirmary. This could mean the rest of his life."

Taylor was silent again. Lee wondered how straight the young man would be, how much he could trust him. "I can tell you this," Lee said, "it was Brad Falon who attacked Blake." He was taking a chance on this. If they locked Falon down, and they sure as hell would, and if Falon had lied to him, Lee couldn't get at him again.

On the other hand, Falon couldn't get at Morgan, either.

Still Taylor said nothing.

"New information has come to light," Lee said. "Evidence that could clear Morgan of all charges, that could free him . . . If he lives," he said softly.

Taylor looked tired suddenly, looked knowing and weary. Lee thought he was going to refuse. But prisoners *were* allowed two phone calls a week, and so far he hadn't made any calls. He looked steadily at Taylor until, sighing, Taylor ran a hand through his crew cut hair, set Storm's card before him and picked up the phone.

Lee and Storm sat in the prison interviewing room. Two folding metal chairs and a scarred oak table, on which Storm had dropped his briefcase. A guard was stationed outside the door. Storm looked like he'd already put in a hard day. His rumpled suit coat hung crookedly over the back of his chair, his tie hung loose, his shirtsleeves were rolled up. When Lee told him Falon had spilled, had revealed where the bank money was hidden, a grin transformed Storm's tired, rugged face.

It had taken the attorney only twenty minutes to get out to the prison from downtown. In that time, Lee had returned to the infirmary hoping to see Morgan, but he wasn't allowed in. He did get one of the medics to talk to him. The freckled, towheaded medic told him, "Blake's alive. In and out of consciousness. We're doing our best to keep him awake, he sure has a concussion."

But no one would let Lee see him. Did they think Lee himself might have bashed Morgan? All Lee could think was, Morgan *had* to recover. They'd come this far, they were so close. Morgan wouldn't give up, Lee couldn't let him give up.

Now, across the table, Storm said, "If the money's there, if the feds and Georgia Bureau of Investigation can find it, can identify it as the bank money, we'll have enough for a new trial. With an honest jury, we'll have enough to hang Falon."

"They'll fly Morgan back to Rome, for a new trial?"

"Let's find the money. If it's there, if we can put together a solid case, I'd rather transfer jurisdiction out here to L.A. I think Lowe would, too." Storm leaned back in the hard, folding chair. "I've talked with Lowe. The picture I get, Rome is a small town with a mind-set dead against Morgan. That can happen, you get that kind of thinking started, it's hard to reverse. Lowe doubted that with the lies and trumped-up evidence, they could *find* an impartial jury. And the federal court in Atlanta is booked six months ahead.

"Another thing," Storm said, "as violent as Falon seems to be, it would be safer to keep him locked down here than to transport him back to Georgia." Storm glanced at his watch. "Nearly midnight in Atlanta, but I'll call Quaker. Once he's contacted the FBI and GBI, I'm hoping they'll head right on up to Turkey Mountain Ridge. Meantime," he said, "I'll call the bureau here, I know a couple of the agents. See if I can get them out here tonight to meet me, to talk with Falon.

"And," he said, "I'd like to know the details of what Falon did to Morgan, I'd like to file a charge."

"As soon as Morgan's conscious long enough to talk," Lee said. "As soon as he *can* tell us. I knew nothing until I saw him on the stretcher, headed for the infirmary. They wouldn't let me near him."

"As for what *you* did to *Falon*," Storm said, his gray eyes amused, "I don't know anything about that."

"While they search for the money," Lee said, "will Falon's transfer be postponed?"

"I'd guess it would. In the morning I'll talk with Warden Iverson." Rising, Storm picked up his briefcase.

"And you'll call Becky?" Lee said, pushing back his chair. "Tell her Morgan's hurt? You can break it to her more gently than when the prison calls. Tell her I'm . . ." He winced at the inadequacy of saying he was sorry. There were no words to undo what had happened. Lee had talked Morgan into this trip, into harassing Falon. He might have talked Morgan into his last trip. Sure as hell, Becky would see it that way.

Leaving the interviewing room, Lee shook Storm's hand, mighty thankful for the day he'd flipped through the L.A. phone book and, with luck and the grace of God, had gotten through to Reginald Storm.

But, stepping out into the hall where the guard stood waiting, Lee wondered if he'd had other help as well. Wondered, as crazy as it seemed, if the yellow tomcat had guided his hand as he ran his finger down the page of that battered phone book and stopped at the name Storm.

Then he wondered if Sammie already knew about her daddy. Had she waked seeing Morgan on the stretcher, awakened from her dream crying out for him?

Returning to his cell, lying back listening to the foghorns, all he could do now was wait—wait until the bureau interrogated Falon, wait until the feds had found the money—hope to hell they'd find it. Wait until he could see Morgan. Wait, and try not to think how this would all end.

38

A single light burned behind the hospital bed, illu-
minating the white bandage that circled Morgan's
scalp. Light caught across his stubble of beard and
picked out the IV tube that ran down his arm, draining
through a needle into the vein of his wrist. Lee couldn't
see Morgan breathing, couldn't see the blanket move,
but each time he laid his fingers along Morgan's free
wrist he found a faint pulse. Morgan had been unconscious all night and it was now nearly noon, the high
sun slanting down through the half-closed Venetian
blinds of the small hospital room. Lee sat in a wooden
chair beside the bed, his knees pressed against the
metal rail, talking; he'd been talking most of the night.
Except for a short break to eat the breakfast an orderly
had brought him, and for a brief nap on the other bed.

A few minutes' sleep, then he'd risen to groggily feel Morgan's pulse and to start talking again.

He had no idea if Morgan could hear him. The constant effort wearied him, but Dr. McClure had said to keep talking; he said the sound of Lee's voice could be a lifeline for Morgan. Said the contact between Lee's voice and whatever within Morgan was alert enough to listen might keep him from sinking deeper into an oblivion from which he could not return.

Lee had no idea if that was so. He had no idea how much the medical profession really knew, and how much they could only guess. Dr. McClure was a strange man. You'd think a prison doc would be hardened, that after the twenty years he said he'd spent at T.I., he wouldn't give a damn who lived and who died. But McClure's sad, dark eyes under those bushy brows had shown Lee a whole world of caring inside that middle-aged, pudgy man. "Talk to him, Fontana. If you're his friend and you want to help him live, talk to him and keep talking."

"But he can't—"

"You don't know what he can hear. There's a lot in this world we don't know, maybe a lot we'll never know. I say he can hear you and that talking to him might keep him alive. Sit here and talk, as long as you can, no matter how foolish that seems."

So Lee talked. McClure had gotten permission for him to stay with Morgan. The orderlies and male nurses moved around Lee doing their work, silently accepting his presence. Lee told Morgan over and over that Falon had spilled, had confessed where the money was hidden. He just hoped Falon wasn't lying. He told Morgan that FBI and GBI agents were already on their way up Turkey Mountain Ridge to look for the evidence, for the proof that could clear Morgan—that could put Falon on trial for the robbery and murder. In between telling him about Falon, Lee talked about anything he could think of just to keep going; he dredged up memories that, after several hours, turned his voice rough and straining.

He told Morgan about life in South Dakota when he was a kid, how he broke his first colt when he was eight. How he'd hobbled the youngster, dragged an old jacket over his neck and back and legs until the colt no longer snorted and bolted, how the colt finally settled down to lead. He told Morgan about spring roundup, how the steers and cows would hide among the mesquite or down in a draw and you had to rout them out. How the ranchers all helped each other rounding up the cattle, separating out their own stock during branding. The scenes of roundup came back so clearly, he recalled scanning the far hills where you could barely pick out a few head of steers, watching them slip away among the brush as a rider or two eased after them. He could still hear the calves bawling during the sorting and branding, could still smell the burning hair and skin under the smoking iron, though it didn't hurt them but for a minute or two.

Sometimes, as Lee talked, he was aware of another presence, a warmth between the comatose man and himself, the touch of rough fur against his hand, and he could hear soft purring as the ghost cat pressed against Morgan. It seemed to Lee then that he could see the faintest of color in Morgan's white, cold cheeks. Lee knew as well when the ghost cat had gone and wondered if he was with Sammie. He remembered Morgan's description of Sammie's sickness when Morgan, after the bank robbery, had been left drugged and unconscious in the backseat of his car, and Sammie herself was unable to stay awake. Now, with Morgan in a coma, was the child again lost in darkness? As Lee kept talking, hoping to reach Morgan, was he reaching out to Sammie, too?

He told Morgan about his first train jobs, when he was barely seventeen, described how his chestnut mare would race alongside the engine keeping close to it as he dove off her back onto a moving car, how he'd taught her to follow the train, waiting for him.

He tried to explain the fascination of the old steam trains, to describe his excitement when he, just a kid, was able to stop a whole train and haul away its riches. He told Morgan that was the life he'd always wanted, that he'd had no choice—but he knew that wasn't true. No matter what you longed for, you always had a choice.

Late on the second afternoon as dusk crept into the hospital room, Morgan stirred. His free hand moved on the covers, but then went still again. His eyes slit open for an instant unfocused, but then closed. At the same moment the shadows grew heavy around them. Suddenly Lee's rambling voice sounded hollow, sucked into emptiness. The walls had vanished into shadows, the floor had dissolved except for the one ragged section that held Morgan's bed and Lee's chair. They drifted in dark and shifting space.

And Morgan woke, staring at something behind Lee.

Lee turned to face the dark presence looming over them, its cold seeping into Lee's bones. Morgan's hand, then his whole body, grew so cold that Lee scrambled to reach for the call button.

"They won't hear it," said the dark spirit.

"What do you want? Get out of here. What do you want with Morgan, what does he have to do with your vendetta against me? He's not of Dobbs's blood." Lee wanted to lunge at the figure but knew he would grapple empty air.

"Morgan's little girl is of Dobbs's blood. She is descended from Dobbs just as you are. There is no finer prize," Satan said, "than a child. Now, through her father, I will destroy the girl. Through her father and soon through you as well.

"Oh, she dreams of you, Fontana. You *are* her kin. She saw you kill Luke Zigler, she saw his smashed face. She saw you and Morgan scale the wall; she was with you on your journey, suffering every misery you endured; she felt cold fear at the sight of the tramp's switchblade, fear not as an adult would experience but as a child knows terror. Her pain, as she watched, is most satisfying.

"She saw you pull the cable around Falon's throat, she felt your urge to kill him, she watched you smile and pull the cable tighter."

Lee's helplessness, his inability to drive back the dark spirit, enraged him. Nothing could be so evil as to fill a child with such visions, to torment a little girl with an adult's lust.

But at Lee's thought, the invader shifted. "*I* do not give the child her nightmares," Satan snapped. "*I* have no control over her dreams."

"How could she see such things if the dreams don't come from you?"

The shadow faded, then darkened again. "*I do not shape her dreams,*" he repeated testily. "I do not control her fantasies."

But then he laughed. "Soon I *will* control them, soon I *will* break the force that gives her such visions, and then," he said, "then I *will* shape the images she sees, I *will* shape her fears until, at long last, I use that terror to break her. To own her," Lucifer said with satisfaction.

"In the end," he said, "the child will belong to me. My retribution will be complete. You might resist my challenges, Fontana. You might have won a bargain, as you put it. But Sammie Blake won't win anything. She will soon be my property. As I destroy her father, so I will destroy her. She is my retribution, the final answer to my betrayal by Russell Dobbs."

39

It was early morning in Georgia, the sun just fingering up through dense growths of maples and sourwoods. A Floyd County truck stood parked in the woods at the foot of Turkey Mountain Ridge, its tires leaving a fresh trail along the narrow dirt road. Agents Hillerman and Clark of the FBI and GBI respectively, and Deputy Riker of the Floyd County Sheriff's Department, had already climbed halfway up the steep slope. Sweating in heavy khaki clothing and high, laced boots, they shouldered through thorny tangles and dense, second-growth saplings. Hillerman was perhaps the most uncomfortable in the hot protective clothing, with his thirty pounds of extra weight. Clark, the youngest, was fit and tanned, blond crew cut covered by a sturdy cap, his ruddy face clear and sunny. Each man wore a backpack fitted out with water, snacks, and the tools they would need if they found the hidden well.

Though the three men wielded machetes, cutting away the briars that tripped and clawed at them, still the thorny tangles ripped through their clothing, tearing into their skin leaving their pants and shirts dotted with blood, their hands and legs throbbing. They had driven up the old rutted logging road as far as the truck would go. When the incline grew too steep they had left the vehicle to climb the eastern slope on foot. Riker was in the lead, a rail-thin, leathery man as dry and wrinkled as if the cigarettes he smoked, two packs a day, were surely embalming him. Breathing hard, he led the two men back and forth, tacking across the steep hill searching carefully, stopping often to study the ground, the surrounding growth, and the mountain that rose above them. He was looking for signs of old, rotted fences, abandoned farm tools. He did not smoke while in the woods, he chewed.

Years ago Riker had hunted deer on this mountain. He didn't remember any old homeplace up here, but often all that was left would be a few bramble-covered artifacts or, higher up the hill, fragments of an old rock foundation and the old well, both long ago covered by heavy growth. As they neared the crest he glanced back at the bureau men, cautioned them again to take care. "You step in a hidden well, you fall a hundred feet straight down." They'd climbed in silence for another five minutes when Riker stopped suddenly, stood looking above them where a dozen huge oak trees came into view, towering above small, scrubby saplings.

"There. That'll be it." He moved on quickly, straight up the ridge until it leveled off to flat ground. There was no sign of a house or of fences or foundation, but Riker nodded with satisfaction, stood wiping his forehead with his bandana. "I'd forgotten this place. Watch your step, the well's somewhere close."

Hillerman, the FBI agent, stared around him searching for signs of a homeplace.

"These big old trees," Riker said, "crowding all together in a half circle? That's where the house stood, in their shade. And the brushy land that drops on down? That would have been cleared, that's the garden spot." The other two looked at him, questioning, but Riker knew these woods. And for the past hundred yards they'd been walking over old, worn terraces.

"There would have been crops here, too," Riker said, "corn, beans, more tomatoes, collards. Off to your right," he said, pointing, "those old pear trees gone wild? Someone planted those." He paused beside a low-branched sourwood, took a small folding saw from his pack, and cut three long straight branches so they could feel ahead through the scrub and grass.

"The well won't likely be near the bigger trees," Riker said, "where the roots would grow in." They moved on slowly, poking ahead, doubling back and forth watching the ground. Near the old homeplace, Hillerman shouted.

Riker and Clark joined him. Kneeling, Riker pulled aside a tangle of honeysuckle, revealing the remains of a crumbled stone curb. Carefully they pulled out long, tangled vines, clearing the stone circle beneath. It was some five feet across, the hole in the center yawning black and deep.

The sides of the well were lined with stone, too, the carefully laid rocks gray with moss where Riker shone the beam of his torch down inside. Tying a rope around his waist, handing the ends to Clark and Hillerman, he leaned down in until his light picked out the far, muddy bottom. He moved the beam slowly, looking.

"It's there," Riker said. "The ammo box."

Hillerman fished a coiled rope from his backpack, a treble hook tied at one end, and handed it to Clark. Kneeling beside Riker, the younger man let the coil play out easy, down and down, the swinging steel claw catching torchlight as it bounced against the well's stone and earth sides. When it reached bottom he let it settle, then eased it toward the dark metal box lying deep in the mud against the earthen wall.

It took seven passes, Clark gently finessing the hook, before he snagged one of the two handles. Slowly he pulled the box up, afraid at every move that he'd lose it or it would pop open and spill its contents. Keeping it clear of the edges, he at last lifted the dirt-encrusted ammo box above the well and out over solid ground.

Hillerman had to use the beer opener on his pocket-knife to pry up the two heavy, rusty latches. When he had pulled the lid open the three men, kneeling around the box, looked at each other grinning.

Within lay the bundles of greenbacks, moldy smelling, each secured with a brown paper collar. They touched nothing. Tucked in beside the money was a tightly rolled canvas bag and a dark blue stocking cap. Hillerman picked this up carefully with the point of his knife, held it high, revealing its length, which would easily cover a man's face. Two ragged eyeholes had been cut in one side. Underneath, where he'd removed the cap and bag, lay a .38-caliber revolver.

Pulling on clean cotton gloves, Hillerman dropped the cap, bank bag, and revolver into clean paper bags. Carefully he checked the serial numbers on several of the bills, lifting their edges with the point of his knife.

"Now," the overweight agent said, grinning, "let's see what the lab makes of this."

"The lab and the U.S. attorney," said Riker.

Latching the lid, they placed the box in a larger evidence bag. The agents fitted the bags into their backpacks and, all three smiling, they headed back down the mountain. Ever since Quaker Lowe had filled them in fully on Falon's long record, on Blake's murder trial, and on comments made by prison authorities, and knowing Lowe's honest reputation as a straight shooter, they wanted to see Falon fry. Descending the ridge on the trail they'd partially cleared, Riker said, "That old parolee, the old train robber? Whatever his reasons, if it was Fontana who made Falon talk, I'd say he's earned the court's blessing."

"And maybe the Lord's blessing," said Hillerman, smiling.

40

The ghost cat, lingering unseen on Morgan's bed, was well aware of the search in Georgia and of the morning's find in the old well. He was as pleased as the three lawmen as they moved down the wooded hill packing out the bank money. The cat, lying close to Morgan listening to Lee's verbal marathon, reached out a soft paw whenever Lee started to drift off. He alerted Lee more sharply to any slightest movement as their patient began slowly to return to the living, his spirit reaching up again from the darkness beyond all dark. The yellow cat, lying close to Morgan, knew that Lee's and Morgan's lives had begun to brighten into the shape of hope.

The two men might not yet sense it, but from the time they scaled the wall, all across country and then into T.I., even to Morgan's present battle, the cat knew that hope touched them. He started suddenly, hissing, when an orderly bolted into the room.

The man reached for Lee, his meaty hand on Lee's shoulder. "Phone call, Fontana. It's your lawyer, he said it was urgent."

Rising, Lee headed for the door not knowing whether the man meant Quaker Lowe in Georgia or Reginald Storm, and not wanting to stop and ask. He followed the orderly to an empty office, the young man staying behind Lee, where he was in control. Stepping into the small space, Lee picked up the receiver that lay on the blotter next to the tall black phone.

"Sorry to wake you," Storm said, "I know it's early. Quaker just called. They've got the bank money. A sheriff's deputy went up Turkey Mountain Ridge this morning with two agents. They found the old home-place, the old dry well, the ammo box there at the bottom. The money, the canvas bags. They found the gun, Lee."

Lee stood grinning, clutching the receiver tight, as if it and Storm's words might vanish.

"The bank has records of some of the packs of bills," Storm said. "The bureau has lifted a number of Falon's prints, that match those from the L.A. files. And ballistics is working on the gun. They even found the mask he wore, that wool cap with the eyeholes."

"I can't believe it, I can't believe our good luck."

Storm laughed. "We're on our way, Lee. We have something to work on, you're on your way to court."

"If anything can rouse Morgan," Lee said, sitting down at the desk to steady himself, "this will wake him."

"This," Storm said, "and the sight of Becky and Sammie, in the morning. They're flying out today, the first flight they could get. Lowe said Becky's been really down, worrying about Morgan. Said with this news, she's not so furious anymore, at the two of you."

That made Lee smile wryly, almost tenderly.

"They have a number of layovers, they'll be in around midnight. I'll pick them up, get them settled in a motel over there near the prison. Becky's aunt paid for the flight," Storm said. "I guess Becky argued, but she didn't have much choice." There was a smile in Storm's voice. "Lowe says her aunt Anne's a pretty stubborn woman."

That made Lee smile. Storm said, "I'll be over later this morning to talk with Iverson, make sure Falon's . . . satisfactorily detained," he said with amusement. "How's Morgan doing?"

"Some better," Lee said. "He wakes a little some-times, and his sleep seems more normal. Maybe this news will bring him around. The wound's beginning to heal, the swelling's going down, they can't detect any inner bleeding. I want to thank you," Lee said, "for getting Iverson to let me stay with him."

"That was Dr. McClure's doing. Maybe by the time we get this on the docket Morgan will be raring to get into the courtroom. I just hope we can transfer jurisdic-tion. Lowe's working with the U.S. attorneys on that. If Falon's arraigned and tried out here, and if he doesn't ask for a jury, that's our best bet. Our L.A. judges are a pretty good bunch."

Returning to Morgan's room Lee stood looking down at him; laying his hand on Morgan's arm, he told Morgan the news, that the law in Georgia had found the money and gun, told him everything Storm had said. He thought a little color came into Morgan's face, a brief spark of awareness. As Lee talked, the yellow cat suddenly appeared beside Morgan, looking up at Lee, flicking his tail, twitching his whiskers, gazing deep into Lee's eyes. They looked at each other for a long time, the cat filled with triumph and goodness; but when Lee reached to touch him he vanished again. Disappeared flashing Lee a cattish smile, was gone as suddenly as he'd appeared.

Sammie's excited cry jerked Becky upright from napping among the plane's pillows. On the hard seat, Sammie no longer huddled dozing against her. "Wake up!" Sammie demanded again, shaking Becky so hard she knocked their pillows to the floor. "Daddy's awake, he's waking up."

"Shhh," Becky said, hugging the child against her, glancing around at awakened and annoyed passengers. Curious faces rose up from the seats ahead, looking back staring at them. Becky turned away, cuddling Sammie to quiet her. They had left Atlanta in mid-morning, had already changed planes in Dallas, with two more stops ahead before they reached L.A., and every moment of the journey excruciating as they worried over Morgan

"He's awake," Sammie repeated, then, "He knows. Daddy knows they found the money. He's waking up and he knows. Oh, Mama . . ." The child's face was alight, she hugged Becky hard.

"Shhh," Becky said again, "tell me quietly."

"*This* is what it's about," Sammie whispered, sounding very grown-up, "*this* is why they climbed the wall."

Every night since Morgan and Lee escaped, Sammie had cried out in her dreams, afraid and often defiant; she had traveled with them all that long journey, not sleeping much, not eating well. But now, tonight, she seemed stronger. Now it was Becky herself who was shaken and clinging, who needed Sammie to hold her.

Around them passengers continued to stare and some to grumble. Mother and daughter were silent, their tears mingling against each other's faces. When Misto pressed suddenly between them warm and comforting, Sammie put her arms around the ghost cat, too, and smiled contentedly at Becky. Everything was all right now, everything would *be* all right. She hugged Misto. What *should* be would be. Their life, despite the bumps and hurts yet to come, was moving on in the right direction, just as her good cat knew it should.

Lee woke at dawn from a short nap on the empty bed, his wrinkled clothes binding him. He swung to the floor—and there was Becky sitting beside Morgan's bed on the straight wooden chair.

The room was barely light. Morgan had turned on his side, Lee could see the rise and fall of his chest, see the IV tube swing when Morgan shifted his arm. He watched Morgan reach up and tenderly touch Becky's face. Lee wanted to shout and do a little dance. Morgan was awake. He sat silently on the bed, looking.

Becky's navy suit was rumpled from traveling, her eyes red from either crying or fatigue, her dark hair limp around her face. He saw no suitcase, then remembered that Storm had put them in a motel last night. Sammie lay curled up at the foot of Morgan's bed, her head on a pillow so she could see Morgan, her blond hair tumbled across the prison blanket. He remembered how warm she had been the times he had held her, infinitely warm and alive. Sammie's gaze didn't leave Morgan. But slowly Becky looked up at Lee.

It was all there in her face, her pain from the long weeks when she didn't know where they were or what was happening to Morgan, didn't know whether he was alive or dead. Her relief when at last Storm called to say they had turned themselves in, relief that Morgan was alive—and then the phone call that he was injured, that the doctors couldn't wake him. She looked at Lee for a long time in silence, then, "Lee? How did you make him talk?"

Lee smiled. "I had a piece of steel cable. After he hurt Morgan, I showed him how to tie a necktie."

Becky thought about that. She didn't ask any more questions. Lee knew the guards would have found cable marks on Falon's throat. So far no one had hauled him into Iverson about it; he wasn't looking forward to that confrontation.

Maybe Storm's friendship with Warden Iverson had stifled such inquiries. He could only hope so. When he looked again at Becky, there was amusement in her eyes. He grinned back at her, rose, grabbed the clean clothes the orderly had laid out for him, and went down the hall to the shower.

When he returned, Sammie lay snuggled in her daddy's arms, Morgan's face buried against her shoulder. Becky still sat in the chair, her hand lying against Morgan's face, below the bandage. Lee looked at Morgan. "What did Falon hit you with, a brick?"

"A sock full of something hard as hell," Morgan said. "Before I woke, you were talking to me. I kept reaching for your voice, trying to come awake, trying to make sense of what you were saying. Something about horses, about cattle. I kept trying to reach up to you, like swimming up through heavy molasses."

"I figured you'd come awake when you got tired of hearing me."

"You made Falon talk," Morgan said. "The money . . . they have the money? His prints . . . ?" He eased up against the pillows, lifting Sammie with him, holding her close. "When do we go to court?"

"Storm's hoping for a transfer of jurisdiction," Lee said. "An arraignment out here, get it on the L.A. docket. You'll have to be strong enough," he said, "so you don't go to sleep in the courtroom."

41

Three hours before Brad Falon's scheduled move from Terminal Island to L.A. county jail on the land scam charges, the federal grand jury in Los Angeles charged him with bank robbery, murder, assault, and attempted murder. He was taken into L.A. for a preliminary hearing, bail was set at twenty-five thousand dollars, and he was incarcerated, as planned, in the L.A. jail but on the new and more serious offenses. The land matter case was set over until the murder trial was resolved. While the L.A. docket wasn't crowded, it took most of one week to select a jury. Falon felt he had a better chance conning a jury than a federal judge; he'd heard nothing good about this group of judges. Some called them hanging judges, hard-nosed and righteous men who would not understand the finer points of his character.

On the day of the trial Morgan and Lee were seated at the attorney's long mahogany table below the judge's bench. Morgan was a prime witness. He approached the table with the thick, heavy bandage covering the side of his head, walking unsteadily with his hand on the arm of an orderly, and with a deputy marshal following. Even riding in the official car from Terminal Island to L.A. had left him shaky, he was glad Lee was there beside him. Storm wanted Lee at the witness table to back up small incidents in the prison and to corroborate what Morgan might have told him. "You both escaped from Atlanta to bring about this trial," Storm said. "Before this is over you'll both be charged for that escape. You've put a lot on the line, Fontana, you have a right to be here."

Two armed deputy marshals were stationed near the bench, three more behind the jury box. Lee watched Falon ushered in, his ankles and hands shackled. His hair was carefully combed, bushy at the sides, which accentuated his narrow face and close-set eyes. He was seated at the next table with his own attorney, facing the jury box. He had buttoned his prison shirt high at the throat so the angry red wounds didn't show. Turning in his chair he looked smugly at Lee until his attorney, James Ballard, nudged him. Then Falon turned away. Ballard was a portly man with a shaggy fringe of brown hair edging a shiny bald head. He continued to whisper to Falon until Falon looked up at the jury, a bland and gentle expression in his muddy eyes. He had pleaded not guilty on all charges: murder, bank robbery, assault, and the intent of murder.

The mahogany walls of the courtroom were hung with portraits of federal judges, some of whom, by their fancy attire, had lived in the last century. Some looked so tough they made Lee smile. Above the paintings, through the high windows, Lee could see snatches of overcast sky. He half expected to see a feline silhouette padding along the sill. But if Misto was present, Lee guessed he'd be comforting Sammie. In the visitors' gallery, she and Becky sat near the front. Becky sat very straight, one hand fisted tightly in her lap, her other arm around Sammie; Sammie pressed close, watching Lee and her daddy, her face white and still. Her dress was pale blue, smocked down the front as Lee's mother would smock his sisters' dresses. The section was half empty. Looked like a few reporters, with their notepads, and a handful of old folks who might have gathered for the free entertainment.

Lee studied the jury: three women and seven men, one of whom would be an alternate. All looked like good steady citizens, neatly dressed, their expressions heavy with civic responsibility. The bailiff ordered everyone to stand. Judge Crane entered the courtroom from a private door behind the raised bench, a big man with a square, sunburned face, looked like he'd be happier on a sailing ship than confined in the courtroom. But there was something haughty about him, too, something withdrawn that made Lee watch him uneasily.

The judge would not decide Falon's innocence or guilt, the jury would do that. But Judge Crane would decide and pronounce sentence. And even if Falon were found guilty, thus overturning Morgan's conviction, both Lee and Morgan still had to face the judge on charges of escaping from Atlanta. When Lee looked again at Sammie, she sat straighter in her seat; she was not so white, and her arms were akimbo as if she held an imaginary doll. Lee could almost feel the warmth himself as her unseen companion eased the child's fears—fear of what lay ahead, fear of this roomful of strangers who held Morgan's life in their hands.

The trial took three days. The U.S. attorneys in Georgia and in L.A. had agreed that the depositions from the bank employees were sufficient evidence, on top of the bank money, the bank bag, and the gun with Falon's prints. They had not required that the witnesses be flown out from Atlanta. None of the witnesses could have clearly identified Falon, whose face had been hidden beneath the navy blue stocking cap with its two eyeholes. Betty Holmes's deposition stated clearly that she had seen the robber shoot and kill the bank guard. The written statements were long and detailed. There was a deposition, as well, from the shopkeeper across the street from the bank who had seen the getaway car and recorded the license number. It was this, the identification of Morgan's car, that had first led police to increase their hunt for Morgan on the night he disappeared, and that had helped convict him.

Lee didn't take to the U.S. attorney, didn't like his offhand manner. James Heller was a slim man with delicately small hands, pale skin, a high forehead beneath soot-black hair. A fragile-looking fellow who seemed too self-centered when he presented the new evidence, though he was thorough enough. He showed photographs of the gun, the ammo box, the stocking cap, the wrapped packets of money. He passed a set of the photos among the jury, along with copies of the fingerprints found on those items, pointing out that copies of all pertinent material had been furnished, earlier, to both the jury and judge. Only one item lay on the evidence table, near where a deputy marshal was stationed: a small, closed shipping box, securely sealed.

Heller read the report from ballistics that matched riflings from the .38 revolver with the bullet removed from the body of the bank guard. He read into the record statements from the Georgia FBI and GBI agents and deputy sheriff who had recovered the evidence from the old well. He presented Becky's formal complaints and police reports on Falon's harassment, the break-in at her aunt's, and the incident on the bridge outside Rome; all to bring into question Falon's original testimony as a key witness against Morgan. When Heller had finished, the bailiff called FBI agent Karl Hamrick of San Bernardino, and that brought Lee alert, staring. What was this? What was Hamrick doing there?

Hamrick was the agent who had interrogated Lee after he was arrested in Vegas for drunk and disorderly, he had no connection to this case. Lee grew chilled thinking about the grilling Hamrick had laid on him. As the agent entered the courtroom from behind the jury stand Lee wanted to run, to get the hell out of there.

But in a moment Lee relaxed, limp with relief. Hamrick had been stationed in Georgia on a temporary assignment at the time of the bank robbery; he was one of the agents who had originally investigated the case. He could have had no notion, then, that Lee would become involved. In Georgia, he had interviewed Falon after the robbery, as the last person who saw Morgan before the bank went down. And he had run the background check on Falon. Now he presented that to the jury: Falon's past arrests and convictions, his incarcerations back to his Juvenile Hall days, the present indictment against him. When Falon's attorney, Ballard, tried to confuse Hamrick's testimony, Hamrick was calm, collected, and certain in his statements. As Hamrick finished up and left the courtroom he glanced at Lee with only mild interest.

When all evidence had been presented, Falon's portly attorney, wiping a handkerchief over his bald head, impressed on the jury that Morgan's prints, too, were on the revolver. He suggested that Morgan had been an accomplice, that the two had planned the robbery together, that Morgan had waited outside in his car so they could make a quick getaway.

Storm pointed out that Falon could easily have put Morgan's prints on the gun while Morgan was drugged. And that, in the deposition from the store owner across the street from the bank, only one man had entered the car, plunging into the driver's seat and taking off fast. The store owner had not been able to identify the man, it all happened in an instant. It was then that Storm asked the Court if he could perform a demonstration.

When the judge gave permission, Storm asked Brad Falon to stand.

Moving to the evidence table, Storm opened the small shipping box, removed the navy blue stocking cap, and nodded to a deputy. When the deputy walked Falon forward to face the jury, Storm stepped up beside him.

"Would you put on the cap, Mr. Falon?"

Falon just looked at Storm. He had to be instructed three times before he sullenly pulled the cap on, adjusting it just low enough to cover his bushy hair.

"Pull it down over your face, please."

Falon didn't want to do that. The deputy stepped forward and adjusted the cap himself. The holes fit exactly over Falon's close-set eyes.

"If the court please," Storm said, "I would like Morgan Blake, who was originally convicted on this charge, to try on the cap."

The judge nodded. His expression didn't change but, Lee thought, was there a smile in his eyes? Storm motioned Morgan forward to face the jury and gently unwound the bandage from Morgan's head. A large, flat rectangle of tape underneath ran from low on Morgan's forehead up over his shaved crown. Storm reached up, Morgan being taller, and pulled the wool cap gently over Morgan's head. Even with his head shaved, with only a flat layer of tape over his healing wound, it was a difficult fit. Storm had to twist and stretch the cap. When at last he managed to pull the mask down, a ripple of laughter swept the jury.

Morgan could peer out one eyehole, but the other eye was covered. When Storm shifted the cap, only the other eye was visible.

Falon's attorney asked permission to approach. He tried to stretch the cap to fit Morgan; he pulled and tugged but was unable to stretch it sufficiently. Morgan could not see out both eyeholes at once, not without ripping the cap. The jurors continued to smile. When Lee glanced around at Becky, she was smiling, too. Sammie's fist was pressed to her mouth, her eyes dancing, her other arm hugging the unseen cat in a frenzy of triumph.

Falon's attorney, in his closing statement, tried again to implicate Morgan, but now the jury gazed through him. Lee watched with interest as the game played out.

The jury's deliberations took less than an hour. Lee and Morgan waited under guard in a small chamber from which they were returned to the courtroom when the jurors had filed in. Becky and Sammie had gotten a drink of water and returned to their seats. Lee thought, from the way Sammie leaned close against Becky, that the ghost cat had left them. Why would Misto abandon the child at this crucial moment?

Unseen on the judge's bench, Misto sat licking his paw. There beside Judge Crane he had a clear view of the jury, of their faces as they filed in to their seats. A clear view of Brad Falon and his attorney as they rose at the judge's direction, Falon flanked by two deputy marshals. Misto shivered with nerves as the foreman approached the bench, as the short, round man began to read aloud from the paper on which the jury's verdict was written:

"In the case of the *People versus Bradford C. Falon,* on the first count, murder in the first degree, the jury finds the defendant guilty. On the second and third counts, attempted murder, the jury finds the defendant guilty. On the fourth count, felony armed robbery, the jury finds the defendant guilty."

In the gallery a wave of murmurs ran through the spectators; they smiled and whispered to each other. Becky hugged Sammie, crying, their arms tight around each other. At the attorney's table, Morgan wiped away tears. The judge's gavel pounded until he had order; silence filled the chamber. Above the judge's bench where Misto drifted unseen, the tomcat found it hard not to yowl his pleasure in the judge's ear.

But suddenly Falon spun around, dodging the deputies, lunging at Morgan. Morgan swung away, overturning his chair. The deputies moved fast but Lee was closer, he caught Falon around the neck, jerked him backward over the table, held him struggling as the deputies pinned him. Judge Crane had risen, tensed to move, as if the big man burned to deck Falon. Misto, drifting higher, watched the drama with pleasure. The devil had lost this one. He'd lost the court battle. He'd lost whatever use he might make of Brad Falon. Misto watched Falon marched from the courtroom, a deputy on either side gripping his shoulder and arm.

The judge waited until everyone had calmed. He thanked the jurors and dismissed them. He set the next day for sentencing and for the nonjury trial of Lee Fontana and Morgan Blake on the charges of escape. As he rose, those in the courtroom rose. The judge turned away behind the bench heading for his chambers. Only then, with his back turned, did Judge Crane let himself smile. He entered his chambers with a sense of well-being, as entertained as the small and ghostly cat was.

42

As Lee and Morgan entered the U.S. marshal's limo for the drive back to Terminal Island, Becky and Sammie headed for the little motel near the prison, to the room Reginald Storm had reserved for them. Storm had loaned them a car, in a concern for them that extended far beyond that of most lawyers. He had picked them up at the airport in the little green coupe, said he'd just bought a new car and hadn't yet sold the Chevy. His new Buick had been waiting for him, parked at the motel, and he'd handed her the keys to the Chevy. The car was comfortable and clean and was mighty welcome, to get around the streets of L.A., where she'd never been. Now it purred right along to the little restaurant beside their motel, where they'd have an early supper. Becky couldn't stop worrying over what sentence Falon would get, and how much time Lee and Morgan would have to serve for breaking out of Atlanta. As they pushed into the steamy café, into the smell of fried meat and coffee, Sammie said, "I can't eat, Mama. I'm not hungry."

The restaurant was plain, the pine paneling shiny with varnish, the gray linoleum dark where traffic was heaviest. The wooden booths were nearly all empty, only a few early diners: a family with three small noisy children smearing catsup on each other, an old man in a canvas jacket with a torn sleeve, leafing through a stack of newspapers.

"Maybe some warm milk," Becky said, sliding into a booth. Sammie sat across from her huddled into herself, pushing away the menu the thin waitress brought.

Becky looked at Sammie a long time. "Your daddy's free. This should be a celebration."

"But tomorrow . . ."

"They won't get a long sentence on the escape charge."

"But that Falon . . . Now, tonight, they're all back in prison together. He already tried to kill Daddy, there in the courtroom. What will happen tonight?"

Becky reached to take her hand. "He'll be in jail tonight, not in T.I. He'll be away from Daddy and Lee. And maybe, when he's sentenced . . . Maybe Falon will be in prison for the rest of his life," she said hopefully. She hated that Sammie had to suffer the long day of testimony, the fear, the waiting not knowing what would happen. She started, then laughed when Misto appeared on the back of the booth behind Sammie. He was visible for only a moment, lying along the wooden backrest nuzzling Sammie's neck. When the tomcat vanished again, Becky knew he was still there, the way Sammie was grinning, the way Misto's unseen paw rumpled the collar of her blue dress.

"He wants me to eat, but I'm not hungry." Misto appeared again, hardly a smear of color along the top of the booth, his tail lashing as he pestered at Sammie, his invisible paw teasing a long strand of her hair and tangling it. He didn't leave her alone until she picked up the menu. "I'll have the fries," she told Becky. "And orange juice."

Becky shrugged. Watching Sammie stroke what appeared to be thin air, she was so thankful for Misto; the little spirit loved Sammie, he cheered Sammie in a way neither she nor Morgan could offer: a playful little haunt, concerned and possessive, driving back the darkness that pursued and terrified Sammie.

When their orders came, Becky wasn't sure *she* could eat, her stomach twisting with nerves. She felt such dread that Falon would be released in only a few years, would be free again to come after Morgan. That didn't make sense. Why would Falon get a shorter sentence than Morgan had received? But still, she worried. Adding sugar to her tea, watching Sammie pick at her fries, she wanted to get Sammie into a warm bath and then bed, to have a hot shower herself and crawl in beside her. She'd like to sleep forever and knew she wouldn't sleep, wouldn't stop thinking about tomorrow, couldn't stop her restless mind from demanding answers that wouldn't come any sooner by lying wakeful.

Strangely, she did sleep, and so did Sammie, a deep sleep huddled together, Misto pressed warm against Sammie's shoulder. Morning came too soon, Becky didn't want to get up, didn't want to return to the courtroom, yet she was anxious to be there, to get it over with.

In the plain little restaurant they managed to get down some cereal and milk, then headed for L.A. When they entered the courtroom everyone was standing. Becky, watching Judge Crane emerge from his chambers, tried to put her confidence in the big, sunburned man. But when Brad Falon was led in, handcuffed between two deputy marshals, fear again turned her cold. The fact that Falon had lost, the fact that he'd been convicted of the murder and all charges, didn't ease her fear of him.

Falon's attorney, James Ballard, approached the bench neatly dressed in a pale gray suit, white shirt, and gray tie, his bald head reflecting the courtroom lights. Presenting his closing statement he nodded seriously to Judge Crane. "Your Honor, my client begs your compassion. He has already endured threats and severe emotional stress in prison, at the hands of other inmates," he said, glancing around at Morgan. "Surely the court will agree that with the trauma he has endured at this time in his life, he should receive only a minimum sentence, that he would not be helped by a longer term. That when he did become eligible for parole, the few years remaining would be meaningless to him, he would be a broken man without purpose."

Judge Crane waited patently for Ballard to finish, then let silence fill the courtroom. At last his look cold as stone, he leaned forward to better observe Ballard.

"How much trauma, Mr. Ballard, did Morgan Blake experience when he was imprisoned for a robbery and murder that he did not commit? How much hope for justice did Morgan Blake have?"

Judge Crane leaned back, watching Ballard. "How much hope did the bank guard have when he was murdered in cold blood?" The judge looked so intently at Ballard that Ballard backed away. The judge said no more. He looked around the courtroom, then dismissed Ballard, and summoned Falon to the stand.

Shackled, Falon faced the bench, trying to look mild and submissive. Twice he moved in a strange sidestep and, with his cuffed hands, scratched at his puffy hair. Each time the deputy marshals crowded nearer. The judge watched Falon, puzzled, as Falon fidgeted and tried to be still; it was some time before Judge Crane spoke.

"It is the judgment of this court that defendant Brad Falon be sentenced to twenty-five years on the charge of armed bank robbery. To life imprisonment without parole on the count of first-degree murder, and twenty-five years for assault and attempted murder. These sentences shall run consecutively, not concurrently."

A ripple of voices; a catch of breath from Becky as she looked across at Morgan and half rose, wanting to go to him. Above them Misto drifted unseen over the heads of the deputies and the judge to crouch high on the windowsill watching the drama play out, watching this one perfect moment, in the endless human tangle, play out the way it should.

In the gallery Becky held herself back from running through the gate and throwing her arms around Morgan; Sammie's small hand squeezed her fingers so hard Becky flinched. *Life plus fifty years.* Falon would never be out again to harm them. Barring some change in the law, he would die in prison just as he had meant Morgan to die, behind prison bars.

As Falon was led from the courtroom he looked back belligerently, straight at Becky, arrogant and threatening. Becky watched him coldly. But when Judge Crane looked over at Lee and Morgan, her heart started to pound again.

Morgan took the stand first, and then Lee. The questioning didn't take long. Both men admitted they had escaped from Atlanta. When, at the judge's question, Lee explained in detail how they had gone over the wall, again there was amusement or perhaps challenge in Judge Crane's eyes. When Reginald Storm made his final statement, his voice was soft and in control.

"Your Honor, Mr. Blake and Mr. Fontana did escape. For the express purpose of coming across the country to turn themselves in at Terminal Island, where they knew Brad Falon was incarcerated, where they knew he wouldn't be able to evade them.

"Morgan Blake wanted the truth from Falon, he wanted to see Falon duly tried for the crimes that he committed, for which Morgan had been convicted.

"That has now been accomplished. Blake and Fontana committed no new crimes coming across the country. They lived on the money Mrs. Blake earned and borrowed. They had a destination and a goal. Their efforts, against all odds, have corrected a grave injustice."

Becky's arm was around Sammie, squeezing her close. Judge Crane asked both Morgan and Lee if they had anything further to add. Neither did. When the judge leaned forward, looking down from the bench directly at Lee, Becky couldn't breathe.

"Mr. Fontana, can you tell me why, at Terminal Island, all of a sudden after so long a time, Brad Falon decided to reveal where the stolen money was hidden?"

Becky saw Lee swallow. "At first," Lee said, "we tried to talk with Falon, tried to reason with him. But reasoning didn't work very well. It made Falon so mad that he went after Morgan, he hurt Morgan bad, I didn't know whether he'd live or die. After Morgan was taken to emergency, I found Falon," Lee said, "and I used a little force on him."

"How much force, Mr. Fontana?"

"Enough to scare him," Lee said quietly.

The judge nodded. He didn't press the question. When he glanced up at the defense attorney, Ballard was blank faced and quiet. Becky expected him to pull open Falon's collar and reveal the red marks Lee's cable had made. Ballard didn't, nor did Falon attempt to exhibit the injury. Maybe they knew it wouldn't make any difference, that this judge wouldn't go soft over Falon's pain.

Judge Crane looked back at Lee and Morgan, ready to sentence them. Becky couldn't breathe. She took both Sammie's hands in hers; they were ice-cold.

"Escape is a serious charge, gentlemen. It is not dealt with lightly by this court. However, the statement that Mr. Storm has made on your behalf, and the circumstances of the situation, must be taken into account."

U.S. Attorney Heller approached the bench. The thin, pale man made Becky uncertain. He was not prosecuting Falon now, he was concerned with Lee and Morgan, with their escape from prison. When she looked at Morgan she could see sweat beading his forehead around the white tape.

Heller's narrow back was rigid, where he faced the bench. "Your Honor, Mr. Fontana and Mr. Blake have confessed to breaking out of Atlanta Federal Prison. Their attorney has stated that this was for an admirable cause." The thin, dark-haired man stood silent for a moment, then, in a reedy voice, "The United States Attorney, Your Honor, declines to press charges. We will not seek prosecution in this case."

Becky felt limp. At the witness table Morgan and Lee were very still, watching Heller. As if they couldn't believe his words, as if waiting for the other shoe to drop, waiting for the downside.

"I move, Your Honor, that in light of the present trial of Brad Falon and the jury's verdict of guilty, Morgan Blake's conviction for murder, robbery, and attempted murder be overturned in its entirety. That it be wiped from the books. With the perpetrator in custody and duly sentenced, Mr. Blake should be left with a clean record. I move that he be released from all charges. That, as of this hearing, Morgan Blake be divested of any criminal record."

Morgan put his face in his hands. Lee's arm went around Morgan's shoulders, hugging him. Judge Crane looked down at them.

"Mr. Blake, Mr. Fontana, it has been only a matter of days since you turned yourselves in at Terminal Island. Since that time, you have been waiting, hoping for this hearing. I sentence each of you only to the time you have already been held in custody awaiting trial. As of this moment, Morgan Blake, you are a free man." He nodded to Heller, dismissing him from the bench.

"As for you, Mr. Fontana," Judge Crane said, "you are a riddle. I have your record. I see what you have done in the past, and I can guess there are many crimes for which you were never apprehended. But there is another side to you. You took a grave personal risk to help Morgan Blake. As far as I know, you had nothing to gain by that risk. Now you have a little time left on the term you are serving. And time will be added on for your escape from Atlanta. I rule that both be added to your parole, that you finish your sentence on the outside. With the hope, Mr. Fontana, that this time you will stay out of trouble.

"You will both be returned to the prison long enough to get whatever personal belongings you left there and attend to the paperwork to transfer you out. Mr. Blake, you will have to be released by the medical staff. And Mr. Fontana, you will be interviewed by a probation officer before you leave. Then you're free to go, you'll be on your own." Judge Crane looked them over. "Mr. Blake, your wife and child are waiting for you."

Morgan and Lee thanked Judge Crane. He smiled and nodded and shook hands with them. The look in his eyes was satisfied, a look that said justice had been done despite the bizarre and questionable manner. Lee would always wonder, even years later, what had gone on between Judge Crane, Reginald Storm, and Falon's attorney, that Lee's use of force on Falon had not been further pursued.

When Morgan turned away, Becky and Sammie ran through the gate, they were in his arms, Becky crying against him. Lee thanked Reginald Storm and, stepping aside with him where they could talk in private, he removed the Blythe money from his pocket, counting out the bills. Storm pushed them back at him.

"When you first came to my office, Lee, you gave me a six-hundred-dollar retainer." He took the folded bills from his pocket. "Every year I do a couple of cases pro bono, cases that I find particularly interesting or rewarding, that move me in some way." Storm grinned. "Looks like I'm starting early, this year. This money is yours and the Blakes'. This one's on me, Fontana."

Lee stared at him. "We can't take this. You did a fine job for us, you saved Morgan's life. You can't—"

Storm shook his head. "I *can*. This is my decision. I enjoyed every minute. As to the six hundred," he said, "I can sell you the Chevy for that, if you want it. Save you looking for transport, and save me the bother of advertising and selling it, now that I have the Buick."

Lee didn't know what to say. He'd need transportation, at least until he could pick up a good saddle horse and a packhorse. But more important than the car or the money, Lee truly liked this man. Reginald Storm was one of the few people who'd touched his life in a way he wouldn't forget. "There's no way in hell to thank you," Lee said, handing back the six hundred. "And I sure could use the car." He watched Storm remove a slip of paper from his pocket, lean over a table, and sign it.

"You can fill out the rest," Storm said, handing it to Lee. Turning, he nodded to the deputy marshals. He shook Lee's hand, stepped over to say good-bye to Morgan and to give Becky and Sammie a hug. Then he moved away out of the courtroom, not looking back.

Lee and Morgan were escorted out to a marshal's car heading for T.I., for their final processing and release. And where Lee would spend a tedious hour with one more federal probation officer no different, no more amiable than any of the others he'd dealt with. But by five that evening they had jumped through all the hoops. They moved out the sally port of T.I. for the last time, to where Becky and Sammie waited.

Crowding into the green Chevy, they headed for their motel, where Becky had gotten a second room for Lee. Soon they sat in the small restaurant for what should be a happy, celebratory dinner. But even approaching the little café, already Lee hung back, distancing himself from the Blakes, feeling heavy and sad and not liking the feeling. Not liking that they would soon be parted. For maybe the first time in his life he didn't relish the fact that he would soon again be alone. It was only when Sammie took his hand and pulled him along faster that he hurried to catch up with Morgan and Becky.

"Can Uncle Lee come home with us? And live with us in Georgia?"

Becky turned, laughing. "Of course you can, Lee. We were hoping that's what you'd want. Come back to Rome, live with us, get acquainted with your family— the family you didn't know you had."

Lee felt a sudden sharp longing, imagining that kind of life. As they entered the café Becky tucked her hand under his arm, looking up at him. But, watching him, she saw it in his eyes. Saw that he wouldn't come with them, that he would soon leave them. She felt hurt and disappointed, but she'd known this was how it would be. Lee had a different agenda. Something urgent guided him. Whatever pulled him in the opposite direction, it was too private for her to ask. What could be so urgent that he would abandon Sammie? Where would Lee's life take him? She so wanted him to remain part of their family and she knew he never would. Nor could she and Morgan and Sammie follow into that other world, the one Lee longed for.

Except, she thought, Sammie might follow. In her dreams Sammie might still reach out to Lee. Becky prayed that would happen, prayed Sammie could know something of Lee as his life played out.

43

As they headed for the Blakes' motel room after a quiet supper, Becky handed the car keys to Lee, but he hesitated to take them. "You could drive it home to Georgia."

"The Chevy's yours," Morgan said. "If we drove home we'd be forever getting across country. This time," he said, grinning, "I'm in a hurry."

Lee dropped the keys in his pocket, fished out the money he'd drawn from his savings account in Blythe and counted out six hundred dollars. Morgan tried to push it back.

"I've still got a couple hundred," Lee said. "Soon enough, I'll be rolling in cash, I'll be fixed up just fine." They both looked at him, but said nothing. He hoped he was right, hoped the stolen money was still where he'd buried it. "I'll take you to the airport in the morning, then I'm on my way."

In the Blakes' small room, Lee and Morgan sat in the two faded armchairs, Becky and Sammie on the bed leaning against the limp pillows. This last night together they were all uncomfortable, reluctant to say good-bye, knowing they might never see each other again. Lee hated partings, hated to string things out. With their long ordeal ended, parting was harder than he'd imagined. He itched to move on, and at the same time he wanted badly to stay with them, to head for Georgia, to be with his family and with Sammie, see Sammie grow up. He couldn't explain that if he stayed in the U.S. he might soon be back in the joint. When Sammie slid down from the bed and crawled in his lap, he wondered for one unrealistic moment if he could go back to Rome and never get caught for the post office heist. Sammie leaned against him, wanting him to stay. When he could no longer stand her sadness he stood up, hugging the child to him, and set her on her daddy's lap. "We need to be up early, need to head for the airport by six. Maybe we can grab a bite of breakfast near there." Not looking at Sammie again, quickly saying good night, he headed for his own room.

Crawling into the lumpy bed, he slept fitfully. He dreamed of crossing the desert on horseback, choking on dust, dreamed of thirst, of fighting rank and unbroke horses. He woke wondering why he'd dreamed that. At five-thirty, he showered and dressed and headed for the Blakes' room.

They left the motel in darkness, the air cold and damp with mist. As they hurried through a greasy breakfast in a tiny café near the airport the sky began to grow light, to brighten the dirty windows. In the airport, checking Becky's bag and the canvas duffel Morgan carried, they moved out to the tarmac behind the terminal where the DC-3 sat waiting, the metal stairway being rolled into place by four sleepy Hispanic men.

In the cold dawn they endured a last, tearful goodbye. Lee watched them ascend the metal stairway among a dozen passengers. He waited, shivering in the cold morning, until the plane backed around, revved up a little, and headed for the runway. Watched it taxi away to the far end of the strip, thinking how the man-made birds had helped to shape his life. Planes not yet invented when he was a boy: helped him steal, helped him escape, carried him to prison, and now carried away the child he loved. Far down the field the engine roared, the plane turned in a tight circle, came back nearly straight at him, lifted over him into the sky. He watched until it had vanished among the clouds, then turned away, a heavy knot in his belly.

He gassed up the Chevy near the airport and headed south out of L.A., taking the inland route against the green hills, direct for San Bernardino and on toward Blythe. All the while, part of him longed to turn around and follow the Blakes back to Rome, to live among his own family. The pain of parting was wicked, of learning to care for someone and then turning his back on them. Walking away as if he didn't give a damn, when in fact it took all he had to do that. The distress of leaving Sammie, just as he had abandoned Mae, was nearly unbearable.

Passing through the little towns separated by stretches of orange and avocado groves, he thought about Sammie's smile, so like Mae's. Such vital little girls, Sammie so filled with joy after the trial when he and Morgan had been freed—but then, at the airport, Sammie smearing angrily at the tears she couldn't stop.

But in Sammie's dark eyes he had seen something else as well. He'd seen a power that startled and then cheered him. In that moment, something in Sammie had shone out as strong as steel—she was born of Russell Dobbs's blood. No matter what turns her life took, no matter what occurred in the years ahead, Sammie would prevail. And maybe he would see her again, maybe somehow he would manage that. The ties that had begun with his memories of Mae and that had led to Sammie, those ties could not be broken.

Moving on past San Bernardino, he pulled up at a little cluster of houses and stores, parked the Chevy before a pawnshop. How many pawnshops over the years, all with the same black iron bars protecting their tangles of old watches, dusty cameras, tarnished jewelry, and used guns. At the counter he chose a .357 Magnum with a shoulder holster that fit nicely beneath his heavy jacket, and ten boxes of ammunition. He picked up a frying pan, a used sleeping bag, a good knife, all the necessities for a meager kit, then he stopped in a little grocery for canned beans and staples.

Leaving the store with his box of groceries he spotted, on down the street, a tiny Mexican café. Stowing his purchases in the car, he stepped on in. He bought four burritos and four tacos, which the accommodating waiter wrapped in a red-and-white-checked napkin and dropped into a brown paper bag with two cold beers.

Driving south again munching on a taco, heading for Blythe, Lee's thoughts turned to the moves he'd have to make slipping in and out of the area, easing up the hills unseen to where he'd buried the cash. That got him thinking about the gray gelding he'd ridden up the mountain when he buried the money, had ridden back down to connect with the crop duster that lifted him fast over into Nevada. Not until the plane had appeared had he turned the gray loose, watched him gallop away over the desert bucking and kicking. Lee knew when the horse got thirsty and hungry he'd head for the isolated ranch that stood below on the empty desert.

The gray had been a good and willing companion; Lee missed him. He didn't like this sadness of being alone, this was new to him, this hollow loneliness.

What he'd planned to do was buy the gray back, if he *had* been taken in by that ranch, buy him if they'd sell him, and take off on horseback for Mexico. But a little thought, a few questions asked, and he knew the land along the Colorado, down into Baja, would be way too hard on a horse. Little if any grass for miles across the desert, little if any water, and much of the Colorado River inaccessible where it ran deep between ragged stone cliffs. Even if he bought a trailer, maybe traded the Chevy for a pickup, it would still be a hard journey, hard to care for a saddle horse. He didn't have any real destination, didn't know where, in Mexico, he'd end up. Somewhere along the gulf, but how much feed could he buy there, how much water could he count on? He'd be smarter to wait, to buy some Mexican cayuse later on.

Well, hell, the first thing was to get the money. If it was gone, he couldn't buy a flea-bitten hound dog.

Parking beside an orange grove he unwrapped a burrito and opened a beer. It was then, as he ate the rest of his lunch, that Misto was suddenly beside him, grinning up at him, yellow shaggy coat, ragged ears, ragged, switching tail. How often had it been this way over their long friendship, Misto abruptly appearing pressing against him, loud with rumbling purrs. Lee stroked his rough fur and offered him a bite of burrito, but Misto sniffed and turned his nose away. Too much hot sauce.

He stopped once more before he reached Blythe, to gas up the Chevy again and use the restroom. The attendant was young and shy, he looked at his feet when Lee addressed him. "Can you tell me the name of that ranch out on the old road to Amboy?"

The young man glanced up at him, turned, and headed for the office. Lee could see him ringing up the sale. Bringing Lee his change, still he didn't look at him. "That would be the Emerson place," he mumbled. "It sets just beyond the little airstrip."

Lee nodded. "That's the only ranch out there?"

"The only one," the young fellow said shyly, studying his boots. But he stood watching as Lee pulled away. The ghost cat had disappeared. The car seemed filled with emptiness as Lee headed for the road to Amboy.

Approaching the old abandoned barn on the Amboy road, he parked behind it and, at the base of a boulder, he dug with a rock until he'd uncovered the little folding shovel he'd buried there, and then the saddle and bridle. There wasn't much left of the rotted blanket. He wiped the leather off as best he could, laid the saddle and bridle in the trunk beside his meager kit. Somewhere down the line, he'd need them. As he headed the Chevy up the shallow mountain the scene came back too vividly, the robbery, returning here in the truck with the dead convict sitting in the seat beside him, the man he had killed to save his own life and who, it turned out, had come in real handy. That day, he had driven up the hills as far as he could, leading the gray with a rope through the open window, the dead man propped in the cab beside him. Picking his spot along the canyon, he'd gotten out, tied the gray at a safe distance, and sent the truck and dead man, with the gun and a few scattered post office bills, over the edge of the ravine, a no-good convict taking the rap for the robbery.

The truck and his companion disposed of, he had moved on up the hills on horseback, buried the money, and ridden back down to the old barn. Had buried the saddle and, when the duster plane came into view, had turned the gray loose, then buried the bridle and shovel. Stepping up into the cockpit, he'd headed for Vegas. No commercial plane to fly him from the empty desert, and the small duster plane left no record. For all intents and purposes, when the post office robbery went down, Lee was already drunk and raising hell in Vegas, cursing and assaulting the Vegas cops, and was thrown in the can there. So far, his alibi had held firm.

Now, heading the Chevy up the shallow desert mountain, he thought he could make it maybe halfway before boulders made the trail impassable and he'd have to walk. Already he could see, high up to the east, the rock formation where the money was hidden.

Before he left the car he backed it around so it was headed down again, the parking brake set, the front bumper secure against a boulder. Moving on up, on foot, the sand hushed beneath his boots with an occasional soft scrape. Lizards scurried away, and once he startled a rabbit that went bounding off. Nothing chased it. Was Misto with Sammie? Would Sammie, in a dream, see him walking up the mountain, watch as he approached the tall rock and began to dig, see him bring up the stolen post office bags? What would she think, how would she judge him? That thought bothered him.

"It's all I have," he told her, wondering if his words would enter her dreams. "All I have, for whatever years are left." A little cottage in Mexico, good hot Mexican food, soak up the hot sun. The money he was about to dig up, that's all there was against an empty future.

44

In the DC-3, as Sammie yawned in Becky's arms, already Morgan had drifted off, his head on Becky's shoulder. Becky couldn't have slept again; her stomach felt queasy from breakfast or maybe from the plane taking off, banking over the city, then lifting fast above the mountains. Below them clouds hung low between the highest peaks, then soon the plane's shadow raced ahead over mountains mottled with snow. Snowcapped ridges tinted gold by the rising sun surrounded a deep blue lake; far ahead, long white ridges marched, jagged, primitive, stroked with gold.

Last night in the motel room Sammie, sleeping peacefully, had stirred suddenly and sat up, her rigid body silhouetted against the motel lights beyond the window. Becky couldn't tell if she was awake or still asleep; but a darkness stood across the room slicing fear through her—a dark consciousness more alive than if they faced a human intruder.

"Leave us alone!" Sammie shouted. "Leave my daddy alone. You tried with Uncle Lee, too. You failed with both of them. Now go away. Go away from us. Go bother someone who *wants* to follow you."

The authority in the child's voice held Becky. Morgan was awake and took Becky's hand. They didn't speak to Sammie. This was not the kind of dream they were used to. Sammie didn't reach out to them, frightened. She seemed quite in control, there was a new power in the child. Her strength seemed to press at the dark presence as if driving it back; it smeared and grew thin. "You couldn't hurt Russell Dobbs," Sammie said boldly. "You couldn't hurt Lee or my daddy. You *can't* hurt us any longer."

Her fists gripped the covers. "You *can't* direct my dreams. You never could, they never came from you! Go away from us, we are done with you!" She was not a child now, something within her seemed ageless, they could only watch as she faced down the dark that stifled the small room. The child waited silent and rigid as the spirit receded. When it vanished, she turned away—she was a child again, soft and pliant, leaning into her daddy, pulling Becky close, pressing between them until soon she slept, curled up and at peace.

They exchanged looks, but didn't speak. At last Morgan slept, too. Only Becky lay awake, thinking about the strength they'd seen in Sammie—and then about the days to come. Home again in their own house. Morgan back in the shop he loved. Caroline with her comforting support. Anne a real part of the family now, Anne and Mariol.

With Morgan exonerated, all charges wiped from the books, would time turn back to what life was before? Would the town's anger be wiped from the books? As cleanly as the legal charges were expunged? Would they be a real part of their community again?

She didn't think so.

Their true friends, who had stood by them, would embrace them. But the rest of the town, that had turned so cruel, why would they be different now? She couldn't be friends again with people who hadn't trusted or believed in Morgan, people *they* could never trust again. And that was most of the town.

What kind of life would they have among people they could never again feel close to, could never respect? She and Morgan had no reason to embrace their onetime enemies. And what about Morgan's customers? Would they return to him or would they remain distant, so business continued to falter? Caroline was doing her best to oversee the work, to make appointments, pay the bills, take care of the books on top of managing the bakery. Even bakery sales had fallen off some. And Becky's own work? The clients she'd lost were, in her view, gone for good. She couldn't hope there'd be new work for her. Now, this morning, heading through the sky to Georgia, were they returning not to their regained freedom, but to a new and different kind of confinement?

As if, though Brad Falon was locked away, his shadow still followed them.

She thought about California, the miles of orange groves below as they'd left the city. The open green hills, the small communities lying snugly along the sea. She thought about the way Lee had talked, over supper last night, about watching the ocean surge so close outside his cell window. Thought about the friendliness of the few people she had met, the waitresses and manager at the little motel, and about the kindness of Reginald Storm—her thoughts filled with the bright mosaic of that world, so very different from what they might find at home.

But then, looking down from the DC-3 at the dry desert of Arizona and then soon at the snow-patterned prairies of the Midwest, her thoughts turned to Lee and to where he might be headed in his mysterious odyssey. Already she missed him, she said a silent prayer for him. Give him peace, give him what he longs for in his last years. And then she thought about Misto.

Would the ghost cat know new earthly lives yet to come? But meantime, would he stay with Sammie yet for a while?

And where would he go when he must return to a new life? Into what place and what time? Must the little cat spirit start over each time as a small and ignorant kitten with only his own strong will to guide him? That seemed so cruel.

But how could she understand the patterns that guided the soul of animal or human? She could only guess. Yawning, she looked at Morgan sleeping against her and prayed that life would be good to him now, would be good to all of them as she and Morgan tried, as best they knew how, to protect Sammie and nurture her.

45

Lee's shovel, striking stone, echoed louder than he liked. Though the desert stretched away empty below him, only scattered mesquite and boulders to conceal anyone observing him. And who would be out there on the empty land alone? But he kept watch as he dug at the base of the tall rock formation, shale falling back again and again so he had to scoop out the hole with his hands. There: his hand stroked hard leather. Quickly he uncovered the saddlebags, hauled them out and dug feverishly into the two pockets.

The stash was there, the packets of money, solidly wrapped as he'd left them. Pulling out several packs of hundred-dollar bills, he found none of them crumbled or torn as if rodents had been at them, no corners chewed by marauding ground squirrels. He tucked a thousand dollars in his left boot, folded a thousand more in his pants pocket, left the rest in the saddlebags, and tied them shut. He covered the hole, scattered sand and debris across so the ground looked untouched.

Carrying the saddlebags, he headed down the mountain, sliding on his heels in a couple of steep places. At the Chevy he shoved them under the front seat, slid into the warm car, and drove on down, thinking again about the gray gelding.

He knew he couldn't take the gray with him, that was kidding himself. But he'd like one last look, like to know the gray had found a good home, know he was all right. Easing the Chevy on past the old barn, he turned in the direction of the lone ranch, the old Emerson place.

It wasn't far, a couple of miles. A pair of stone pillars supported a wrought-iron sign: J. J. EMERSON. Parking the Chevy across the road, he slipped in through the gate, shutting it behind him, and headed on foot up the long, rutted drive. Strange, even with all the hill-climbing and digging, his lungs weren't bothering him too bad. Maybe it was the adrenaline rush of having the money safe. Rocky hills rose behind the ranch house, sparse with brown winter grass. A herd of Hereford cattle was being moved, worked slowly down toward the corrals that surrounded the faded ranch house. He saw the gray, a kid was riding him, likely one of the rancher's boys, a slight youngster of twelve or so. The three riders pushed the herd in between board fences that funneled them into a catch pen. Lee watched the kid spin the gray to turn back a reluctant steer, hustling the steer on through the gate but never tightening the reins. He watched the way the gelding moved, loose reined and easy, and the sight put a grin on Lee's face. He hungered to have the gray back, to have him for his own.

The two older riders began to separate the cattle, moving the younger steers into a long chute. The gray's rider moved away as if their part of the job was done, eased the gray into a small corral without lifting the reins, dismounted, pulled off the heavy saddle and slung it on the fence. Reaching up, the rider took off the wide-brimmed hat that provided shade from the desert sun, releasing a cascade of long blond hair, bright and clean looking. Lee watched the girl pull off her Levi's coat, revealing a slim female form beneath her Western shirt. A child of maybe thirteen, a little older than Sammie. A child living the life Mae had wanted to live, the life Sammie had never been exposed to, and that was a pity. Lee watched this young girl doing what she loved, doing what she was meant to do. He watched her remove the gray's bridle, slip a rope halter on him, and tie him to the fence.

She left the corral, returned with a bucket and carrying a sponge and rags. Lee watched her fill the bucket from a tap and hose next to the fencepost, watched her sponge the gray, starting with the sweaty saddle mark, sloshing the sweat off real good, the gray flicking his tail and tossing his head with pleasure. He liked it even better when she turned the hose on him, sloshed him all over, washed his face and wiped out his eyes, the good gelding snorting and shaking himself and asking for more. Lee looked him over, the good shape he was in, well fed but not fat, his hooves neatly trimmed and shod. The girl knew he was watching, but she gave no sign. She swiped the excess water off the gray's back and rump and neck with a rounded metal tool. She hugged the gray, soaking the front of her shirt, hugged him again, removed his halter, slapped him on the rump, and laughed as he spun away, running the length of the corral.

At the far end he lay down and rolled, twisting this way and that, making a muddy mess of himself. When the girl turned to look at Lee, her gaze was wary, questioning. Lee knew what she was thinking: This horse had appeared at the ranch running loose, no brand, no mark of an owner. They'd taken him in, a nice horse like this. Maybe they'd looked for the owner, maybe not.

Did she think Lee was the owner, that he'd found the gelding at last, after all this time, and had come to claim him?

It was strange they didn't know where the gray came from. Lee had bought him not that far away, out on the other side of Blythe. Ranchers, horsemen, they knew every horse for miles.

Or maybe these folks did know who'd owned him? Had old bowlegged Rod Kendall, who'd sold him the gray, had he for some reason not wanted the gelding back? Didn't have the money, or the man's health was failing? The girl watched Lee, assessing him, her look far older than her youth.

"Rod Kendall died last fall," she said. "You the fellow who bought the gray from him? Smoke. I call him Smoke." Lee was silent, watching her. "He's not for sale," she said. "I don't know how you lost him or why it took you so long to come for him. I figure, you abandon a horse like that for over a year, it's finders keepers. He's not for sale."

Lee laughed. "I didn't come to buy him. Where I'm headed, the way I'm traveling, I couldn't take him with me. I just wanted a last look, see what kind of shape he's in."

Her look eased. The gray trotted back across the corral to shake mud over her, but when he saw Lee he nickered and trotted over, leaned over the fence nuzzling at him, stirring a pain in Lee's heart. Lee scratched his neck, scratched under his forelock and behind his ears, then gave him a little push, moving him back toward the girl. The gray laid his head on her shoulder, pushing mud into her pale hair. She scratched his ears absently.

"Just came for a last look," Lee repeated. "Have to be on my way." He looked the gray over good, filling up on the sight of him. He looked hard at the girl, wishing Sammie could live like this, with a good horse to love, free of the hard times, free of the haunts that plagued her.

"Means a lot to me," Lee said, "that you love him, that he's with you and cared for." He reached through the fence and they shook hands solemnly. Then Lee turned away, walked back up the road, got in his car feeling old and alone, and headed for Mexico.

He wasn't alone long when the ghost cat settled beside him, warm and purring, and Lee knew, hoped he knew, that the spirit cat would stay with him for a while, maybe continue to move between Lee himself and Sammie for as long as he remained in ghost form. Who knew how long that would be, until Misto must return to the world of the living? However long, Lee was glad for his company.

So it was that Lee and Misto worked their way south until they crossed the border to travel along the Mexican side; skirting Arizona, moving down into Sonora, Lee looked south across sage and mesquite to the distant gulf, imagining a small village right on the shore, a little empty hacienda waiting for him.

Each night he slept in the locked car, gun at hand. On a night when he'd parked beneath a grove of tamarisk trees, as he lay dozing, the moon filtering light down through the lacy branches, the ghost cat brought him awake, rubbing against Lee's face. "Just for a little while," Misto whispered. And he disappeared, gone into another element. Only his last words lingered. "Sammie's lonely, too, she needs a snuggle, too."

Misto would return to ride with Lee, watching over the old train robber as Lee headed at last where he longed to be. And though sadness filled the ghost cat that the old man traveled alone, he knew that could change. This night as Misto departed, willing himself back to Rome, slipping beneath the covers into Sammie's arms, she woke and hugged him. "Lee's all right?" she whispered. "You'll keep him safe, you won't leave him for long?"

He pressed his nose against her warm cheek. "I will return to him, I will travel with him, just as I will be with you."

"I saw him dig up money," she whispered. "Lots of money. Will that put him in danger? *Will* he be all right? Oh, Misto, will he be safe? And happy?"

"The gods willing," Misto said, "I will tell you how he fares, and I can bring him messages. Will that please you?"

"Oh, yes," she whispered, hugging him tighter. "But what happens when you must be born again? Then what will happen to Lee?"

"My life on earth is but an instant, in the eternal warp of time. But always, as spirit, I am with you and with Lee, I can move anywhere, into any time. Always I will be with you, we belong together. Wherever I am, my spirit self is near."

Yawning, Sammie kissed Misto's nose. Holding him close, she drifted into dreams where for a few moments she felt herself a part of eternity, was lifted up into an incomprehensible freedom that buoyed and strengthened her. "Wherever I am in endless time," Misto repeated, purring, "I will be with you, forever I am with you."

About the Authors

In addition to her popular Joe Grey mystery series for adults, for which she has received eleven national Cat Writers' Association awards for best novel of the year, SHIRLEY ROUSSEAU MURPHY is a noted children's book author who has received five Council of Authors and Journalists awards. Two of her children's books were written in collaboration with her husband, Pat.

PAT J. J. MURPHY spent his career as a federal probation officer in California and Oregon, as well as the chief USPO in Panama and Georgia, where he retired as chief probation officer for the Northern District of Georgia. The Murphys retired to their home state of California, settling with their two lady cats in Carmel, California.